Different Drummer

by Catherine Gigante-Brown

Cover layout by Vinnie Corbo
Cover Model - Allison Sciulla
Author photo by Vinnie Corbo

Published by Volossal Publishing
www.volossal.com

Copyright © 2015
ISBN 978-0-9909727-8-5

for Debbie
(1955-2010),
who lived through this

Table of Contents

Garland "Chin Lieu" Song
Sous Chef, Temple Lev Simcha

She was like a fire. I stood at the kitchen door, watching. Even above the clatter and chatter of the kitchen, I heard her. The drumming. Like the constant knocking on a door that refused to open. Like the beating of an angry heart that was about to explode. Only different. Persistent, yet in perfect rhythm. Rising and falling like anxious breath, swelling then subsiding like the ocean. I was drawn to the doorway, held fast there.

Her movements were so rapid that her hands were little more than a blur, moving from drum to cymbal back to drum again in a flash, as thoughtlessly as other people breathe. As swiftly as a flame engulfs a house or a tree, that's the way she moved. As though it were natural. Organic. As easy and effortless as walking, because for her, it was.

Of course, I'd noticed her earlier, carrying her equipment in through the kitchen as I molded ovals of stuffed derma in my palm, one after the other, and placing them onto baking sheets. She came through several times, each time carrying a bigger parcel, like hat boxes, only larger. And every time, she either smiled or nodded, acknowledging the kitchen staff that was so often ignored by musicians and magicians alike, as if we were an extension of the battered pots, pans and wounded spatulas which created a hundred dinners in one evening, sometimes more. It was as though she somehow surmised that the raw, brown hands of the Mexican boy washing dishes sometimes held an artist's paintbrush. Or that the old Chinese man salting the matzo ball soup might also create haiku in the wee hours of the morning when he got home and everyone else in his humble house was asleep, his dreams locked into syllables of 5-7-5. She gave us all that respect. The respect of not knowing, the respect of…perhaps.

It was this way every time she worked at the Temple Lev Simcha. She was cordial and polite and above all, kind. I took notice and gave her an extra slice of derma, which she liked for some reason. I did this instead of spitting into her food, which I sometimes did to the others. Especially the bandleaders.

So, I stood in the doorway, arms folded, watching her. Why? For the same reason we are unable to pass a burning shell of a building without stopping. For the same reason we study the sunset. It fills us with excitement and wonder.

The way this girl played the drums, she became part of them. It was difficult to tell where instrument ended and woman began. She no longer looked exactly human. She was a slick, sweaty form in a worn tuxedo, a shape that did not appear to be made of bone and muscle and tendon stretched just so. Perhaps this was a new electrical device from Norm's Music on Kings Highway. But no. This was a person.

A crowd had gathered on the small, carpet-coated stage. Still others were drawn into the vortex of noise. One or two peered over my shoulder from the kitchen. She played with a kind of desperation, a determination. She rounded the amber-colored cylinders and crashed into the brass cymbals as though in a trance. Eyes lightly closed, sticks quickly touching the skins in an uneven rhythm. Always moving, never breaking the spell. At times, her drum solo sounded like confused hearts beating. First with love, then with power, then with hate.

I watched as the fire caught from the girl to the crowd of observers. As if to be included somehow, they seemed to have a need to make noises of their own. It began with a pair of hands timidly clapping. Then four, then six. Then the entire room quaked with applause. Arms flailed above heads stiff with hairspray. Old women raised their gowns to their meaty calves and younger ones lifted their Spandex hems well above their thighs. Bodies writhed. Grandma Wasserman was ushered to the ladies' room in her swollen orthopedic shoes, overcome with excitement.

At some point, the drummer opened her eyes and the magic was broken. She suddenly seemed to become conscious of her hands. She appeared to be thinking about what to do next. Perhaps she worried that the sticks might go flying from her perspiring fingers. Perhaps her arms felt heavy like a boxer's might get after so many rounds. Slowly, she circled the drums one last time and ended with a short, snappy roll on the smallest one.

There was more applause. There were whistles and war whoops, as though the audience had been the ones to accomplish something instead of her. The girl didn't seem to know how to respond. She dipped her head, shyly smiling, awkward as a giraffe in an elevator. Like Judy Garland, she didn't seem to know what to do with her hands. She nodded and grinned until the clapping stopped.

I didn't clap, though. However, during meal break, there would be the most perfect slab of prime rib on her plate, a generous dollop of mashed potatoes, crisp broccoli and not one, but two, circles of stuffed derma. That was my applause, my gift to her.

At the end of the evening, this girl always tipped the waitstaff, even though it wasn't her wedding and she was hired help just like the rest of us. And I was sure that the awful men who posed as bandleaders didn't pay her very much or treat her fairly. But the good ones, we all do whatever we can for each other, in little ways, in small joys, in tiny kindnesses, to make up for the shit.

1/1/79

I play society music. Club dates. Weddings, *bar mitzvahs*, christenings, anniversaries, "Parents Without Partners" mixers. Whatever you want to call them. You name it, play it. And most of the time, it sucks. But it helps put food on the table. It gives me pocket money for demo tapes and studio time. It lets me pursue what I love, which makes the rest of it bearable.

I'm writing this because Michael said I should. He said that it might help if I put my feelings down on paper. For something other than angry songs, he meant. Michael said I was one of the most pissed-off people he's ever met and that maybe if I wrote down what was going through my head, I could get rid of some of the anger. Exorcise myself from my rage, he said.

I was "fraught with rage..." were his exact words. I never heard anybody use the word "fraught" in a sentence before, so I figured he meant business. Maybe he had a point. He cared enough to say something, at least. So, even though Michael's not part of my life anymore—not really—I figured I would give it a shot.

Technically, we're not seeing each other these days but that doesn't stop him from calling me for a "rekindle" when he's lonely. That's what Buffalo, one of the firefighters who hangs out at Captain Walter's, calls it. A rekindle is when a fire you've put out flares back up again. In relationships, rekindles are when you start up something you left for dead. Usually for a quick *schtump*. Sometimes more. Nobody likes rekindles, especially not firefighters. It shows that you didn't do the job right the first time. As for Michael and me, I don't know what these rekindles mean exactly, if they're good or bad. But they just are. Kind of like this journal.

I haven't kept a diary since I was something like 10. And I don't think I was very good at it, even back then. This one is a plain old black and white marble notebook, not hot pink and furry, no lock and key. I stopped writing in my old diary right after I picked up my first pair of drumsticks, even though girls back then didn't do things like that. Play drums, I mean. Sometime in June of 1960, I'm pretty sure it was. I started playing hokey stuff like "Alley-Oop." The Everly Brothers' "Cathy's Clown." Paul Anka and "Puppy Love." I'm still playing some of that crap now, almost 20 years later.

Although even back then, my taste went more for the gritty, the soulful stuff. I'd pick "The Ice Man" Jerry Butler over Percy Faith any day. Damn, I'd still take Fats Domino over Pat Boone. Roy Orbison wailing "Only the Lonely" like his heart was truly broken, which I'm sure it was. This is the music that molded me, made me feel different, made me feel hope, made me feel like I had a chance, made me feel that maybe if I practiced hard enough, I could break out of the Brooklyn hellhole that was my life.

Even at 10, I knew that they could call it a "garden suite" all they wanted, but it was a still a basement apartment, pure and simple. You could put perfume on shit but it was still shit, right? And that's all my mom could afford after my dad left. Shit.

Anyhow, that day, I picked up my cousin Solly's drumsticks when he wasn't home. I was nosing around his room one afternoon when my Aunt Iris was watching me. My mother was in the hospital because of her bum hip and her baby sister was looking after me until my mom got out of the Hospital for Joint Disease. I found the drum sticks wedged between Solly's mattress and box spring like some forgotten girlie magazine. Which I had also found: a creamy blonde centerfold on red satin. But even the pink-nippled model didn't impress me as much as Solly's drumsticks. Louie Bellson 5A's, with wood tips. Light and smooth. Even smelled good: fresh, clean. I could twirl them between my fingers from the get-go. Felt so right, I stole them from Solly without even a second thought. I don't think he ever noticed.

My mother wasn't supposed to move around a lot right after the surgery. Aunt I or Mrs. Morowitz across the street would come over to tidy up and bring food. My sister Aileen and brother Irving weren't much help. I'd make my mother Kosher green Jello and take her plates of pickled herring, courtesy of Mrs. M. Then I'd disappear back into my room, close the door. Lock it even. Like I was doing something bad. Which in her eyes, I was.

"Always with the tap, tap, tapping," my mother would yell through the thin walls, pausing only to take a drag on her Chesterfield, her voice coarse and mean as gravel. "At first, I thought it was a woodpecker, but then I said to myself, 'There are no woodpeckers in Sheepshead Bay.'" She still lives there, in that Godforsaken Coyle Street basement. God help her.

Another deep drag then more berating. You would think I was in there with a hand mirror propped between my knees (that came much later) or my dad's long-dormant, left-behind electric razor buzzing me off into oblivion (that came later too, if only just to spite them). But no, I was only drumming. And in her mind, that was a thousand times worse.

Little did Edie know that I lost my virginity in my cramped little Coyle Street bedroom. To the accompaniment of The Beach Boys' "Pet Sounds" while *The Sands of Iwo Jima* blasted on the "Million Dollar Movie" in the living room. As Stanley Morowitz (who was even nerdier than me) fumbled with the buttons on my blue gingham Western shirt, I gritted my teeth to the sickly sweetness of "Don't Talk" then became more interested in the drum line of "Sloop John B." Without losing his boner, Stan flipped the album to Side B on my old Decca and I was finally popped during "God Only Knows," though the jingle bells in the background got on my nerves. In retrospect, I think the drum parts and chord changes interested me more than Stan did. Then he put on The Mother of Invention's "Freak Out!" and I was never the same again. I think I liked Stan's eclectic record collection more than I liked him.

So, here I am, a couple of decades later, still pounding away on the skins. Getting nowhere except angrier. If that's possible. But it is. I know it is. Because I'm getting more and more pissed off the more I write. Maybe it's because I have to go back to that bullshit temp job tomorrow. Then again, maybe not. Maybe I just like being pissed off.

But however you look at it, this is it. My last chance to make it. And by "make it," I mean get a record deal, make a name for myself in the record business. I refuse to become part of the 1980s without a record deal. I'm 29 already. I'll be 30 at the end of the year, on Frank Sinatra's birthday, ironically enough. I always thought it was a sign, a lucky day for musician to be born. Now I'm not so sure. And if I'm not signed by December 31st that's it. It's over. I swear on my life.

Marty Karroll
Bandleader/Keyboard Player, Ste-Mar Orchestra

She's not a bad-looking chick. But admit it, girl drummers are hot by definition, even if they look like Bea Arthur or Aunt Bea or whatever. No matter how shapeless the *tuchus* or how flat the tits, a chick with drumsticks is a winner. Especially if they know how to use them. And Cara does. But a singing, female drummer...a singing female drummer is off the charts.

I knew Cara when she was Carol. Carol Finkelstein. Skinny, fuzzy-haired, mouth full of metal (braces courtesy of the crappy orthodontist who took her crippled mother's Medicaid plan), nose too big for the rest of her and a family too poor to fix it. But the best drummer, girl or boy, that Sheepshead High had ever seen. Couldn't get into her pants even back then, desperate and butt-ugly as she was. Can't get into them now, even though I keep trying. And I ask you, what's the harm in trying?

But that's okay, I've got Beryl. And dumb as she is, Beryl ain't bad to look at. She cleans up nice, even if it does take her forever to get ready. Even if she is high maintenance. Beryl looks good on a dance floor and face-down, tush-up on a mattress. Just don't talk to her too long or mention anything that might require her to rub two brain cells together. Something like the Pol Pot regime, for example. Beryl is so stupid, she thinks Pol Pot is a new line of Farberware. But I've got no problem with that. I have no desire to fuck an Einstein, who was smart as shit but definitely not a looker, even for a guy. Besides, with a snort or two of coke, Beryl looks better and better. Just so long as she keeps her trap shut.

But Cara…man, she just doesn't know when to shut her fucking mouth and play. That's my main gripe with her: she doesn't know how to play the game. It's her biggest problem, if you ask me. Like when I tell her that it wouldn't kill her to wear a low-cut blouse or a gown on a gig. (Or to give me a hand job once in a while.) "It would get caught up in the bass pedal," she whines. Or "I can't *schlep* around a drum kit with my boobs hanging out." Bullshit. Cara insists on wearing a black tux to gigs, just like us. Got it from the same Zeller's we go to on Avenue U, tailored to fit. With that worn spot near the knee where it rubs against the snare. Has the same powder blue ruffled shirt, just like the rest of the band, like she's some big, bad dyke, which she's not. Oh, and the hand job would be unprofessional, she says, serious as a heart attack, before she slams the car door in my face.

There's no question that sometimes Steve and me sell the band just by virtue of Cara's playing and singing alone. She sings "Shalom" as good as a cantor's wife and kicks ass on The Commodores' "Brick House." But would it be any skin off her ass to give the *bar mitzvah* boy's father a half a hard on or the new groom a woody by showing some cleavage? According to Cara, it would. I made Beryl offer to take her shopping down at Kings Plaza, not once but twice, and each time, Cara rolled her eyes, remembered some mysterious appointment and gave some lame excuse about why she couldn't make it.

And her hair! She keeps it short, cropped so butchy that it stands on end. "I want to keep it out of my eyes or else it bothers me when I play," says she. "And I can't keep brushing it away when I'm playing."

And play, she does. Like nobody I ever seen. Not in this business, anyway. The club date trade is filled with hacks, myself included. And let's not even talk about the way Steve strangles his trumpet. But with a little flash, glitz and fancy footwork, you can easily bamboozle people into thinking you really can play. Especially if there's an open bar and the Stoli isn't watered down. Especially if the price is right and the package deal for five pieces, non-continuous is cheap enough. But it's all about money. Don't let anybody tell you any different. Talent, schmalent. It's greenbacks that pay the bills. Period.

1/5/79

I hate this place! I'm so glad it's not a real job for me, or else I'd shoot myself in the head, I swear. Just biding my time, just making a few extra bucks to supplement the bullshit wages Ste-Mar gives me. In my 9-5 gig, I pretty much come and go as I please. I call the shots. I just tell Payton People, the temp agency I work for, the days I'm available and they take it from there. For some reason, they like me as much as I hate the corporate crap. At an advertising agency, no less, the worst corporate slime of them all.

Today I'm sitting in the black box of a black reception area. The walls, ceiling, carpet, even my desk, are black. It looks like a perverse jungle with tall silver lamps positioned just so on the floor, next to a row of uncomfortable black chairs. I try to look busy. And I must do a good job because I look so busy that nobody asks me to do anything but answer phones that hardly ring. I guess they assume somebody else has given me a ton of work. But the folks at Benson & Bowe like me—they keep asking for me by name. They keep putting me in this same windowless closet on the 38th floor but it might just as well be the basement because I can't see a thing. I don't even know what the weather's like outside.

No one seems to come up here except for messengers. One of them is sweet on me. The nuttiest, craziest one of them all. Michael says I'm a "nut magnet," because I keep attracting people who are a little bit off, the type who are one taco short of a combination platter, if you know what I mean. What does that say about Michael, then? Not much.

Anyhow, this bike messenger guy started off by complimenting my shoes, which he had to crane his neck to see behind my Wailing Wall of a desk. Arnold said that he wanted me to walk all over his back in my sensible pumps and then asked if I wasn't adverse to giving a bad boy a sound spanking. I almost freaked out since I was all alone in this black hole, nobody within earshot to help me. But then I got my shit together and told him in my most stern, mistressy voice (mimicking my mother, who is the Queen of All Verbal Humiliation) to leave immediately. I swear, Arnold practically skipped in delight at the thought of getting a free dose of oral S&M. But at least he left. I don't think I'm going to accept any future assignments at B&B. That guy creeps me out.

I know my mother hopes that I'll get a "nice" job, a "real job" in a fancy high-rise office building like the World Trade Center. Once or twice, firms have offered to buy out my contract with Payton People and asked me to come work for them full-time. But I've always politely turned them down. "See? I always told you to learn how to type," my mother likes to say proudly. "It opens up all kinds of doors. You never know who you might meet in a nice office building." But those aren't the sorts of doors I want to open. I'm a musician, not a secretary. I don't want to be somebody's wife. I don't want somebody to take care of me. I can take care of myself, thanks. Besides, I've always marched to the beat of a different drummer, no pun intended.

And I'm not like you, Mom. I'm nothing at all like you—lost without a man and no idea how *not* to chase them away. *I'm* the one who leaves. Ask Michael.

Sitting at the reception-desk prison at B&B, now I'm scribbling in my marble composition book, looking very industrious. But other times, I tap out lyrics on the brand-spanking-new IBM Selectric. I bang out my angst and watch the silver ball twirl this way and then the other, typing my sorrows away.

Thank God this week has passed quickly, a short workweek no less. I have a gig tonight, a cheap PWP dance at the Baron DeKalb down on Emmons Avenue. It starts at 8:30 so I won't have to rush home from the city like a maniac. In the winter, the D train crawls along the frozen tracks like a crippled baby.

At least Marty's picking me up, so I won't have to wrestle my drums into one of Marine Park Car Service's crappy little Pintos. Besides, it's always fun watching Marty fight for a parking spot with some *schmo* and his wife out for a Friday night bite at Castle Harbour. But I'll probably have to fight off Marty, peel his hand from my behind like an unwanted growth, dodge his double-entendres with a wink and a smile, and hope he doesn't short my pay too much for giving me a lift.

Marty's what my mother, the great Edith Finkelstein, who never has a nice word to say about anybody or anything, would call a *schnorrer*. A taker, a sponge, a parasite. *Schnorrer* might be the most disparaging Yiddish word of them all. But in Marty's case, it's true. He's a snake, a real piece of dog shit. And then there's the gig. I think these PWPs are the worst. Parents Without Partners…they all seem so desperate. It's like, when they have a few hours without their stinking kids, they feel compelled to cut loose and go wild. Some

women do nothing but talk to each other and eat. Others just cry. The men seem
to prowl, like they're in some warped, Knights of Columbus jungle gym.

Then there's the guy the band nicknamed "The Humper." He's a big lug,
about six-two, and shaped like a bowling pin. He fancies himself light on his feet
but he's anything but, more like one of those dancing hippos from *Fantasia*.
The Humper grabs himself an unsuspecting partner, gives her a twirl, lifts her up,
then proceeds to dry-hump her in mid-air. He manages this in an awkwardly
graceful gesture. It could be a very Alvin-Ailey move if he was a
beautifully-chiseled black man instead of a rotund Guido from Bensonhurst.
It might be oddly stunning if it weren't so pathetic. Which it is.

Michael Galante
High School English Teacher

She doesn't know I'm here. I'm watching her from the doorway at the Baron DeKalb, tucked behind the doorframe, actually. She's so wrapped up in her music, I don't think she'd even notice me if she stared straight at me. Somehow, a samba led to a drum solo and now she's lost in it. But that's just how life with Cara is—sudden, extreme, filled with things you don't expect.

As skilled as she is, I never like watching her do a drum solo. It's too uncontrolled. Too unbridled. Too much like a freak-out. It looks too much like pain. Then there's that moment when she comes back down to earth, becomes conscious of what her hands and feet are doing. Becomes self-conscious, in a sense. Then it ends. Suddenly. It's like that when Cara makes love, too. She becomes lost in it, consumed by it. Then afterwards, reality is a rude awakening.

When Cara's eyes open on the bandstand, they look suddenly sheepish, wounded almost, and she blends back in with the other musicians. Or tries to. But Cara never blends into anything, not really. Maybe that's part of her problem. It's been a rough week for her, I can tell, just by the violence of her drum solo. I could feel it coming, building, even through the insipid chorus of *Copacabana*, a song she truly hates, a song so unlike the songs she writes.

And then Cara took flight. Eyes closed, there was no way Marty could grab her attention to wrap it up, though he tried several times. It ended when she was ready for it to end, just like everything else does.

I haven't seen her for a week or more. Just after Christmas, it was. I was still on school break. I managed to get some of my own writing done, even with all of my students' essays to grade—"Who do you love best and why." I didn't pick up the phone to call her once, though I wanted to, though I had to practically hold back my hand from dialing her number. I had to honor her wishes, break it off for now, and wait, just wait for that lonesome 2 am call after a gig. It always comes eventually and I always let her come over.

So it begins and so it ends again.

This is a closed party for "those PWP freaks" as Cara fondly refers to them. Parents without Partners, or "Perverts without Prospects," she says drolly. But since I am neither, I got in because I went to Fort Hamilton High with a guy who tends bar here. Dave let me through the door, no problem, no questions asked.

I just needed to see her. Not in that crazed "Son of Sam" kind of way, but just as a friend, even though Cara and I can never be just friends. I want more than that from her and she can't give it. Not right now, she says. Well, I just wanted to see that she was all right, which I can tell she isn't. Cara is never "all right." But sometimes not all right but alive is the best you get from her. And for now, I'll take what I can get.

1/6/79

I thought I saw Michael at the Baron gig last night. But I was good, I didn't call him to find out for sure. Anyhow, it would have been tough to meet up with him since I was squeezed into the back seat of Marty's Caddie, between his wife Beryl and my bass drum. There isn't much difference between the two of them except the drum is probably smarter than Marty's wife. And quieter. That girl never stops yapping, even when there's nothing to say. Sometimes I feel like grabbing her by her 24-karat tricolor Italian gold hoop earrings or yanking her by the neck of her poncho and flinging her across the room.

Michael…it seems like ages since we first met but it's only been a couple of years. At a gig, no less. His niece's Sweet 16 party. Gina dragged him onto the dance floor and forced him to do the Pony with her. To "I Saw Her Standing There." I couldn't help but laugh as I was singing. He looked so uncomfortable, like a Chihuahua wearing a hat. But handsome: smoldering brown eyes, Italian good looks. Our eyes met and locked, and that was that. I started talking to him in the buffet line.

Michael…I hope I can get through this day without calling him. Shit, it's halfway over as it is. And then there's the gig tonight, way out on the ass-end of Queens. Booked for five hours, and with any luck, we'll get an hour overtime. But with me and Michael, late at night, after a gig, that's the danger zone. The testing ground. To call or not to call, that is the question during those dead-tired, weak, desolate hours after a gig. Packing up as the busboys strip off the stained tablecloths, after aunt and niece duked it out over who got to take home Table 10's gross floral arrangement.

I don't know what gets to me, what makes me call him. Maybe it's all those hours of watching strangers hold each other tight in their arms, kiss and smile and hug and love. And live. While I supply the pleasant background music to key events in their lives. Maybe it's wanting to have a life myself. Those bleak, empty hours when I pack up after a gig…that's when I find myself at a pay phone near the powder room, dialing Michael's number. Or just stopping by. He always lets me in, no matter how late it is. It's almost like he's been expecting me.

And it isn't only the sex, which is good, incredibly good, but it's the after sex stuff I crave. I mean, Michael and I can talk. About anything. But we don't even have to talk. We can just be. Michael's the only guy I've ever been with who I don't want to throw out after the deed is done. Who I don't mind sharing a cup of coffee with the next morning. Sometimes he even goes out to Meshuga Phil's and brings home bagels while I'm still asleep. And I'm always happy to see him come back with an onion bagel or two, still warm. He's the only guy who makes me feel good just seeing him walk into the room. Then why do I push him away so much? If I knew the answer, then maybe I wouldn't do it.

Saturday afternoon. Michael's probably sitting at his kitchen table with his "Naughty Elephants" or "World's Best Teacher" coffee mug cooling at his right hand, a pile of papers to grade at his left. Tortured poetry. Essays filled with teen angst. Pop quizzes. Creative questions intent on soul-searching and digging through emotional *schmutz*—like "If you could do one thing to change the world, what would it be and why?"

If I had a teacher like Michael when I was 16, I probably would have turned out better than I did. I definitely wouldn't be so fucked up. Now I have the chance to have him as my boyfriend, more even, and I throw him away. And not just once. Several times. Go figure.

So, here I sit with my notebook open, scribbled lyrics to an almost-song on a sheaf of junk mail and The *Village Voice* opened to the "Musician Classifieds" section. I'm looking for that perfect connection and never seem to find it. A kick-ass band inches from a record deal whose drummer OD'd or freaked out moments before they signed the contract. Something like:

> *"Exceptional blues band with Columbia deal seeks*
> *gifted drummer…"*

Or:

> *"We've got the connections, just need drummer to*
> *complete the band. Call…"*

But instead, there's just:

> *"Promising garage band seeks drummer with van…"*

And:

"Need drummer for local gigs. Must have transportation…"

Or:

"Talented drummer sought to showcase for…"

And you call, right, and it's all bullshit. There are no gigs, no paying gigs anyway. Just a percentage of the door at CBGB's on a Wednesday night. And really, who the hell goes out on a Wednesday night? Any *schmo* could get booked at the Bowery on a weekday night. And when you do the gig, no one shows. Not the Warner Brothers A&R man who supposedly loved your demo tape. Not the creative director at Larva who went to college with the bass player's brother's sister-in-law. Not even your friends, who have respectable 9-5 jobs and get up at 6 am but still beg to be put on the guest list. Shit.

By the time you throw a little something to the sound man and pay off the lead singer's bar tab (who conveniently left his wallet home), you end up owing the house about 10 bucks a head. You see, I've been there before. There and back and there again.

So, why do I do it? There's nothing else for me to do. Why am I even writing this bullshit when I could be finishing up that song, adding yet another to the hundred or more collecting dust in that old Dellwood milk crate in my bedroom?

Or I could be snug in bed next to Michael. But I promised myself I wouldn't call him. Only what does it matter if you break a promise to yourself? I mean, who really knows about those silent promises? Only you. But maybe that's the worst kind of promise to break.

Steve Spinelli
Bandleader/Trumpet Player, Ste-Mar Orchestra

Shit on a stick. That's what the musicians call this place. Terrace on the Park is in the middle of Flushing Meadows-Corona Park. Near the Trylon and the Perisphere (which are still there) from the '36 (or is it the '39) World's Fair. It's about 10 stories high, not far from LaGuardia Airport. Impressive-looking but shoddy-ass construction. You can actually feel the airplanes coming in for a landing. The whole dance floor shakes when the audience does the *tarantella* or jumps up and down for "Shout."

Plus it sucks getting your equipment upstairs. For me, it's not so bad. All I've got is my trumpet and my briefcase. But they always give Cara a hard time at the Terrace. A few months back, one of the waiters actually pulled a knife on her. Pulled it straight out of a baked ham on the way to the carving table in the main dining room. The fucking Rican said that Cara was hogging all the space in the service elevator with her drum kit so he couldn't fit in his cart. A bus boy had to hold him back, pleading to him in Spanglish.

Cara didn't say a word but looked horrified—and scared. I felt sorry for her. Usually do. Especially when Marty treats her like shit. But then again, Marty treats everyone like shit. Even me. But then again, nothing much bothers you after a blast or two. And I always have a few toots on hand. Makes my upper lip numb, but what the hell, I ain't much of a trumpet player anyhow.

But I am something of a businessman. I got the gift of *schmooze*, as Marty likes to say, which is why he keeps me around. I know the right time to smile, when to give a warm pat on the back when the bride's father is sweating the details of a contract and worrying about his bankbook. Whereas Marty is a snake in the grass. He'll turn around on the bandstand and snarl at everyone for coming in too late on the chorus of "Feelings," then turn back to the audience with a slick smile on his face that fools nobody.

I try to help Cara whenever I can, grab her hi-hat cymbals or her snare case, though she doesn't usually like anybody handling her snare. Says it's delicate and expensive. Whatever. I still try and help her just the same. I keep telling Marty we should pay her more since she sings and plays. Cara's a great selling point and has a nice ass which nobody gets to see because sits on that drum stool all the time. Nobody but us. Me and Marty save big bucks by getting an incredible female drummer and singer rolled into one. We should be paying her a little more than everyone else, whether we have to pick her up or not. After all, we're getting two for the price of one and she's not even getting time and a half. But Marty won't have it. The less we pay her, the more for us, he says.

To me, Cara's like that guy in the *Li'l Abner* comic strip. You know, the one who always has a gray rain cloud hanging over his head. Joe something or other. Stuff happens to Cara that doesn't happen to anyone else. You wouldn't believe it. Like, for instance, if three people are parked illegally, she'll be the one to get towed. (Maybe that's why she doesn't have wheels anymore.) If she makes a demo tape, the masters will get ruined in a flood. Marty says she brings this crap upon herself with her piss-poor attitude, but I don't know. I think it's just the luck of the draw. Born under a bad sign or something like that.

And her mother's a piece of work. Nothing's ever good enough for her, not even a daughter with a kind heart, great talent and promise. No wonder her pops left when Cara was just a kid. The old bitch drove him away. If she's not careful, she'll do the same thing to her daughter. One day, Cara will get tired of being a whipping boy and she'll book. The only question is when.

1/8/79

Well, Saturday night was another memorable gig. If your definition of "memorable" is sucky. The one bright spot was getting to hang out with Steve's wife Denise. The only smart one in the whole motley crew of club-date wives and girlfriends. She's funny, too. And Denise has a *real* job, not a disco hostess or some crap like that. She's an X-ray technician for an outfit in Mill Basin. Denise actually does something, helps people and knows her shit. You can just tell.

How Denise ever ended up with Steve is anybody's guess. My guess is that she met him at a gig, her cousin Lenny's *bar mitzvah* or Aunt Minna and Uncle Heshie's 50th anniversary party. Steve turned on the smarmy charm during "Perdido" and that was that. She was hooked.

Dennie comes from a good family, successful folks who built up their business from the bottom up. Transcribing reports to go with X-rays, something like that. Built it from scratch, or from scraps, as Edie likes to say. Real cool people. They have money, but they're not stuck up. Dennie was born on an Army base in Alaska when her dad was enlisted. Somehow, 25 years later, she ended up in Brooklyn (by way of New Jersey) with this *schmuck* of a husband while Mom and Dad stand by cringing but letting their oldest daughter make her own screw-ups. That's the only way you learn, supposedly, by screwing up and not making the same screw-up twice. I, however, am living proof of just the opposite. But that's about to change.

Dennie's good to talk to while wolfing down dinner on a 10-minute break during a continuous gig. The only breath of sanity in this insanity. Tall girl (taller than me) with a big, curly mop of dark hair, brown eyes that spark with intelligence, an easy laugh, quick wit. The mirror opposite of Beryl, who's dumber than a stump. Beryl and Dennie are thrown together at these gigs but instead of being bummed, Dennie seems to enjoy it, seems revel in hanging with that halfwit for sheer entertainment value, if nothing else. At least Dennie could find Vietnam on a map. Beryl, on the other hand couldn't locate it, not even if it bit her on the ass.

Why am I writing about Dennie? To avoid writing about myself, I guess. And Michael.

*

Busy weekend, so I didn't take a temp gig today. I wanted to chill on this Billy Holiday-esque Gloomy Monday. Even though the *Post* was asking for me again. Besides, I hate working in the executive offices, and hearing that asshole Rubin Murphy bellowing at someone or other. I've worked there a dozen times, filling in for a secretary who was taking a personal day or three, and every time I've seen Murphy, he was yelling. Plus I've only seen that Aussie asshole from behind, shouting on the run, chasing someone down. Like the poor fool didn't even rate high enough to get reamed out face-to-face. Or else Rubie couldn't wait to get to their office before he started chewing them out. What a spoiled rich bastard.

So, instead of listening to this millionaire Murphy's crap, I opted to hear a Welfare lady's crap. Not Welfare, exactly, but Disability, which is Edie Finkelstein's only visible means of support. You see, my mother broke her hip when she was just 19, her first job, in the rag trade. Rushing to get a sample, she tripped over a dress rack and fell, fell hard, shattering her hipbone into a million little pieces. Well, according to her anyway. It was the late 1930s and medical miracles weren't what they are today. Many surgeries later, including a fused spine—Oy, don't ask—Edie still walks with a bad limp, mostly with a walker, especially on particularly sucky days. And even Aunt Iris, who never says bad things about anybody, noted that Edie's attitude got worse with each surgery.

For some reason, my mother couldn't bear to marry a guy she was crazy about since she was "damaged goods" (her words) after her accident, so she married a guy she didn't love. My dad Jake was no prize but hard-working. He was in the printing business, had a good job even after the War, bought Edie a brand spanking-new dollhouse on Sunny Lane in Levittown with a loan he'd gotten on the GI Bill. But still, it wasn't good enough for Edie, who found fault in everything Jake did because he wasn't "the one."

I came along unexpectedly when my mom was the advanced age of 29, which, in 1949 was ancient. The pregnancy didn't help her hip or her mood much. I say "unexpectedly" because as per Edie, she avoided sex as much as she possibly could. But there I was, evidence that she hadn't. Was it on some romantic Passover evening when she'd consumed far too much Manischewitz after working elbow-to-elbow with her sisters Sarah and Iris in the kitchen, producing matzo balls so deadly they could have been dropped on Germany and ended WWII. Not to mention their potato kugel, which could double as spackle. (It's a running family joke which Edie doesn't think is very funny.) Or maybe Little Edie was just horny...or lonely.

Yeah, there I was, colicky and cranky, like I had channeled my mother's dissatisfaction through the umbilical cord somehow. Even her breast milk was sour. They tried formula after rancid formula and finally a beige, smelly soy concoction worked. It cost a lot, too. "You had expensive taste from the get-go," Aunt I likes to joke, as my mother looks on, scowling.

My childhood memories are sparse and not exactly happy: my mother standing me on the kitchen table to dress me every morning because it was easier on her bad hip. Sobbing, bony and naked except for my bloomers, as the neighborhood kids rode their bikes up and down Sunny Lane. (I was sure they could see me through the sheer, lime-green café curtains.) Me, struggling to fall asleep in the pitch-blackness of my room because a nightlight wasted electricity and was "stupid" and I was being a "baby" at age three. Shit, I *was a baby*. My parents' gravely, raised voices in that dark I was so scared of. Chesterfield versus Marlboro. Finally, Chesterfield won, Marlboro moved out, and I was stuck growing up with this empty cigarette pack of a woman who didn't like me, let alone love me.

Jesus, I can't believe how long I've gone on about my mother. Or how long I've gone on, period. What time is it anyway? Doesn't matter. I have no gig, no rehearsals, no Michael.

So, today, I walk into my mom's dive on Coyle Street and she's sitting at the kitchen table, staring into space. Cold cup of coffee on the stained oil cloth, worn-off red nail polish, cigarette burning away. My guess: enough Vicodin to take away the pain but not enough to curb her tongue. Not even dressed, still in a button-down housedress which didn't look all that clean.

The minute I saw it on the table, I should have turned and run and not looked back. "It" being that old shoebox from Thom McAn, green with the fancy cream-colored script on top and "America's No. 1 Shoe" on the side. That old shoebox filled with even older memories and none of them of me. Well, I can't really say that because I never got a good look at what's inside.

My mother glanced over at me when I walked in and just sort of rolled her eyes. That's "hello" for her. She grudgingly offered me her cheek, which I kissed. It tasted sour and felt dry against my lips. I put the bag I was carrying on the table. "Chinese food," I smiled, determined she wasn't going to get me down. The happier I was, the more miserable it made her.

"Chinese food?" she barked. "For lunch?"

"For lunch, ma. It's lunchtime. I'll get the non-Kosher plates."

Edith Finkelstein was a food hypocrite of the highest degree. Like many semi-religious Jews, she had separate dishes, pots and silverware for meat and dairy, and stashed away in the back of the cabinet over the Frigidaire were four plates and utensils to be used only for culinary contraband. Oh, Edie wouldn't cook non-Kosher but she would certainly eat it, and with more relish than she did anything else. I often thought that if she had gone down on my father with the same gusto as she worked on a lobster claw, they would still be together today.

I set one Melmac sunflower plate in front of Edie and one at what had always been my place while she tore into the paper bag, already stained with sweet grease. My mother lined up the white cartons like soldiers and unwrapped them one by one, folding back the waxed cardboard edges so that they stood open of their own accord. Shrimp with lobster sauce (two forbidden fruits in one) and roast pork with mushrooms complimented by pork fried rice. You could never have too much pork, especially when you were violating Jewish dietary laws.

In between messy bites, my mother managed to complain, give a cursory chew, take another gluttonous mouthful and complain some more. Our conversation went something like this:

HER

You never call.

ME

I called this morning.

HER

Yeah, but before that. It's been...

(Edie shovels a glimmering mountain of fried rice into
her mouth. I pick up what she drops on the table
and throw it in the trash.)

ME

Ma, I tried. You refuse to let me hook up that
answering machine I got you last Hanukkah.

HER

Ba!

ME

Because if I did, you'd have *bupkis* to
complain about.

(With that, I get one of Edie's epic eye-rolls combined
with a world-class sigh. She stabs three peas innocently
swimming in lobster sauce, thoughtfully mashes them
with her molars then tears into me with renewed energy.)

HER

You never visit.

ME

I'm here now, aren't I?

(A disgusted shrug followed by more cold shoulder, Fairbanks, Alaska cold.)

ME (cont'd.)

Ma...I'm working two jobs.

HER

Instead of one decent job.

ME

Who says working in an office is a decent job?

HER

You could have gone to college...

This is how Edie and I spend the first 15 minutes or so of any visit. Never any "Good to see you's" or "Your hair looks nice" or "Thanks for bringing lunch." Just wasted moments of what I *didn't* do. Sometimes I imagine a June Cleaver or *Ozzie and Harriet* type of exchange. Even that would be more normal and productive. Something like this:

HER

It's so nice to see you, Carol.

ME

You too, Mom. Sorry I haven't...

HER

No need to apologize. I can only imagine how
busy you are. I'm so happy you make the time
for me.

ME

You're my mother! Of course, I make time for you.

HER

And this lunch! What a feast! Thanks for
bringing it.

(Edie reaches for her change purse.)

HER (cont'd.)

Can I give you...

ME

No, mom. It's on me. My pleasure. The least
I can do.

HER

But you work so hard, temping during the day,
playing gigs at night, doing your music...

ME

My music...sometimes I think it's just a
pipe dream.

HER

(holding onto my hand)
Carol, what else do we have but our dreams?
Besides, you've got talent, real talent. And...

See what I mean? What bullshit. So far left field of the truth, it's more a lie
than a fantasy. In reality, my mother and I end up having an argument about what
I'm not and what I don't do, and she winds up crying in an asthmatic rasp that is
both heartrending and annoying at the same time. And I end up leaving.

Which is exactly what happened.

Michael

She called. Late. After a Baron DeKalb gig. I know I shouldn't have gone but I picked her up with the Colt. She looked so forlorn standing there in the cold next to her drum cases piled up on Emmons Avenue like so many black hat boxes. Marty was packing up his keyboard and amps, and barely gave me a nod hello. I hate the bastard: his oily smile, his slimy, sleazy ways, nickel-and-diming his musicians, his lack of respect for them. Marty respected no one, not his customers, his wife, his business partner. I felt like grabbing him by the collar of the Members Only jacket he had changed into. I knew he was a big reason why Cara was so miserable. Marty's put-downs and Semitic misery only compounded what Cara's mother had laid on her for decades. To an outsider like me, and a *goy*, it seemed like a Jewish tradition—making someone feel like shit so they felt too low to even try and escape.

But there was Cara on Emmons, looking so tragically beautiful as well as despondent. Her dark hair standing up in defiant shocks, her purposely-smudged eyeliner accenting her "please don't drown me" chocolate-brown, puppy eyes. Shivering in an oversized black leather jacket. Garland, the old Chinese chef, gave her a small bow as he left and she bowed back. He worked at the Temple Lev Simcha besides doing side jobs at the Baron. Nice guy.

"Thanks," Cara said to me, heaving her bass drum into Colt's hatch. "Thanks for coming."

In my car, there wasn't much to say. Her wordless sigh said it all. I drove silently through the deserted streets that looked frozen, hopeless, laced with the scattered remnants of old, gray snow. Cara's snare drum case was on her lap and she tap, tap, tapped the hard cover in an irregular beat. She did this when she was nervous or upset or both. It felt good to have her beside me again, good to look across the console and see her worried profile, her strong nose, her delicate chin.

The Belt Parkway was almost empty that time of night. The Verrazano-Narrows Bridge, its lights strung against the indigo of the clear, winter sky, looked like a glowing pearl necklace, breathtaking, but still, no words from Cara. Bay Ridge is a pretty safe neighborhood but we still took her drum kit inside, piece by piece, piling them in the hallway like a tiered, black wedding cake.

Cara took the snare drum inside. "It's easy for some skell to walk off with it," she explained, plus she'd finally found one she liked. We squeezed past the drum pile and up a few steps to my apartment. She put down the snare. I hadn't even gotten the door closed when she not so much as fell into my arms but more like melted into them.

The sharp angles of her hip bones. The softness of her inner thighs. The smolder of her eyes. Slightly crooked front teeth, biting down on her lower lip, on me, almost drawing blood. Wet, tense, fluttering, like a sparrow trapped in a pillowcase, then gone.

When I woke up the next morning, the bed was empty and Cara was curled up in an armchair, wearing one of my flannel shirts, scribbling furiously in the notebook she always had in her backpack. "Glad to see you're keeping a journal," I told her.

"Who says it's a journal?" she said.

"Fair enough," I answered. "You staying?"

"Breakfast?" she asked. I made my way to the kitchen. "Maybe longer," she tagged on.

I took out a carton of eggs, piled the butter dish and a tin of Maxwell House on top, and balanced it over to the table. "How much longer?"

"You have someone else coming over?" she wondered.

"There is no one else. You know that," I told her.

Over breakfast, Cara dove right back into it, as though we'd left off in mid-argument three weeks earlier and she was picking up after a sentence. She stabbed an egg yolk with the corner of her toast until it oozed. "I can't keep doing this to you," she said. "It's not fair."

"Fair, shmair," I said, channeling her mother. For the first time since I'd picked her up, Cara smiled, then laughed. "I'm the one who went and got you, remember?"

When did my journal take a crazy left and turn into a novel? And a bad novel at that. I'm the one who's always telling Cara that she should write down her thoughts and here I am...

Yeah, I know she's gotten the shitty end of the stick most of her life. Yeah, I get it that the years of living with her witch of a mother's negativity and sorrow has taken its toll. Yeah, I understand that Marty and Steve are each scumbags in their own right, but I don't understand why she doesn't just get the hell out of that band and move on.

But then again, why don't I? Move on, I mean.

Why is it so easy to take Cara back into my bed, into my life? It'll be good for a few days, a few weeks, even, then it will start again. That dark, pervading sadness that gets into everything around us, like smoke. And no matter what you do, no matter where you go, it's always there. Like "The Thing That Wouldn't Leave" from the *Saturday Night Live* skit. And that nameless *thing* is in Cara so deep that I can almost taste it on her skin. After a while, it invades me. Like *The Blob* or *Invasion of the Body Snatchers* or any of those 1950s B sci-fi movies Cara loves so much. I can almost feel it sitting on my chest, so that I can hardly take a full, deep, cleansing breath. Then, before I know it, I start to realize that the bad outweighs the good, that the tears outlast the laughter, that the anger turns Cara's body into a cold, hard fist which even love can't penetrate. But I keep holding on for dear life until Cara pushes me away.

1/15/79

I haven't written in this thing for a week or so, and I must admit that it felt good…at first. Then I found myself jonesing for it like I sometimes jones for Michael. And I really felt messed up about that: about both joneses.

Well, it's on again. With Michael. And it's good. Oh, it's always good at first. Then I start to get to him. And not in a good way. He starts to want more and I start to pull back. By more, I mean marriage, a family, the whole bit. Michael swears he'll be okay with me gigging, recording, trying to make it. But I know he'll start to lose patience with the lifestyle, the late hours, seeing each other like ships passing in the night while he works days and I work days, nights, weekends and holidays. The aloneness will get to him. It always does.

Besides, I don't fit into the pigeonhole of being a "wife." At least not in the Beryl sense of the word. Or like my sister-in-law. Cooking, cleaning, making nice even when I don't want to. No, thanks. If I were really honest, I only feel right when I have a pair of sticks in my hands. And that's pretty screwed up. Or is it?

And kids? I love my nephews, I really do. But having kids of my own. Being pregnant, squeezing one out… I could never picture that, even before I ever sat behind a kit or picked up a microphone. Maybe because of the kind of mother I had. Still have. I'm so scared of being like her.

Plus I'm not cool with the thought of taking care of anything. Not even a plant. I can barely take care of myself. How could I take care of a kid and a husband? I'd be a shitty wife and mother. I just know it.

Let's face it—kids are one big ego trip. When it comes down to it, how is it a reflection on you if Little Murray got an A on his science report or nailed his haftorah at his *bar mitzvah*? It's all about them, not about you, and it's all a crap shoot anyway. Besides, I wouldn't want to get stuck with a moody mook with all of my own worst qualities who'd only grow up to hate me. Let's be honest, that's parenthood in a nutshell.

Saw an ad in the *Voice* today. Will probably call but it's probably just the same old bullshit.

JR Cloud
Keyboard Player/Bandleader, Aircraft

I knew she was the one the minute she walked into the studio. Skittish like a bird on ice, clutching her snare drum like it anchored her to the gray, stained rug. Slightly unsure of herself until she got her bearings, until she made eye contact. Then she turned all badass, stared me down, hard, unblinking. "You JR?" she said, both asking and telling me in the same breath. Her voice was hard and soft at the same time. Broken glass dipped in hot fudge.

Without waiting for an answer, she made her way toward me, hand extended. All swagger and attitude, like Buddy Rich with tits. But way prettier, in a rough and tumble way. "Name's Cara," she told me. "Carol, really."

I met her hand, calloused in the palm where she cradled the stick, Louie Bellson 5A's, I later learned. "JR Cloud. Real name's Wilmot Clapowitz, Jr. Only my wife calls me 'Willie.' I guess you and me both named ourselves better than our parents did."

She didn't answer, just gave a crooked, whiplash smile that I could easily picture on the front of an LP. "You wanna hear me play?"

I shuffled through a pile of sheet music on the beat-up piano. "I don't read music," she told me without apology or excuse. "But I've got a good ear." She was already unhooking the studio snare and snapping hers into place. "And perfect pitch," she added for good measure.

"Anything else?" I asked.

"And a five octave range," she shrugged.

Cara sat behind the kit, waiting, sticks in hand, silently bidding me to show her what I had.

I ran through "China Doll" once on piano, barreling my way through the words and music I'd written myself. Well, my wife Fern pitched in with the lyrics on that one. Cara nodded throughout, making mental notes to herself, biting her lip, then letting it go and nodding some more. "Nice," she said when I was done.

When the guys came back from their smoke break, reeking of weed, we ran through the song again after hasty introductions. We'd been through at least a dozen auditions in the past two days, Cara being the last. Some sucked and could hardly keep a beat. Some were just okay. One or two were exceptional but none had that spark. No one fit. You know, picking a new band member, it's like meeting a chick and knowing that this is the one you're going to marry. It was like that with Fern, so intense that I didn't want to see her again because I knew someday, she'd be my wife. And it scared the hell out of me.

But when I watched Cara shake hands with Roy, Danny and Mongo, I had the same feeling. Something clicked. They joked around, then got down to business.

Cara was deep, watching, listening, absorbing my silly, little song through her skin. After the first chorus, she jumped in mid-verse, not missing a beat, throwing in tasty snaps and rolls that immediately found their place and lived there. It was like she'd been playing with us for years instead of just minutes.

The guys looked at each other, nodding and laughing out loud but the music drowned out the sound of their laughter. Cara's eyes were closed, so she didn't see at first. Third verse, she opened them, like coming out of a dream, and she was grinning, too. By the last chorus, she was singing harmony like she'd wrote the song herself.

There were high fives all around when we were through. "So, we rehearse three nights a week..." I began.

Between Cara's day gig and society gigs, I didn't know how she'd manage but she swore it would be no problem. "Family? Kids? Boyfriend?"

She kept shaking her head. "Nothing. No ties."

But that could be a problem, too. No roots, no responsibilities, no loyalty. She could be out of here in a New York minute. Just like Jimmy after that "Star Power" audition. The producer loved him, hated us, and in the blink of an eye we were without a lead singer and he was in the quarter finals. Rat bastard.

But where would Cara take us? Aircraft was about to find out.

1/22/79

I had a feeling as soon as I walked into the studio. Nothing special about the rehearsal space, same shitty worn-out equipment, gray egg cartons on the walls, half wall around the kit, like they're trying to trap the drummer, contain him. Because let's face it, nine times out of ten, it's a him.

The ad in the *Voice* was nothing special either. Same blah-blah-blah about contacts, demo, record deal waiting in the wings. Dumb-ass name too...Aircraft. I mean, what the hell is that supposed to mean? Is it a band or an airline? But I overlooked it and figured what the hell, I would check it out anyway. It's only a couple of hours out of my life. You never know. But I knew, the minute the studio door closed tight behind me. I knew it was right.

The lead guy was the only one there. JR. Not much to look at but he had this intensity in his eyes, this hunger. Not a hunger for me, but a hunger to make it. JR didn't look at me like a piece of meat or some pussy he could get over on like Marty did, but like an equal. Someone who could help him get where he wanted to be. There was no bullshit about JR. It was down to business right away, but he seemed to have a heart, too. You could tell by his music.

He played a song for me on the keyboards. On the surface, JR's song was a catchy enough ditty about some hot Asian chick but if you sliced down through a few layers, it was all aching and longing and loss and more loss.

When the three other guys got back from a break, we tried out the song together. I thought JR would come in his pants when I played, easing right in with them, kicking ass with backing vocals on the chorus. JR didn't even say I was in, he just filled me in on the rehearsal schedule and showcase gig at CBGB's in a couple of months. He didn't have to say that I made the band—I was already *in* the band.

This feels right, better than any group has in years. The other guys seem pretty cool, too. Lead guitarist like a big, dopey puppy. Bass player bald as Kojak and with no eyebrows either, but I don't think it's from chemo. Pretty-boy lead singer, with flowing hair, chiseled chin, dreamy, blue eyes, a poor man's Robert Plant, but from Michigan instead of Oxford or wherever the hell Plant is from.

I'll have to bust my ass to keep up but I've done it before. And hopefully, it will be worth it. Don't know where Michael fits into the picture but whatever. If he believes in me, he'll still be there if I want him to be.

The clock is ticking, 11 more months and then it's over. Really. I swear it.

*

I've had a lot of time to write today. The Accounting bozo I'm pretending to be secretary for is in meetings most of the day. The other secretaries…the ones who insist on being called "administrative assistants," the permanent ones, and not lowly temps like me…they pretty much ignore me. They think I'm too dumb to hold down a full-time job and pooh-pooh the fact that I refuse to wear Polyester monkey suits to work. Bad enough I have to wear a costume to club dates so I'll be damned if I wear one to my day gig, too. Don't get me wrong, I don't look like a *schlub*. I have a bunch of bright, colorful skirts from Joyce Leslie (no pinstripes, thanks), lots of black, and nice shirts, but no one would mistake me for a corporate bimbo. I'm out on the fuck-me pumps, too. For me, it's sensible heels from Payless that I could run in if I had to.

Ellis, my boss at the *Post*, doesn't mind if I write music, poetry or porn on my down time. He just wants a warm body to answer his phone and get his messages straight. I have this carbonless Write n' Stick message pad—and I would love to tell him where to stick it!

He's actually pretty cool, I guess, even though he looks me up and down like he's wondering what planet I'm from. In his 50s, thinning hair, pants too high up on the waist, shrew of a wife, fuck-up of a daughter. Thinks he can lecture me because his horror show of a kid won't listen to his bull. But I just listen because I have to, I'm paid to, and my ass is glued to this chair for eight hours a day, five days a week (minus breaks). I don't care if he's dictating a letter or pontificating, it's all the same to me because I'm getting paid. I feel like a corporate hooker.

Last week, Ellis was looking over my shoulder as I was at the Selectric, ball spinning so loud, I didn't hear him come up behind me until he was already there, breathing pastrami breath down my neck. He wanted to see the poem I was writing, so I eased it out of the roller and handed it to him:

I took a bright, green ribbon
and wrapped it around
"Summertime,"
and gave it to you
for no apparent reason
except that I love you
like its melody:
slow and easy
and timelessly.

All the guy wanted to know was why the ribbon was green, why the word "Summertime" had a line to itself and why I didn't say "timeless" instead of timelessly. Not 'Why am I shelling out $10 an hour to Payton People for you—of which your cut is $8 or so—to write shitty poetry.' Poor cocker has no sense of rhythm. I bet he can't even *schtoop* to a beat. He probably never had a poetic thought in his life. Number crunching pain in the ass!

When things get boring, I walk by the loading docks and watch the truck drivers heave stacks of newspapers onto the paneled trucks for the afternoon run. After morning deliveries, those guys sit around doing nothing until they hear "Get your belts on!" over the loudspeaker. Which means the conveyer belt will start rolling any second—and also that they should be wearing their heavy-lifting belts—so they'd better look alive. And they do. No matter what they were up to before, bullshitting with each other or flirting with a female who was passing by, they start stacking their bales of newspaper into their truck, grabbing them from the conveyer belt as they pass, working in tandem, fast, never missing a beat or a pile of second-rate tabloid papers. Now that's poetry. Poetry in motion.

When I go into or out of the the *Post*, I tend to take the Catherine Street entrance. Maybe because it's closer to the F train. Maybe because it's a pretty name for a street, as opposed to Market or Peck. But going down Catherine Street has become something of a ritual.

One afternoon, I happened to be coming down the block in the middle of the truck-loading madness. It was like stumbling upon on a secret ceremony in the midst of a hidden forest. I was captivated by the action, the electricity, the movement of the belt, the strength of the drivers loading up their trucks, the urgency. I couldn't help but stop and watch, even though I was already five minutes late. Ellis was out for his usual liquid lunch, so what was the rush?

Soon after I started at the *Post*, a driver named Howie began chatting me up. Then I learned that a bunch of the drivers were vying for my attention and it had become something of a game among them who could get me to smile or say hello. Now, I'm no great beauty, I know this, but I've never been thrown out of bed either. And women are scarce here. Not only is this crappy rag an old boy's club, but most of the females here are secretaries, and they think they're too high and mighty to talk to me, let alone a sweaty truck driver.

Just for ha-ha's I started talking to the truckers. Even saved 10 minutes or so of my lunch hour for conversation. Timed it so that it wasn't "press time" when I passed, so we could chat. It was so boring up on the fourth floor that this was something to look forward to, something that helped make the day pass. And it was a pisser watching them trip all over each other to get a word with me. Guess it was more boring on the loading dock than it was in the executive offices. Plus it did wonders for my battered ego.

Early on, Howie and a freckle-dusted guy with a chestnut-colored shag haircut named Tom started jockeying for position. Hands down, they were the Alpha Males of the loading dock. Although Howie was okay-looking with his Jewfro, hairy chest (so hairy it peeked out through the neck of his long johns) and gold chains, Tom seemed a little bit smarter, not so much of a lech, and had these wicked blue-green eyes that made me melt when he looked at me dead on. Howie and Tom pretended to be the best of friends in each other's presence but would bad-mouth each other when the other one wasn't there:

Howie: "Tommy's all right, but he doesn't know how to treat a woman. Not a woman like you."

Tom: "Jews don't know how to fuck. You know that, right? Meanwhile, the Irish are short but enthusiastic."

Howie: "Tommy's a little bit of an ass. But you're a smart girl. I'm sure you noticed."

Tom: "How many fucking times is Howie going to pull out that *Playboy* clip from the Plato's Retreat story? If he does it again, I'll puke." (It was true, Howie carried around this frayed page from a *Playboy* article, folded into eight squares. It showed him naked from the waist up, hands firmly planted on some anonymous blonde's hips. I'd seen it so often, I had it memorized.)

Howie: "I told you I've been to Plato's Retreat, right? Hey, if you ever want to check it out…"

And on and on.

I didn't care if they talked rough. It was Saturday at the *shul* compared to the garbage that went on in Ste-Mar. Besides, I thought it was funny as hell that two guys were fighting over me.

Well, the party's over. Here comes Ellis, looking shell-shocked from his luncheon meeting with Murphy, his comb-over askew, his tie slightly loosened. Like I said before, the only time I've ever seen that insane Aussie, it's been from behind and he's been yelling. I've got to give my boss his five highly unimportant messages and pretend that I give a shit.

Denise Weinstein-Spinelli
Radiologist/Steve's Wife

I noticed something different about Cara the second she walked into the Lev. Like a weight had been lifted off her shoulders. And even listening to 45 minutes of bullshit as Marty drove her from Sheepshead Bay to Great Neck couldn't kill her high. I was glad for her. Cara was good people. She deserved good things but kept getting crap. Not that Steve was any help. I mean, he's my husband and I love him, but he doesn't have the strongest backbone in the world. Even though he isn't the one treating Cara like shit, he doesn't put up enough of a stink when Marty tries to take out too much of her pay for gas or doesn't give Cara the fair share of a tip. What do they call it? The sin of omission?

Well, that's my Stevie. He doesn't like to rock the boat, doesn't like to make waves. But I try to tell him that you pretty much sell your soul to the Devil (aka Marty Karroll) when you let him step all over your band members like that. I also know that Steve can't bear to hurt someone's feelings or say 'no.' So instead, he yeses people to death, even if the yes turns out to be a lie. He hates to tell the bride's goo-goo eyed sister that he's married if it means he might lose a sale. And he doesn't wear his wedding ring for that very reason too—appearing to be single gets more single girls up to dance and flirt with the trumpet player with the bee-stung lips. He flirts back, smiling behind the mouthpiece, winking, sometimes more.

To get a sale, Steve might go a little further. I know that. I've told him it bothers me. I've told him it isn't right and it hurts me like hell. But then he turns on the charm, telling me, "Dennie, baby, what's the difference if I have a snack on the way home, so long as I still have an appetite for dinner with you?" I don't know what it is, his crinkled smile that makes me melt or the words I so much want to believe but I always end up forgiving him, no matter how many nights I end up spending alone, no matter how late he turns up long after a gig is over.

That's what I admire so much about Cara—she never sells out, she never gives in, even if it means losing money when she's on the balls of her ass. Plus she's funny as all hell and smart, not book smart, but street smart, body smart. Cara found something she does well and she does it, no matter what. No matter how many guys leave her because she's not like the other girls. No matter how long and hard and loud her harpy of a mother bitches because she doesn't have: a) a career; b) a husband; and c) a baby; or d) all of the above.

If it weren't for Cara, I would lose it at these God-forsaken gigs. Some Saturday nights, I just don't want to be alone, so I go with Steve to the El Caribe or the Lev Simcha, especially the Lev because it's full of ferret-faced Temple Girls—high school seniors wearing Sephardic versions of the proverbial French maid outfit, only a tad more pious with an inch or two more of black satin skirt. (Before Beryl and Marty's wedding, one Temple Girl spread STDs like peanut butter, so that poor, stupid Beryl had herpes on her honeymoon. Thankfully, Steve was unscathed, though I know he went to the party, too. He probably wore a rubber.) Yeah, these Temple Girls are real whores but whores can often sell a catering hall, even a religious one.

I would freak out with only Beryl to talk to while Steve went *schmoozing* with the *bar mitzvah* boy's aunt to get in her good graces for her own pimply spawn's upcoming party. Cara knows it's all a joke, that it's all a game, pure bullshit. That's why she's so fun to hang out with.

Our favorite thing to do at these gigs is goof on people, practically to their faces. Why does Grandma Nesserman think Spandex was a good idea? ("It's a privilege, not a right," Cara has been known to quip.) Should we tell the bride that she's trailing a ten-foot section of toilet paper as she leaves the bathroom? (Nah.) Is it possible to wear one's pants any higher than that guy in the brown suit? (Probably not.)

And sometimes Cara and I laugh until we practically piss ourselves, usually at Beryl's expense. I.e. Beryl thought *The Andromeda Strain* was based on something that really happened "on one of those Apollo thingies."

I couldn't even get mad at Cara when she looked at me in the mirror in the Lev's prissy pink ladies' room one night as we were both fixing up our eye makeup, and she suddenly blurted out, "Why do you take it?"

I knew exactly what she was talking about but played dumb, stroking on the Great Lash until one eye was noticeably more Liza Minnelli than the other. Then I went to town on the other. "You're too good for him," Cara said, undaunted. "You deserve to be treated better."

Then our eyes met again in the mirror. Mine were hard like black marbles while hers were warm and gooey like caramel. Instead of getting pissed off at her, I burst into tears and the next thing I knew, we were sitting side by side on two of those velvety little toadstools that frilly ladies' rooms always seem to have. She smelled like Tigress and sweat, which wasn't a bad combination. Her arms wrapped around me like she didn't care who saw. And she didn't.

"But I love him," I managed to choke out.

"That's no excuse," she said. "No excuse at all."

How could you not like someone like that? How could you not root for her?

After I calmed down, I splashed cool water on my face and reapplied my Maybelline to the tune of Olga, the washroom attendant, cooing, *"Ay, chica…"* and Cara saying, "It will be all right," even though I knew she thought it wouldn't.

Cara and I were soon back in the Sinai Ballroom just as Bob Ackerman was finishing up acoustic guitar music to accompany the stuffed cabbage *et al* during the main course. I think it was one of those obscure 15th century Spanish madrigals Bob's so fond of. Basically, nobody gave a damn what he played just so long as it wasn't obtrusive and didn't get in the way of the *kasha*. Nobody seemed to notice that Ackerman was a God-damned genius or else, they did and nobody cared. To them, he was just a math teacher who played guitar on weekends. Nothing more. But he was a lot more. We all are. More. More than what people think we are.

Steve was still MIA but Marty, fucking Marty was out of his head, thinking Cara went AWOL, too. "Where the fuck were you?" Marty snarled as she slipped behind the drum kit. Then he turned to the audience with a nauseating, Saccharine smile and announced "More than a Woman." I hate that rotten bastard, hate him with same blind passion I love Steve with.

"Powdering my nose," Cara told the back of his head.

"That's some fucking nose," Marty snapped, then was all sweetness and light for the *bar mitzvah* boy and his overpaying family, bucking for overtime, no doubt. Damned SOB even masked a snicker when they almost dropped the poor kid as his drunken uncles were dancing around with him in the banquet hall chair they lifted over their heads.

Stevie magically reappeared on the bandstand, his Dry Look, shellacked hair just slightly out of place. He grabbed his trumpet and grinned at me. Then I noticed that Sandy, one of the curviest Temple Girls, had just reappeared in the dining room, straightening her hem. Cara looked at me then looked away.

One thing that brought my head up—besides Beryl not being there—was how happy Cara looked, even with Marty berating her. While she was setting up that night, she told me that she'd just auditioned for an amazing band and nailed it. "Why doesn't that surprise me?" I told her. She didn't hear good things about herself nearly enough. Would you believe she blushed?

"This is it, Dennie," she beamed, her face bright red. "I can feel it."

Now, I'd heard this from Cara more times than I care to admit. She said it with every half-assed original band that welcomed her into the fold, and every single time, she was let down. Hard. I hoped to God she was right this time.

52

1/30/79

It's been a hectic few weeks. End of the year tax crap with the *Post*, which means I actually have stuff to do—and so does Ellis. I've been rehearsing two nights a week, sometimes more, with Aircraft. They're getting all bent out of shape about that showcase gig when there's no need to. We sound phenomenal, like we've been playing together for a decade, not weeks. Besides, I've been down this road before. Everybody and their grandmother says they're going to show up at CB's but when the day finally rolls around, there will be two bums from the Paradise flophouse upstairs, Captain and Tennille's former roadie and an indie A&R man's drunken assistant/girlfriend. Instead of getting a record deal, we end up getting stuck with their bar tabs.

But I'm trying to be more positive. I really am. I promised Michael I would. Not that I've been seeing much of him since that rekindle soon after New Year's. I think he is alternately put off by me and turned on by me, sometimes both at the same time. I think it messes him up—and then worries him because it messes him up so much. Here's a guy who's always in control, a guy whose lesson plans are pretty much done before the end of August. A guy whose markers he grades papers with are carefully thought out: red's too aggressive and angry, green's too wishy-washy, yellow too hard to read, and blue (indigo blue) just right because it's straightforward yet sincere. I kid you not.

I think Michael needs a white-picket-fence kind of girl: conventional, with slightly-thick ankles and sturdy, childbearing hips. Even though he considers himself a rebel, Michael's pretty conventional himself. I think he thinks he wants me but he also believes that maybe I will end up destroying him. That I will end up chipping away at him, at the things he loves, and then he will become something he hates—in addition to hating me. But nobody can tell Michael anything. He has to see it for himself. He also wants me to meet his family but I've held off on that, too.

So, Michael stays away. Winter marking period, winter break, whatever. He distances himself from me until he needs another fix to feel all quirky and radical when he's really just a button-down guy at heart. But that's okay, I just roll with it. We give each other what we need. Sometimes.

It's been cold as all hell lately. Like I said, work's been insane but tiresome. I'm not a numbers kind of gal, even though I temp in Accounting. It's gotten so nuts at the paper that I seek out the company of jerks like Howie and Tom down at the loading dock, anything to get away from the click of the adding machine or those dry, yawn-filled letters I have to type. It's so boring there that Ira (the guy under Ellis) and I made up a rumor that we're having an affair. And I'm pretty sure he's gay. People are starting to look at us funny, which is hysterical, because they have no clue we started the gossip-party ourselves.

Ira and I also started this fun thing where we throw all of our pocket change into a jar, our mad money, we call it. Actually, we're saving up for a nice lunch at Forlini's, a great Italian place on Baxter Street, in the shadow of the Tombs. When we have enough, we'll sneak out like we're going to some sleazy Chinatown hotel, and sneak back in like we just spent the past two hours sliding between greasy bed sheets. Even Howie thinks something is up with Ira and me.

Ira is a cool guy. He hates the *Post* even more than I do because he's an actual employee. Hates it with a passion because he's stuck here, makes a decent salary but can't stand the people he works with (except for me) and is too chicken-shit to up and leave and go someplace else. Or take his piddly savings and chase his dream—which is opening up a card store in Florida called "Hi I." That's not much of a dream but at least it's a dream. And it's sad as hell that he's not man enough to chuck everything and chase it.

I'm really digging the Aircraft songbook. Everything else is such shit that I look forward to our rehearsals. In a way, it's the only thing that's keeping me going. We're still getting a feel for each other's styles, still testing the waters, but given the fact that we've only been playing together for a few weeks, we are pretty fucking impressive.

Bass players and drummers traditionally have a groove because their instruments are so hinged on each other. And Mongo and I are really starting to mesh. JR is a hell of a songwriter, really complex stuff, like late Beatles meets a not-so-trippy Floyd. He's no slouch on the keyboards but his writing really shines. Not much of a voice but he's solid on the harmonies. When we play CB's in March, we'll be ready.

January is a slow month for the club date trade because it's too unpredictable weather-wise. Prospective brides, grooms and *bar mitzvah* parents are scared shitless that it's going to blizzard on their parade and ruin their special day, even though there are deep discounts. And everyone knows how Jews love their discounts. (I can say that because I'm Jewish. Besides, it's true.) That's when Marty and Beryl spend 10 days at her parents' St. Maarten timeshare—even though I doubt Beryl could even find the Caribbean on a map of the Caribbean. And I get a break from the Ste-Mar bullshit. But I do miss the pay.

I'm starting to think it's serendipity or karma or whatever the hell they call it, that I found Aircraft now. We'll be gigging by spring and hopefully have a record deal by the summer if things go the way JR says they will. In a couple of days it will only be February, so there's still time.

Henrique "Mongo" Martinez
Bass Player, Aircraft

Like I always say, the drummer is the heartbeat of a band. And in a way, Cara's got my heart already. Now keep your mind out of the gutter. I don't mean she's got my heart in *that* way. I got Zelda for the lovey-dovey shit. Cara's no bow-wow but she's a little too androgynous for my taste. Stringy arms, tight as rubber bands. She could probably take me in an arm-wrestling match. Calloused fingers from years of holding sticks. Cropped black hair. Miles of attitude. Picture Pat Benatar and Chrissie Hynde's love child and you've got Cara Funk.

Didn't even have to play a lick and I knew she was the one. The minute I got a look at her in that dingy rehearsal space, holding her snare like it was a time bomb, ticking away, I knew. She looked me straight in the eye when we shook hands, no bullshit, just a "what you see is what you get" bare-balls look. It's kind of hot when a chick knows what she wants, what she is, and goes for it.

Mi abuela would say, "You come from the same *barrio*." Even though we don't. Even though Cara ain't a Rican but a Jew through and through. We both come from a kind of ghetto that we're trying like hell to get out of. From a life we're trying to right and change. There's a mark we've got to make, and we're busting our asses to make it.

At first, JR and Roy were thinking: "Girl drummer…great gimmick," and wanted to run with it. Danny and me were trying to tell them to fuck the gimmick angle, she was just a kick-ass drummer. Cara slid right into "China Doll" like sweet butter, eating up all those wild chord changes, tempo shifts and whatnot like it was nothing. Like she relished each one, couldn't wait for the next chance to prove herself. Cara and me kept looking at each other, nodding, laughing even. It felt right. So, yeah, we are from the same *barrio*, the same place, the same hood.

When rehearsal was done, Cara said, "Mongo, huh? Like the big guy in *Blazing Saddles*?"

I had to admit she was right. "Kind of a family joke," I told her.

"What's your real name?" she wondered. The guys in the band never even bothered to ask.

"Henrique, after my grandfather," I told her. "But no one's called me that in, like, forever."

"Mine's Carol," she said. "But no one ever calls me that except my mother." And the way she said it, kind of with a snarl, I knew never to call her "Carol." No matter what.

2/3/79

Another shit gig in another shit catering hall. Marty's on the rag, probably because Beryl is. I can't do a fucking thing right even when I do. He's snapping at me between his teeth like a mad dog to slow the tempo, then to stop dragging it, then turning around to the *bar mitzvah* boy, sweet as pie, and complimenting him on his *haftorah*. And Marty, the lying son of a bitch, wasn't even there to hear him stumble through his pained Brooklynese Hebrew, weighed down by puberty and braces. I swear, one of these days I'm going to throw a drumstick at his fat, fucking face and hope it gets him in the eye.

But the craziest thing happened after the *bar mitzvah*. This sweet, little, old Jewish lady hobbled up to the bandstand while I was packing up. "You're very good," she told me.

"Thanks," I told her back, continuing to throw my drum stands in the case.

"No, really, really good," she continued. "And I should know," she said, fumbling for the big, gold heart-shaped locket around her neck. When she opened it, to my surprise, there was a picture of Gene Simmons inside, of him wearing his crazy Kiss face makeup. "I'm his mother," she smiled, and walked away. I almost fell over. That almost made the night and almost made the awful gig worth it. Almost.

I don't know why I've been in such a rage. I'm not on the rag, even though Marty asks me every other week if I am. The truth is I've had it. With his bullshit, with his band, with everything. I know I should keep my head up, that it's just a matter of time before Aircraft makes it. Yeah, I know, we haven't even had our first gig. But some things you just know. You just feel it in your gut. And some things you don't. Like me and Michael, for instance.

I can't see us getting settled down and married. I can't see where we're going but I have a feeling where we'll end up. Maybe because I'm sabotaging us every chance I get. Michael doesn't ask for much from me. He doesn't mind that I'm working most weekends. He doesn't try to shove me into a little box of what he thinks a girlfriend should be. He doesn't ask for much except respect and honesty, and I've pissed all over that. More than once. I'm sure I'll do it again. Flirting relentlessly with Tom and Howie. Putting music before him. It's just the way I'm built. I'm a piece of shit, pure and simple.

Edith Finkelstein
Cara's Mother

Oy! If I had a dollar for every time she said she was going to make it, I wouldn't be living in this *facocta* basement apartment. It's too cold in the winter, too hot in the summer. You can hear every footstep over your head, day and night, every flush of the toilet. No, I'd be living in a fancy-shmancy condo on Knapp Street, looking down on the fish and the stink of Emmons Avenue instead of across the street from that noisy high school.

"Ma, when I make it, I'll buy you a nice little one bedroom in The Emmons Avenue Condominium," Carol promised, when I was *kvetching* this afternoon. I had on two sweaters and thermal bloomers and I was still frozen solid. Because my hip was throbbing, I dragged my leg like Boris Karloff in one of those crappy monster movies Carol loved to watch as a kid.

Then I just lost it. I don't know if it was the pain or the cold or just listening to the same *dreck* over and over again from my daughter but I let her have it. I hated the sound of my own voice, scratching and screeching like some lunatic. I watched Carol's face collapse, fall into pieces, just like it did when she was little, but I didn't care, I just kept right on lacing into her. It felt good before it started to feel bad. Sometimes I think the one thing in my life that I have power over is making Carol feel bad.

You may wonder why don't I stop acting like this if I feel so guilty about it? But it's not me who should stop. It's Carol who should stop doing things that get me so angry. Besides, it's a mother's duty to look out for her children. If they do something stupid, you should tell them it's stupid, right? Who else is going to tell them? And if it hurts their feelings, too bad. So be it.

It wouldn't have been so terrible if Carol fought back, if she would say *something, anything*. But she just sat there, staring back at me in shock, like it was the first time I ever did it instead of the thousand and first. Carol unwrapped the roast beef sandwich she'd brought from Roll-N-Roaster, put it on the waxed paper wrapper and said nothing. Every time she visited, she brought us something nice to eat, something she knew I couldn't afford or get to (because I can't walk far and don't drive), shrugging and admitting, "Jews don't cook," when she set it down in front of me.

"What do you mean, I cooked every night when you were growing up," I told her. I had a feeling she was going to give me nonsense about feeding her Hamburger Helper all the time but she didn't. She didn't say anything.

Then after a while Carol said, "You'll see." I tried to keep eating but the way she looked at me, disappointed, defeated, took away my appetite. "I've been hearing that *meshugaas* talk since you picked up those stinking drumsticks," I said, and not kindly.

Carol was already reaching for her jacket, the crummy leather jacket that's falling apart at the seams. It's not nearly warm enough for the winter. She stood there, playing with her hair, twirling it, then pulling it like she does when she gets real nervous, just like she did when she was a little girl. And that hair! Chopped short like she just got liberated from Auschwitz. Better she should wear a *sheitel* than go around with hair like that.

"Enjoy your sandwich, Ma," Carol said in that same small voice she had as a kid. I could tell that she was about to cry.

Instead of thanking her for bringing the food, I told her, "How can I enjoy my sandwich with you talking *narishkeit* at my table?" Her arm shot down the jacket's right sleeve and then the left. One step to the door, then another. "And it's not even Kosher!"

A wounded look. How many was that now? Carol's hand was on the doorknob. When she turned it, I swooped in for the kill. "And why do you always insist on bringing *traif* into this house? This is a Kosher home! Is it because of your boyfriend…that *goy*…"

"Michael's not my boyfriend," Carol said as she stepped out the door. Then she ducked her head back in. "See you next week."

"I might not be here next week!"

Then she laughed. "And where would you go?"

"I might be dead!" I screamed. "Dead, I wouldn't have to deal with a daughter like you! You're *gornisht*…" And just in case Carol didn't remember her Yiddish, I was nice enough to translate it for her. "You're nothing, *gornisht, gornisht helfen!*"

That did it. Carol turned and left without even closing the door. I had to get up and do it myself, cursing and grabbing onto furniture as I went. Cracked Formica kitchen table, breakfront, doorjamb, wall. My walker was in the living room. Even though Carol was moving fast, I managed to get a glimpse of her, hunched against the cold, rubbing at her nose, her eyes. Her shoulders were shaking as she cried. She wasn't even wearing a hat, let alone gloves.

My fingers couldn't light the Bic as I fumbled with the cigarette, even though I wasn't supposed to smoke. I always kept a pack hidden in the cutlery drawer and another in my nightstand. I finished Carol's sandwich, then mine before digging into the cole slaw and "fries-n-cheez" meant for us both to share. I was ready to bust by then and even madder. That's why I was such a big, fat blimp. Because my daughter made me so *verklempt*. What else could I do but eat to feel better? It was her fault, her fault, her fault.

I dragged myself over to the sink, cursing Carol again for helping me into the kitchen when it was time for lunch instead of making me use my walker. Then I took the stopper out of the sink so it wouldn't clog and jammed my finger down my throat, feeling the hot acid of not-so-fast food come rushing up. When I was done, I washed the orange mess down the sink, splashed my face with water, pulled myself back over to the table and lit up another Chesterfield.

Carol...I refused to call her by that *shiksa* name she gave herself. Cara...Not the name the rabbi gave her when she was eight days old. How dare she disrespect my mother, G-d rest her soul, who she was named for! Carol gave me more trouble than the other two put together since Day One, from before then, even.

I had a boy and a girl and we were all happy, even Jake. Irving and Aileen were such good children, still are. I didn't want a third child. We couldn't afford it and the place was too small. I couldn't go out to work, not with two little ones at home and my bad hip. And my good for nothing husband could barely provide for us. Besides, I couldn't bear the thought of Jake on top of me, flopping around like a flounder out of water, so all of the above were good excuses to keep him away.

Too much *Pesach* wine, I blame it on, and a husband with no self-control. Dr. Kessler warned me that having another baby would do me in. The hip and all couldn't take the pressure, the extra weight of being pregnant. But did Jake listen? No. He was as thick-headed as his daughter turned out to be. Refused to use protection, "Just this once," he begged, "It's Passover, Eidala." And look what happened! I never let him near me again.

I was in a wheelchair the last few months of the pregnancy, could barely make it to the toilet myself. I felt like such a *schnook*. Then besides everything else, Carol decided to come a month early. I wasn't ready! I don't know if I ever would have been ready. Jake was glad to get the tax break in 1949 rather than have to wait a whole year to save a few *shekels*. I was mad at that. Come to think of it, I've been mad ever since.

Carol was such a scrawny, little thing, pink and hairless like a baby rat. All arms and legs and long, long fingers. Piano-playing hands, Jake said. But did a no-good *schlemiel* like him have money for piano lessons or anything nice? Ha! We were lucky we had food in our mouths with him. If it wasn't for my father, G-d rest his soul, I don't know what we would have done. Poppa was always slipping me a twenty here, a ten there. And it wasn't just because I named Carol after Momma like my sister Sarah said. Poppa would have done it anyway. I was always his favorite.

Not that Carol could ever say that she was *my* favorite. From the first time the nurse made me hold her—I was so weak from the Cesarean and the drugs, I was afraid I would drop her—she squirmed away from me. And she's been squirming away from me ever since. Cried from colic and there was nothing I could do but sit there and cry with her in my arms. She, red in the face, fists balled up, me red in the face and sobbing, too. Once it was so bad, I pictured what it would be like to throw her against the wall. I was so horrified with myself that I put her down in the bassinet and lay on the bed with my hands wedged under my body. Praying, praying for the crying to stop. It never did.

Then, the hip got so bad that Dr. Kessler said I would have to have surgery. I was in the Hospital for Joint Diseases for months, in traction, until I healed from them fusing the bone in place. Sarah and Iris took care of Carol, who I barely recognized when I got home. Chubby cheeks, dimpled arms, big, brown curls. She was even smiling. But the minute I took her in my arms, she squirmed and cried. Maybe she knew. Maybe she knew I didn't want her, that I still don't.

Then things went sour with Jake, not that they were so great before Carol came along. But if you love somebody, you'll go through thick and thin with them. And we didn't. Love each other, I mean. I married him knowing I didn't love him; I thought I might grow to love him. Women did things like that in those days. But I never learned to love him. Jake was a good man but not a good man for me. When I was still a teenager, I was sweet on someone else. Then I took a tumble over a metal dress rack when I was running to get samples in the sweat shop and shattered my hipbone like an eggshell.

The doctors didn't think I would ever walk again, didn't think I could have a normal life, kids, nothing like that. So, I settled for Jake, a nice guy I grew up with, instead of marrying the man I was keeping company with. I married a man who was crazy for me instead of one I was crazy about. I couldn't be the right kind of wife for Herb so I stopped seeing him. Just like that. Worst decision I ever made in my life—besides having a third child.

"You should understand, Ma. You, of all people, should understand," Carol tries to tell me. Understand what? Living with regret? Giving up? Having no dreams? I understand better than anyone but I tell her I don't. Why can't my daughter be like everyone else? Why can't she just settle, settle down? Why isn't "good enough" good enough for her?

2/7/79

I have a boatload of work to do but I don't feel like doing it. All day, I've been pretending I have a bad stomach and have been running to the bathroom, just to get away. I sit in that green-and-black tiled stall, look at flecking gray paint on the back of the door, breathe deep and try not to scream. Then I go back to my desk, look at the spread sheets that are piling up in my "In" basket and feel like screaming all over again.

I don't know how long I can get away with this disappearing act, so I took my journal with me this time. Maybe unloading my crazy thoughts into it will make me feel better and not feel like grabbing someone, anyone, by the neck and squeezing, squeezing hard. Or giving somebody a good throat punch.

It's been colder than I ever remember, even as a kid. So cold that boots and long johns and tights under my skirt don't even cut it. Getting off the F train, with the wind whipping up from the East River, I cursed this stinking job and having to walk down stinking (literally, it smells like fish and Chinese rot) Catherine Street to the stinking *New York Post* building.

This morning was no different. I was feeling crappy to begin with and in no mood for Howie and Tom's bullshit, stepping all over each other to get to me. Finally, I told them to cut the bologna and put their money where their mouths were. "Meet me on the corner today at one," I said.

"Which one of us?" they asked, almost at the same time.

"Both," I told them.

Then I just walked away. Left them with their mouths hanging open.

When one o'clock rolled around, I was there and they weren't. Well, not at first. Catherine Street is way out in the open and it seemed colder than it was at nine in the morning. Even after a few minutes, I was ready to go, pissed off that both of those bozos had stood me up. Then I heard a horn beep and noticed a green *New York Post* panel truck idling across the street.

Tom was behind the wheel and Howie was nowhere to be seen. When I got in, Tom handed me a cardboard cup. I was about to work off the top and take a sip when he stopped me. "Nah, like this," he said, and ripped two little slits in the lid with his teeth, then peeled back a notch in the plastic cover. "Drink it like a truck driver," he told me. "So it doesn't spill."

Tom's gift was a steaming hot cup of tea, flooded with milk, just the way I like it. For the next few minutes, I gave him shit about him and Howie giving me crap every morning, flirting with me just because they could, with no intention of following through. Tom was speechless, not used to women speaking to him like that, I guess. Then he got hold of himself. "Secretaries don't even talk to guys like us," he said.

I told him that I wasn't a secretary, I was a drummer. And that got Tom harder. I could tell he was turned on by the way he talked, by that soft edge to his voice. And I was turned on because he was turned on.

We were way up in the cab of the truck so I doubted that the few people passing by on the street could see. It was so freaking freezing that any idiot who was out walked by with their heads down anyway, steeled against the cold. I was still in a foul mood and decided to call Tom's bluff. "I'm not going to get busy in the front seat of a truck," I said. He almost cried with joy, showing me into the back of the van, pulling up the gate and helping me inside, offering me a hand, almost chivalrous.

It wasn't as dark as I thought it would be but it was almost as cold inside as it was outside. Slivers of daylight shone through the truck panels. "I only have 15 minutes left on my lunch hour," I told him. He sat on the wheel bed and I got down on my knees, icy floor seeping through my thick tights. Fished him out of his pants and long johns, peeled him out of the layers like an artichoke. I was still wearing my gloves so it was tough to manage but I didn't want to take them off. That's how frigid it was. I think Tom kind of liked the feel of scratchy cotton alternating with mouth. Every so often, I took a sip of my tea, letting it heat my tongue, then got back to work.

Was I turned on? Sort of. Did I get off? Not technically. I think the power of the whole deal got me off more than anything else. Having complete control over him, over the situation, of whether he came or not. And come he did, partly into a wad of Dunkin' Donuts napkins, and the other part arcing through the cold air of the empty van and onto the floor to harden like ice.

"Howie's gonna *plotz*," he laughed. "He was pissed off enough as it was that they sent him to Queens to make a late delivery."

Always the gentleman, Tom offered "to do something" for me but I refused.

That would have ruined things in a way, break a hole in my veneer. I felt high enough just from doing him, sneaking off in the middle of the work day without anyone knowing.

I wiped my mouth, finished the last of the tea and went. And wouldn't you know it, Howie was pulling into the garage as I was walking down Catherine Street. Just by the shattered look on his face, I knew that he knew. And it killed me a little bit.

That's when the bad feeling started, from Howie's face and from thinking about Michael. Why did I do it? Boredom. Feeling pissed off. Wanting to feel like I was in charge of something. But the more I look over what I wrote, this poor excuse for a *Penthouse* letter, the worse I feel.

I still don't know why I did it. Had nothing to do with horniness or desire. I fucking hate it when guys say, 'It just happened,' because nothing *just* happens. You have to *let* something happen.

*

It's late. Midnight? 1 am? I'm not sure. All I know is I can't sleep. Michael called tonight and I blew him off. I can't see him with another man's pre-come still digesting in my belly, can I?

That old Spinners' song keeps going through my head. The one with the tasty guitar hook at the beginning. I think it's called "It's A Shame." You know, the one about how it's a shame the way you mess around and hurt your man.

Shit, it keeps playing on an endless loop, and it just won't stop.

After I slinked out of the can at the *Post* with my journal, I managed to keep myself together until 5, then I got the hell out of there, even though there was enough work to milk into OT. I could have done a couple of hours and still made it to rehearsal but I didn't feel like it. I was still reeling from seeing my mom a few days ago. It will be a long time before she sees my face again. I'm trying to stretch it out to Passover but the *kvetching* about not seeing me will be worse than the *kvetching* when she sees me.

Rehearsal was good. Those guys get me, appreciate me. Even when someone gives me a lift home, there's no bullshit like there is with Marty. There are no double entendres, no ass-grabbing. They see me as an equal, as a musician, not as a piece of tail.

I know my family and friends are tired of hearing me say it, but this time, I'm going to make it! I know I am. Just watch me.

Michael

I feel strange, detached, watching Cara from afar. (This time, with her permission, and not sneaking a look from the back of the Baron DeKalb or some other club-date nightmare.) Like I'm watching a movie of someone else's life.

Cara seems so in control, so in charge of herself. She knows just what to do, when to put in a roll and when not to, when to ease off and when to charge full on. Not showy but captivating, always noticeable, demanding attention just by being...doing. She couldn't stay in the background if she tried. Even though she's not the front man...or woman, I should say, she is always front and center. She's the one who commands attention. And it's not just because she's my girl. I would think the same thing if I never laid eyes on her before.

My girl. Is Cara really my girl? Does she belong to anything but music?

Cara holds the band together, that much is clear. No lie. But instead of being more together herself, off stage, she's unraveling even more than usual. She's more volatile, more angry, yells easier, cries easier. I wonder if something else is going on underneath the surface. Something besides her mom—Cara just saw the old battle axe last week, and it always throws her for a loop, even though she swears she doesn't care. Is it her job? Or should I say both jobs, which I know she hates equally and alternately. Something else, maybe?

Watching her perform, Cara is all angst and hard angles. I can hardly believe she's the same person who curls against me in sleep, that is, when she can sleep. Most nights, she has a tough time settling down. Even after sex. It's like something inside of her is always moving, that thoughts are always rattling around in her head. Even when Cara's sitting still, something is always in motion—she's tapping a foot or a finger, always.

Why do I keep hanging around, many people ask? A lot of women are easier to deal with, more together. But I never liked easy. I was always the kid who brought something home from someone else's trash, a treasure that just needed to be fixed, to be loved, then it would be fine. Good as new.

Not that I think Cara's trash. She's not, even though she treats herself as though she is. I like the challenge of her. I like the fact that she's never the same, ever. From one minute to the next. I like never knowing what to expect with her. But there are times when she's volatile, scary. I just hang on tight, weathering the storm of Cara like a nor'easter. And when it passes, there's that achingly beautiful blue sky again.

Cara's the one who asked me here. I was shocked when she did but I tried not to show it in my face. I tried not to make a Federal case out of it, but it was a big deal. She'd been rehearsing with these guys for almost a month. I'd heard a lot about them but never saw them in action. Being with Cara for almost two years off and on (but who's counting, right?), I've seen lots of bands come and go. I've heard all about the record deals, the promises, sweated through a dozen showcases. I've heard her swear that this one or that one was going to make it, only to see them fail. But it's never her fault. It's always a lead singer with a coke problem or a guitarist who got shit-faced before a record company audition or a manager who splits with the demo tapes. True, every word of it. I am not making this up.

I could go on and on. I never tell Cara that I'm getting tired of hearing it. Tired of *it*, not tired of her. I'm sick of how she beats herself up over it, how she blames herself, how she gets into that dark place for weeks and pulls a no-show. I would be cool with her playing and gigging if it didn't take so much out of her. But I guess it is her. It *is* what she is. Cara the Drummer and Just Plain Cara are inseparable, indistinguishable. Besides, I'm not sure there is such a person as "Just Plain Cara." Being a drummer is who she is *and* what she is. It defines her. It is her. And until I accept this, it's not going to work. If it even is working. I don't know anymore.

But watching Cara is amazing. I tried to disappear into the back wall of the studio, which is basically JR's basement. One weekend they soundproofed it with egg cartons and whatever else is nailed to the walls. They stuffed the bass drum with old rugs to muffle the sound. Renting out real studios for rehearsals was eating into everyone's pocketbooks. JR's house is detached, brick, and right across from the Belt Parkway, so I guess the noise gets absorbed by the constant swish of traffic. The neighbors don't seem to care. Two, maybe three days a week, Cara comes here and practices the songs for their set at CBGB's.

Although I hate to admit it, they are pretty damned good. JR wrote most of the songs with his wife Fern, who seems pretty nice. Complex keyboards, decent, solid lyrics, amazing harmonies, which Cara adds a beautiful layer to, melting into them like they've been singing together forever.

I've always been floored at how people make music, that people actually *can* make music. For me, it's always been the written word, the spoken word. Turning a blank page into one covered with thoughts and ideas, has always been easy for me. But turning silence into song, pulling on a string, hitting a drum, blowing into a horn and actually making music from it, never ceases to amaze me. And Aircraft or Airborne or Cargo, or whatever the hell they're calling themselves this week, is pretty fucking amazing.

Even though it's the middle of February and freezing in this concrete hole, Cara is sweating. Her hair is glued to her forehead, perspiration is dripping down her neck, and there are stains ringing the armpits of her T-shirt. The top of Mongo's bald head shines as he nods and smiles at her and plucks at his bass. Roy is lost in himself, his fingers a blur. JR stands at the keyboards, lunges at them as he plays, nodding. Danny's voice reaches notes I didn't think were humanly possible, and Cara's meets him on the harmonies, tangling like the tails of two kites, like two falcons sparring, becoming one, now pulling away, then meshing and leaving again.

When the song is finished, "Charade," something Cara wrote with JR, they seem almost embarrassed. Like almost-strangers after unexpectedly explosive sex. They laugh because there isn't much else they can do. It's just past nine, not late, but they don't continue. How can you keep practicing after a song like that? Practicing means you need to get better at something.

At that point, I'd already put away my notebook. "You weren't listening," Cara said later. "You were writing." I told her that I was listening with my body.

Cara wasn't as quiet as usual on the way home. She wanted to go to Nathan's in Coney Island. I gladly complied. On the way, she was jazzed, ecstatic, high, bubbly even. It's a Cara I wish I saw more of instead of the dark, self-effacing, brooding Cara. But I'll take any Cara I can get. She is truly unlike anyone I've ever known, man, woman, anybody. I will weather the storm of her as long as I can.

It wasn't hard to find a parking space on Surf Avenue in the dead of winter. No Coppertoned bodies, crunch of sand, Daisy Dukes, hot-dog eating contests or flip-flops. Nathan's Famous is strictly hardcore in the winter. Solely for those craving a frank that snaps back when you bite it and French fries fried in the same grease since 1916. Or for people dying to eat frogs' legs…I never really could figure that one out; it doesn't seem to go with the rest of the menu. Craving enough to brave the unapologetic ocean wind, the huddled bums, the ruined starkness of Mermaid Avenue. Nathan's is a truly strange place with the doors closed (it's pretty much open-air in the summer), trying to capture these big chunks of humanity in a small, tight, oily space.

There were more people than I thought there'd be late on a work night. Cara and I had our dog and fries standing up at one of those tall silver tables, trying to keep a safe distance from the nutters. In the 10 minutes we were there, a hooker mooned the counter staff when they refused to serve her because she was drunk (in truth, she was, drunk or high or both), a homeless man complimented Cara on her "snazzy haircut," one person was pick-pocketed and another almost knifed. Cara loved it, her eyes on fire, laughing. "The food's good, hell of a floorshow, though," she said when we got back into my cold Colt. I wasn't surprised when she stayed the night, though it was the first time we'd been together in weeks. But I was glad it wasn't at 2 am after a few drinks and a gig. She smelled of French fries and tasted of not-so-Kosher hot dogs.

I had to go to work, where I am now, but I left her at my place sleeping, with a key on the kitchen table to lock up after she left.

2/13/79

It's the day before Valentine's Day, but luckily, like me, Michael doesn't go in for that pretentious emotional marketing ploy that is February 14th. How does it prove that someone loves me because they give me a sappy Hallmark card and an artificially-flavored chocolate heart? I do love the chocolate, though. Got an interoffice envelope at the *Post* yesterday with a 50¢ box of Conversation Hearts in it, nothing else. From Howie? Tom? Damn, I thought a BJ would get me at least a tin heart of Russell Stover's.

I feel slightly guilty as I write this because I'm still at Michael's place, scribbling away in bed. His bed. He's already gone to work. I'm dragging my behind because my boss will be in late and he told me to take some extra time to make up for the late hours and busy days that will come pre-tax season. (He's only approved to pay me a certain amount of OT each week, the rest he gives me in time off. But mum's the word—Ellis actually used that expression—because Payton People and the *Post* would have a cow if they found out about our little arrangement.)

Even though I've been lugging around this journal for less than two months, it's pretty beat up. Takes a lot out of you to keep up with me, I guess. Even if you're just a dimestore notebook.

I'm feeling almost normal with Michael. If I try hard enough, I can convince myself that the Tom thing last week never happened. To me, it meant nothing, but I know it would mean something to Michael. Would I care if he went down on some chick? Maybe. I'm not sure how I'd feel unless I was in the same situation.

But things like that don't happen with guys, do they? They're perfectly fine with a girl going down on them without reciprocating but do they ever think of giving a cutie some head without anything in return? Not likely.

Am I trying to justify what I did? Possibly. But justify to who?

*

I took a break after trying to sleep some more, but couldn't. So, I got up and got myself a cup of brown gold that Michael thoughtfully kept heated up in the Mr. Coffee. Why does he have to be so nice? I don't deserve it. He even left a key on the kitchen table. I couldn't miss it on the cheerful orange plastic placemat. No note, thank God. But the significance of said key was implied. And not just so I could lock up.

It's almost 10 but I don't feel like going to work. If I get there by noon, I'll be fine. In spite of the hellishly slow commute on the RR train, I should have more than enough time if I leave here by 11. I still have to shower. Nobody would notice if I have on the same clothes from yesterday. They barely give me a second glance there. I think I'll skip putting on my soiled undies, though. I'll just shove them in my pocket to rinse out at home later. I'll resist the invitation to put them in Michael's hamper for him to scrub, and God knows to do what else with. Leaving a pair of panties behind might signify to him that we're back "on" again. Instead of just that I just got lazy and wanted him to do my laundry. And I wouldn't want to get his hopes up.

Last night, before he drifted off to sleep, Michael said something about watching the Grammys together. That maybe we could. I think they're in a couple of days. I broke it to him as nice as I could that it would be hell for me to watch that crap, even with him. Rich people patting each other on the back. Poor musicians making rich producers even richer. Fuck that shit! Elvis fucking Costello. A Taste of fucking Honey. No thanks.

This weekend, there was another depressing as hell PWP gig at the Baron DeKalb. St. Valentine's Day dances are the worst, with everyone scrambling around for that last ditch stab at love the Saturday night before so they can convince themselves they're not as desperate as they actually are. There were foil hearts on every available surface, red crepe paper falling down from the ceiling tiles, blood-colored roses on each table, and a sea of too-tight dresses in varying shades of crimson.

Sitting there behind my kit, I was reminded that:

(a) red is not a flattering color on most people; and

(b) Spandex is a privilege and not a right.

There were more rolls on the Baron DeKalb's dance floor than at Alba's Bakery. Plus guys with their ears perked up like a German Shepherd's waiting to hear their master's key in the door. Except with these hopelessly single dads, instead of a key in the door, they were looking for a sign, a smile, a nod. Anything to signify that maybe they wouldn't be alone again that night. It actually made me feel kind of sad. Even though most of those guys were idiots.

Marty was more obnoxious than usual. Maybe he sensed that I wouldn't be around for long, that I truly didn't give a flying fuck about his stupid society music band. He bulldozed his way through "Le Freak," muffling Ackerman's funky rhythm guitar hook by slobbering all over it with his frenetic (and not in a good way) keyboards. I kept shooting Marty pissed-off looks as I sang and he had no clue why. Plus he bitched like hell when I said I wanted to learn the song. Hey, "Le Freak" has only been # 1 on the *Billboard* charts for something like three out of the past four weeks, but who am I to say? Everyone was grooving to the song. Even the dreaded Humper momentarily forgot his horny pumping and got a little funktified. I swear, I don't know why I bother sometimes. I don't think anyone notices or cares. But the point is that I do. *I do.*

I guess I can't help but bother. It's music and it moves me. Even pop music. It's like I have no choice but to pour my heart and soul into it, whether it's a ditty by the Bee Gees, an R&B band from across the river or one of JR's unbelievable Aircraft songs. Somehow, the music takes me over and I'm lost. I'm just barely aware of the way my hands move, the way the words come out of my mouth. It's almost second-nature, like breathing. It just is.

Ste-Mar is the mirror opposite of Aircraft. With one, I feel stifled, like I'm playing with my right hand strapped behind my back. With the other, I feel so incredibly free. As close as I can get to happy. With Ste-Mar, the musicians are so marginal, less than okay, except for one or two. With Aircraft, there is so much talent in that cramped, little basement that the music just transcends it, breaks down the brick, roils over the Belt Parkway, past the rusting overpasses, ricochets off Dead Horse Bay across from Kingsborough, under the Marine Park Bridge and out into Long Island Sound. If that makes any sense.

Denise was at the Baron DeKalb gig, ever the dutiful wife. She tried not to notice when Steve disappeared out the side door, soon to be followed by a swish of blonde in red satin. I watched Dennie watching, then looked away as her face crumbled, cowardess that I am. Even if she said something to Steve about it later, what would be the use? He'd only deny it, make up a half-believable lie which she'd force herself to believe because it was easier than not believing it.

I put down my sticks, pretended to listen to a Soccer Mom's request for "Too Much Heaven" and went to Dennie's side. We slipped out the back door to the terrace that looked over Sheepshead Bay. Despite its cheesy interior, smoked mirrors and fading glitz, the Baron boasted one of the best views in Brooklyn. It was freezing out there but so worth the fresh air and inky blue sky that seemed to go on forever. It didn't take much to convince Dennie to share a joint with me. Not that I smoke much but Roy gave it to me at the last rehearsal. Figured it was as good a time as any to light it up.

Dennie's face glowed hot red when she took a drag. "You've got something cooking, I can tell," she said in a choked voice, letting out a blast of reefer. "Something more than what you told me the last time.

"I always have something cooking," I said, taking the joint from her fingers.

"You know what I mean," she added. "Something real this time."

I just shrugged in response and hugged my tux jacket around me. "I told you about that new group, right?"

"Get out," she told me flatly. "Get out of Ste-Mar before it's too late."

I handed her back the J. "I could say the same to you."

Dennie took the roach between her bitten-down fingernails, sucked on the moist paper then shook her head. "It's too late for me. But you…get out before they crush you, Carol. Before they take your dreams away."

"No one can do that to you unless you let them."

A car door slammed. There was a flash of blonde and red, of a stocky man with tinted glasses and a black tux hustling into the Baron's front door. "I let them," Dennie admitted in a tiny voice, like a broken, little girl. "But you… you've got to do it…for all of us. For all the people who let them."

Dennie crushed the roach under her red, patent-leather heel, squeezing the light out of it, kissed me on the forehead and left me standing there, alone.

*

I hate to read over the things I write. Makes me feel empty and wonder why I'm doing this. Makes me question what I'll get out of it or what anyone else will get out of it. Makes me feel mad all over again. But maybe that's a good thing. Mad does stuff. Mad doesn't stand still. Mad gets out.

Roy Hammerman
Guitarist, Aircraft

The showcase at CBGB's is less than two weeks away. In the beginning, I had my doubts that Cara was good enough for us. Now I wonder if we're good enough for her. I can tell she tries to hold back, to keep in the background, but she can't. She keeps bursting out, exploding, in spite of herself. Even though I haven't been to church in ages, since I was a kid and my undertaker father forced me to go, Cara reminds me of the Scripture that basically says, "Don't hide your light under a bushel basket." But Cara, she can't hide; it's impossible.

I got past the novelty of having a female drummer pretty quick. Got past wanting to fuck her. Honestly, she scares the shit out of me. Too intense. Wound up tight like a top. Like Keith Moon with a vagina, only prettier. Lots prettier.

The girls love her, the band wives. She poses no threat, I guess, and is so damn likeable. Tragic. All the Shakespeare sob stories rolled into one. Weepy Cordelia, crazy Ophelia, bitchy Lady Macbeth. It's almost like other women want to take care of her, feed her, give her a good home, like a stray kitten. That's what Cara reminds me of...a stray cat. Lost, doesn't fit in wherever she goes, not a hair in place. Yet scrappy and strong and steady in a "don't fuck with me" sort of way.

Her guy Mike seems pretty cool. Quiet. A schoolteacher, I think. He seems like the type of fellow who likes to make everything all right. So it's a good mix. It works. For now, at least. But when Cara doesn't need fixing anymore, when she moves past what he can give her, I think she'll move on, too. Seen it happen lots of times before.

But who am I to judge? Just a casketmaker's son. A pretty smart casketmaker who saw that he could make a lot more money by changing his business model and taking a bigger piece of the grief pie. My dad went from just supplying the coffins to offering "the full funeral experience." He has three memorial chapels and counting. And it's served my Pop well. He has that house in Florida plus a condo in the Bahamas. Two bitching Beamers and a Karmann Ghia in Bimini.

I've got to admit that the old man is pretty generous with his kids. Sends a check once a month, which really helps because I'm not making shit with Aircraft. Though I love the music and I believe in them. Roy, Sr.'s contributions help pay the rent and buy a few demo tapes. God knows, I can barely make ends meet with that exterminating gig. Which I hate. But who doesn't hate their job?

Damn, I just realized that everything I have, I got from other people's misfortune. Bugs, vermin, death… But somebody has to, right?

2/20/79

I can't believe it! I can't fucking believe it! JR goes and sets up a practice gig a little more than a month before our showcase at CB's. And on a Tuesday night no less! Who the fuck goes out on a Tuesday night in February? Especially in the 11:45 time slot. Nobody, that's who. And that's who's here. Practically nobody.

When we all belly-ached, JR was his stoic self. Unmoved, like a thick, Polish wall. He just raised his hand to silence us (which, amazingly, it did) and simply said, "We need the practice." He didn't want the showcase at CB's to be our first gig, ever, which it would be. Until tonight.

Pretty much, I'm scared shitless. There's literally no one here. Well, no paying customers, at least. Most of the trusty wives are here: JR's Fern (short for "Fernanda") and Roy's Annabelle. Plus Danny's groupie girlfriend of the moment, whose name I didn't bother to learn. I like Fern, a big-nosed, big-assed Italian girl from Dyker Heights, and Annabelle ("Anna," for short), who's from Ohio, Iowa or some interchangeable non-New York place. Mongo's main squeeze, Zelda, is holed up with their two "crumbsnatchers" (as Mongo so lovingly refers to his kids) in Cobble Hill. Couldn't get a sitter on such short notice. I didn't tell Michael about this gig. Didn't want to. I'd be even more terrified with him here.

These places are all interchangeable. The Bottom Line. The Bitter End. Same old, wooden beer stank. Same crumbling brick wall behind the stage. Same ratty carpet covering the stage. Slightly different banners behind the stage: Paul Colby's Bitter End at that one, for example, with the kit shoved between two brick chimneys, also crumbling. Similar accessories: beer/water/coke on a concrete block within arm's reach, narrow, decrepit bathroom with a daisy pattern of floor tiles (white with black/green/orange, take your pick).

I've stolen off to a dark, sticky table in the corner of Kenny's Castaways. It's a dive showcase bar on Bleecker Street which squeezes in bands like doctors squeeze in appointments, every half hour or so apart. I'm scrunched in here with my kit around me, waiting for some God-awful country-disco band to cease and desist. When they're done, it will be like playing "Beat the Clock:" waiting for the CW band to hurl their stuff off the tiny stage then rushing the platform, carrying my drums like weapons, screwing the mounts into place, slapping the stands open, wedging in the amps, plugging in the mikes, and starting. No soundcheck. No announcement except Danny's intro, and away we will go.

I'm sweating so bad I'm afraid the sticks will fly out of my hands and attach themselves to some rummy's head. I keep wiping my palms on my Sergios but it doesn't do much good. To calm myself down, I'm writing in my journal, only it isn't working. I'm still nervous as all hell. Once Fern asked what I was writing and I told her, "My last will and testament." She laughed and didn't ask again.

This place looks like a bordello gone wrong. It has swinging saloon doors on either side of the stage with an M and a W marking each restroom and a parade of losers going in and out of them. I have the feeling it's due to doing lines of coke rather than weak bladders because practically everyone comes out rubbing their noses. There's a burgundy velvet curtain messily pinned up behind the stage. Round, chipped, black tables are mixed in with a few small, rectangle ones. Dark paint a few shades deeper than dried blood covers the walls. There's a long bar on one side of the room, with a bouncer up front, his big bottom squeezed onto a stool that's half its size. Typical dive bar.

As scared shitless as I am, I have to admit that I am looking forward to this gig in one way. We were promised part of the door, only no one but wives and girlfriends came to see us. So it can't really be called a gig because we're not technically getting paid. And with the bar tab Roy is ringing up from sheer nerves, downing the Dewar's like Tab, we're likely to leave deep in the red.

Writing this shit down is the only thing keeping me from screaming with the hopes that screaming will stop my hands from shaking. One knee is working like it's at an invisible sewing machine, and try as I might, I can't keep it still. My left hand is tapping at the table while my right hand flies across the page, writing.

What the hell am I so nervous about? That I'm wrong, yet again? That, if I'm wrong, I'll have to live up to my promise to myself and stop gigging? Leave music altogether? What would I be without it? Will I cease to exist? Is that all I am? A drummer?

Danny Galen
Lead Singer, Aircraft

I thought it was a mistake, a big mistake. Playing a nothing gig, our first gig, a month or so before the showcase at CBGB's. But there's no swaying JR once he has an idea in his head.

At first, there was no one but our tiny, sad entourage in the audience, minus a few. The wives and girlfriends but no Zelda and no...whatever the heck Cara's boyfriend's name is. Mick...Mike...Michael, that's it. No Michael. Plus some girl I met last night at the Peppermint Lounge showed up. But that was it. Kenny's is small, not counting the upstairs, which looks down on the stage like it's a pit where they used to sacrifice the Christians to the lions. It was such a slow night, they even closed the upstairs. I mean, shoot, it was a Tuesday.

But I tried real hard not to let this get me down. I'm a professional, gosh darn it! I sing my butt off whether it's to an audience of two or 2,000. Not that I've ever sung for 2,000. Yet. With this group the way it is now, I have high hopes. We've never sounded so good, so complete. I've been taking care of my voice, quit smoking, quit drinking. Do a line of the white devil every now and again, but a guy's gotta have some vices, right? But I think the way we sound now has a lot to do with our new drummer, Cara.

So, we started the set with our most kick-butt song, "Killer," and just exploded onstage. Even the bartender couldn't help but notice us. And barkeeps don't usually give a rat's behind about anything. Except tips or tail.

I could be all stuck up and say it was because of me but I'm not that egotistical, even for a lead singer. I know it was Cara. Nobody ever stopped dead in their tracks and took notice of us like this before. Not even when I was smoking hot, in the zone. This girl just grabs you by the shirt collar and forces you to listen. Whether you want to or not.

"Killer" starts with a short drum solo, just a few rolls, like a march or a dirge. But in Cara's hands, it comes alive and transforms into something you've never heard before. Now I'm not talking about a tired, old "Fifty Ways to Leave Your Lover" rip-off, but something fresh. Unique. I'm not sure I can put it into words. You just have to take my word for it. Or come see us.

It was cold as a witch's left ninny outside but hotter than the backdoor to hell inside. I guess that's why the bouncer decided to keep the front door propped open with a chair. At first, I thought it was a bad idea but soon, I knew it was genius. Every schmo on their way to the A train at Waverly Place seemed to pop in. And not just duck their head in to check us out, but they actually stayed. A while. Ordered a drink or three. So, when it came time to settle up, the club ended up owing us something instead of the other way around. For once getting "part of the door" was profitable. And I have a feeling it won't be the last time.

Cara was red hot. She slipped from one song to the next like she'd been playing them for years, like she'd written them, lived them. And maybe she had. Even her vocals were dead-on. She perfectly complimented mine, not too loud, not lost in the background but just right. She knew, she sensed it, without anybody telling her. It was like we were lovers or something, that's how connected we were.

And afterwards, Lisa, the girl I'd met last night, acted kind of teed off at me. It took a heck of a lot of convincing her that Cara and I weren't an item in the sack. Not that the thought didn't cross my mind. But no. It's like Pop used to say back home on the farm, "You can't let the hogs poop at the dinner table." (It sounds better when he says it, I promise you. Pop doesn't cuss either.) Mongo might say, "You can't shit where you eat." There, I said it.

And with Cara in the band, I have a feeling I'll be eating caviar with a shovel before long. Not that I even know what caviar tastes like.

3/1/79

It's been a while since I've written in this thing. I can barely read the chicken scratch I scribbled onto the page in the half-light the night of the showcase at Kenny's. We've been busy as hell getting ready for CBGB's at the end of the month. Rehearsing three, sometimes four times a week now.

JR's wife turned the music studio into a photo studio on Monday so she could shoot some publicity shots of us. I was expecting Fern to come out with a Polaroid or a Kodak Instamatic but she had the real deal, lenses and all. Plus she knew how to use them. I have to admit, the pictures came out pretty good. Fern is a lot more than just a babymaker, I'll tell you that. (She and JR have a cute kid named Jessica who's two or something.) Fern set up a screen, lights, had us wear a bunch of outfits, even brushed us with face powder, which the guys bitched about. But Fern said we all looked shiny and sweaty, so we let her powder our faces with her Covergirl TruBlend.

I felt really comfortable in front of Fern's camera, something that's not typical for me. I'm usually like those native peoples who think you're going to steal their soul when you snap their photo so they always look stern and guarded. That's me. Maybe it stems from all of those awkward family pictures, my mom growling at Irving and Aileen and me to stop slouching and looking like *schlemiels* so she could take the *facocta* picture already. Or else male photographers looking at me like I was lunch, copping feels when they arranged my body this way or that.

Fern took some pictures of me alone when the guys were having a smoke break. (I don't smoke anything besides the occasional joint. I'm too scared my voice will disintegrate into a scratchy mess like my mother's.) Real leather and lace stuff against a raw brick wall in the basement's laundry room. Unlike most women, most people, for that matter, Fern gets me. She understands me. She's not just somebody's wife and mom, she's somebody. She's not just JR's partner but his writing partner, too. I recently found out that she's the one responsible for lots of Aircraft's lyrics. And that "Linda" isn't a love song in a traditional sense, but a love song to their daughter. (Linda is Jessica's middle name.) It's pretty cool.

I've been avoiding writing about that night at Kenny's Castaways. I don't know why. It went well but it made me feel strange. I'm used to crowds watching me at *bat mitzvahs* and weddings but this was different. This time, I wasn't just a side dish to the main course at somebody else's party. This time, I *was* the party. We were, I mean. When I looked up during "Killer," I couldn't believe that people were crowding through the door, at midnight on a Tuesday, listening to me. Us.

I somehow managed to calm down before we hit the stage but then I was all jumpy again. It hit me that I might make it after all. This might really happen. I might actually get my chance. Then I'd have to prove it. That I'm good enough. That I'm better than good enough. Then I'd have to stop my bitching and belly up to the table.

Michael asked me once why I was so hell-bent on making it. "It'll mean I'm worth something," I told him, after some thought. He just shook his head.

"Don't you think you're worth something anyway?" he wondered. When I started to balk, he added, "I'm serious."

"It would mean that someone believes in me enough to put money into me, to give me a record deal."

"I believe in you," he said.

"But that's different," I struggled to explain.

"So, making it, getting a record deal, means success to you," Michael said, trying to get his head around it. "Then you'll finally be happy."

"Maybe not," I told him, "but it would be a good start."

*

Work still stinks but it's a necessary evil. There's OT if I want it but I don't want it. This week, I stayed late a few days, so long as it didn't interfere with Aircraft rehearsals. With the fiscal year ending in April, there are boring bucketloads of papers to be filed. And with Marty and Beryl, Steve and Denise away at the timeshare they share in Aruba—yes, this is in addition to Beryl's folks' St. Maarten timeshare (Are they stupid rich, or what?)—there were no gigs this past weekend. Which doesn't bother me at all except I'm low on cash. Chipping in for film, developing and postcards advertising our gig at CB's has whittled away at my discretionary funds. Who am I kidding? What discretionary funds?

To cut back on costs, I've been sneaking photocopying flyers for the CBGB's gig at work. Just 20 or so at a time, every time I have to go to the Xerox machine. But it adds up. Not sure if Ellis is onto me but he's pretty cool, as long as I get his work done. He doesn't give a rat's ass if I wrangle a few pennies of Xeroxing away from old man Murphy's crates of dough.

I'm writing this at my desk, as most of the staff is at a big quarterly meeting. But since I'm technically not staff, and just a lowly temp, that's fine with me. Ira and I are still creating—and spreading—rumors about our imaginary affair. It's the only thing that keeps me going here sometimes.

Andrew Ellis
Chief Accountant, New York Post

Cara's a good egg. I could tell from the first day she started here. Thorough, professional, takes pride in her work. Doesn't look like the other secretaries, what with her hacked-off hair and all. Almost always dresses in black. Not that it doesn't look good on her. But what difference does it make if she doesn't look like the typical administrative assistant? She gets the job done.

I don't get the feeling she's very happy, though. Seems to have a permanent scowl like those...what do they call them? Punks. Punk rockers or something like that. My daughter listens to that crap. Anyhow, I know Cara plays music but I'm not sure what kind. Whatever it is, I'm sure she's pretty good at it. That's just the type of person she is. Always pitches in when we're on deadline—although I suspect it's more about the cash than from pure dedication.

I also don't get the feeling she's in it for the long haul, even for a temp. I think she'll be up and out of here the second she has the chance. She's been in Accounting a little more than a month, which isn't bad for a temp. But I don't have the budget to hire someone permanently. Not that she'd take it. This one, I can tell she doesn't like being tied down, even in relationships. Especially in relationships. These cubicle walls are thin and you hear an awful lot, even when you don't want to.

Seems to get on well with Ira, who I suspect is "half a fag" (as my son would say). Me, she just tolerates, like a father, like a boss, which I am. But it doesn't stop me from chewing off her ear. It feels good to have someone who will listen to me. Even if they're just an employee, and have no choice.

For some reason, I like having Cara around. I'm not sure why. Am I attracted to her? Not in the traditional sense. She's young enough to be my daughter. But still, something draws me to her. For some reason, I want Cara to like me, to accept me. I don't even know why I'm telling you this. You didn't ask. And you're not going to use any of it, right? What's this for again?

3/7/79

I have no time to write, yet when I don't write, I feel like I'm cheating on myself. Keeping this journal weighs on my head. I feel that it's something I'm *supposed* to do, and if I don't, I feel empty. Panicky. Wrong. I'm not even seeing Michael anymore, but I still feel the pull to write in this damn thing. Even if I don't have much to say. Maybe I'll put it down for a while. Put it away in a drawer somewhere so that it doesn't silently accuse me of neglect. Maybe then I won't long for it. Maybe then I won't feel the need to tell my story, to explain.

What else? JR had posters made for the CB's gig. He had his friend Jed run off tons of copies of our demo tape. More expenses. Between OT at the *Post*, rehearsals and weekend gigs with Ste-Mar, I barely have time to breathe. Or think. Which is good in a way. But at least there's a little extra cash flowing around. Which is good, too. But it's going as quickly as it comes in.

*

Can't sleep. Which is bad. Got in from rehearsal about 1 and have been wound up like a top ever since. I have work tomorrow and it's only Thursday, so I have to stumble through two more days until the weekend. Thank God there's no Baron DeKalb gig on Friday because that would really do me in. And if I were still seeing Michael, no doubt he'd feel neglected, that's how hectic things have been lately. I have no time to even do my laundry, let alone do a boyfriend. I'm down to one semi-clean pair of panties, so I've got to do a load or two tonight. Damn. I wish there was an all-night laundry nearby.

*

3 am. This is getting ridiculous. If I don't get to sleep soon, I'll be dozing off over the spreadsheets tomorrow. Ellis is a good boss but he's only got so much patience. I don't know what it is. I'm wired like I did a few blasts of coke. My heart is racing, my breathing is ragged. Maybe I'm having a heart attack. Nah, I don't have any other symptoms. Anxiety? No. Everything is going good. Well, good for me. I can't seem to relax my mind, blank out and think of nothing, no matter how I try. I keep going over the harmonies for "Killer" or the drum licks for "40,000 Feet." Will I be ready in a few weeks? I have no choice, I've got to be. This is it.

*

4:20 or so, still wide awake. (I'm afraid to look at the clock.) I picked up the phone two or three times and almost dialed Michael's number, then hung up. It's hard to stay away from him. I'm afraid I'm losing it. Sleep deprivation is getting the best of me. Okay, I admit, one time, I actually dialed Michael's number but then I hung up before...I mean, after he answered. I didn't say anything but he said, "Cara?" anyway. That's when I hung up. I will not, will not call again. I swear...

Marty

This chick never ceases to amaze me. She'd been bitching about how we do the same old boring shit (meaning love songs) and said we needed to get funktified. "No pun intended," the Divine Ms. Funk told me. "'Songs in the Key of Life' only topped the charts for 13 weeks in '76 but who am I to say," she nudged. I finally gave in and said we'd learn "Isn't She Lovely" but the bitch didn't go for it.

"'I Wish,'" she said.

"No fucking way," I said.

"Why the fuck not?" she asked.

"It talks about Christmas, Sunday school, and church. We play mostly Jewish gigs. That's why the fuck not," I told her.

"I'll make it work," she told me. "Just learn the music." I glared at her. Who the hell was she to tell me what to do? I was the God-damned bandleader, after all. "Trust me," she said.

I did. Damned if she didn't make it work. She swapped out *Christmas, Sunday school* and *church* for *Hanukkah, Hebrew school* and *temple*.

Then my only worry
Was for Hanukkah what would be my toy...

And:

Mama gives you money for Hebrew school,
You trade yours for candy after temple's through.

Fucking genius! Worked like a fucking charm. The crowd loved it. We did it for the first time tonight and she kicked ass. I hate to admit it but Cara has a knack for making shit work. Except shit for herself.

But even Stevie Wonder himself couldn't save this last wedding at the Grand Marquis. It was without a doubt the worst gig I ever had. And I'm talking about a shit career of cock-sucking gigs. We were breaking in a new guitarist, who was hot to get his wife to sing a tune. Then the asshole groom actually pulled a gun on his brand-spanking-new father-in-law. His soon to be ex-father-in-law, if the dimwitted bride has any sense whatsoever. Which she probably doesn't. You could tell by the wedding gown she chose—a tight, strapless number that made her look like 10 pounds of shit in a five-pound bag. And the bridesmaids' gowns were even worse. Fuchsia satin with puffy sleeves and Parson's hats. You'd think Stevie Wonder picked them out.

Anyway, I swore to the SOB groom that I would learn "In-A-Gadda-Da-Vida" for the first dance. Which, of course, I didn't. Who ever heard of something so stupid? Who the hell can slow-dance to that? I promised him we'd play that dumb-ass Iron Butterfly song because I thought the druggie would be too out of it to remember or care by the time the first dance rolled around. When we tried to sneak "Just the Way You Are" past him, the dude went berserk. He left his tubby bride standing in the middle of the dance floor by herself and screamed, "Are you fucking kidding me? Billy Fucking Joel?!"

He was all coked up, you could tell. Kept running off to the bathroom, rubbing at his nose and twitching his upper lip, which was probably numb as Beryl's brain is. That's probably why he went so ape-shit on me.

The Mrs. burst into tears, raining tons of Maybelline spackle all over her hideous gown, snot running down her face, as the Mr. began fumbling for the .22 he had tucked into back of his powder blue tux pants. Luckily, the mother of the bride was a Corrections Officer at Rikers and managed to tackle him and disarm him before any real damage was done.

There was more hysterics, more drama and general pandemonium. It was great. Really shaved a lot off our playing time and the father of the bride was too upset to ask for a partial refund. But I don't doubt they'll ask for it somewhere down the line. Jews hate to be parted with their pennies. And I know, because I'm a cheap Jew myself.

The cops pushed their way onto the dance floor and ended up cuffing the groom. Instead of being smart and going quiet, he put up a stink. Before you knew it, he was being dragged off with the bride shrieking like a Kosher pig on the way to the slaughter, and her asshole husband yelling something about Charles Manson.

Instead of being upset by the general panic, Cara was cool as a cuke, looking at the scene like she just didn't give a shit anymore. I mean, she almost crapped a brick when a waiter pulled a knife on her at that Queens gig a couple of months ago, but here, with a gun being waved around, she barely batted an eyelash. Like she was above it all.

I took advantage of the general mayhem and the crush of bodies to sidle up close to Cara. "Can you believe this shit?" I said to her, cupping one of her glorious ass cheeks in my hand. She gave me the hard eyes. I stared her down then grabbed my dick through my tight tux pants, for emphasis.

"There's a lot I can't believe," Cara told me, removing my hand like it was a bug. That's it. No yelling, no cursing.

That's when the asshole guitarist actually had the balls to let his wife get up and sing…without my OK. She was pretty good and not hard on the eyes either, so I let it go. Nice set of tits on her. Some sort of dark-skinned spic chick.

Beryl was right there at the table with Denise, so maybe Cara didn't want to make a scene about me grabbing her ass on the bandstand. Not that Beryl would care. We do stuff with other couples. Just so long as it's not behind her back, she's cool with it. Beryl thinks Cara's half a dyke anyway. Any chick who doesn't wear Lee Press-On Nails is a rug muncher in Beryl's book. And as you can imagine, Beryl's "book" is almost blank.

Cara sat down next to Denise, her stuffed derma going cold on the plate. She had a strange look on her face as she watched the guitarist's chick sing. Then Cara rubbed at her eyes and bit her lip. I saw Denise whisper something to her, then Cara laughed. Later Beryl told me what Denise had said, which was: "Get out of here while you can. They'll eat you up alive."

Imagine that. I have no clue what Denise was talking about.

3/21/79

I thought that gig at Terrace on the Park was the worst one ever but the latest at the Grand Marquis this weekend had it beat. Hey, guns always trump knives, and boy, was the groom packing. It was a mess, complete with hysterical bride, cops, handcuffs, the whole bit. The only thing that saved it was a song.

We had a replacement guitarist for the gig because Ackerman had double-booked himself. He sent a guy in his place who I'd never worked with before, Lars something or other. A Swede, I think. Long and gangly, curly brown hair cut short and the most amazing, piercing blue eyes I've ever seen. Lars was rangy and edgy, constantly moving, even when he was standing still. Kind of like me but even more intense. And a lefty, just like Hendrix.

In fact, on a break, Lars told us a story about being up in the Borscht Belt with his family when he was a teenager. Up around White Lake. He's tossing around a Frisbee when three guys with trippy clothes and wild hair come up to him. Lars starts playing Frisbee with a tall, thin, black dude. They're having a great time. One of the guy's friends tells Lars, "Hey, kid, do you know you're playing Frisbee with the great Jimi Hendrix?"

Lars stopped and shook Hendrix's hand—left-handed guitarists shaking right hands. Then, Lars's brother Irwin arrived, breaking the spell. After the dudes left, Irwin said, "No matter where we go, you're always hanging around with niggers. I'm telling mom."

But Lars didn't care. "That was no nigger…that was Jimi Hendrix," he told his brother.

Why am I telling this story? It has nothing whatsoever to do with me. Maybe I'm trying to avoid what I'm getting to.

Anyway, Lars had his wife with him, a beautiful, dark-skinned Cuban girl. Amaryllis, but everyone called her "Amy." A little chubby but she wore it well. Kind of looked like Billie Holiday in the face. We talked on breaks. She was pretty cool. Amy was also learning how to sing but she had never sung in public before.

Lars was getting ready to play some Main Course Music when all hell broke loose with the cops arriving. He stood there, not knowing what to do. The crowd couldn't seem to settle down, even after the groom was carted away, even though their prime rib was congealing on the tables. Lars started playing a beautiful song on his guitar, full of trills and dips. Soon he took off, soaring like there was no one else in the room. The song sounded oddly familiar but I couldn't place it at first. Then I realized it was that song from *M*A*S*H*. Aka "Suicide is Painless."

Lars motioned to Amy, who shook her head "no." Then he motioned again, and she reluctantly got up. She stood beside him, scared and wooden, and started singing in a small voice. Amy sang with her eyes closed at first, too afraid to open them. I never realized how beautiful the lyrics to that song were. It's all about how life is a game and how hard it is. And how suicide brings change and takes away all the pain. Either you take life as it comes or you leave it. The choice is yours.

Almost immediately, the room got quiet and all eyes were on the lovely brown woman standing tentatively beside her husband, singing her heart out with closed eyes. ("So they can't hurt me with their eyes," Amy confessed to me later.)

At first, I thought, 'What a weird song to sing at a wedding.' But somehow it fit. The simple beauty of the melody, the stark truth of the words. I just sat there in shock at first, then was moved by it. Floored by it. My eyes filled up immediately. I tried to blink away the tears but they wouldn't go. I don't think anyone noticed, nobody except Denise. She told me to get out of there, to leave Ste-Mar, that they'd only end up destroying me. "Like they're doing to me," she whispered.

That was hours ago and I'm still haunted by what Denise said. Haunted by Amy's song, too. I can't sleep and it's 4 in the morning. I'm exhausted but my mind is racing. Yet again. I might have to snatch some more of my mom's Percocet so I can get some rest but I'm trying to save them up.

Why did that stupid song affect me like that? I know exactly why. It's something I've been trying to avoid. In this journal. In my life. Suicide.

I'd be a liar if I said I never thought about it. I think about suicide a lot. I've heard that people in AA have a saying, "Never go into that dark room." The unspoken part is, "Because you may never find your way out." Well, I live in that dark room. I've lived there as far back as I can remember.

It scares me, how I look at suicide. Relief. Release. From everything. From all of this shit. Making it, not making it. Punishing the people who treat me like crap. My mother…Marty…the music industry… From Michael's painful, unconditional love. Going out in a blaze of glory. Making people feel bad. All of that. Sometimes I just want it to be over. The empty feeling I get when I know a manager is lying to me. That panic I feel when I realize an A&R man is never going to call. The ridicule in someone's eyes when I tell them that this time, I'm going to make it. That this time is the last time I'm ever going to give it a shot. And then it's over.

But it's true. This is it. I just can't do this to myself anymore. I can't try anymore. I just can't watch other people make it who have less talent in their whole bodies than I have in my pinkie toe. People who don't deserve it, who don't appreciate it. I'm just tired. I'm almost 30 and I'm tired of listening to myself.

I've even thought of how I would do it. Quick, painless. Just like the song says. If I had a car, I would do it in a car. Not crash the thing, too unpredictable, too many variables. What if I didn't die and just languished. What if I was paralyzed. That would be even worse than death. No, I would do it with carbon monoxide poisoning. Slow, gentle, reliable. The sweet, putrid gas filling my lungs. Just like going to sleep, they say. Only permanent. The big sleep. But I don't own a car anymore. I got rid of mine because it was too expensive. And to borrow Michael's Colt to off myself in it would be maudlin and mean besides. He's such a sensitive soul that he'd probably never recover from it.

Jumping from something high, the Brooklyn Bridge, for example, or the Verrazano, would be suitably dramatic but too damned scary. The long way down would be terrifying enough and if the fall doesn't kill you, then drowning is a positively sucky way to go. I hate getting water up my nose even when I'm unexpectedly downed by a wave at Coney Island. Could you imagine what breathing in cold, murky water would feel like?

No. My suicide would have to be as pain-free as possible and not messy. I never was one for making other people clean up my mess. I guess I can thank my mother for that one.

No slit wrists in the bathtub. ("*Oy*, can you imagine how hard it is to get bloodstains out of porcelain?" I can just hear Edie *kvetching*.) No gun to the gut. What if I missed? And how the hell could I get my hands on a gun anyway? I suppose Tommy or Howie could help me out in that department but I wouldn't want to get them in trouble in any way. ("Sure, drag yourself down into the *dreck*," Edie would drawl, taking a drag on a Chesterfield like it was giving her life instead of sucking it away, "But don't drag those poor *schlemiels* into it!")

Without a car, I would just do it simple and easy, a nice OD. I've been swiping pills from Edie, Percocets and Vicodins, little by little, two at a time every time I visit, so she won't notice. They're right there in her crowded medicine cabinet, in the black and pink tiled bathroom. I see it in my mind, clear as day. The bars right next to the toilet bowl to help Edie get up and down to pee and shit. The shower grab bars, grimy with soap scum. Come to think of it, her bathroom always smells slightly of piss, probably from what splashes onto the pink crocheted toilet seat doily that some almost-forgotten friend made for Edie so her fat, wrinkly behind wouldn't get a chill from sitting on the can. Then there's the jungle of her medicine cabinet, the mirror decorated with spit and toothpaste splotches. My mother never notices that the pills are gone, or else, I would hear it from her. I've got 20 so far.

Would you listen to me? I sound so messed up. Talking about suicide. If anyone read this, I would be committed. 100%. "*Oy*, a daughter like this! What did I do to deserve a daughter like this?" Edie would bellyache to whoever would listen. Only I wouldn't be there to listen anymore.

But who am I kidding? I wouldn't give her the satisfaction. Marty either. That's why I have to make it. Revenge? Maybe. But to show them, to show them all that they're wrong. About me. About everything.

JR

CBGB. I don't know which smells worse, the bums outside or the urinals in the men's room. Probably the urinals. The winter air and dirty snow somehow eases the bum stink.

There were only about five people in the place when we carried our equipment through the audience. And none of them from a record company. That's the only way into this place, through the audience. There's no separate band entrance. You have to carry your shit through the front door, weaving your way through the junky tables and graffitied walls that say *Suck My Balls, June Bug vs Hurricane* and *Jesus Saves* and whatnot. The band stickers are like wallpaper and the paint is peeling off in chunks.

But still, this is the cream of the crop for New York City rockers. Blondie. The Ramones. The Police. Patti Smith. Joan Jett. Talking Heads. They've all played at CBGB. The name stands for "Country Bluegrass and Blues," which isn't exactly accurate. It's more punk these days than anything else. I think punk is the gum on the bottom of the shoe of the music industry, the dog crap you can't get out of the ridges of your Keds. But hey, that's only my opinion. And stinking pisspot or not, CBGB matters.

Hilly, the owner, was sitting in the front office. He just noded as we passed, lugging in speakers, guitars, pieces of the drum kit and assorted other equipment. He was sizing us up, trying to figure out how much money we might make him in the future or if we'll be just another flash in the pan, a do-nothing, go-nowhere garage band wasting his time.

I lost count of how many times Cara puked her guts up, kneeling on the floor of the shitter off the dressing room. About as many times as Roy has gone in there to do a line or two "just to get right," as he put it. Fern sprayed Cara with Lysol (which she made me buy at a corner *bodega*), especially her hands and knees. This made Cara have to hurl again. My wife rubbed Cara's back while she puked, telling her not to worry, that she'll do fine. Better than fine. I picked me a good one in Fern. Yes, I did. After that Cara calmed down. Or maybe it was just that she had no puke left in her.

We were fifth in the lineup. I couldn't tell you anything about the other bands. All I noticed was that people started spilling in through the double doors. At first, it looked like tourists from Idaho, hoping to get an authentic New York City music experience. Then I noticed a slick-looking, chubby dude slip in and take one of the reserved tables. Jordache jacket. Leather jeans. Longish hair but expensive cut, definitely not Lemon Tree. Hilly gave the guy a little nod. I figured he was the A&R guy from Larva but I didn't tell Roy or Cara. It might lead to more coke/puke.

It was just past 11 when Hilly took the stage. Not a bad-sized stage for such a long, narrow place. Took up the whole back wall. You had to pass it on the way to the can. Hilly gave us a great intro, reading straight from the press release that Fern wrote and typed…with her fingers crossed that there would actually be some press at the club and that people would actually listen. Turns out we didn't need to cross our fingers or anything else. Hell, we *owned* CBGB after the first note. We took it over.

Cara got some whistles and cat-calls when she sat behind the drums. She was the first one onstage. I must admit, she looked hot wearing ripped Spandex tights, a torn black t-shirt with a corset choking her waist and black construction boots. She looked like a punk rocker's wet dream. Roy was next, rubbing his nose on his wrist. Me and Mongo followed with Danny coming on last. Cara counted off and exploded into the drum solo that starts "40,000 Feet." And that was fucking that.

3/30/79

Waiting on the sidewalk with the equipment after the CBGB gig, a bum stumbled up to me. "You're pretty but you're poor," he snarled, for no apparent reason, and then went into the Paradise rooming house next door. When JR pulled up with our rented van, I forgot all about it. Until now.

It's 3 am and I can't sleep. I didn't drink, well, except for that shot of tequila. Didn't have a line of the coke even though it seemed to be as plentiful as snow in January thanks to Roy. JR and the guys were so stoked after the showcase at CB's that we decided to grab a few sacks of sliders at White Castle on the way home. Even more amazing, Roy treated. I'm surprised he could eat after doing so many lines but we all ate like starving dogs. I must have had at least 10 of those deliciously greasy mini-burgers, chased by onion rings and a chocolate thick shake so thick you needed a spoon to eat it. My stomach was bone empty from puking my guts up from nerves before we got onstage.

Why the hell was I so nervous about this gig? I play in front of people all the time. But this was different. This was *it*. This one would make or break me. And it scared the shit out of me.

What am I doing writing about puke and food and fear?! I should be talking about how incredibly amazing Aircraft was. It's hard to put it into words. I find it a lot easier to bitch and *kvetch*. But good stuff, I find it tough to write about.

I was nervous as shit the minute we carried our stuff into CBGB. I'd been there for other people's gigs before but never once thought I might be taking that hallowed stage myself. Dreamed it, sure, but I never really figured it would happen. Not with my track record.

We had to tough it out through a bunch of other acts. I passed the time vomiting everything I'd ever eaten in my entire life, including a few chunks of manna the Israelites brought while crossing the Sinai. JR's wife Fern was a doll, sticking by my side the whole time, encouraging me. She has that real "mommy" gene, and not just from being a mom, but from something deep inside her. Something my own mother doesn't have. And I doubt if I have it either.

Anyway, if my hair was long enough, I bet Fern would have been holding it back while I barfed. I was so terrified of taking the stage that I felt like I was heading to the guillotine. In a way, maybe I was. This was my "shit or get off the pot" moment. Sink or swim. Put your money where your drumsticks are, bitch. If we crapped out at this gig, it would probably be all over. For me, at least.

Then it was like somebody flicked a magic switch. I guess I just realized that this was what might be my last chance and I better not fuck it up. I rinsed out my mouth, popped in a chunk of Freshen-Up (Marty delicately refers to it as "the gum that cums in your mouth" because of its gooey jelled center) and touched up my makeup. Dark Cleopatra liner and red hooker lipstick.

Right after Hilly's intro, I bounded onto the stage like I was going to steal something. The rest of the guys followed with as much determination as me. Danny looked like he could have strangled someone, but in a good way. Then we just took off like a rocket. JR had the balls to write a song that starts with a drum solo, and that's what we started with. "40,000 Feet." Nonsense lyrics about a pilot being "40,000 feet in love" with a slutty stewardess. Kind of like The Beatles' "Lovely Rita" but in the sky instead of with parking meters.

And we all nailed it. Danny's voice was in prime form and he used every single octave in the eight-octave range he brags about. I swear I saw smoke coming from Roy's guitar strings. Or maybe it was just coke residue. JR's hands were a blur as he smeared them back and forth across the keyboards and Mongo stood there all solid, stoic and "Mongo-like," plucking and snapping at his bass like he was picking a lock.

I couldn't really describe what I played like. I was so lost in it, I have no clue. All I can say is that I didn't have to think about where my hands went or when to do a roll or when to hit the snare. My arms just moved and the rest of me just followed. It was almost like I was outside of my body, watching from above, anxious to see what I was going to do next. I never experienced anything like it before. It might have been scary if it hadn't been so fucking cool.

When I was conscious of my surroundings again, I looked up and saw everyone on their feet, heard the applause. Danny must have gone down to his knees on the impossibly high note that ended "40,000 Feet" because he was getting up off the gritty stage, turning to the rest of us and laughing. Then the rest of us started laughing and smiling like mad. We nailed it. Even Hilly came out from his cramped little office to see what was going on. He nodded, folded his arms and went back inside.

We had to wait a minute or two for the clapping and cheering to die down before we bounded into "Killer." We were only supposed to play three songs but the sound guy let us do a couple more. While the rest of us packed up, JR sat with the A&R rep from Larva, who was grinning from ear to ear. His cash cow had just come in and its name was Aircraft.

Actually, Bruce seemed like a really cool guy, more polished and together than the other record company execs I've met. Sincere almost. Plus he didn't look at me like I was something on the menu. A meal ticket, maybe, but at least not like I was lunch. And the Aircraft guys were cool, too, never once hinting that it might help our chances of getting signed if I took Bruce back to the dressing room, alone. Stuff like that always made me bristle anyway. The quality of my blow job had absolutely no reflection on the quality of musician I was.

Bruce insisted on buying us all shots, and not house tequila either. It was Patron for this puppy. A class act all the way. While Bruce couldn't guarantee a record deal, he made it clear that he didn't want anyone else to grab us. Plus he never threw us lines of crap like we were the best thing since ribbed condoms. Yadda-yadda-yadda. I've heard it all before but somehow, Bruce's rap felt different. Real. True.

For a second, I wished Michael was there. Through all the smoke and haze, I thought I saw him. But after I downed a shot of tequila, the guy was gone.

Bruce said there would be a contract hand-delivered to JR within the week and that we should get a lawyer to look it over. It wasn't a record deal per se but an exclusivity agreement or some such shit. Basically, it says Larva has first dibs on us. At least *somebody* wants *some* dibs. That's the furthest I've ever gotten.

We'll see...we'll see...we'll see.

I wish I had someone to share this with.

Michael

I wouldn't miss it for the world. How could I? The CBGB gig was all Cara talked about for months, even before we drifted apart. I had to see it for myself, see her. Not in a *Night Stalker* kind of way but like a buddy. An ex-lover. Whatever. I just wanted to see that she was okay.

By the way Cara looked when she walked through the door, snare drum in one hand, hi-hat in the other, I could see that she was not okay. Scared stiff. Like she had to remind herself to breathe. And how to breathe. I was in a corner at the far end of the bar, behind a big, blonde woman. Or at least I think it was a woman. It was too dark to tell.

I didn't see much of Cara until she went onstage. Aircraft was all tucked away somewhere in the back. But when I did see Cara again, the transformation was amazing. She was all black and leathery and shiny and confident. Like a gladiator with only music as armor. Like an ebony butterfly that had burst out of its cocoon. She was magnificent. Not beautiful in the traditional sense. Cara was all sharp angles...nose, chin and cheekbones like they were carved out of dirty ivory. But she was captivating all the same.

And then she started to play. With a fury. Everything that ever hurt her, every nasty comment her mother ever made, every record deal she never got, every promise that was ever broken, every shortchange from Marty, every lie she was ever told, every broken heart...they all came out of her body, through her hands, through her feet and were let out into the air, unchained, unprotected, unleashed.

And the expression on her face—it looked like she was being beaten and being made love to, all at once.

Now I'm not much for the drum terminology. I know when it's good and when it's not. I can't tell a paradiddle from a drag or a flam. And it's not like Cara didn't try to teach me. But what came out of Cara that night was unexplainable, unnamable. It's what separates her from everyone else. Whatever it is.

Aircraft did a bunch of songs. More than the other bands who played before them. The group that came on after them didn't have a chance. After she left the stage, Cara was dripping wet. Her hair was soaked and sticking up. Her mascara was running like she'd been out in the rain. Aircraft pulled up chairs at this well-dressed, heavyset guy's table. He looked like money, dressed like money. I guess he was from a record company.

Even from a distance, I could tell it was going well. Lots of smiles, nods, head shakes and pats on the back. A round or two of shots. Fancy Man was looking Cara up and down like she was dessert. I had to admit that she wasn't hard on the eyes. Even all disheveled and sweaty. That might be her best look: leather waif. And she wore it well.

I knew it was time to go. I saw what I'd come to see, and besides, I was too close to getting caught. So, I downed my Heineken, even though it had warmed to the skunky taste of horse piss, zipped up and was out of there. I took one last look at Cara. She was laughing with her head thrown back, like she didn't have a care in the world. But I knew better.

Why did I do this to myself? Damned if I know. Damned if I'll call her. But if she calls me, well, that's another story.

4/7/79

I swear, I wish I could quit this fucking job right now. Just say, "I'm out of here," and walk out the door. The look on Ellis's face would be priceless. Worth it. The Larva deal seems like it's in the bag. There was a hearty back-pat, a handshake and talk of a contract in the mail. Supposedly. I'm trying my best to be positive because... Well, because I'm so negative.

And Howie, besides being into threeways and Plato's Retreat, is always going off about negativity begetting negativity and positive energy reaping good vibes, and all of that crap. He's also been trying to get me to go down on him ever since he heard about me and Tom in the back of the delivery truck. I still can't believe I did that. Still don't know why. Boredom? Maybe I'm just plain bad. If I said I didn't think of Michael and how it would hurt him, I'd be lying.

Sometimes the H-Man gets me a cup of tea and we sit in the cab of his truck, which is usually parked on Cherry Street. The days are getting warmer, so we can roll down the windows or at least roll them partway down. Howie's stuck on me, so he'll listen to me talk about anything and everything. Even music. Sometimes he even has helpful things to say about following one's path and "the way" finding you instead of the other way around. It might be a load of crap but still, it feels good, sounds good.

Howie's philosophy is the mirror opposite of the JMOT (Jewish Mode of Thought), which might go something like this:

"Stop being such a *schmendrick* and get a real job..."

"Enough of this *facocta* music nonsense. One more word and I swear, I'll *chalisch* ..."

"*Oy*, to me it's just noise... Now, the Barry Sisters, *that* was real music."

Growing up, The Barry Sisters were always thrown in my face. They were a Semitic version of the Andrews Sisters but not nearly as good. Plus Claire and Merna (born Clara and Minnie) were not as pretty as Patty, Maxene and LaVerne, who stole their hit *"Bei Mir Bist Du Schön."* Or as my mother referred them, "those Andrews witches." The Barry Sisters (nee Bagelman—they changed it to seem more white) could do no wrong in Edie's book and I was forced to listen to the music of these Yiddish jazz princesses until I was ready to *plotz*. Imagine, "Raindrops Keep Falling on My Head" (or as they sang it, *"Trop'ns Fin Regen Oif Mein Kop"*). Klezmer crap with no percussion to speak of. Although "We Belong Together" wasn't as terrible as most of their albums.

But I digress. Howie. Not that I can picture anything happening with him but he helps make a terrible situation (i.e. work at this awful place) almost bearable. Sharing boxed lunches (succulent roast pork on a bed of white rice in a tin from a Chinatown butcher, all for the bargain price of $1) or black and white milkshakes from Carvel. Someone to pass the time with here at work. At least when Ira's not around. Especially since Tom started acting weird after that BJ.

I can't help but notice the bulge in Howie's jeans sometimes. Can't say I'm not tempted. But I don't want to be labeled the *Post's* whore. Or do I? Once it looked so painful that I gave him a rub and a tug—all for the price of a cup of tea from Li's Bakery up on East Broadway. Another time, I sat there looking straight ahead toward the *bodega* while he fished out his goods and stroked. This was upon Howie's request. He didn't want me to touch him. Didn't even want me to look. He just kept staring at the side of my face. I could hear the soft, wet sounds—and I can't say they didn't get me soft and wet. He was so far gone that it only took a couple of minutes before I felt him tense up on the seat beside me and make a tiny groan that sounded so vulnerable I almost reached over.

Does that make me a whore anyway? Maybe. Probably. Yes.

Anything to make the minutes go by and make me stop thinking about the fact that Passover is little more than a week away and I'll be at yet another unbearable Pesach dinner with the fabulous Finkelstein family. If it weren't for my nephews, all five of them, I wouldn't go at all. Irving and Aileen did good for themselves, married a nice Jewish girl and boy (respectively), unlike yours truly. And I'm constantly reminded of this fact by my mother, every chance she gets. It helps that Robin and Stew's families are well off. But then again, everyone's well-to-do compared to the Finkelsteins. I can't think about it anymore. It's much too depressing. Especially surrounded by cubicles.

I guess I should get back to work.

1:35 pm

I can't believe I have almost 4 hours left at this stinkhole. I have a boatload of work, which I don't feel like doing. Ira took a sick day today, which makes it even more hellish here. There's no one to goof on my idiotic co-workers with. At least it helps pass the time. That chick Bing is always good for a laugh or two—and not just because of her name, which probably means something nice in Chinese. Hopefully. Because in English, it's just a cherry.

2:15 pm

JR just called. I had to sound all businesslike and professional because everyone can hear everything I say in these freaking cubicles. The *Post* is so cheap that they didn't spring for 6 footers; these cube walls barely go up eye level. Tall people can see over them as they walk by. In fact, especially annoying ones, like Bing, will say stupid things like, "Oh, you're having a banana?" as they pass. Yeah, asshole, or is the banana having me?

Anyway, JR said that Bruce was messengering over a contract tomorrow. Just for an EP. And in case you've been living under a rock, an EP stands for "extended play" record. Like what you get when a 45 and an album have a baby. Not a record deal really, just enough for 4 songs or so. A taste. Something to test the market when a record company doesn't have the balls to back you all the way. An EP is better than nothing, I guess, but still, not what we were all hoping for. What I was hoping for.

Damn. Fuck. Shit.

3:40 pm

I'm counting the minutes like a death row inmate. Except at 5, I get set free. I've been cross-checking rows and rows of numbers until they all look like they're running together, bleeding like black blood onto the page. I've grown to hate Ellis's squiggly chicken scratch. The numbers seem to mock me, almost vibrating if I look at them too long. And I've been looking at them too long. Even with all the breaks I've been taking.

JR called an emergency meeting tonight to talk about what Larva is offering us. No matter how much Ellis bitches and moans, I'm not staying late. I can't. This is too important.

5:30 pm

It never, ever fucking fails. Whenever I have something to do, Ellis has some crisis. He took a 2 hour (probably liquid) lunch or else went to that handjob-heaven tittie bar on Wall Street and I've got to pay for it. Came back to an urgent message from old Rube about numbers he needed ASAP. Looked like a whooped dog when he got back from the executive offices because I'm sure he was chewed out by that wacky Aussie. Probably deserved it, too. What it all boils down to is that I've got to type up the most recent year-end stats from every single department. Xeroxing Ellis's wavy columns of scribble just wouldn't do for the big boys. So, now I'm typing with Ellis breathing his sour gin breath down my neck, which is almost as bad as a gun to my head. Especially when I should be on the D to Brighton.

7:39 pm

I think I could walk faster than this train is going. It's been crawling all the way from DeKalb, stopping in the tunnels, the heat clicking on and off. But at least I've got a seat. I'm wedged between a fat, smelly Hasid and a pimply teenager so emaciated I can feel her hip bone cutting into me like a switchblade. She keeps nodding off on my shoulder and I keep jerking her away. Hasid Harry keeps shifting from the worn *Talmud* in his hand, trying to read my notebook. Then, he abruptly turned away when he read this. Or maybe it was when he saw, "MIND YOUR OWN DAMNED BUSINESS!" which I wrote at the top of the page, bold as I could.

I'm only at Kings Highway and the D's going local. I thought there was going to be a riot when some drunken, red-faced Irish idiot shouted out, "All the niggers always get out at Newkirk Avenue…" But alas, most of the blacks were already gone and there were just a few pissed-off stares from whites. Two more stops till Neck Road. I'm always the last one at rehearsal but then again, I'm the only one with a traditional 9-5 job, a "real job" as opposed to my "fake" job playing plastic club-date music.

11:35 pm

Well, I was overruled. I wanted to call Bruce's bluff and hold out for a better deal but the rest of the guys were pussies about it. Every single one of them. Mongo even accused me of being scared. "Of what?" I asked him, almost yelling.

"Of succeeding," he told me.

"That's bullshit," I shot back.

"Is it? Look, Cara, I love you, but you do a pretty good job of pushing away everything that matters to you."

"You're crazy, Mongo."

"Am I? Think about it. Your boyfriend. This record deal. Do we have a better offer? Huh? There's nothing waiting in the wings. Hell, I'm pushing 30 and so are you. J's starting to lose his hair. This is it…"

But he'd already lost me at "your boyfriend." I pushed Mongo. Hard. JR had to step between us. "Drop it. Both of you. Just drop it," JR warned. I stepped back. Fern put her hand on my shoulder but I shrugged her off. Maybe I shouldn't have. It proved Mongo right. Maybe I do push people away. Sometimes literally. But I couldn't bear to be touched. Not right then.

JR looked like he might cry. "Listen, we've worked too hard. All of us. All of our lives. People have told us we should just give up. Our families. Our friends. But we can't. And now…now we really have something. It might not be exactly what we want but it's something. We've gone through too much to throw it away."

I shook my head. "J, all I'm saying is that we should call their bluff. We've got nothing to lose."

"No, *they've* got nothing to lose," JR insisted. "We've got everything to lose. And I'm not going to lose it again."

About 8 years ago, JR had been so close "I could taste it," he always said. But then the deal fell through because the lead singer's voice went wonky. The record company wouldn't give them a chance to put a new singer in his place and shelved the record deal. Then there was the time, just a couple of years back, when that TV show "Star Power" turned them down but invited their lead singer back onto the show. Son of a bitch made it to the quarter finals.

"I've been losing my whole life," I told JR. Told all of them.

"Not anymore," he said.

Mongo grabbed me in a bear hug and gave me an Indian Head Burn, which he knows I hate. (In Michigan, where Danny's from, I learned that they call it a Quaker Rub.) "Friends?" Mongo asked.

"Yeah, friends," I said reluctantly.

I've been in at least 20 bands since I was a teenager but no band has ever felt like this. I'd say it feels like family but my family is so messed up that it never felt like family.

Aircraft kissed and made up then sat down to figure out which three songs we should do for the EP. Four if we could do them quick and cheap and good enough. Fern even talked about writing a new song for the occasion. Yeah, she wrote most of our material with JR in addition to taking kick-ass photos.

So it boiled down to this playlist:

"China Doll"
"40,000 Feet" and
"Linda"

It was a no-brainer.

And the fourth song was something Fern was still working on. She called it "Under the Mask." It was about me.

Fern Cloud
JR's Wife, Lyricist/Photographer, Aircraft

I never met another person who was so at war with themselves. Cara makes Willie look like he's normal. Almost normal. She's so high-strung that she never relaxes. She reminds me of a tigress pacing in her cage, back and forth, trying to get out but not knowing how. Cara never stops moving either. Hand, foot, face... something's always jiggling.

Oh, and I don't go for that JR crap. I call my husband "Willie." The rest of his family and his friends call him JR. It's short for "Junior" because Willie was named for his dad Wilmot. A nice enough guy but my husband is so original, so one-of-a-kind, I don't like that he was named for someone else. So, I call him "Willie." Marrying Willie made me "Fernanda Clapowitz," which is quite a mouthful. But I like it. I like being Willie's wife.

Enough about me. Back to Cara. I like her. A lot. I did from the first time I heard her sing and play. Willie did too but he worried that she might snap. Might go off the deep end without warning. I mean, drummers are volatile by nature—I guess it goes with the territory of hitting stuff for a living. But Cara seemed volatile and vulnerable at the same time. It wouldn't surprise me if I heard she'd stabbed someone. Or killed herself. It wouldn't shock me one bit.

Then again, she's so good with Jess. So patient and gentle. Like she's giving another kid what she never got. And loving it. If I hear that damned "Bein' Green" from *The Muppet Show* one more time, I think I'll scream. But Cara has the patience to sing it with Jess until she falls asleep in her arms. Or she'll scream that song "Mah Nah Mah Nah" while Jess runs around in nutty circles then drops from sheer exhaustion, the kid's hair in sweaty ringlets. It's all or nothing with Cara.

She had a nice guy, a teacher, I think, then suddenly, he was gone and Cara didn't want to talk about it. Willie says I'm not happy unless I'm psychoanalyzing the shit out of a situation. But I can't figure Cara out. We've never met anyone from her family. Nobody ever came down to one of her gigs. And I know she has siblings plus a slew of cousins who live in Sheepshead Bay. Would it kill them to come to a gig or a rehearsal?

I worry about Cara. She beat herself up before the CBGB gig, power-booted for about 30 minutes straight. And now she's balking at the EP deal. Cara's her own worst enemy. A few weeks after she joined Aircraft, I started writing a song about her. Working title: "Under the Mask." I don't know if she'll love it or hate it. JR suggested I shorten it to "Mask." I have to roll that one around a bit, see how it feels. Yeah, "Mask" might have a better ring to it. Short and to the point, like her.

This is what I've got so far:

Eyes, dark with pain, dark with longing.
Don't get too close, I'll cut you down without warning.
Eyes, dark with pain, dark with rain,
I'll leave just when it gets good, you're all the same.

Because I live under the mask,
Don't ask me to stay.
Because I've been hurt before, know the score,
And I'm already gone anyway.

Not a bad start. Willie already has a melody bouncing around in his head. He keeps bugging me to finish. I peck away a line here and there when Jessica is sleeping, in between imaginary tea parties, sitting on a tiny plastic chair in her purple princess bedroom. "Mommy, stop," she tells me when I try to sneak off and write. "Mommy, play."

It was easier to write when Jess was littler. I could nurse her and cradle her with my left hand and wrestle a pen and paper with my right. Wrote the song "Linda" that way. It's her middle name…I just couldn't compete with Dickey Betts' "Jessica" even though it doesn't have words. But his song's so gorgeous, it doesn't need them.

Now it's getting harder to find the time but I still write. I don't know how not to. Things jump out at me, no matter where I am. Even if I'm in the frozen food section of Waldbaum's or at the Homecrest Playground. It's been like that as far back as I can remember, from when I first learned how to write at OLPH. When I learned my ABCs, I began putting letters together into words, and putting words into poetry. I used to get into trouble for doing it instead of reading those stupid

"Dick and Jane" books like everyone else. But I could write and still listen, still spit back lessons into Sister Mary Hewer's face, much to her dismay when she pulled on my ear and said I wasn't paying attention. She usually found a reason to make me sit in the corner anyway. But I didn't care. I could still write in the corner.

Willie was the only person who ever took my writing seriously. I went from scribbling verses of lovesick teenage angst to song lyrics. It was an easy leap. I liked this dark-eyed, moody musician the minute I saw him in the schoolyard near Grady. A Bishop Kearney Girl, I was way out of my turf, slumming in Sheepshead Bay. Willie was playing stickball with my friend Daria's brother Pete. "What's in the notebook?" Willie asked, not even saying hello. It was the first thing he ever said to me.

"Just stuff," I told him. "Personal stuff." And I opened it up for Willie to see. I'd never shown it to anyone before—no one had ever asked. We've been together ever since.

I don't worry about Willie wandering. Even with someone like Cara. Willie and me, we're like facing pages in a book; we complete each other, we validate each other. He's in awe of Cara and her talent but she also scares the hell out of him. He likes nice and easy and calm, and she's anything but.

Willie wasn't sure about keeping Cara in the band. There's no doubt that she blew him away, that she blew all of them away at her audition. But the very same fire that makes her so unique threatens to make her crash and burn. Cara's volatile, self-destructive, doesn't play well with others. She'll blow up during rehearsals for the least little screw-up—mostly something she does herself. I've noticed that she's more forgiving of others than she is of herself. She's been known to flip a drum stick across the room in frustration because she misses her cue. It's scary but it's also a little bit exciting. Like watching a hurricane from the balcony instead of behind the safety glass.

Roy and Danny wanted to let her go—several times. As for Danny, I think he feels threatened because Cara's voice is just as strong as his is. Lead singers have frail egos anyway. And add to Cara's "plus" side that she also plays a musical instrument, when Danny's only instrument is his voice, and he's running scared. Roy is too much of a drunk and a cokehead to have a solid opinion about anything but he always sides with Danny. Always did.

I managed to convince Willie that Cara's plusses outweighed her minuses. And that she was their ticket to the top. They've never been any closer than they are right now and it's all because of Cara.

She's one of the few people I liked the moment I met her. Willie says that I immediately dislike everyone and then eventually (sometimes) come to like them. (He might be right.) But not Cara. I don't know why. She gives you so many reasons not to like her but at the same time, something draws you to her. The same way an approaching car's brights draw you to cross the double-yellow line or the same way you slow down to look at a kid having a temper tantrum on the sidewalk when you know you shouldn't stare.

Willie thinks Cara and I are a lot alike. The first time he said this, I jumped down his throat. How dare he think I was that explosive, that hopeless, that desperate. But the more I thought about it, the more I knew he was right. I am all of those things—without him. Without the life raft of Willie in my life. He holds me steady. Keeps me honest. Keeps me from being all sorts of terrible things: a coke whore, a crazy cat lady, a Star Wars groupie. Willie saves me from myself.

But Cara...Cara has no one. No one but herself. And I ask you, who's going to save her?

4/12/79

Holidays at Edith Finkelstein's are never what you'd call pleasant but this one was surreal. The only way I can write about what Passover dinner at my mom's was like is to write about it like I'm writing about someone else's life. Or writing a play. But I haven't done that since I was forced to in Drama Class at Sheepshead High. This might not be pretty but here goes:

Setting

Shabby Brooklyn basement apartment. Inhabitant is clearly "not from the cleaners." The place is neat but not clean. The furniture, threadbare and several decades out of style, has been shoved to the sides of the living room to make space to accommodate a large, rickety, aluminum folding table. A noisy *Erev Pesach* (Passover Night) dinner is in progress.

Time

Present day

Characters

EDITH/EDIE: The matriarch of the family, a sullen, angry, gray-haired woman in her late 50s, wears a housedress and walks with a limp. Picture Julia Waldbaum (her portrait is on the store's canned peas, etc.), only more pissed off.

IRVING: Edie's eldest, dark-haired, brown-eyed, going gray and bald, in his 40s, smiles a lot probably due to the fact that he's a furniture salesman at Jennifer Convertibles.

AILEEN: Edie's middle child, petite with sharp, birdlike features and an uncharacteristic turned-up nose in a sea of Semitic honkers. Dental assistant turned unhappy housewife.

ROBIN: Irving's wife, cute enough but tends to *kvetch* about everything, mom to their super-cool boys: Shawn, Evan and Rowan. ("Don't these people know they're Jewish? Why do they give their kids such *meshuga goyim* names?," as per Edie)

STAN: Aileen's husband, overweight, overemotional, everything's a tragedy. Fell into his father's plumbing supply business and hates it. A blonde Ralph Kramden clone, but not nearly as funny. Father to two semi-cool sons: Jared and Stewie.

CARA: Drummer/singer, black sheep of the family, never quite fit in.

ACT ONE
SCENE ONE:

(As the curtain rises, the Finkelsteins are in the middle of a heated discussion around the rickety dinner table.)

EDIE
Oy! Stab me in the heart, why don't you!

IRVING
It was a joke, Ma!

EDIE
A joke? A joke, he says. I've been slaving in the kitchen for two days and you insult my cooking!

CARA
Ma, these matzo balls could bend a spoon.

EDIE
You too? What ungrateful, rotten bastards I raised.

(The children CHUCKLE softly at their grandmother's cursing.)

EDIE (cont'd.)

Don't you laugh at me!

IRVING

All I said was that if they dropped these matzo balls on Germany during the war, it would have ended in a second. I was kidding.

CARA (whispering to Irving)

Her matzo balls *and* her potato kugel and they'd be begging for mercy.

EDIE

Again with the matzo balls. As if once wasn't enough. I will not have you making jokes about the Holocaust at my *Pesach* dinner table. The thought of…

CARA

Hey…everyone…did I tell you about the showcase my band has in a few days? We…

EDIE

Showcase, schmocase. I'm tired of hearing about that *facocta* garbage you call music. Now, the Barry Sisters, that was real music.

AILEEN

Momma, Carol is very talented. You should be *kvelling*. You should be proud.

CARA

It's Cara, not Carol. And thanks, Ai. Not like you've heard me play in, what, at least 10 years.

AILEEN

You know I don't go to the City.

EDIE

Enough already with this music talk. What happened to your *goy* boyfriend?

CARA

Michael is a friend. Just a friend, Ma.

EDIE

Would it kill you to go out with a nice Jewish boy for a change?

CARA

Probably.

IRVING

Stop picking on Carol, Ma. Can't you take a break on holidays?

CARA

It's Cara, but...

EDIE

Don't tell me what I can and can't do in my own house!

(There's a brief, uncomfortable silence, then...)

EVAN

I heard something interesting in school. About Rod Stewart.

EDIE

Rod Stewart? I don't know from Rod Stewart. Is he Jewish?

ROBIN

Probably not. He's a popular singer, Ma. Everybody knows Rod Stewart.
(to Evan)
What did you hear, *bubbala*?

EVAN

Well, did you know that he was in the hospital recently?

IRVING

No, what happened?

EVAN

They had to pump his stomach. They found 30 gallons of sperm in there!

(Matzo balls and utensils go flying across the table. The kids
LAUGH hysterically while the grownups stifle their laughter.
Edie is in shock and grabs her heart, gasping.)

EDIE

What?! At my Passover table? Is that any kind of talk for...

ROBIN

Edie, he's only 8. He doesn't know what he's saying.

EDIE

He gets that kind of dirty talk from you.

ROBIN

From me?

(Stan throws down his fork and stands.)

STAN

Aileen, I've had it with your fucking family!

(Stan storms off. Aileen runs after him to try and
placate him.)

EDIE (scowling at Evan)

See what you did?

(Evan begins sobbing.)

EDIE (to Robin)

I hope you're happy now.

ROBIN

Me?! Irving, your mother is out of control.

EDIE

I'm out of control? Well, you're the one…

(Cara grabs her jacket from the back of her chair and exits
stage left.)

CURTAIN.

See what I mean? You just can't make this shit up. I didn't even say goodbye
to anyone, just walked out. As Ricky Ricardo might say, "That 'splains a lot,
Lucy." Explains why I'm so messed up. And that's just the tip of the iceberg.

Afterwards, I thought of calling Michael but I didn't. He was probably away
anyhow because of spring break. He used to love to get out of Brooklyn, even for
a day or two, to a little bungalow colony near Kingston called Twin Lakes. As the
name implies, there are two lakes, ponds really, but it was quiet and peaceful with
lots of trees and woods around.

One time we went up there with Steve and Dennie without telling Marty, just
to chill. We were having a great time. Steve's a completely different person when
Marty isn't in the picture. Laid-back, pleasant, even. At 2 in the morning, I wake
up to car headlights lighting up the cabin like it's 12 noon. Somehow, Marty
figured out where we were, found out which cabins we were in and drove up in a
rage with Beryl in the middle of the night. He couldn't bear the thought of Steve

going anyplace without him or give the poor guy a break. No, he has to be up Steve's ass 24/7.

Steve went out on the grass in his boxers and tried to get Marty to calm down. It didn't work. Marty was cross-eyed drunk. I don't know how he drove on the Thruway like that. Poor Dennie was so terrorized by Marty and his antics that she burst out crying. Michael couldn't believe it. He finally saw for himself what an asshole Marty was and what I was up against at those club date gigs. But I think he was actually a little charmed by Marty's insane performance. "I feel like I'm in the middle of a Marx Brothers movie," Michael told me the next day.

It wasn't so charming, though, during breakfast, when Marty asked Michael, "What's a waitress's worst joke?"

When Michael innocently asked, "What?" Marty opened his mouth, which was stuffed with chewed-up bagel, lox and cream cheese. I think Marty'd been spiking his tomato juice with vodka, so he was already in rare form. Only then, after Marty went back to the buffet table, did Michael admit, "You're right. He is an asshole." And that was before Marty slurred even more nonsense, asking why I was wasting my time with a *goy*.

I didn't bother to answer. I would have ended up screaming. Michael and I just left, jumped in the Colt, headed for the Thruway and went home.

But that was a long time ago. Last summer or the summer before. Seems like a world away.

2:10 am

I still can't sleep. I thought I could write myself into oblivion and fall asleep with the pen in my hand but writing only seems to get me more agitated. My mind is racing with thoughts of what the next couple of months could be like: recording studio, "real" record deal instead of just an EP, quitting this half-assed job at the Post, leaving Ste-Mar once and for all, etc.

My brain started doing back flips from one thing to another. I also had visions of making enough money to get my mother out of that dreary basement apartment—not that it would stop her *kvetching* about life or about me—and buying Michael a flashy Dodge Charger so he could get rid of that clunker of a Colt. I would have someone tow it away and replace it with a mint, black Charger, have the keys delivered to Michael's classroom. That would really be something.

Damn, I wish I could calm myself down. My mind is running wild, my heart feels like it's going to beat out of my chest... I feel like I did an anthill of coke but I didn't do anything stronger than a half glass of Manischewitz at Edie's failed Passover dinner.

What the fuck is wrong with me? And who the hell am I writing this for? Half the time it sounds like "Dear Diary" drivel and the other half, it sounds like I'm performing for an audience. I try to put it aside but then it calls to me. Like a siren on the rocks. And I can't put these thoughts out of my head, so I put them down on paper. Maybe now I can sleep.

Steve

I swear, this business is eating away at my soul. If I had a soul. I don't really mind the slow times—January, February and March—and the Jewish holidays. It gives me a breather, time away from Marty, time away from smiling so hard it makes my face hurt and bullshitting so much it makes me nauseous. Lying about one thing—like playing songs at a gig you know the band will never learn—makes it so easy to lie about another. Making nice with the *bat mitzvah* girl's unhappily divorced mother and lying to Dennie about it makes it so easy to lie to Dennie in general. I manage to convince myself that I've never done the things I have and that I've done things I haven't.

It's not that I'm unhappy with my wife. I *am* happy with her. Denise is great—sexy, witty, hardworking. The perfect partner. The problem is that *I* suck. The more someone gives, the more I take. I don't know why.

Anyhow, I've been loving spending more time with Dennie and less time with Marty. I almost feel normal. I've been almost monogamous.

One person I miss hanging out with is Cara. Even as sour as she can be sometimes, she's funny as all hell and has this unusual take on the universe. I've felt that Cara's been more detached lately. Looking at all of this from a safe distance, if you know what I mean. I've grilled Dennie about it but she's not talking. I'm pretty sure she knows what's up but she's keeping it to herself. I can't even worm it out of her when I'm going down on her. You know, stopping and starting, tormenting her, making her beg. But Dennie's kind of girl who can finish off by herself, turning the tables and torturing me.

Speaking of torturing and begging, Dennie has been pleading with me to leave Ste-Mar, to branch off and form my own club date band. "You don't need him," she says. "You're the one with the gift of gab. You're the one all the musicians love. Ask Cara." Then, "You don't need him. He needs you." But the truth of the matter is, I'm a lazy fuck. Having my own band sounds like a good idea but it also sounds like a lot of goddamn work.

Ste-Mar had its first gig in a long time, after two weeks or more, this past Friday. "Hitler's birthday," Cara quipped. Which also happened to be Marty's birthday. "Same thing," she shrugged.

While we were sharing a J outside the kitchen door of the Oriental Manor, it seemed like Cara was about to tell me something but stopped herself. "What?" I asked her. But she shook her head.

Then when we were going back inside, she said, "It's been fun." Just like that. Nothing more. Then she added, "Most of it."

I never really thought about it before but Cara has been something to me that no other woman has been—a friend, pure and simple. Dennie is a hell of a lot more than a friend. And just about every other woman, I fuck, in one way or another. But Cara is different. Just going for a bite at the Mill Basin Deli after an early gig, sharing a noodle *kugel*, talking about what we want in life, where we see ourselves in the future…no one else is like that with me, asking nothing in return. I'll miss Cara when she goes, and I know she's going. In some ways, she's already gone.

I wish I could be there more for her, stand up for her. Like when Marty rips her a new asshole if she forgets to shut off her snare and it buzzes during "Feelings." I should tell him to shut the fuck up but I don't. I just let Cara stand there, looking alone and abandoned. Like a kitten in the rain. I should tell him to go fuck himself when he calls me a dumb dago. I should go off on my own like Dennie says. But I don't. I don't do anything. And sometimes, not doing anything is as bad as doing the wrong thing.

4/25/79

I never knew what "tired" was before today. I'm literally burning the candle at both ends holding down two jobs. Or is it three? We've been laying down tracks for the EP at a recording studio on the Upper West Side. Sound Lab is top of the line, a class act all the way. And expensive. But as JR likes to say, you can't cheap out when it comes to your career. So, what we've been doing is taking the time slots no one else wants. Like 3 am on a Tuesday night.

More than once, I've laid down my drum tracks, then caught some z's on a broken-ass couch in the back of the studio while the guys do the guitar and keyboard parts. Then they wake me up to lay down the background vocals. I catch a few more z's then change into my work clothes, heels, wraparound dress and whatnot. I carry my snare drum like a briefcase. It took me forever to find one that I liked—a Pearl. I happen to think Pearl makes the best drums in the world, but not because Louie Bellson named them after his wife Pearl Bailey. (And imagine, loving someone so much you name your drum company after them.) I think they're the best because they are.

To me, studio work is like watching paint dry—boring as hell. You're laying down the same tracks over and over again, singing the same lines so much that you feel like screaming. I'm isolated in a Plexiglas cage wearing headphones, the band and the sound guys watching me from the booth like I'm a crazed animal. Sometimes it's hard to get into the music isolated like that. But then I just close my eyes and I let it carry me away. When the sound tech puts it all together, it's a miracle. It sounds pretty good. No…it sounds fucking great.

After a recording session, when I take the D to Grand Street and walk down to the *Post* on the East River, swinging my snare case, I'm practically walking on air. Then in a couple of hours, I crash. I'm so exhausted that sometimes I fall asleep at my desk when Ellis is in a meeting. Once, he caught me with my head resting on my Selectric and he really got his panties into a twist. "You're not doing drugs, are you?" he wondered. I told him that I haven't been sleeping well, which is the truth.

Aircraft has been getting gigs, too. Last minute gigs. Sometimes, when the opening band flakes out at the eleventh hour, pulls a no-show or the lead singer walks off a balcony in an angel dust haze. Bruce must have some pull because when this sort of thing happens, they call him. Then he calls us.

Last night, we had a gig at the Peppermint Lounge, opening up for a band called The Lost. I'd never heard of them but apparently they're pretty big. The lead singer has a mass of pink and blue and peroxided hair (think cotton candy gone wrong), big, scary red lips and stuffs her boobs into these fishbowl-looking things. Gale something or other. Gale, like the wind. What a crazy name. She must have made it up. I think she's married to the guitarist, a wussy guy with a pompadour and eye makeup. It looks like she can take him in a fistfight in a heartbeat, whip his prissy ass without a second thought. I bet she does.

During sound check, I heard her sing...if you can call it singing. She has a high-pitched, squeaky voice and sounds like Betty Boop on acid. Plus her singing style is full of robot-like moves and jerky head bobs. She pulls all sorts of crazy faces, too. I couldn't help but laugh a little bit and I think she saw me. Gale also slathers her face with Maybelline war paint: purple triangles, blue stripes under her eyes. Why, I don't know. Maybe to detract from the fact that she can't sing.

I ran into Gale in the bathroom. She was rearranging her boobs in her fishbowls while I was washing my hands. "You think it's easy?" she snarled, giving me a whiplash smile. It was like she was posing as that Billy Idol guy from Gen X, except he's a lot better looking.

"I know it isn't easy," I told her. And then she was gone, just like that.

For some reason, Aircraft didn't get a sound check. I think it had something to do with her.

So, we were The Lost's opening act and it was going pretty good, sound check or no. I mean, we were rocking out. No one ever heard of us, so what did we have to lose? We didn't care, we just went with it. The crowd, who'd been booing us off the stage at first and shouting for The Lost, suddenly changed their tune and started cheering us on. It was an amazing shift of the weather.

As I was singing the opening harmonies on "Mask," I saw Gale watching us from backstage. She didn't look very happy. She flipped me the bird then disappeared.

JR shouted back to me that someone from the audience wanted to join us on stage. Was it Gale? No way in hell.

"Do you know any Led Zeppelin songs?" JR wondered. I nodded, still playing "Mask." He kept on, "Which ones?"

I told him, "All of them." Next thing I know, Robert Plant is making his way up to the stage. He's tall and handsome and curly-haired and for some reason, is wearing a Jets jersey. Plant picks up the mike and we're ready to start "Whole Lotta Love" when it all goes black, literally. Seems that Gale got one of her roadies to pull the plug on us. She suddenly remembered that there was a clause in their contract that specified no opening acts. Funny that she had amnesia until we got onstage…and won over the audience. Bitch.

Plant made his way back to his seat and left soon after. We didn't even have a chance to thank him. We never seem to catch a break. Never, ever.

Garland

"Cunt...whore..." those are the choice words I heard from the skinny one with the thinning hair. His name is Morty or perhaps Marty. I try not to pay much attention to that one because a litany of evil words always seem to be coming out of his mouth (except when he is in front of a microphone). Words like "Chink," "Guinea," "Nigger." Words that wound. Tonight was no different. But these bad words were directed at Cara.

"Shush...chill...there are still people in the ballroom..." It was the fat one with the glasses. The one who chases pleasures and doesn't let anything get in the way of them—he goes with women, men, does cocaine, smokes marijuana. Any port in a storm. He was trying to calm down the evil Marty character. Steve, his name is. Steve had his big, chubby hand on Marty's chest, trying to keep him away from Cara. Her eyes were downcast.

"I don't give a fuck!" Marty screeched. "She's trying to destroy me. And right before the busy season. Bitch!"

Cara's eyes met his. Dark and brown and burning. "Then why do you always treat me like shit? Huh? If I'm so important?"

"You're not," Marty spat. "But you make us money."

"That's all I ever was to you, right? A paycheck. Well, I'm cashing out."

Marty struggled to get past his partner while Cara held onto the small, flat drum, snug in its case like a hat box. She was never without that drum. Then Marty took a swing at her, lurched past Steve's reach and smacked her across the face. Cara tried to lift the drum to shield herself, but it was too late. "Nobody leaves me, understand?" he yelled. "Ever. I'm the one who does the leaving."

"Not this time," Cara told him, eyes glistening. With tears or hatred, I couldn't tell. I stood there behind them, scouring the range with Brillo, listening to every word. It was better than Sino TV, even if it was in English.

"Let her go," Steve told him. "She deserves to go if she wants."

Marty let out a bloodcurdling scream, like something caught in a trap. It was clear he wasn't used to things not going his way.

"Pay her for tonight's gig and let her go," Steve said but Marty didn't move.

At this point, Steve's wife came into the kitchen. A nice lady who doesn't deserve such a man. She's a nurse, I think, and very kind. "What the hell is going on? We can hear you out near the coat check room," she told them. Then she saw what was going on. Perhaps Cara had confided in her, this sad girl with so few friends. "Oh," Denise said. "Oh."

"Five hours continuous plus overtime," Cara announced. "Give it up and I'm gone. You never have to see me again." She and Denise locked eyes, then looked away from each other.

"What's the matter, Karroll? Breakups suck, don't they?" Denise told Marty. "Pay the lady."

Marty went into his pocket and peeled a few bills off a large wad like he was tearing the petals from a paper flower. He threw the cash into Cara's face. It spilled onto the kitchen's red tile floor which was spattered with chicken grease, dishwater, drips of coffee and other unpleasantnesses. Then Marty stormed out the back door and into the parking lot with Steve following close behind, murmuring quietly like a beaten-down girlfriend trying to calm her batterer.

Cara put down her drum and fell to one knee, careful not to dirty her pant leg in the muck. Denise joined her, not caring so much. Pantyhose, even expensive ones, could be easily replaced. Denise and Cara put the money into one pile and stood. "Make sure it's all there," Denise told her. "It's just like that SOB to short you." Cara counted and nodded.

"Well, I've got to get Steve home...before he goes home with someone else," Denise stated. She was only half-joking. I'd seen it happen, and more than once. Before Cara could lift her drum, Denise took her in a hug. "I'll miss you, kiddo," she told her.

Cara hugged her back and did not let go. "I'll miss you, too. You're the only thing that made all of this bearable. Well, you and Garland's cooking," she smiled at me over her friend's shoulder. It was the first any of them had acknowledged my presence. I thought I was like a fly on the wall or a smudge on the wallpaper. I bowed my head and smiled, then busied myself with another kitchen task.

When the women parted, they looked into each other's eyes, which were full of emotion. "We'll see each other again," Cara said.

"No, we probably won't," Denise told her.

"Yeah, you're probably right," Cara agreed. Then they both laughed. Denise smacked her friend gently on the bottom then rushed out the delivery entrance, pulling her rabbit jacket close to her thin body. Her face was wet, her eyes red.

Cara bit her lip, stuffed the damp money into her pocket and picked up her drum. Before she could leave, I pressed a small, brown paper bag into her hand. "What's this?" she asked.

"Something you like," I told her. "Something good."

"Thank you, Garland," she said simply.

"Because I hope never to see you again," I said. "At least not in this place."

4/29/79

It wasn't as bad as I thought it would be. But it was still bad.

Of course, Karroll overreacted, as he overreacts to pretty much everything. Called me every name in the book. Well, every negative female-inspired curse word. Right in the kitchen of the Lev. I felt sorry for Garland who looked like he felt sorry for me. Who else was going to compliment his noodle *kugel*? But I think it was more than the fact that I complimented his *kugel, kasha varnishkes* and stuffed derma. I think he really likes me. Maybe he knew I wasn't just another White Devil—or worse, a White Jewish Devil—in this Godforsaken place. But then again, everyone thinks they stand out, that they're special. Even assholes like Karroll.

Steve didn't say much. Never does. Hates confrontation. Will allow himself to get stepped on, pushed around, put upon, just to avoid going up against someone. Maybe that's why he's taken Karroll's bullshit for so long: to avoid a scene. Plus he's as lazy as they come, except when it comes to trying to get laid. And I'm not taking about with his wife. Anyone else but.

Speaking of which, Dennie walked in on the middle of the scene from the ballroom door. It looked like she wanted to duck out the second she realized what was going on. Not that she didn't have an inkling. I as much as told her what I was planning to do. I don't think she believed me, though.

Garland left as soon as he could, giving me a bag of stuffed derma to remember him by. He said he never wanted to see me again, but I know what he meant. Not there. Not onstage with Ste-Mar.

Last in was poor, stupid Beryl, looking like a gaunt, perplexed Teddy bear in her fox coat and that ridiculous Farrah Fawcett flip in her hair. Sometimes I just wanted to choke her by her gold rope chain and put her out of her misery. Beryl looked even more confused than usual, chewing on one of her pink Lee Press-On Nails like it was lunch.

Karroll stormed back into the kitchen, looking for his wife, avoiding looking at me. Finding Beryl, he smacked her hand out of her mouth, to which she responded, "What?" Unfazed, like it happened all the time. It probably did. I felt sorry for her because she had to go home with the guy. No doubt, he would probably do up a pile of coke, blame it on me, then fuck her raw just out of pure meanness. Dumb-bunny Beryl. But she chose the king-sized bed she's lying in.

After Beryl and Marty left, I stood in the kitchen alone. I made my way home too, grabbing a ride from Ackerman, who was happy to do it but sad to see me go.

How do I feel? Relieved, I guess. Numb. Shell-shocked from all of the name calling. But I feel kind of high myself. And a little sad. I'll miss Denise most of all. (And Garland's Jewish soul food.) But it's not like I can't call her and get together with her now and then. Who am I kidding, though? It never happens like that. Oh, sure you say, 'Let's keep in touch' when you leave a job or move. But you never do. Ever. Life kind of gets in the way.

I will miss the extra money, though. Just biding my time until I can leave the *Post*. That probably won't be until after the EP is mixed, pressed and out there. Weeks, probably months. In the meantime, JR is getting us gigs in every shit little club in Manhattan, and some good ones, too. Besides CB's, the Mudd Club and even a new place in the East Village called The Pyramid Club. Just to get practice, to keep our chops sharp. Meaning, so Roy can get his shit together and not be so terrified to perform that he has to get wasted to do it.

I don't get as scared anymore. I haven't barfed since the CBGB gig. I'm ready, ready, ready. I don't know about the rest of them. Don't care. I'll leave them in the dust if I have to. All I need is myself and my kit. No man, no nothing. Just me.

*

Took a break, went for a walk. Reread what I just wrote. I don't want to sound coldhearted but... Hey, I don't give a damn how I sound. It's my journal, for no one's eyes but mine. Right?

Tom McCole
Truck Driver, New York Post

Alls I know is that she was hot. Had all of this attitude, a way of strutting down the street, like Mick Jagger does onstage. It was like this shitty little edge of Chinatown was her stage. The whole world was. It was like she owned it. And she did.

She never wanted to talk much, just get down to business. I was never really sure whether she liked sex or not or if it was just another thing she had to conquer. Master. Get the best of. You know? Not that she wasn't good. She was intense. With a hard, lean, muscled body that didn't quit. But not dykey. Feminine even though she didn't have much on top. But what she lacked in the tits department she made up for in ass. Her arms were strong, so she could get you off with a few strokes. Strong from carrying her kit and playing drums all those years, I guess.

Not that I ever saw her play. We weren't like that. I never saw her outside of work. Back of the truck. Front seat of my car. It was like she didn't want to mix her worlds. Oh, yeah, and the one time she came by my place late. And that was all right with me. I wasn't looking for a wife or even a girlfriend. Just some tail. I didn't care if it was a hand job in the front of my Buick or a blow job in the back of my delivery truck, so cold, I could see her breath around my cock as she sucked me off. There's no such thing as a bad pop, if you ask me.

Did she get off? Couldn't tell. Did I care? Not particularly. And she didn't seem to care either. Just seemed to get off on the idea of doing it. And I had no problem with that. Especially when I was on the clock. No better way to stick it to Murphy than to hit him where it hurts. In his wallet.

I don't want you to think I'm some kind of sex monster, some *Looking for Mr. Goodbar* maniac. It wasn't all about getting my rocks off. Sometimes she just sat in my cab and we talked, no sex, no touching, even. I'd bring her a tea, hot and light and sweet, just the way she liked it. I'd sit there and listen to her talk. Bitch about her boss on the fourth floor. Bitch about playing gigs for weddings and christenings. (Yep, once some Guidos from Bath Beach actually hired a band to play a christening party at Fiorentino's. I remember her telling me how she looked for the bride and groom and then noticed a baby in a bassinet. I kid you not.) Of course, she'd bitch about not "making it." A lot.

I'm not a philosopher. Fuck, I'm just a truck driver…I'm in the union though, so I'm not a total piece of shit. I'm not a college boy but I guess I got some common sense. I'd try to talk some sense into her, tell her that it's not all about "making it" but the shit you see on the way up there, on the road to success. And if you never make it, so what? You still saw and did some pretty amazing stuff along the way. At least you got that going for you, right? Wrong. In her book at least, it's all about making it. Every breath, every movement, everything she did. Ever.

She'd sit there staring out the dirty windshield or fiddling with the top on the to-go cup, shaking her head 'no.' The more I talked, the more she shook her head. There was no talking to her if she didn't want to hear what you had to say. So, I gave up after a while and just listened. She talked a lot about leaving. This place, the *Post*, which I couldn't blame her for. She had a shit job, stuck in a cubicle all day with assholes, old Rube yelling at everyone whenever he felt like it. She yapped about leaving club dates…which I heard she actually did. Leaving Brooklyn. Leaving New York. Just leaving, checking out.

I started to wonder if she was talking about offing herself but I never had the guts to ask her. Jeez, what would I have said if she'd said 'yes.' Look at me, I ain't anybody's savior. Not even my own.

5/5/79

I never realized how playing music, even crappy club date music, took the pressure off everything else. Banging on the drums, even to a half-assed version of "La Bamba" with Marty tormenting the keyboards and Steve alternately mangling Spanish and his trumpet, took the edge off of life. Instead of being more calm—Ha! There's a word people rarely associate with me—I'm more bitchy. If you can imagine that. My fuse seems much shorter and I'm a lot easier to set off, and at the stupidest littlest things. Like missing a train or Edie's latest nonsense.

Cookie, a sax player Ste-Mar sometimes used, called me about filling in on a *Cinco De Mayo* gig tonight—and I jumped on it like a chubby chick on a sleeve of Oreos. It wasn't just the money, which was a lot better than Steve and Marty used to throw me. I think the reason I was so stoked about the gig was the idea of getting to play in front of an audience again, the instant gratification applause brings. Even from drunken Mexicans in a bucket of blood bar like the Mambo Lounge in South Brooklyn.

Not that I'm unhappy with Aircraft, but it isn't moving as quickly as I'd like. Seems to be at a standstill, a deadlock, even. We finished the EP a few days ago, after we laid down the tracks to "Mask." Since Fern wrote it about me, JR insisted I sing lead on it. That's just the kind of guy he is. No ego involved, just what's best for the band. "You have a stronger voice than me," JR said simply. (We'd already decided to mix it up and have someone else besides Danny sing lead on one song to show our versatility.)

Then JR added, "Besides, it's your song." And that was that. I'm not sure Danny shared J's enthusiasm, but screw it.

We dropped off the master at Larva on Wednesday. Here it is Saturday, and still nothing from Bruce. We tried to hand it to him in person but we couldn't even get past the receptionist. "He's in a meeting," his assistant Trini smiled sweetly when she came to the front desk to get the tapes. Meeting my ass! It's a power play, that's all it is. Bruce was all over us at CB's, messengered the contract within days, then when he's got us on the hook, he pussies out to offer us an EP instead of a full album. Who knows what else he has up his sleeve? I don't trust any of them. They're all bullshitting liars out for themselves.

At the Mambo Lounge, the first Margarita went down soft as silk but that was all I had. I have to be careful not to drink too much and get messy behind my kit. It's a small place (probably without a cabaret license for drums or horns) so Cookie told me to only bring three pieces and my mike. As happy as Cookie is to be playing his own gig, he's also scared Steve and Marty will find out he booked something behind their backs then never hire him again. "I thought slavery went out with Abe Lincoln," I told Cookie but he didn't seem to get it.

"I got four kids from three different broads," he said on a cigarette break. "I need all the gigs I can get."

Even though I never heard the song before, there I was harmonizing with Cookie like we were lovers. Crazy lyrics about the Figaro cha-cha-cha.

Cookie is like an excited little kid on this gig. He just discovered that he could sing a few months ago and he is thrilled with his new toy: his own voice. He's not half bad, especially with the Latin stuff. And the crowd is pumped. The dancing at the Mambo Lounge is a joy to watch, not like the Humper at the Baron DeKalb. Here, you see huge Hispanic people as light on their feet as if they're dancing on air. It's been a long time since I enjoyed a society gig like this.

Some people were actually weeping when I sang "Before the Next Teardrop Falls" en *Español*. An old *abuela* sighed, pinching my cheek, *"Ai chica, mas bueno a Freddy Fender."*

"She says you're better than Freddy Fender," Cookie was nice enough to translate for me. When Cookie told them afterwards that I was Jewish, the applause swelled even more.

Is my ego so fucked up and wounded that this makes me feel amazing?
Yes.

Why can't I just find the pure joy in making music? Why can't it be like this every night? Why do I have to gauge everything against "making it?" Because I'm a messed-up piece of shit, that's why. Nothing is ever good enough for me, not even happiness.

Mongo

I've said it before and I'll say it again: I've never met anyone like her. In good ways and in not so good ways. And I thought I was a sour, sorry-assed son of a bitch. But Cara makes me look like a cock-eyed optimist.

I mean, anyone else would be happy as *en cerdo en mierda* with this record deal, but not Cara. Definitely not a pig in shit, she keeps poking holes in it. First she was pissed that it wasn't an album deal.

"At least it's not for a single," JR said hopefully.

"But it's not an album. It's just an EP," Cara was quick to point out.

Just an EP! Does she realize that each of us would give our right nut for this! For someone else footing the bill, for once! For someone else thinking we're good! For someone else setting up a tour!

"I wouldn't call it a tour, Mongo," she said. "Just a few gigs." A few gigs in different states, a few gigs we didn't have to set up ourselves. Or that JR's wife Fern didn't have to set up, locked in the bathroom, trying to sound professional, with the kid banging on the door, wanting to watch fucking *Sesame Street*. Shit. Give me a break!

Of course, I didn't say any of this out loud. JR gave me "the look" and shook his head. Anything to keep the peace. Anything not to fuck up this record from getting released. Anything to keep us from breaking up. I swear, I don't know what JR would do if that happens. He poured his heart and soul into this thing for years. They're his songs—well, his and Fern's. They're his blood. His breath. His life.

In the beginning, I tried to be sympathetic to Cara. I felt for her. I really did. I knew where she was coming from. I've been through a lot of shit in the music business myself. Who hasn't? But as I got to know her, I saw that it was always the worst case scenario with Cara, the deepest, blackest "what if." Yeah, we have gigs in Jersey, Pennsylvania and Rhode Island. Rhode fucking Island. Half the guys I grew up with can't even find Rhode Island on a road map! Remember, I'm just a Rican from the projects. Shit! 'Yeah, but the gigs are in small houses,' Cara complained. Damn! I'll play a gig in some bozo's house if it pays and they buy EPs. We're fucking nobody, that's why they're in small venues. We're fucking nobody until we're somebody. That's how I look at it. That's how we all look at it, except for Cara.

Bruce is talking about getting us some gigs out on the West Coast, too. "I'll believe it when I see it," said Cara. I had to hold back from rapping her right in the mouth! But then I reminded myself that I don't hit girls.

In my eyes, it's perfect, for now. We get to test the waters, feel it all out, and we don't have to quit our day jobs. Not that I'm crazy about working for FedEx but it's not terrible. After I set up my deliveries, I'm out driving a truck most of the day, nobody up my ass. At least I'm not stuck in a brick box from nine to five like Cara. Maybe it does something to your brain, to your spirit. I don't know.

I swear, sometimes she sounds like a crabby, ancient Jew. I should know, I deliver packages to them all day long in Brighton Beach. "Nice day today, Mr. Yankowitz," I say.

"But it's supposed to rain tomorrow," they say.

'And you might be dead tomorrow, you rotten, old fuck!' I don't say.

Come to think of it, Cara *is* a crabby old Jewish woman—her mother. Not that I ever met her. But I heard enough of the one-sided conversations she has with her mom to know. And I've seen how deflated, defeated Cara comes away from them. Sometimes I can hear the yelling from the other end of the line, even though Cara tries to mash the receiver against her ear so no one else will hear. But somebody always hears.

In my mind, the worst thing you could ever do is become your parent. I haven't seen my old man since I was three, and that's when he was walking out the door. I'd be damned if I turned into him. I'd rather be dead.

Joyless. That's how I'd describe Cara. If someone put a gun to my head and said I had to describe her in one word, it would be "joyless." And that's pretty fucked up. But I like her. I really do. Only, it's almost as if she's trying to destroy this one little good thing we have, this one little thing that could easily become one big, good thing. If she would only stop picking at the scab and let it be.

Cara just better not fuck it up for the rest of us. I worked too hard to get to this point. To get out of the PJs, those fucking housing projects that smell like piss and puke and disappointment. To get out of a dead-end job where the people get grayer and fatter every year. Just to get out.

Where is she going to end up? Dead? Alone? Both? I'll be damned if she takes me with her.

But I like Cara. I really do.

5/13/79

I couldn't believe it when JR told us that Bruce called. Not to give us a release date for the EP but to ask us to lay down additional vocals for "Mask." He thinks it's our strongest song and our hit. I took this as the music business screwing with us once again while JR, as always, was able to see the sunny side of the street. "He just wants to make it better," he told me. I guess I might have had a look on my face that said I was going to give him shit. Maybe that's why JR's eyes just kind of pleaded with me not to. So, I didn't.

There we were, harmonizing our asses off at 10 on a Sunday morning when Paulie buzzes me from the sound booth, "You got a phone call, Cara." I don't know how my sister found me. I didn't think I told anyone where I'd be. Maybe I mentioned it to her kid Jared but how could he remember? I went into the sound booth to take the call.

"I think Mommy's having a heart attack," Aileen said, without even saying "hello."

"Think or know?" I asked. Then Aileen started screaming, just like my mother. These health scares have happened before. Heartburn = heart attack in Edie Finkelstein's book, just to get attention. Pimple = skin cancer. You get the drift.

I held the phone away from my ear, not caring if Paulie heard my sister's tirade. "The ambulance is on its way," I heard Aileen say.

"I'll be there as soon as I can," I told her. "I'm in the middle of something." Then I just hung up.

Paulie looked at me in disbelief. "No more calls," I told him.

"But it's your fucking mother," he said.

"Have you met my fucking mother?" I asked Paulie, heading back to the studio. "If you did, maybe you'd understand."

PS, I laid down my vocal track in two takes then was out of there like a shot. I'm writing this on the Q train, which is taking its sweet time to get to Coney Island Hospital.

2:15 pm

Turns out it *was* a heart attack and now I'm screwed. My sister and brother will never forgive me. Hopefully, they won't tell Edie how long I took to get here or else I'm triple screwed. "You chose your music over your mother," Aileen snapped at me through gritted teeth as I pushed through Emergency's swinging doors. I almost snapped back at her but I managed to hold it together.

Now, I'm in the vinyl waiting room on the ICU floor sandwiched between a crack whore and a wino. My family has banished me here with their killer looks, impressive sighs and dramatic eye rolls they perfected as understudies of the great Edith Finkelstein. It's okay, I'm used to being ostracized for one reason or another.

At least my nephews still love me. Jared and Stewie have been taking turns sneaking off to report things like: "She's breathing on her own now" or "Grandma Edie just called the nurse a *meshuga* when she tried to take her blood" or "She just pulled the *facocta* oxygen thingy out of her nose." Like I thought, Edie was going to be fine. She's too mean to kill. There's a lot more pain and suffering she needs to bestow upon the universe. Albeit her own tiny universe. Aka, me.

3:45 pm

"What the hell are you writing?" Aileen's voice boomed above me. I slammed my notebook shut and shoved it in my hippie bag, as she calls it.

At the moment, I'm on the B-36 crawling down Avenue Z toward Sheepshead Bay, scribbling where I left off when my sister interrupted me.

"A song," I lied to Aileen.

"I hope it's about your dying mother," she snapped.

"How is she?" I smiled at Aileen. "Still dying?"

"She wants to talk to you," my sister said. "Alone."

"Uh-oh," I responded. Still no smile from Aileen. Screw it. If she was going to punish me, I was going to punish her.

It was a crummy room, I'll give you that. Not even semi-private but more like a ward, the kind you see in those B-movies starring Ida Lupino that are set in women's prisons. Edie was surrounded by ladies of different shades of brown dressed in shabby hospital gowns lying in high, steel hospital beds, buzzing with machinery. The smeared window looked down onto Ocean Parkway. I found my mother next to a woman who moaned constantly, somewhere between pleasure and pain. When I moved to kiss Edie on the forehead, she pulled away.

"I want you to do something for me, Carol," she said, her voice more raspy than usual. Her breath reeked of old Chesterfields, medicine and fear.

"Sure, Ma, anything," I told her.

"Anything?" she snarled.

"Well, anything within reason. What?"

"I can't trust your brother or your sister," she whispered harshly. "They're both itching to get their hooks into what little I have."

"Ma, I don't think..."

She shushed me fast. "No, don't think, Carol. Listen." My mother took a deep, dramatic breath, worthy of Camille or Carmen or some other opera diva. "There's a box under my bed at home. A shoebox. From Thom McAn. An old one. I need you to get it and take it to your place. For safekeeping."

"Sure. What's in there?" I asked, even though I knew what was in there: her life.

"Things," she told me. "Just things. Papers and things. I can't trust either of them." I must have flushed a little with pride or embarrassment. "I'm not sure I can trust you either," she added, for good measure, just to hurt and keep the upper hand, I guess. "But you're too dumb to cheat them or me or anybody."

"Thanks, Edie."

"You know what I mean."

"Yeah, I do, unfortunately," I told her.

"I don't want to talk about it here. The walls have ears." So did the homeless people and the Welfare mothers. *"Oy,"* she said, "Doesn't that one ever shut up?" she added, gesturing to Mona the Moaner with her head. Then, before I could answer, she swallowed hard. "I would kill for a Chesterfield. Even a Parliament."

"That's part of what put you here," I told her as gently as I could. I braced myself for the shit storm that would follow.

"Did I ask you, Carol? Huh? Did I ask you?"

No answer required.

"Now go," Edie told me.

I went. Past my brother, past my sister, past the kids, who, at least, kissed me on the cheek as I passed.

6:00 pm

The dust bunnies under my mother's bed must have moved in soon after we moved there, which was soon after my father left her. Us. Without much trouble, I found the Thom McAn shoebox. I didn't even need a flashlight, although my right arm was coated in ancient powder. I cleared a space on the Formica kitchen table, first piling up the old copies of *The Daily News* that were spread across its surface. (Edie didn't read schlock like the *Post*.) I wouldn't dare throw her newspapers away or Edie would go ballistic when she got back, lamenting her unclipped coupons (pronounced "kew-pons"), sweepstake games, and unrealized riches of some sort. I dumped the trash, which was starting to stink, emptying the overflowing ashtray into it before I did. I opened a window, even though it was cool and starting to get dark.

I needed something to get through this, something stronger than Waldbaum's Cream Soda, so I felt under the kitchen sink cabinet until my hand rested on the familiar squarish tapered bottle and long neck. Manischewitz Blackberry Wine, Edie's old standby. Still almost full. Poured a jelly glass halfway, took a quick sip and thought of cough medicine. I opened the box.

Bruce Lask
A&R Director, Larva Records

I'd never seen anything like her. And I've been in the record trade more than
20 years. She just blew me away. Looked like a big, hot mess: lawn-mower
haircut, bargain basement clothes from Domsey's, scrappy, pissed off. But
Larva's creative team could work with that. Hone it. Polish it. I mean, take Patti
Smith. She's no looker but she's got something and she's going somewhere.

Officially, the initials in my title stand for "Artist and Repertoire," though
some call it "Find and Sign." And that's basically what I do. Find artists and sign
them. A&R people have a reputation of being cut-throat and I guess we are, but
it's a cut-throat business. Hey, generally speaking, any business is. I go to the
bottom of the barrel, searching the dregs of the earth for new talent. Once in a
great while, I find it. In piss-soaked bars. On ghetto street corners. In West Islip
garages. The kid next door's grandmother's nephew. Everybody thinks they've
got "it." Everybody thinks they're going to "make it." But the truth of the matter
is that very few have "it" and very few will. And if they do, it's not going to be
like anything they ever imagined.

Am I a bottom-feeder? Do I prey on other people's desperation? It is what it
is. By the time I come along, the artist will pretty much sign anything, even if it's
not remotely what they wanted. At least it's something, right? That's what they
think. But usually, it's nothing. Usually, they're shelved and their demo never
sees the light of day, never gets the push it deserves, or they think it deserves. But
that's just the nature of the business. What's that stat—something like 90% of

everything is crap. Sturgeon's Law, I think it's called. Well, my job is to weed the crap from the rest. And out of the rest, maybe 1% gets push, radio play, fame and fortune.

They don't understand it, though. The artists. They think you're just being a bastard, that you're cold, heartless. But if you don't bring marketable material to your record company, then it's your ass—and your job. And all the A&R folks are swimming in the same gene pool, looking for the next big thing. But I think I found it with Cara. In fact, I know I did.

Don't get me wrong, Aircraft isn't a bad group. Decent songs. Good musicians. Not much of a look but they have that kick-ass female drummer. That's what everyone's talking about, the drummer, not them. Not only the way she plays but the way she sings, wrapping her lips around the mike like it's someone's dick. Maybe yours, if you're lucky.

Do they have what it takes? I personally don't think so but I've been wrong before. Look at The Knack. I didn't see much there but the boys at Capitol grabbed them like they were their last meal. But Aircraft...they might, just might, find fame as a B-music group. Like Kansas, Boston or one of those interchangeable place-name American rock groups. Would they achieve the fame of a Led Zepplin or the Stones? No, I don't think so. But who does?

Why did I sign Aircraft, then? Simple. Why do you kiss up to the ugly, fat chick? To get close to her hot, pretty best friend. Right? I signed Aircraft to get close to Cara. I needed to see if she had the right stuff, if she could cut it. She didn't have her own demo or her own material, so essentially, I made Aircraft her backup band. That's why I made them go back into the studio to rerecord those tracks on "Mask." Her song. To my ear, that's the hit single. But only with her as frontman. Or frontwoman. Whatever.

Was that a scumbag move? Maybe. But it's common. It's standard. It's business, nothing personal. Aircraft will have very little choice in the matter. There's a tiny clause in their EP contract that they probably didn't even notice or if they did, didn't pay much attention to. Most musicians don't. I told them to have a lawyer look over the contract but I will bet cash money they didn't. Bands rarely do. They don't want to shell out the extra bucks. Couldn't imagine anyone would want to screw them over. Let's face it, musicians are mostly ego, anyway. I mean, they all think, 'We're so flipping great, why would any company sign us and not distribute us?' They usually gloss right over this gem:

21. CONDITION SUBSEQUENT. If Company does not enter into a binding contract for the distribution of the Recording during the Distribution Period, the assignment and license from Artist to Company granted pursuant to Sections C. and D. hereunder shall be deemed rescinded by the agreement of the parties.

As for Cara, she'll have a couple of choices:

1) split with the group and go solo;
2) front Aircraft; or
3) none of the above

Will Ms. Funk go for it? Well, what do you think?

5/14/79

12:15 am

I've been sitting here for who knows how long, going through that damned box. I can't believe it's after midnight now. I lost track of time. I've been helping myself to the Manischewitz as I go along. Filling up the jelly glass midway to Fred and Wilma Flintstone's chests. Pebbles is totally submerged in the darker-than-blood fluid.

I guess it's time to go.

There's all kinds of crap in this box. An Aetna life insurance policy for my mother in the grand sum of $5,000—with all three kids as beneficiaries. One for my father, same amount, of which Edith was still the beneficiary, paid in full on October 9, 1959, with the check register receipt still attached. (Jake died a few months before my 10th birthday.) Edie's birth certificate—Aileen, Irv and I were ceremoniously handed ours when each of us moved out. Edie's yellowed, bent Social Security card, still inside the envelope it was mailed in, postmarked October 24, 1934. In her maiden name, Edith Schwartz. A copy of her lease. A copy of her Medicaid card, just in case she lost the original.

I took them all out methodically, one by one, flipping them over onto their faces, so as not to upset the order. I don't want to get Edie's considerable knickers in a knot for making a *facocta* mess.

And then came the stuff I didn't expect. Shit that floored me: locks of hair from all three of us, preserved in cellophane that had long gone sepia, Edie's wispy handwriting on scraps of paper inserted into each. Mine said, "Carol

Sylvia, first haircut on her first birthday, 12/12/50." I carefully unwrapped the plastic wrap. The curl inside was the color of wheat, still soft, finer than thread. I couldn't help but run my fingertips through my own hair which, was now black and stood up like a wire brush.

Next were tiny paper envelopes of baby teeth, carefully marked. They were pretty gross, dried blood and roots against ivory white chips of tooth matter.

There was the blue velvet *yarmulke* from my parents' wedding, with "Edith & Jacob Finkelstein, June 9, 1945," printed on the inside in faded gold lettering. "Your father did them himself at the plant," my mother had once told me, proudly. Tucked inside of the *yarmulke* was the white lace head-covering my mother had worn under the *chuppah* at Temple Beth Elohim for her wedding. She was a blushing bride of 25, considered elderly in those days.

Then there was a photograph, black-and-white, scalloped edges, my father with a crisp military haircut, fresh from some undisclosed location in the European Theatre, my mother looking young, toothy, hopeful, and almost pretty in her simple white shift made by her sisters Sarah and Iris.

Underneath the wedding debris was an envelope filled with pictures I'd never seen before. My parents on an extended trip out west, in Tucson. Or maybe they lived there, tried to make a go of it outside Brooklyn. I was never clear on the facts and my mother got upset whenever I asked. "The past's the past. What does it matter?" she'd say.

But I know it was after my dad was discharged from the army. My parents looked happy. Fresh-faced, in love, even. There were long captions written on the backs of the pictures, dated and documented in my mother's frilly hand. One floored me. In it, my mother was smiling so wide and true that it didn't even look like her. It was dated July 19, 1945 and said, "Me, holding lilacs and laughing."

I don't know why the picture affected me like that. I felt like crying but wouldn't let myself. What the hell happened to that woman? Then I realized— *we* happened to her. She had kids one after the other, three in less than five years. Being pregnant put wear and tear on her bad hip and it got worse with each pregnancy, ending with me, who landed her in the hospital for months.

I don't know why, but I slipped the lilac picture into my pocket.

I poured the blackberry wine empty and took out the last item. It was a 5x7 Manila envelope with a clasp. It seemed a lot newer than the box's other contents, yet it was shoved way on the bottom. What I found inside was me: everything I had ever done, musically and otherwise, was inside that envelope.

There was a program from a performance at the Sheepshead Bay High School Assembly with my name listed under "Percussion." I'd played the Beatles' "Boys" and sang behind the drums for the first time in public. Edie managed to hobble across the street with her walker even though she'd gotten out of the Hospital for Joint Diseases days before. She told me I was good but complained that my hair was "a mess." She'd sighed, "*Oy*, so sweaty and stringy."

There were clippings from various local papers and *The Village Voice* announcing where bands of mine had played. L'Amour (self-proclaimed "Rock Capital of Brooklyn," as per its awning), 2001 Odyssey (yes, even *I* had a disco phase) and dives like Lauterbach's on Prospect Avenue. Kenny's Castaways, CBGB, and Penny Arcade way the hell up in Rochester. Everything since my first gig back in high school. It was all there.

My hands were shaking when I closed the envelope. Probably from the wine. My stomach felt sour, too. I had seen enough. I'd reached the bottom of the box and there was nothing left to see except for a few wisps of dust. Why did my mother act like she hated me? Why was she so cruel all throughout my life, from as far back as I can remember? Why did she act like she didn't care when the Manila envelope showed just the opposite?

I have the overwhelming desire to call Michael. Not for sex, just to talk. But it's too late and I have work in the morning.

Michael

She called. It was after two in the morning but she called like it was nothing, like it was two in the afternoon. I was still up, grading papers for practice finals. They were spread out across the bed and I was almost finished with the Heineken I'd been nursing all night. I heard it in her voice that she'd had a few, more than a few. It was thick, lazy, slow. Not her usual squirrel-on-acid timbre.

"Do you think my mother loves me?" she asked when I picked up the phone. No "Hello" or "How are you?" No "It's been a while" or "Sorry it's so late."

My first impulse was to hang up but that would have been a sucky thing to do, even to someone who was calling you at 2 am. And besides, I used to love her. Maybe I still do. "What's not to love?" I told her.

"Michael..." she drawled. "I'm serious."

"So am I," I said. Then I took a deep breath, "I think your mother loves you as much as she's able."

"I guess that's all you can expect from anyone, huh?"

"You okay, Cara?"

"Yeah," she told me, finally. "As okay as I can be." Then, after a beat. "Edith had a heart attack."

"Sorry to hear that. Will she be all right?"

"As all right as she can be," Cara shot back. "She asked me to get this box that she keeps under the bed."

"A strongbox?"

Cara laughed. "You know Edie, she's too cheap to buy a strongbox. It's a shoebox. If it's free, it's for me." I waited for Cara to continue. "My whole life is in a little box…You wouldn't believe the things she kept."

"I bet I would," I told her. I listened as Cara went on about the various items she found in the Thom McAn box. And as I listened, I told myself that I wouldn't ask where she was. I wouldn't ask if she wanted company. I wouldn't ask her if she wanted me to pick her up. I wouldn't ask her if she wanted to come over. And I didn't. It had been months since we'd been together (not counting the time I watched Aircraft at CBGB—as far as I could tell, she still didn't know I had been there), months since she'd called.

Plus I started "seeing" someone from work. A pretty, smart Social Studies teacher named Marnie. Not that we'd gone very far, just coffee, dinner, a movie here and there, and a little kissing, all very pleasant. But I don't want to screw it up. I had to stop myself from comparing Marnie to Cara, from constantly comparing everything and everyone to Cara. No one will ever have her fire. But you know what they say about fire.

After the box, Cara moved on to music, to the EP, to her singing lead on one of the songs, "Mask," I think, and Danny, the lead singer's quiet but well-noted hissy fit. That brought us up to date, to tonight, or, more closely, this morning. "I guess that's it," she said. "How have you been?"

"Pretty much the same," I told her.

"Just minus me," she added.

"Yes," I told her. And that was it. Cara hung up soon after. I guess she got what she needed out of me. I can't say that it wasn't nice getting a call from her. I can't say that I didn't get a charge out of hearing her voice again. But I was also glad when she hung up the phone. Relieved.

I wasn't getting on that train again because it led nowhere. But it was a good ride while it lasted. A wild ride but a memorable one.

5/14/79

Later

I didn't go to work today. I called in sick. Haven't done that in, like, ever. Just didn't have the heart to be with people or deal with any more crap that's not already on my plate.

After Edie's, I went down to Captain Walter's, box in tow, tucked under my arm like a Bible thumper. For some reason, I didn't feel like putting it in one of the ancient plastic bags from Edie's unruly collection, so I walked with it under my arm, just like that. I did put a rubber band around it, though. I didn't want the contents of my life spilling onto the broken concrete.

Thankfully, the Cap's Open Mic comic's night was over and no one I knew was there. I didn't feel like talking. I just felt like drinking, which is rare for me. I just went with it. Jerry was tending bar. He's a decent guy and doesn't yap when it's clear you just want to sit and be quiet. And it wasn't crowded. Just a handful of people, who, like me, didn't want to have conversation. Except for a couple falling all over each other at the end of the bar, it was silent, just the jukebox. ABBA, then Lou Reed, then Barry White. Then I don't remember.

I felt this infinite sadness. For me? For Edie? I don't know. Maybe for both of us. But I felt this big, black hole where my heart should be. I filled it up with rum and Coke.

Soon, Jerry told me that the Cap was closing and I found myself making my way home. It wasn't far, only a bunch of blocks, less than a mile. I don't know. It didn't matter. My feet moved like they were on a conveyer belt. It was almost like I didn't have to move them myself. They just knew where to go. Kind of like my hands and feet do when I'm playing. Then suddenly, I was home, squeezing my way past my kit, piled high like hat boxes, in the hall. I wasn't hammered, just a little numb. And still sad.

I flung myself on the couch, pulled out my notebook and started to write. That's when I decided that I wasn't going to work this morning. I didn't have to lie, really. I left a message for Ellis about my mom and made it seem a teeny bit worse than it was. Plus I was feeling a little queasy from mixing the Manischewitz and the rum.

After that, I started scribbling.

Things to do before I die
1) Make it
2) Make it
3) Make it
4) Stop worrying about making it
5) Make it—by any means necessary
6) Stop thinking about what people think about me
7) Stop giving a fuck
8) Make it
9) Stop bitching—I'm sick of listening to myself and everyone else is, too
10) Just make it, already!!!!

Oh, and I called Michael. No big deal. We just talked. That was it.

Then I shut off the ringer on the phone and turned down the volume on the answering machine. When I got up this afternoon, there was a message from Bruce. I'll give him a call when I get the nerve.

Edith

I guess you could say I'm glad to be home. Even though I'm alone. At least there's no one poking at me, stabbing me with needles and waking me up at 4 in the morning to take my temperature. I'd rather be home by myself than go through that nonsense again.

"At least you're alive, Ma," my daughter Aileen tells me.

"Am I?" I tell her. "You call this living?" As usual, she doesn't know what to say. Doesn't know *bupkis*, that one.

My son Irving's a *shmendrik*, a grinning, stupid idiot. He can barely support his own family, just like his father. But I don't want to get into that right now. And Carol, Carol finally made it to the hospital, they tell me, after a few hours. Seems no one could reach her. That's just like Carol. Only thinks of herself. My sister Iris says it's because Carol was on her own at such a young age she developed some sort of defense mechanism. I was in and out of the Hospital for Joint Diseases so much when she was a little girl, Carol never knew who would be taking care of her or when I would be out, so she made her own little dream world, her own little fortress. I think that's *mishegas*, but Iris, who took a psychology class 20 years ago, thinks she's Mrs. Sigmund Freud.

But why is Carol the only one out of my three children who I trust? She's not interested in getting what few scraps I have, while the other two, that's all they ever seem to think about. I bet they can't wait until I'm out of their hair. I trusted Carol with my life, which happens to be in a shoebox.

Carol's also the only one with half a brain. If only she would stop with that music *dreck*, she'd be all right. There I was, almost a week in the hospital, and when Carol came over to see me when I got home, she asked if I wanted her to wash my hair. Aileen was here every day, day in and day out, and it never even occurred to her. "Why didn't anybody tell me?" Aileen snapped, then stormed out. Like it was a big secret we were keeping from her. Use the brain G-d gave you. Wouldn't you want your hair washed after more than a week?

Carol was so gentle, bending me over the kitchen sink as easy as she could. I didn't even care that she got water down my back from the sprayer. She brought some fancy green shampoo, Herbal Essence, or something like that. Smelled nice, like Pine Sol, only nicer. Her fingers were like tiny fairies, tickling me. She used one of my good towels, the ones I save for special times. Except I never end up putting them out because nothing seems special enough. "Don't you think you deserve it, Edie?" she asked me when I told her this.

"You should be a nurse," I told her when I sat down at the kitchen table, out of breath from walking even a few feet.

"Thanks," she said. "But I already have a career. I'm a musician."

I literally bit my tongue not to say something bad. Not something bad, but something honest that I knew would hurt her.

Carol toweled down my hair and ran a thick comb through it, all with so much care. Not the way I used to do it when she was a kid, angry-like, pulling at the tangles, making her cry. Maybe that's why she keeps it so short now—no tangles. I guess I was always good at making her cry. I don't know why. I was always so angry. I still am.

Carol threw in a load of laundry while a pot of coffee was brewing. "You still have that box?" I asked her.

"Of course I do, Ma. Do you think I'd throw it out?"

"Throw it out, no. Lose it, maybe." We both laughed. It was a long time since we both laughed together.

"Some of the things in there," she said. "The pictures. You looked so happy with Daddy."

"*Feh!* With your father? Ha! Never." I wouldn't even give her that.

"Come on," she said. "The one with the flowers."

"I don't know what you're talking about, Carol." She got up and poured the coffee. Better than Maxwell House. Said she grinds up the beans herself because life is too short to drink cheap coffee. Fancy pants girl, she is. Even brought half-and-half, which I never get. Too expensive. Skim milk is fine for me, I always thought. Except it isn't.

"The lilacs. In Arizona or someplace."

"Oh, *those* flowers. It was Texas. We might have been content for a time. For a short time. A very short time." That seemed to make Carol happy. It takes so little to make this one happy. Or a lot. I'm not sure which.

She put some rugelach onto a plate. My good Kosher China. But I didn't say anything. Chocolate and apricot both. I looked at the box. "Leon's on Knapp Street? That's out of your way."

"Not really," she said. "I know they're your favorite."

The rugelach was heaven. I don't know which flavor was better. After we polished off the plate, she said, "The things you saved. In that box." I looked at her like I didn't know what she was talking about. "Our baby hair, our baby teeth."

I shrugged. "*Nu?* I'm a mother. That's what mothers do."

"The clippings," she added.

"So?" I told her.

"So...I didn't think you would, that you cared."

"I'm your mother. Of course, I care. I'm proud, Carol. Of you. Only..." With me, there's always an "only." I can't just say something nice and leave it at that. It's like Carol was a dog, waiting for me to throw her a scrap. "...only I wish you picked something easier. It's not that you're not good..."

"I'm a little better than good, Ma..."

"So I'm told. But it's too hard to make it to the top. My friend Bertha Siegelman told me it's not how good you are but who you know."

"I know a lot of people."

"You know what I mean, Carol." She poured more coffee without me asking. "I just hope I live to see it."

"I hope so, too." That's it. I said nothing nasty. Nothing sarcastic. And it felt good. It also felt good when she hugged me. Carol was always a good hugger, even as a kid. She put her whole body into it. I guess that's the way she did everything. Maybe that's why she gets me so mad sometimes. If you put everything into something, you can lose everything. Am I right or am I right?

5/22/79

I think Bruce is stringing me along, bullshitting me. First, he leaves a message on my answering machine, telling me that he has "a proposition" for me. Then, he's MIA. What the hell gives? It looks like he's full of it, just like everyone else in the music business.

Of course, I haven't said anything about Bruce's message to JR or to anyone else in Aircraft. But I don't think, J has heard from Bruce either. We're hanging by a thread here, waiting, always waiting. Supposedly Bruce is out of town. That's what his secretary says when I call her. Every day. Out of town, scouting, Trini says. Can't be reached. Will give him your message when he calls. Yeah, thanks. I'll wipe my butt with that message. It's been more than a week and *nada*.

Michael always told me to think positive. But it's hard. Especially considering my track record. "You have two choices," he used to say. "You either can be miserable or be happy waiting, thinking the best."

"But expecting the worst," I'd shoot back. I'm not good at being a happy idiot. I know how it sounds. I'm surprised Michael put up with me for so long. I wouldn't even put up with me if I didn't have a choice.

What else has been going on? Work at the *Post* sucks as usual but at least tax season has come and gone so it's not crazy-busy anymore. And the weather has been nice. Not so hot to bring up the Chinatown stink from clams and whatnot. Even the Fulton Fish Market, which is just a stone's throw away from the *Post*, doesn't smell too bad. Sometimes at lunch, I take long walks along the East River or else I sit on the pier right across from the *Peking* at South Street Seaport, reading, writing, thinking. It's hard to believe that flimsy-looking thing used to sail around Cape Horn. It is graceful and pretty, though.

Yesterday, I met Tom for lunch at that building across from the Fish Market. It's not elaborate, like a big garage with food stands and crafts stands. Supposedly, they're going to develop this whole area into one huge indoor/outdoor mall but I just don't see it. I don't see how they can get rid of the fishy stank. It will always be there, even if they open up a Gap or an art gallery. They'll be selling fancy pants that reek of crotch rot.

Anyway, the food is cheap and good but you're lucky to find a place to sit. We did. I sat and held our table while Tom waited on line, brought us fish and chips in paper cups and a couple of Cokes. His treat. This was the first thing he ever bought me besides a cup of tea. Maybe Tom's turning into a gentleman. Somehow, I doubt it.

I knew he had something up his sleeve but I couldn't figure out what it was. I thought maybe wanted some more pipe because we hadn't gotten together in his truck for a while. I felt like I was beyond that, and honestly, I was a little embarrassed it ever happened—several times—in the first place. Halfway into the fish and chips, Tom said that he was worried. About me. "I can take care of myself," I told him. He ignored me and said that he was afraid I was about to crash and burn. I had been taking off a lot of days lately, it was true, but I had time coming to me from all of the OT I worked in March and April, I shot back.

In a way, I was touched by Tom's concern, though unwarranted it was. But in another way, I was pissed off. Who the hell was he to judge me and think I was the fucked up one? Look at him, a truck driver with a GED, living in an illegal studio apartment, drinks too much, thinks too little... I could go on and on. And *he's* worried about *me?*

"It's like you're trying to off yourself," Tom said.

I couldn't hold back a snorty laugh. "With what?" I asked him. "Music?"

"Well, yeah," Tom told me. I could tell this was hard for him and I should have been kinder. But screw being kind. I'm done with being kind. No one's kind to me. "It makes you mad. And a little mean," he added.

I took a thoughtful sip of my Coke, which was already watery from the ice. The fried fish tasted like ash in my mouth. "Mean is good," I said. "Mean gets shit done. Nice girls finish last."

"But at least they finish." Even though I knew it was tough for Tom, I took a strange delight making it harder. Not a real cerebral guy, he wasn't much for talking. This was epic for him. He cleared his throat. "Me and Howie...Howie said to me one day, 'It's like she's trying to kill herself, using music to do it.' When Howie told me that, the hairs on the back of my neck stood up because I knew that the crazy fucker was right."

What do you say after a guy tells you something like that? I picked up my soda and my half-eaten fish and I threw it in the trash. "Thanks for lunch,"

I told Tom, and walked away. I'll be damned if I'll be psychoanalyzed by a couple of grown up newspaper delivery boys!

I was surprised that Tom didn't try and follow me. I walked through the wide-open double doors of that food warehouse, past secretaries and stockbrokers, high-rollers and bums, and into the bright blue day.

Damn, maybe I should have been a writer. In a sick way, I guess I am. Even if it's just this half-assed journal.

Not much else going on. Just playing the waiting game. Waiting for everything.

JR

It's coming apart at the seams. I can feel it before it happens. There's no heart in our rehearsals. Danny flies off the handle at the drop of a hat, accuses me of giving Cara the best songs. In front of her, no less. Roy thinks nobody notices him sneaking vodka from the flask that's attached to his hip pocket. Mongo is just Mongo, all smiles and positive vibes, like a slim, Puerto Rican Jesus. He's the Yang to Cara's Yin. She's all furrowed brows and hard knuckles and a tight, set jaw. Fern says I should write a song about it but I'm afraid that I'll just piss them off more and the band will implode.

That's what it feels like. Like the walls are about to cave in. Or that moment just before you feel your old man's fist on the side of your skull. Or when your girlfriend crumbles right before your very eyes and tells you it's over. The way the air crackles with emptiness before something ends.

I've been trying to keep everyone up. Me and Fern, we never saw ourselves as cheerleaders but now it's all we can do. There's Worst Case Scenario Cara, all but telling everyone that we're being shelved by Larva. Then Mongo, smiling and patting backs, saying it's going to be all right. Then Roy disappears to take a swill while Danny gloats in the corner about the fact that he doesn't sing two out of 20 songs. I swear, it's like babysitting at the zoo.

If I did write that song, I think I'd call it "Things Fall Apart." About all the things that do. Friendships, marriages, bands. Bands can be the worst because nothing holds you together but the music. There's usually no love, no real commitment. You're just strangers, basically, who come together to make something that's holy. You speak to each other through the music. And when the music is over…either because of a fight, a contract being broken or you're just not feeling it anymore…it's over. Like a marriage, held together only by the children. Well, sometimes the children just aren't enough.

I feel worse for Fern than I do for me. The songs are her babies. She does a great job with Jess, all of the endless dress-up games and trips to the park, but I know she needs more. She needs to create, to write, to hear her work performed, not just sit in a dresser drawer. Fern looks more and more devastated each day Bruce doesn't call. Like a teenage girl waiting for her crush to phone, she springs up and gets it on the first ring, breathlessly, trying to sound like she wasn't. Then Fern'll roll her eyes and mouth to me, "It's my mother" or "Your cousin Anne Marie."

At least I can get a break from it during the day. Working construction isn't the best job in the world but the pay is good and the day starts early enough so I'm free at night to rehearse or gig. The work can be feast or famine, so you just take it when it comes. It slows down in the winter and in the bad weather. Days off aren't hard to come by, though. I've got plenty of time coming to me and if push comes to shove, I can just take a day off with no pay. No sweat.

It's backbreaking work, hauling bricks and putting up drywall, whatever the job is, but it's the kind of work that keeps your mind free to do other things. I can't tell you how many melodies or keyboard licks I've written while painting or plastering. There's a strange sort of peace that comes with manual labor, and for me, that peace opens up my head for writing music. I find working with my hands very Zen.

I'm not the kind of guy to be stuck behind a desk with a necktie choking the life out of me. I tried that and it sucked. I came home with a headache, felt like there was nothing left for me at the end of the day because I spent hours upon hours thinking so hard for other people. Crunching numbers, whatnot. I always had a knack for numbers. My brother Jerry made a killing working in the Stock Exchange—also got a hell of a coke habit, but that's another story. Yeah, I tried a desk gig for a while but it wasn't for me. I like working with my hands and keeping my brain for myself, thank you very much.

Fern doesn't care what I do, just as long as I'm happy. Well, almost happy. The construction work isn't fulfilling or satisfying. Not like music is. Though little can compare with the satisfaction that comes with building something out of nothing. Looking at a house or a loft and remembering the blank space that was once there and the matter that's there now, and knowing that you had something to do with it. But could I do construction all my life like my dad and feel satisfied? No, I honestly don't think I could. But I might have to.

5/26/79

Bruce called today! He apologized for calling me on a Saturday. And on Memorial Day weekend, no less. ('Are you kidding me? You can call whenever the hell you want,' I felt like saying, but didn't.) LA's a circus, he said. A three-and-a-half ring circus, he said, and it was the first chance he's had to breathe, let alone pick up a telephone. It was a little after 9 am New York time, which is the crack of dawn California time. "But those tinsel people don't get up with the sun…They're afraid of it," he said.

I had a feeling he might have been up all night doing coke but didn't say that either.

For a guy who took his sweet time calling me, Bruce didn't seem to want to get off the phone. He talked up a storm. I could barely get in a word edgewise. Mostly stuff about how fake LA people are, how sincere and down to earth New York people are. That springboarded him onto Brooklyn people—his grandfather was born in Bushwick—and how Brooklyn pizza was better than Queens pizza. Then it ricocheted to Jewish girls vs. Catholic girls and somehow back to "LA bullshit." Maybe it was because I hadn't had a cup of coffee yet but I found him kind of hard to follow.

Finally, Bruce got around to the real reason he called. The Aircraft EP wasn't working, he said. "Well, that's not true," he corrected himself. "Only one song is…the song you sing… 'Masked?'"

"'Mask'," I corrected him gently. He didn't seem to notice.

"'Masked'…that's the hit. And the rest of the band, they're okay. But they're not on par with you. Know what I mean?" He didn't give me a chance to answer. "Maybe that guy, the keyboard player…Jason?"

"JR," I told him.

"J," he said. "He's good. Pretty solid. Has an unfortunate hairline but his chops are solid. He can stay."

"Stay?"

"Look," Bruce said about 30 minutes into our conversation. "I hate doing business over the phone. I want to talk to you about a deal. Make you an offer. In person. I'll be back in New York next week. How's Wednesday at 2? My girl Trini will call and firm up the date. Okay?"

I was in shock but I managed to choke out, "Sure," before Bruce hung up and I was faced with the dial tone. And a pang of guilt. What the fuck just happened?

Five minutes later, Trini called "confirming Wednesday, 2 pm, Mr. Lask's office." That girl was at his beck and call whether he was in the same time zone or not, holiday weekend or not. I would have to call in sick on Wednesday or else take some of the time the *Post* owed me from tax season.

After talking to Bruce, I was bouncing off the walls. I couldn't bear to face JR and the guys (Bruce asked me not to tell them about our meeting), and we were supposed to rehearse tonight. I managed to choke down some coffee and a bagel but I wasn't sure it would stay down. I was feeling what the Chinese call "happy-sad." That's what Garland told me anyway—when you feel happy and sad about something at the same time.

I went for a walk before 12. Couldn't stand being inside any longer. Besides, the weather was nice. A Top 10 Day, as Michael would say. Wandering around, back and forth, up one block and down the other, I found myself near my old school, Sheepshead High. It was a stone's throw from Edie. Literally across the street. Things were looking so far up, I was convinced that even she couldn't bring me down.

I knocked on the door. My sister Aileen answered. "Oh, it's you," she said. (Not even "hello.") "Somebody else can take over for a while." Aileen was out the door in a flash. "I've got to go to Waldbaum's. I have a boatload of people coming over for a barbecue tomorrow."

My sister paused, knowing she hadn't invited me. I ignored it. "Kosher?"

"Of course, Kosher. You know Stanley makes me keep Kosher. It's bad enough she made me drive on *Shabbot*." The evil *she* being Edie. Then Aileen was gone.

Even though the kitchen was dim, I could tell that the Sabbath candles had burned down to puddles in my grandmother's tarnished old *menorah*. What did Edie have against letting in some light, some fresh air? My mother was sitting in a chair by the stove, a battered Magic Chef in avocado green. A cigarette burned down almost to her knuckles. Smoking again, even after her heart attack.

"*Oy*, it's terrible about that little boy, the missing one," she said.

"Etan Patz?" I wondered. She nodded. "They'll find him. He's just lost," I told her.

"Nah," my mother said knowingly. "He's dead. Gone. Some *momzer* got a hold of him and he's..."

"Why do you always have to think the worst of people, Edith?"

"Because they stink," she said matter-of-factly.

"Fair enough, but I still think he's alive."

"What kind of parents would let a seven-year-old walk to school alone?" Edie rasped, lighting another Chesterfield.

"He's six," I told her.

"Even worse."

"And it was to a school bus stop."

"Same difference," she puffed, then coughed. "And what kind of haircut is that. I mean, the kid looks like Ray Charles cut his hair," Edie continued.

"It's the style," I offered.

"Style, schmyle," she barked then took another drag.

I twisted the cord on the Venetian blinds, which were caked with a fine gray dust. Edie waved her hand impatiently, like she was dismissing an annoying waitress. I ignored her, opened the blinds and the window too. "What are you, a vampire?" I asked her.

No answer.

"Are you afraid of the sun?" Still nothing. "When was the last time you were outside?" Edie shrugged, too *verklempt* to answer.

I made her a fresh pot of coffee, ignoring her grating and *kvetching*, "Just heat up what's there," and washed the syrupy gunk down the drain.

"Life's too short to drink crappy coffee," I told her. I thought I saw a slight flicker of a smile as I dug her tin of Bokar out of the Frigidaire. "A&P's finest." I noticed that she'd run out of the good stuff I had brought a few weeks back.

After the coffee had perked, Edie and I sat in the areaway in front of her apartment with our chipped horoscope mugs—not even our own zodiac signs, bought, no doubt, at a white elephant sale. Mine was Libra, hers was Aries. It was a minor ordeal, getting Edie safely into the webbed folding chair with a chorus of *"Oys"* and ultra-dramatic sighs. She faced the spring sun, smiling slightly into it. "See?" I told her. "Nice."

Edie shrugged, almost admitting that it was. Then she frowned. "Why are you so good to me?" she asked.

I didn't know what to say. "Because we're all we've got," I answered, finally. That seemed to satisfy her. I didn't tell her about Bruce or the meeting or the EP, which was crumbling before it even saw the light of day. It was just me and my mom, sitting in the sun. We didn't say much. Didn't have to.

"That little boy," she sighed. "They'll never find him. I know it."

"They might," I told her. "They just might."

"You always were like that," Edie conceded. "Always looking on the bright side of things. Always thinking the best of people."

It was my turn to shrug. "Without hope, what else is there?"

At one point, my mother reached for my hand and just held it, no explanation, no nothing. Then my sister Aileen came back, broke the spell and I was gone.

Bruce

Cat on a hot tin roof doesn't even begin to describe her. Fluttery like some crazy, exotic bird ready to fly off at the slightest movement or sound. I would say she was all coked up but I'm pretty sure being that jumpy is SOP for Cara. Jittery. Skittish. But the question is: what made her so uncomfortable in her own skin. Probably life in general. The music biz. People like me.

I took the Red Eye in from La-La Land last night. Touched down at LaGuardia at 6 am. Maybe I dozed, I don't know. LaGuardia is a sucky, small, little airport. Short runways that dump right into Flushing Bay, literally, if the pilot's not too careful. But still, without traffic, I can be at my place in Tudor City in 15 minutes.

Yep, Bruce Laskowitz (now the WASPish "Lask"), former guttersnipe from Hunts Point in Da Bronx, now lives within spitting distance of the UN, in the first residential skyscraper complex in the world. Though I'm probably more suited for when the area was known as "Goat Hill," when squatters and ruminants ruled the roost. I guess, when you look at it, I'm a squatter at best. I lay claim and stay put until the other guy gives. But it's always worked for me.

At its most raw, base level, that's what the music industry is. People with no talent whatsoever (i.e. me) jumping on the backs of people with more talent than sense (i.e Cara Funk). Or not. Or a look. Or very little talent but something, often unnamable, that's marketable. The French call it *"Je ne sais quoi,"* which is literally, "I don't know what." Well, I don't know what it is either, but if it's profitable, some *schmuck* like me will know how to sell it. Or at least try to.

I could tell that Cara was impressed with Larva when Trini showed her into my private office. Made sure to keep her waiting in the reception area for at least 10 minutes even though I was ready for her. It gives me the upper hand, makes her feel vulnerable, sitting there, looking around, trying to give the impression that she's cool and relaxed when she's ready to run. It also gives her a chance to take in all the gold records and album covers on the walls around her. From Blondie to Huey Lewis to once-wases like Ten Years After and Tull. I knew she was salivating, moistening her skintight Levis, thinking, 'Could I be the next Deborah Harry?' Only Cara was better than Dirty Debbie—she could sing *and* play drums. She could even wipe the floors with Pat Benatar, the new chick that shit-stain Shopman just took on. I'll show him. I'll show everybody.

By the time she got to me, Cara was wide-eyed from all the music porn covering Larva's walls. I made sure she ran into T Bone Burnett in the hallway, who, of course, she'd heard of. Trini did like she was told, gave a quick introduction of Cara to T Bone as my "newest protégé." I imagine Cara liked that a lot, that it gave her chills, got her wetter. So, that by the time Ms. Funk reached my corner office, she was melting. She couldn't take her eyes off the windows, of the picture postcard of midtown shimmering below. The view still grabbed me and I was used to it.

I'm perched a block from Central Park, looming over it, with peeks of the Pond, the Plaza and a shitload of trees, right in the center of Manhattan. When I invited Cara to take a closer look from the floor-to-ceiling windows, I noticed that she held onto the wall with one hand. Scared of heights. She looked so vulnerable it almost made me feel sorry for her. Almost.

My Stickley chair practically swallowed her up. The creamy brown leather clashed with Cara's worn black leather, no doubt gotten wholesale at Orchard Street a decade or so earlier. Her hair was a dark cockscomb, like she'd slept in it and hadn't bothered to even run her fingers through it. But in reality, I bet she spent an hour perfecting it. Her eyes were a slutty smear of mascara and liner, deep, like ink, hard to read. Her mouth red as fire-engine paint. Yeah, I could sell her. And sell a lot of her.

I had Trini bring Cara a Perrier even though she said she didn't want anything. Just being polite, I figured, like her momma taught her, when Cara was probably so dry from nerves that she was spitting cotton. I sat across from Cara in a bigger, taller Stickley, an El Dorado, I think it's called. Named after the lost city of gold or the Cadillac, not sure which. I had a mug of coffee, black, when I really wanted a few lines of coke to set me right after the Red Eye. There was at least an eight-ball in the lacquer box on the glass table between me and Cara but I didn't even break it out. I was afraid it might put her off.

It was quiet for a few seconds, a nervous silence between us, on her part. As for me, I never get nervous. I'm the one who makes people edgy. I've cultivated

it, pruned it, turned it into an art form. I could probably write a book about it...
getting the upper hand by instilling fear. Hey, maybe I should.

So, I leaned forward and said, "Let me guess, it's probably 'Carol.' Am I
right?" She visibly jumped, almost imperceptibly, more a flinch than anything
else, but I noticed it.

"But no one ever calls me that," she conceded. "Except..."

"Except your mother." The little twist to her mouth told me it was so. "Yeah, I
had one of those too. A *yenta* and a half. Till the day she died, she never forgave
me for chopping off the end of the family name."

"Mine's still alive and kicking, and she hasn't forgiven me yet...for anything,"
Cara admitted, settling back further in the Stickley's lap. "Probably never will
either." She wrapped her mouth around the Perrier bottle and took a deep slug,
not bothering with the glass Trini had laid beside it.

"You're probably better off," I told her. "Queens, right?"

"Brooklyn," she sneered. The inferior borough of Queens is an insult to a
Kings County girl. Queens is a mess. I mean, who in their right mind would put
163rd Street right next to 163rd Place? Right? What did they run out of names and
numbers? Take it from me, nobody likes Queens unless they were born there.

"Sorry. This Bronx boy should have known better," I apologized.
"*Saturday Night Fever* country?"

"Bay Ridge? Nah. Sheepshead Bay. I was born in Long Island,
actually. Levittown."

"Levittown. Better than a Trump monstrosity," I said. "But leave it to the Jews
to name their Meccas after themselves. Fred Trump. William Levitt."

"Tell me about it." My smarmy charm was working. Cara was loosening up.
Get people to talk about themselves and they start relaxing. "I grew up on a street
called Sunny Lane but life was anything but sunny there. My folks split when
I was little. My mom, my brother, sister and me moved to Brooklyn after the
divorce. My old man died a few years after that. Colon cancer."

"That sucks."

"It did."

"But you don't. Far from it. You're the most impressive musician I've seen in
a long time."

"Aircraft's a solid band..."

"Plus you got a great voice. That's golden."

"They're letting me sing a couple of songs and..."

As I leaned forward, Cara pressed back into the leather. "Enough about them.
Let's talk about you." At this point, Cara actually held her breath. I wanted to tell
her to let it out, to breathe, but I was afraid she might bolt. Instead, I reassured
her, "This is about you." I put my hand on her knee, not in a creepy, sexual
way (I hoped) but to gain her confidence. I could feel the muscles twitching
underneath my fingertips.

"What about me?" she said, sounding totally unconfident.

"You're a hell of a lot better than them," I told her. "Than all of them put together."

Cara swallowed hard. "Thanks…I think." I waited for more. The ball was now in her court. She took a shot. "Then why did you sign us?"

"To get close to you." Behind the shock on her face, there was a glimmer of a smile, which she bit away by chomping on her lower lip. Made her look all the more vulnerable. Fuckable.

"To me? Then why did you give *us* a contract?"

"To get to you," I stressed. She wasn't stupid, she just had no visible means of self esteem. "Besides, contracts are made to be broken…or rewritten."

Cara ran both hands through her hair and rubbed. It looked even wilder when she finished. "It would kill them," she said, finally. "Especially JR."

"Life is full of disappointments. You just have to roll with them."

"I feel like I've been rolling with them my whole life."

"Well, that's all about to change." I got up and grabbed the contract from my desk. Handed it to her. Cara took it gingerly, like it might be hot, like it might burn her or something. I watched her eyes dart across it.

"I've got to think about this."

"What's to think about?"

"I need to show this to a lawyer."

"Do what you have to do."

Then she put the papers down on the glass table between us, as though they'd hurt her. "I can't. I just can't. The guys have been nothing but good to me."

"And you can be good to them."

Cara screwed up her mouth. The red was beginning to wear off, some on the Perrier bottle, some on her teeth. "How? By screwing them over?"

I've thrown people out of my office for saying less. But this was different. I wanted her, needed her. It had been too long since I'd signed a winner. A year, maybe two? Aircraft was a long shot but Cara Funk was a sure thing. I'd bet my career on it. Shit, I *was* betting my career on it. I took a deep breath, "By taking them with you," I told her. "They could be your backup band. You'd have full creative control. It says it right there." I pointed at the contract for emphasis.

"But contracts were made to be broken. You said it yourself."

"You have my word."

"Ha," she offered, almost spat it in my face.

I flushed, pissed off at her in an instant, this nothing, this brat from Brooklyn, almost past her prime, shitting all over what might her last chance to make it. "You have my word," I said again.

Another deep breath. "This is your chance," I began, grasping at straws, "to prove them wrong."

Cara's eyes narrowed slightly, a raccoon deep in thought. "Them, who?"

"Them. Everyone. Everyone who said you couldn't make it. Everyone who ever treated you like dirt…Your mother."

"How do you know what my mother's like?"

"Because I had one too. Like that. Nothing was ever good enough. *You're* never good enough. Not for her." Cara looked at me, waiting. "But you know, after a while, I finally realized, it was *she* who wasn't good enough for *me*."

Cara took the contract from the coffee table, folded it messily and shoved it into her pocket. "I'll think about," she said, then turned. No handshake, no "thank-you." Just the back of her leather and her swagger, maybe a little stronger than when Trini had shown her in.

And that was that. But she'll be back. I know she will. Guaranteed.

5/30/79

Ask one person and they say, 'Go for it.' Ask another and they say, 'Don't screw your friends.' But is this technically screwing? I didn't seek it out; it just came to me. Sort of. But if it weren't for JR and the guys, Bruce never would have seen me in the first place. Well, I can't say never for sure. He might have. Somewhere else. But where? At a wedding gig? At the Baron DeKalb?

And are the Aircraft crew really my friends? Do we go out for drinks? Afternoon tea? To the movies? I did go with Fern to see *Manhattan* a few weeks back but that was only because she was hot to see it and JR hates Woody Allen. I guess going out to the movies with someone constitutes a friend, but... Fern technically isn't in the band. Even though she writes just about all of their songs. She even wrote one just for me.

Shit...Fuck...I really am a terrible human being. A piece of dog crap on the curb. How can I even think... Wait. I've got to stop beating myself up over this. It's only natural. Anyone in their right mind would at least give it some thought. Especially after how long I've been plugging away at this. Damn it.

Why don't I just tell them? Come clean with them? Because Roy would have a shit fit. Danny, too. Mongo would just look at me like he was incredibly disappointed in me, like my mother did all the time when I was growing up. Like she does now. And JR, I wouldn't even be able to meet his eyes. They would be so wounded, so crushed, shattered. Like a kid whose puppy just got thrown under a bus. He's the puppy and I'm the bus.

But not really. Bruce is the bus. Then am I the puppy? No, JR's the puppy. JR's definitely the puppy. Bruce is the bus and I'm the bus driver. Or is it the other way around? Wait a minute, I don't understand how I even have to be on the fucking bus. I'm just an innocent bystander. I'm standing on the curb, watching the puppy wander out onto Sheepshead Bay Road when the B-49 comes whipping around East 15th Street. I'm standing right near the candy stand under the train tracks, minding my own business, looking at the Tic Tacs when this dumb ass little dog races into the street...

Why am I doing this to myself? Why am I torturing myself? This is what I've been wanting my whole life, as far back as I can remember. They'll understand. Hell, I'd understand. No, that's bullshit. I wouldn't understand. What's to understand? I'm abandoning them. How could you expect anybody to understand that? Does a baby understand when their mother leaves them in a dumpster? Even if someone finds them. Even if it makes the news and it's a happy-ending story where the childless but lovable tattooed ER nurse at Kings County Hospital adopts the baby and names her "Lauren" after herself and she loves that baby to pieces. That kid still lives her whole life as though she was still in that dumpster. That dumpster becomes a part of her. She becomes the dumpster and then...

What the fuck am I saying? I've lost it. I've finally lost it. I really have. I can hardly bear to look at what I wrote. Then don't. Don't look at it, you stupid bitch. Don't look back. Just look forward. Don't even look, just leap, just move. Just do it already, you dumb cunt.

Maybe I should ask Michael. He's always so pragmatic, so levelheaded. He always knows what's right. But I can't keep doing this. Using him. Using him like a crutch. I should be able to think for myself. Make my own decisions. Not run to daddy whenever I get confused or don't have the balls to make a stand. My old man was never there for me. He was out of the picture before I was even five. I never knew what it was like to have a man to watch over you, to take care of you. Except when I was with Michael. And I made a mess out of that, didn't I?

Still, I could give him a call. I don't think he minded hearing from me the last time. Even though I was drunk. And a little high. Like I am now.

As I was leaving today, Bruce managed to give me a tiny Ziploc bag with a few lines in it. "Just a taste," he'd smiled, "to celebrate."

"Celebrate what?" I'd asked him, taking it.

"To celebrate life," he shrugged. "Whatever you want."

And it was good stuff. Barely cut. But you're a real lowlife if you snort alone, if you have no one to get high with. Michael isn't into the stuff. Random drug tests at work, and all. And besides, Michael and I aren't a couple anymore. We are over.

I don't care that tomorrow's a Thursday and I have to see Ellis's happy mug at 8:55 am. (He likes me in early and that's as early as he's going to get.) It isn't late, just a little past 7 and all the blow's gone. All I've got to show for it are crusty boogers, a metallic drip down my throat, the shakes, and a guilty conscience.

My brain is bouncing back and forth across the events of today like a set of Click Clacks gone berserk. My nephews have those things, which are crazy, an accident waiting to happen. Acrylic balls attached to string, whacking against each other at high speeds. More than once, an innocent thumb has gotten caught in the crossfire. Or an annoying younger brother's head was thunked. Served him right, probably. The little bugger.

Back to today. Bruce. The contract. What am I supposed to do? And where the hell is that cat? The cat that shit on my tongue. Why does coke have to make your mouth taste so bad? And be so dry? I've been drinking so much water I bet I'll be up half the night peeing. I hope I actually wake up to pee. That is, if I can sleep. Still wired but it's still early. Earlyish. Getting close to 8. Should I go down to Captain Walter's and gulp down a few rum and cokes? Nah. I think Thursday's Open Mic Night. That could be dangerous. Either it's great or it sucks. It's a crapshoot. Not like that's the only bar in the Bay. But the Cap has a nice feel. It's okay for a chick to go there alone. Nobody's swooping in for the kill and Jerry's a cool guy. I feel like he's got my back when he's tending bar. But is it his night to work? Changes every week. I can never keep track of that confusing firefighter schedule. Apparently, many of the wives can't either. That's why the guys can get away with, 'Honey, I'm working a double...' when they're really working away on some chippie.

How did I ever get off onto this tangent? Captain Walter's...right. Sometimes Silva's there and he's been known to have a bit of blow to sell. He's an unlicensed pharmacist, not a hardcore dealer. Just a nice, dumb stoner who still lives with his mom at 30-something, no visible means of support. Momma doesn't ask questions and Silva doesn't volunteer answers. Perfect relationship.

I don't really feel like leaving the house, though. I tried looking at Bruce's contract but then bugged out about it. Seems pretty straightforward and gives me a lot of control. That could all just be a bullshit smokescreen. What did Bruce say about contracts being meant to be broken? That would mean this contract, too. Would he screw me over if he had the chance? Probably. Why wouldn't he?

Maybe I should show it to Irv. My brother's not the brightest bulb in the box but he has more experience with legal contracts than I do. After all, he's part owner of a furniture franchise and has a house. A shitty townhouse in a cookie-cutter subdivision in New Jersey, but it's still a house. Nah, I don't really want Irv knowing my business. Then he'll go running to Edie. It's happened before. With just about everything. Been that way since we were kids. Yep, Irv's a big blabbermouth. But he's all I've got. Him, Aileen and Edie. When it comes down to it, they're it. Blood. What do they say—that blood's thicker than water? If you think about it, just about anything is. Thicker than water, I mean.

I guess I've got Michael, too. No matter how many times I've pushed him away, I feel like he's still there, like a ghost or a Hiroshima shadow. Back in high school, I remember hearing that shadows were burned into walls when the bomb was dropped. Where people once stood, there were outlines of their bodies after they were vaporized. Sometimes I feel Michael is like that for me: there but not. I'm sure it would change if he had a girlfriend...when he gets a girlfriend, I should say. He's much too nice to be alone. And handsome. And considerate. And fucking hot. Then why the hell am I not with him? That's the million dollar question. But I think I know the answer: he's too good for me.

Jesus, I can barely stand to look at this junk I've written. Talk about a coked-up rant! I just need to put down the pen and go to sleep. I wish I could. Sleep, I mean. I wish I could stop my hands from shaking. My throat feels like it's ready to close up. I'm having a hard time swallowing. I brushed my teeth three times already and my mouth still tastes like crap. Then there's that drip, which tastes like medicine and snot somehow had a baby together. And it's going into my stomach, drip, drip, drip. I've got to get out of here. Out of my head. Out of this apartment. Just out.

4:45 am

Technically, it's already tomorrow. The last day of May. I'm finally starting to come down from the shots of tequila I let myself have at Castle Harbour. I didn't want to go to Captain Walter's. Couldn't face Jerry or anyone else in the crew. I'd been to Castle Harbour a couple of times for dinner, never high, and this time, the stuffed, taxidermied animals freaked me out. Especially the lion. The crocodile and antelope were kind of bizarre, too, but not like that lion. I didn't know anyone there and besides, no one seemed to notice me. The bartender didn't care about me and I didn't care about him. He just kept my glass full of Patrón. Didn't mind that I sipped it slow.

And now, here I am, back in this dingy walk-in apartment. Tired, finally. I hope I can sleep. If I don't start thinking about that kid again. That poor, little, lost boy. Etan Patz. It's been five or six days and they still haven't found him...

Roy

I know they think I drink too much. And drug too much. Hell, back in high school, my nickname was "Hammered Man." A play on my last name. Get it? Yeah, I didn't think it was too funny either.

So, we still haven't heard back from Bruce. We keep rehearsing, though. Twice a week. Tuesdays and Thursdays like clockwork, unless something comes up. Once in a while, Mongo has to work late in his FedEx gig. Did you ever realize that there's an arrow between the E and the X in the logo? I didn't either until Mongo pointed it out. Some people see it and some people don't. I don't.

I've never seen JR so down before. Well, not down exactly, just quiet, sad. Like he had the life knocked out of him. Cara's been acting weird lately. More jumpy than usual. Tries to avoid looking you in the eye and when she does, she turns away quick. I feel like something's up. Maybe they're hatching a plan, JR and Cara, without the rest of the band. But why the fuck would they do that? I mean, what did any of us ever do to them?

A shot of hooch now and again makes it better. Takes the edge off, know what I'm saying? I try not to let them see. But a nip of Jack here and there during rehearsal never hurt anyone, did it? And a pinch of blow when I can get it, when I can afford it. When my dad sends a check up from the Sunshine State, I always take a little bit off the top for me. Just to take off some of the pressure. I deserve it, don't I? It's not like I'm not taking care of my wife and kid. They get what they need. And then some. I need what I need and everybody's happy.

But if I were totally honest, it doesn't feel right, cashing those checks from Pop. Like I've failed in some way. He's just spreading the wealth, I try and reason, sharing what he's got with me. And that's a good thing. I bet it makes him feel proud to be able to do that. Besides, Annabelle is great at sending him thank-you postcards and pictures of Little Roy playing with the things we get for him with the dough Pop sends. Busy Boxes...that freakish Cabbage Patch Doll that looks like the kid. Shit like that.

It's not so much the money that gets to me but those notes my old man sticks into the envelopes. Sometimes on Mom's pastel index cards that she uses for recipes. Sometimes longer letters on a lined pad. All about how they're getting older and they'd love to have us live closer to them in Naples, that there's a job waiting for me when I'm ready, blah-blah-blah. That he needs help running the family business and wants to open another funeral parlor in Pelican Bay. How he wants to spend more time on the golf course or in Bimini. How Little Roy would love the beach. Blah-blah-blah.

The last thing I want to do is be a casketmaker and have my kid be a casketmaker's son like me. But I've got to admit, there is money to be made. Pop saw that funeral parlor owners were making a killing (excuse the death pun) and decided it would be better to have two pieces of the pie by supplying the boxes *and* the bereavement centers. It's worked like a charm for him so far. Smart son of a bitch, my old man.

He's never put too much pressure on me, before now. Even growing up, my dad let me find my own way, make my own choices. He always let me pursue music and was damn proud of me, coming to all the gigs he possibly could, talking me up to his friends. But ever since I passed 30, his attitude slowly changed. Especially since Annabelle had the baby. It was like, 'Okay, haven't you got this nonsense out of your system yet?' But the thing is, to me, music isn't something you can ever get out of your system. It's part of you. It's in you. It *is* the system...the thing that makes you *you*. Nobody seems to be able to understand this. Not even my wife. Nobody but the guys in the band. And Cara.

I wish I knew what was going on in her pretty, little head. But for some reason, I don't think it's good.

5/31/79

Of course, I didn't make it to work today. I can barely lift my head off the pillow. I can barely get up to pee and puke. I know I'm supposed to hydrate to feel better but I can't even stand the sound of the water coming out of the faucet. It makes my head ache worse. And eating might make me feel better too but just the thought of it makes me retch.

I called Ellis at 8:45. He was already at his anally-neat desk and probably on the adding machine for an hour or more and down to the bottom of his coffee-stained "World's Best Dad" mug. I told him that I must have a bug or something because I still felt like crap. (I took yesterday off too, for that Bruce meeting, but Ellis said the office has been dead because it's a holiday week.) "It's Thursday," he said brightly, "Why not take tomorrow off too? You have the hours from Tax Season. I'll sign off on your time sheet." Why was he being so nice to me? Was he canning me? Who else would want to do my boring-ass job? It made my head hurt too much to even think of it.

I find it so strange that this button-down, by-the-book accountant had no problem falsifying my pay documents...well, not falsifying but fudging. Even though he wasn't authorized by the *Post* to pay me (or the temp agency) overtime, he had no problem banking my OT hours and having Payton People (and the *Post*) pay me for days I didn't work. Even the most upstanding citizens have no problem with little lies. It's the big ones that give them trouble. The oversized moral dilemmas.

Fuck them. I'm going back to sleep.

11:45 am

Fuck me. I can't sleep. I put on the TV but the lights, the noise, the jumping and the screaming of *The Price is Right* is just getting on my nerves. Weekday morning television sucks. No wonder housewives are so fat and screwed up. People need to get off their wrinkly asses and do something.

Where the hell are my sunglasses? I can't face this bright, sunshiny day without them. Shit...damn...

2:00 pm

Well, so much for the old wives' tale about how eating a big meal heals a hangover. I guess they didn't factor coke into the equation. No sooner did I step out of the Mill Basin Deli after scarfing down a pastrami on rye (with mustard), sweet potato fries on the side and a cup of matzo ball soup thrown in for good measure than I power booted into a trash can outside the joint. It didn't even look like I'd chewed the fries. It was *déjà vu* of me, puking my guts up before the CBGB gig. A little blue-haired lady walking a yapping Yorkie asked if I was all right. When I could catch my breath, I told her that I was. Then she nodded knowingly, "That happened to me when I was pregnant too...*oy*." The old broad was so caring, cute and cuddly that I didn't want to burst her bubble and tell her that I wasn't with child, but merely a coke whore recovering from a binge.

Was I a coke whore? I took coke from Bruce knowing that it symbolically sealed the deal, then did it alone in my bat cave like a paranoid Dick Grayson. Why do I feel the need to put labels on myself? Why do I need to call myself anything?

Anyway, on the corner of Avenue T and East 59th, I barfed my guts up then grabbed a ginger ale from a *bodega*. (I couldn't bear to go back to the deli with the smell of brisket and chopped liver leaking onto the street.) I couldn't bear the thought of going home so I walked. I walked up T, down U then found myself outside the Temple Lev Simcha. Man, that's one ugly-ass building. It looks like a bunker. Dirty blonde brick with a red brick *menorah* built into the wall. Like Hitler and some unimaginative rabbi designed it.

Who would be there on a Thursday afternoon, I wondered? Probably no one. But I tried the kitchen door anyway. It was open.

I was only half surprised to see Garland standing in his stainless steel prison, chopping with relish. He was even humming. "Cara!" he beamed, looking like a beneficent Kitchen God, then hugging me with knife and onion in hand.

I returned the hug gingerly. "I was in the neighborhood and I..."

"No excuse needed," he smiled. A pot of water boiled away. He had a teapot already waiting on the stove. "I was just about to have some tea. You look like you could use a cup." I didn't argue. Tea, I could probably keep down, especially tea from Garland.

We sat and sipped and talked about what had gone on during the past month or so. More curses from Marty. More smiles and lies from Steve. More tears from Dennie. More unspeakable acts from the Temple Girls, whose skirts had amazingly grown shorter as the owners' prices for parties became larger. "And your wages got better, right?" I joked.

Garland made a phlegmy sound of contempt in the back of his throat. "Not from that evil man," he said.

"What are you doing here on a Thursday?"

"Israeli bond drive," he said. "Like they need more money."

"But it makes New York Jews feel like they're doing something," I told him. "Plus they get to eat your good Chinese soul food."

Garland insisted on heating up a slice of stuffed derma in a frying pan for me. I wasn't sure I could keep it down, but he said it was an ancient Chinese hangover remedy. I wasn't sure how he'd known I was hurting. Then in the next beat, he admitted, "You look like something on bottom of shoe. Skin gray, eyes red." He held my wrist, dropped it. "Kidney pulse sluggish." He put the plate in front of me. The *kishka* went down easy.

I told Garland about the band, how Michael and me were no more, how I was counting my days at the *Post*. "But...," he said.

"There's always a 'but,' isn't there," I responded and gave him the *Reader's Digest* version of the "but" in between bites of beef intestine. Yum.

Garland sat there thoughtfully for a few moments as I finished. He took a sip of tea and a bite of chocolate rugelach. He chewed, nodding. "Sometimes things come into our path for a good reason. Because they're right, because they're meant to. Sometimes things come into our path because they're wrong, to tempt us, to test us. Pretty girl or boy. Easy money. But I think maybe this is the first one."

I was surprised. "So, you think I should do it?" He nodded, taking another bite of pastry. "But what about friendship? Morals? Duty?"

Garland shook his head. "Fuck duty," he told me. "Sometimes you just have to say 'fuck it' and go for it."

I was even more confused when I left Garland's kitchen than when I'd come in. And just as happy when I almost ran into Dennie, literally, on Avenue U. She and Steve lived practically across the street from the Lev. She looked even skinnier than I remembered. The dark circles under her pretty eyes almost drowned out the spray of brown freckles across the ridge of her nose. She was still wearing her scrubs, with her head down, bounding along the avenue. "Half day?" I asked.

Dennie was startled. She jumped then smiled. When she grinned big and wide like that, she looked light years younger. She hugged me with her whole body. "You look like shit," she said, "but you feel good."

"Thanks," I told her. "I love you, too." How could someone look so sad when they smiled? Dennie somehow managed it. "How are things?"

"Same old crap," she sighed. "The only way they'll change is if I change them."

"Are you ready to?"

"Maybe," she shrugged, surprising me. "I met someone. We didn't do anything yet. I'm not into that kind of thing, cheating. Lord knows, I've been cheated on enough and I know it's crap."

"But…"

"There's always a 'but,'" Dennie said. "I met a guy. Doug. At a friend's house. He's Lana's roommate. Big, a biker, kind of rough around the edges, but a good man. And he makes me laugh."

"Musician?" I asked.

"Hell, no," Dennie gasped. "A carpet layer of all things. I like him. A lot."

"Are you going to leave?"

Dennie took a deep breath, let it out. "I think so."

"Does Steve know?"

"I think so."

"Does he care?" I wondered.

"Probably not. Except he'd hate to lose his housekeeper, the person who irons his shirts, the one who waits on him. But I don't think he cares, not like a husband should."

I gave Dennie another hug. It looked like she needed one. "You better give me your number," I threatened, muffled by her shoulder.

"I will. You're a keeper," she said, still hanging on.

I heard a car screech to a stop. "Lesbian love, always so heartwarming." And Marty's sandpaper-on-silk voice.

Dennie and I broke apart. "They have a gig tonight," she whispered.

"I heard." Then I started walking. "Talk to you soon." I hoped that was true. I wanted to keep track of Dennie, even if she moved around. Dennie was a keeper, too. But Marty was like a bad penny. A bad penny that someone had swallowed, crapped out then stuck back up their behind. He followed me down the block at a snail's pace.

"Made it yet?" Marty wondered. I could hear the sneer in his voice, though I refused to look at him.

"I made it the minute I left your band," I told him. Then I turned down East 67th, heading down toward the Basin.

"You'll never make it," Marty sneered. "Do you hear me? Never!" He was yelling at this point, cursing. I just ignored him and kept on walking. But he kept following me and ranting, going the wrong way down a one-way street. I guess that's how mad I made him.

Then I heard a blip and looked up. A blue-and-white had come up the street and was nose to nose with him. Marty had no choice but to stop. "He bothering you, ma'am?" the cop behind the wheel asked.

"Always," I told him. "He said something about that missing kid, Etan Patz, is it?" I kept walking even after I heard the cop tell Marty to put his hands on the steering wheel and not to move.

"You fucking bitch…" was the last words I ever heard from him.

5:15 pm

I managed to sleep a little bit. Maybe Garland's tea was the magical cure. But I think it was pure exhaustion. Aircraft is supposed to rehearse tonight but I'm not sure if I can go. Physically, yes, but mentally, I don't think I can face them. I've got to put up a front, though, put on a happy face. At least until I figure this whole thing out.

Danny

I said, "Look what the cat dragged in." And meant it. Usually Cara's groomed to the max. Punked out, for sure, but carefully done up. Her haphazard look isn't an accident. Lots of work goes into the spiky hair, the smudged eyeliner, the blood red lips. No, I'm not gay. I just pay attention. My girlfriend Alice babbles about this stuff and I can't help but absorb some of it. Born and bred in Iowa corn country, she's fascinated by Cara. And no, she's not gay either.

Anyway...it looked like Cara had been out all night and she wasn't trying to hide it. She showed up to rehearsal—more than an hour late, mind you—wearing clothes she could have slept in. And she's usually meticulous about the way she looks, down to the thoughtfully-torn jeans and perfectly-worn leather jacket. But that night, Cara's hair seemed like it stood up because it was dirty, not because it was molded with Dippity-do or bear fat or whatever the heck she puts on it. Her eye makeup looked she got caught in the rain after a two-year-old put it on. Her lips looked bruised instead of sharp and sexy. See, I'm not gay. Ask my girlfriend. Ask the groupies Alice doesn't know about.

We stopped in mid-song when Cara arrived. JR's keyboards let out a groan when he rested his hands on it, his mouth open slightly, dropping the rhythm of "Suicidal," the new number we were working on. "What?" Cara asked. And that's when I said it, about the cat dragging her in, sounding like my father back on the farm.

"You're just a little late," JR told her, covering my jibe quickly. Cara breezed past him to take a seat behind the kit. I swear I smelled something strange on her. Not liquor but medicinal. Not Aqua Net or Pert but a slightly sour scent. The not-so-great unwashed? I didn't have time to think about it because JR was beginning the intro in the key of G and I had to concentrate on hitting the insanely high note that "Suicidal" starts with. Cara missed her part and came in late. Twice. Something she never does. Then her drumstick broke and a piece of it went flying toward Mongo. He ducked and flipped her the bird. She threw the other stick at him and missed again.

"I'm just feeling a little under the weather," she mumbled.

"Hair of the dog?" I suggested.

"Cats…dogs…what the fuck is it with you and animals?" she croaked. "Next you'll be talking about barnyard critters, Farm Boy."

The guys always rib me about not cussing. About being a nice, Bible-fearing Methodist who made his way to Sin City and sold his soul to the Devil at the crossroads for an eight-octave range. "You sound like Jim Nabors when you talk," Cara liked to joke. "All Gomer Pyle and shit, but you're the real deal when you sing." It was a compliment coming from her.

I like Cara but I didn't appreciate being cussed at. This time I let it go. Something was definitely going on with her. I guess she deserved a pass. At least one. We all do now and then, right? Cara's usually a lot tougher on herself than she is on anyone else. But lately, I noticed that she had this edge. Not just in her music but in everything she did. Even in the way she stood there or came into a room. Even when she walked into rehearsal late. *Especially* when she walked into rehearsal late. Like she did today. All attitude and bravado, none of it false. I know it was only us and it was only rehearsal, but still.

Fern always reminds us that's what being a drummer is all about—making noise and making people notice. I swear, Fern could find the good in anybody. Especially Cara. They're a lot alike. Cara is what Fern would be if she had the gumption to get out onstage. If she had a talent besides writing unbelievable lyrics. Those two could be sisters, the good girl/bad girl side of the same coin. And guess which one is the evil twin?

Not that I've been on my best behavior lately. I've been accused (more than once) of having hissy fits. I admit, I've come up a little bit short in the patience department recently. The pressure of doing these showcases, of waiting for feedback from record companies, of wondering. All of those what-ifs. Wondering if it's true, what the folks back home in Grand Rapids said. That I was good enough for Michigan but maybe not good enough for New York. I reasoned that Pop just said that because he didn't want me to leave, but still, the words cut deep. Still do. They left a scar, I think.

The guys say I'm jealous of Cara, that I feel threatened by her. But that's not it. Not exactly. I've been in this business too long to trust it. I've seen things go sour on the honeymoon. And this band is still on its honeymoon. They can drop you in a heartbeat, like an egg out of a chicken's hoo-ha. No warning, then splat!

"They" being the record company, the promoters, whoever. I know I should be happy because we have a deal signed, sealed and delivered. But Bruce has been like a ghost lately. Flying in and out. Now you see him, now you don't. It's wearing thin. On all of us, I think.

I'm not afraid that Cara will push me out of the band. Should I be? Heck, she's got a great voice but then again so do I. And even though I don't play an instrument, I think I still hold my own. I'm different. I stand out. So does she but in a whole other way.

All during rehearsal tonight, she kept avoiding my eyes, looking the other way when I looked at her. It was weird. Usually Cara stares me down, stares anyone down. That's just the way she is. But this wasn't the same. If I had the guts to ask her what she was trying to hide, I could just hear Cara saying out of the side of her mouth, 'Aren't we all trying to hide something?'

Roy's been worse than usual, messing up his fingerpicking, forgetting chords and lyrics, edgy, yelling more than he normally does. He's been just plain sloppy. Threatening to go back home to Florida if this doesn't work out. I haven't even considered it until now. This not working out. Leaving. Where would I go? I can't stand the place I grew up. Besides, it never felt like home to me. This is where I belong, where I'll die. I just hope it's not soon.

And JR, he just looks hurt, bruised on the inside. He has such sad eyes anyway but now they look half dead. Like he's defeated already. Like he knows something I don't. Fern is good at keeping his spirits up. He'll usually crack a smile at little Jessica's antics. We all do. She's cute as a button. But I haven't seen JR smile, not recently. Not since Bruce and that contract. I swear, instead of making things better between everyone in the band, it's made things worse.

Maybe it's my imagination, but Roy seems to be drinking more. I'd swear he shows up to rehearsals drunk. Tries to cover the smell with tons of Old Spice but I can still pick out the liquor underneath the cologne. Mongo is his usual chipper self, even more so. Makes me want to punch him sometimes, he's so cheery. And Cara just…is… Reminds me of the way a girl acts when she wants to break up with you but doesn't have the nerve. Distant. Steely. Not enough heart to look you dead in the eye. And when she does, she turns away in a flash.

But Cara couldn't avoid me on the way home tonight. Even though she'd bolted out of rehearsal a few minutes before me. Nope, she couldn't avoid me on the dark, empty stretch of Shore Parkway. She'd stopped to use the pay phone under the Belt. She was just hanging up when I rounded the corner and almost walked into her.

"Calling a friend," Cara explained. "He wasn't in." We started walking in step together without missing a beat, almost like we harmonize in the band.

"So, what's up?" I asked.

"Nothing," she told me. "Nothing new."

"Same old, same old," I said.

"How's Alice?" she wondered.

"Nothing new."

"Same old, same old."

But something was weird. It was like Cara had already told me, told me she was leaving, without words. We walked in silence to the Sheepshead Bay train station where it crossed above Bay Road. "This is where I get off," I told her, fishing out my token. "And you?"

"I think I'll walk home. Nice night. Maybe stop off at the Cap's," she said. "Wanna come?"

"Thanks, but no," I told her. When I looked back after going through the turnstile, she was already gone.

6/9/79

It's prime wedding season but I don't miss the gigs. I miss the do-re-mi, though. I'm getting by with what I make at the *Post*. Peyton People pays okay. It'll hold me over until I get my advance. Bruce says it should be within the week.

That's right, I signed the solo contract. My hand was shaking as I did it. From excitement or fear, I'm not sure which. I haven't told anyone yet, not Edie, not the band, not Michael, my brother or sister. It still feels like a dirty little secret, which is kind of nice. Something that's mine and mine alone.

I tried calling Michael to run it by him. Again. He never seems to be in. I left a few messages on his machine. Maybe he's standing there, listening to me stammer, laughing at me with his new girlfriend by his side, if he has one. Well, screw him. And her, if there is a her. Screw everyone. I'm doing what's right for Cara for a change.

At the end of the year, I'll be 30 and I promised myself that if I didn't make it by then, if I didn't have a record out by then, if I wasn't touring by then, that I would give up. But I couldn't live if I didn't play. And I couldn't deal with being a failure. So, you know what giving up means. Giving up on life. On everything. I could look at this as a life-saving measure instead of fucking over my bandmates.

How the hell am I going to tell them? Not show up for rehearsals…ever? That's a real lowlife move. And say what you will about me, I'm a lot of things, but I'm not a lowlife.

As slow as things went when Bruce was dragging his heels with Aircraft, that's how quick they're moving now. He sat me down in his office with files and files of musicians to choose from for my backup band. My band! I can't get my head around that one. I'm thinking I'd like to use JR and maybe Mongo. Definitely not Roy. And though he's got a killer voice, I have no need for a lead vocalist. And I don't think Danny would agree to singing background vocals for me. As a matter of fact, I *know* he wouldn't. But later for him. I'm a hell of a lot older than he is and I've been trying to make it a hell of a lot longer. He'll find something else. Easy. And if he doesn't, it's not my problem.

I'm my problem. I'm responsible for me. No one else. No one looks out for me, do they? And if I think Bruce cares about me, I'm kidding myself. All he cares about is the money he'll make by being attached to me, the name he'll make for himself standing on my shoulders. A chance to prove he isn't a coke-head has-been loser like everyone else says he is. It's about him, not me. But I don't really care, as long as I make it. At any cost. What is it Malcolm X used to say, "By any means necessary." But you see where that got him, right?

Fern

I don't know why she included me in on it. I mean, I'm not part of the band. Well, not officially. I feel like a phantom member, if anything. There but not. It's not as if JR wouldn't have told me anyway. Maybe Cara thought it would be easier, that I would cushion it for her. For Willie. I guess she was right.

The three of us met upstairs in our living room instead of in the basement, in the rehearsal space JR had so lovingly, so thoughtfully created with his own hands. That was easier too, I suppose. Except upstairs, we were like friends instead of business associates or band members. A band is family when you think about it. Dysfunctional and crazy, for better or worse, close, like family.

I was afraid of what Cara was going to say the minute Willie told me she was coming by to meet with us. So, I made sure I put Jessica down for a nap before Cara got there. She brought a box of rainbow cookies from T&D. A peace offering? I don't know, but we never ended up opening them. Cara knew they were Jessie's favorite, which is probably why she brought them. She's really thoughtful that way. But really thoughtless in others.

JR threw the cookie box in the trash after Cara left. Actually, he hurled the box onto the kitchen floor and I quietly threw it into the trash afterwards without saying anything to him. Then Jessie woke up screaming and Willie stormed out. It's been more than two hours and he's still gone. I beeped him four times on his pager and nothing. I hope he didn't throw his Pageboy in the garbage because it cost an arm and a leg.

Anyway, I gave Jessica some pastina for supper. I didn't feel like cooking and I didn't have much of an appetite. Then…

Let me go back to the beginning. About what Cara said. I seem to be trying to avoid it. You could just imagine what Cara said. That she was leaving the band. That Bruce had offered her a solo contract and she was taking it. That she wanted JR to come with her and be part of her band. I watched my husband's face when Cara dumped all of this crap into his lap. It looked like he'd been slapped, punched even. The shock was as clear as a streak of blood on his cheek.

Why hadn't he seen this coming? Maybe he was in it too deep. Maybe he had so much hope that he was blind to it. But in a way, I expected it. This EP deal was too good to be true, too easy. Things were going too well. Then Bruce pulled his disappearing act and I started to get that cold, gnawing ache in the pit of my stomach. I didn't say anything about it to Willie. If I had, he would have said that I put a jinx on it, that I always put a jinx on things by thinking negative. Somehow, this would all be my fault. I guess he needed someone to blame. It was easier than just admitting that it was life, just the way the cookie crumbled sometimes. Even though it sucked.

Right after Cara told us, I reached for Willie's hand. He took my hand but dropped it immediately. "What about Aircraft?" he asked her.

Cara opened her mouth but nothing came out. "Don't you get it?" I jumped in. "There is no more Aircraft."

"Look, it's not personal," she said. "I want you in my band. I want to use some of your songs."

"Use," I said, trying not to yell because Jessica was sleeping in the next room. "That's a good choice of words."

"It's just business, Fern," Cara began, but I cut her off.

"I thought we were friends," I said, a little louder. "You used us!"

Cara stood up. "Everybody uses everybody," she told me. "Every day. They use each other to eat, to work, to get by. It's the way things are." Cara started for the door. Willie still hadn't said anything. "Think about it," she continued. "My offer. I want you in the band. Backing me up. Maybe Mongo, too, if he'll come."

"You can tell them at rehearsal tonight," JR said, his voice sounding weak, tired, defeated.

"I'm not coming to rehearsal," Cara said as gently as she could, grabbing the door knob. "Think about my offer," she said. "Please."

After the door closed, I tried talking to JR but he lifted one finger to his lips, shushing me up silently. Then he threw the cookies across the room and left. And I haven't seen him since.

6/13/79

I haven't heard from JR yet. Rehearsal was last night so he must have told the guys. I figure there's a 50/50 chance he'll go with me. I'm still not giving up. I'm sure I could find good material somewhere else. I'll bet Larva has a stable of songwriters to choose from. But there's something about JR and Fern's songs that I connect with. A kind of desolation and emptiness that redeems itself and comes full circle in three verses and a chorus. And then there's "Mask," the song Fern wrote about me, which Bruce thinks is a hit—if he could only get the name right. Will they agree to let me use it? They'd be stupid not to.

I'll give JR another few days. I owe him at least that much. Then I'll move forward without him. Hey, in this life, it's every man for himself. Even if you're a woman.

Tomorrow Bruce wants me to go over costumes, hair, stuff like that. Costumes? I just dress the way I dress. I never gave it much thought. Bruce keeps telling me that it's not just about the music. It's all about merchandising. He's talking to Kmart about a "Cara Funk" line of clothing. Can you believe that?

And hair. I just go wherever it's cheap. Lemon Tree. Supercuts. The Astor Place Barber Shop if I'm in the neighborhood. Just a quick chop, nothing too complex. Sometimes I even trim it myself. Except now Bruce is going to have a consultant from Vidal Sassoon come in, give me a once-over and size up my head. Oh, joy.

Same thing for makeup. I just buy what's on sale. I don't care about the brand. Maybe it's Maybelline if there's a special at Rite Aid, otherwise CoverGirl or whatever I can grab at the bargain bin at Dee & Dee. Deep crimson lipstick. For eyeliner, it's got to be black, dramatic. Besides that, I don't care much. But Bruce is talking Estée Lauder, who was just plain Josephine Esther Mentzer from Queens until she got married and they jazzed up her new name, Lauter. Kind of like me. Except for the married part.

To me, it's all bullshit. To me, it's all about the music. But apparently, music is more than just music. That's what Bruce tells me anyway.

I haven't missed much time at work. Not yet. Usually our meetings are after hours—Bruce is a late riser, no surprise there. He probably gets up about noon, gets into the office even later. He actually prefers meeting after 5, when the office is almost empty. The fashion/hair people don't seem to have a problem with that. After all, salons and stay open late, don't they?

But Bruce says that pretty soon my two lives will overlap and I'm going to have to make a choice. "Shit or get off the pot," he's said more than once, after a blast. "How would it look if it got out that a Punk Princess like you was a secretary?"

"An administrative assistant," I'd correct him. "A temp."

"Temp, schmemp, whatever. It's not sexy."

When my advance comes in, I promised Bruce I'd quit the *Post*. I haven't told Ellis yet. Lately, it seems like I've been breaking up with everyone who's been good to me. I've been forced to make choices. But life is all about choices, isn't it?

I don't mind all the meetings with Bruce, even if it's for bullshit reasons. It's kind of fun, surreal, though. The only thing that bothers me is that Bruce always seems to have a mountain of coke on hand. And he does it constantly. I'm no doctor, but he's a fat fuck and it can't be good for his health. I try to stay away from it as much as I can. But it's tough to turn down when it's flowing as free as Perrier. "Don't worry, it's not coming out of your advance," Bruce tells me, pinching his nostrils shut after a blast, when I pass on doing a toot.

I want to keep my wits about me. Especially when I have to be making all of these important decisions, even if it's just about mascara or t-shirts. Not to mention which songs to put on the album. I don't have anyone to bounce things off of, no one to ask. In a way, I miss the consensus of being in a band, although I don't miss the crap that comes with five different opinions

In a lot of ways, Bruce is like that tiny devil in cartoons, whispering in my ear, poking my shoulder with his little pitchfork. I don't know who the tiny cartoon angel would be. Maybe I don't have one. I'm on my own.

If it's not coke, then Bruce has a candy dish of pills to choose from. Sometimes he'll pop a couple to come down off the blow. Then he'll need to do a few lines to get high again after a meeting is over and he wants to get nice. Only he gets sweaty, wild-eyed and stupid. Who can take him seriously when he's like that? I wonder if it's true what they say about him, that he's a has-been or a never was. Maybe he's just using me. But then again, I'm using him, too. Right?

Most of the time, I turn Bruce down but others, I think, 'What the hell?' and do a line. Or three.

JR

I walked to Sheepshead Bay. That's where I go when I'm pissed off or need to think. Or both. Cara's news hit me like a left hook. Fern kept saying something was up with Cara. She didn't know what but she had a feeling. And it wasn't good. Fern was right. She's always right.

I give my wife shit sometimes. A lot of the time. But the truth is, I don't know what I'd do without her. She's like my arm. Something I use constantly but never think about. Something that's a part of me, like a heart; it pumps blood, but you never give it a second thought until it stops working.

I'm really at a loss. I know what I *should* do but I don't know if I can do it. If I can do it and live with myself, I mean. So, I walked. Walked to the Bay, sucked the stink into my lungs, watched the fishing boats come and go. The Amberjack. The Brooklyn VI. The Norma Jean. Captain Tony, who's known my pop since they were five, gave me a nod. I nodded back but moved on. I didn't feel like talking.

It wasn't too crowded for a Sunday night in June. The weather hadn't turned summery yet. I went down Emmons on the side of the fishing boats, hands deep in my jacket pockets, passing the litany of shops across the street, leaning one against the other. Then came the places like Captain Walter's, Randazzo's Clam Bar, Lundy's. Took the footbridge over to Manhattan Beach and right down Exeter Street to the Esplanade.

There's a house at the end of the block that I love. I stand there and look at it whenever I feel down. I picture myself living in it. Well, me, Fern, Little Jess and maybe another baby. A son, this time. The windows are wide and long, stretch from ceiling to floor. Red brick, ranch, flat roof. In the "Frank Lloyd Wright does Manhattan Beach" style. At night, the light inside glows golden, I don't know why. But it doesn't look like any of the other houses on Exeter, inside or out.

I imagine the three of us living there instead of the perfect blonde family that's in there now. Sure, there would be more convenient places to live, places with easier access to the City and all. But even townhouses in the Village aren't like this. With a perfect, unflawed view of the ocean. There's nothing between you and it except a small grass yard. You could watch the cruise ships come and go, the freighters, the fishing boats. You could sit there for hours and be happy, not thinking, just sitting there and staring, just *being*. I want to give Fern and my family something like this, something beautiful, something perfect. Something no one else has.

I bet the people inside that house lead easy lives. Uncomplicated. I bet the guy does something normal, like is a lawyer or a banker, instead of hammering nails by day and playing music by night. Anything's got to be easier than what I do. Living on hope, on dreams, on lies, on false words. It's gotten so that I can't tell the difference anymore.

I thought Cara was the real deal, and I trusted her, like family, like a sister. I let her in. I trusted her with my dreams, my songs, my words and music. Not only that but my wife and my kid trusted her, too. Never in a million years would I have believed that she could screw me the way she did. Never in a million years would I have thought she could do it. But here she is, doing it. Leaving the group to do her own thing. I don't believe she pursued Bruce. Cara's not like that. But I do believe he was leading her on, showing her the carrot through us till she was hooked, then pulled it away and offered her a bigger, better carrot. Instead of standing firm, she folded.

I'd be lying if I said I didn't understand where she was coming from. I do. I know the quiet desperation. I know the desire. But is it worth it having your wishes come true, only to lose everything? Your morals? Your integrity? Your soul? That girl is going to die alone. Mark my words.

Not that I'm religious—far from it—but all of this reminded me of something I heard in church once. I doubt Cara knows of it. She's not a New Testament kind of gal. Old Testament, all the way, full of vengeance, bloody wars and that "eye for an eye" crap. Besides, I think Cara might be Jewish, non-practicing, probably. The only thing she practices is her music. That's her God and her devil.

But the passage that keeps running through my head goes something like, "What good is it for someone to gain the world but lose his own soul? What will a man give to exchange his soul?"

The answer? Everything.

But still, Cara didn't leave me flat; she made me an offer. Can I refuse it? Can I screw the group, my group. I think I can convince her to take Mongo with us but definitely not Roy and Danny. I feel like I'm pushed up against a brick wall.

Just now, the man of the house, *my house*, came out the back door, slid it open quietly so that it didn't make a sound. I don't know if he saw me standing here in the dark but it didn't seem like he did. He just stood there, stock still, and looked out at the lights on Breezy Point. Then he lit a cigarette and smoked, still looking. I could tell he was smiling.

By then, I'd started crying. I hadn't cried since the day Jessica was born. Before that, it was when Fern said she would marry me. I tried not to make any noise. I didn't want the guy in the backyard to hear me. I didn't want to ruin his moment even though I hadn't had a perfect moment in more than two years, when he probably had one like this every night, staring out at the sea. Still, it wasn't his fault my life was fucked. But the shit of it was that it wasn't just my life. It was my family's life, too.

I was crying so hard, I jammed my fist into my mouth. Tears and snot and blood mixed together into a horrible cocktail. I swallowed it down, wiped my face on my shirt and started back across the Bay to my tiny house near the highway.

It was then that I decided I was going to say 'yes.' I had to. 'No' was not an option. I'd had a lifetime full of 'no's', a lifetime full of doing things for other people. This is my time.

And if it doesn't work out, I can just go back into construction with my old man. At least I'll know that I tried everything, everything in my power. No…I can't think that way. It has to work out. It's going to work out. Because it's all I have.

I don't know what time it was when I finally got home. Fern was in a deep sleep. I'm surprised she wasn't waiting up for me with that expectant look on her face, like a puppy at the door who doesn't think you're going to show up but is so happy when you do.

Fern's pretty exhausted from taking care of Jessica, the house and everything else, plus squirreling away time to write when she can. I just got undressed in the dark and slipped into bed next to her. She curled around me and nestled her head into the crook of my neck. "Take it," she whispered. "You don't have much choice." Then she fell back asleep.

6/18/79

I've been getting nosebleeds at the most inopportune moments. Not that there's ever a good time to get a nosebleed. But in the middle of my commute on the D train (that's one good way to get a seat) or in the middle of handing Ellis his phone messages. Those are just about the suckiest times to get a gusher. Luckily, Ellis took it well and was able to read his Rediform messages even spattered. I made some lame excuse about the hot weather giving me a nosebleed but the truth of the matter was that it was from all the coke I did with Bruce the night before.

I feel like I *have* to do a few lines with him now and then, just to look like I'm being sociable, like I'm not uptight, like I'm cool. Also, like I'm not judging him. But damn, even my big Jewish honker can't take the blow like his can. "Cauterizing is key," Bruce tells me, almost proudly. "I have a good ear, nose and throat guy. Hymie doesn't ask questions, he just cauterizes."

The last few days have been a swirl. Looking at a heap of pictures: of hairstyles, of shirts, of leathers, of jeans (snakeskin and otherwise) of boots, of makeup. Maria, a nice Italian girl from Mott Street, even used my face like a canvas and tried out foundations, false eyelashes and a rainbow of eye shadow. Brands I never even heard of, that's how expensive they were. Even more expensive than Max Factor. When I got a good look at my *punim* in the mirror, it was like I'd been done up at Torregrossa & Sons over on Avenue U. "When's the *shivah*?" I could almost hear Michael saying, if Michael were still talking to me.

Larva has an in with Jordache and Bruce thinks I might have a good chance of being a spokesmodel if I play my cards right. Imagine my ass on the small screen in Jordache jeans, and me prancing around like a crazyperson?

JR even came with me to today's meeting. That's right, he gave in and said he'd be part of my band. Nobody was more surprised than I was. I can see that he's still pissed off at me. We don't have the closeness we once did, that easiness, like favorite cousins do. (I won't say like brothers and sisters because mine are assholes.) It's like JR was holding back, like he was more guarded with me. Man, that was one uncomfortable train ride. At one point, I pretended to be asleep just so I didn't have to deal with the silence.

I could tell JR was impressed when he stepped off the elevator and into LarvaLand. Even though it wasn't his first time here. Those gold and platinum records will do it to you every time. Bruce treated JR like a prince, clapping him on the back, shaking his hand. I was relieved when Accounting took JR off to do some paperwork. That's when Bruce whipped out the coke again. I only did a couple of lines but he was shoveling it in like a ditchdigger. Then Bruce started getting all weird on me. Didn't touch me—although groping me would have been almost understandable. Normal, even. But Bruce is some kind of freak. He just sat behind his desk and asked me to turn around so I had my back toward him. (I had a Vietnam flashback of Howie in the truck.) Then he asked me to bend over and not to turn around, close my eyes and not look at him. What else could I do?

I could hear Bruce shuffling with his clothes and the scratch of his zipper coming down. I knew exactly what he was doing. I closed my eyes tight, so tight tears started coming down. Why did it always come to something like this? Why did something always have to ruin it? Did this ever happen to guys? Somehow, I doubt it. But maybe it did. Maybe it wasn't just me.

There was the sound of a drawer opening and closing. Bruce was getting out lube, no doubt. Did he do this a lot? So much that he keeps a stash of K-Y in his desk? Did he do this with Pat Benatar? Somehow, I doubt it, too.

Then came the sounds that really made me cringe. The wet sounds. Of a greased hand on greased skin. Small moans. Then a big one. At least this meant it was over. Did this make me a whore? Not really a prostitute because I didn't do it for money. Well…yeah. Yeah, I did do it for money, in a manner of speaking. What choice did I have?

JR came back soon after but by then, Bruce was all zipped up and acting like nothing had happened. I hope he doesn't try this again but he's bound to. What, with the coke and the drinking and all. Plus the time we spend alone.

I don't want to think about it but I can't help it. The picture, the sounds pop into my head, especially when it's quiet. Like now, when I'm trying to get to sleep. That's why I'm up writing and not snoring. Not that I snore. It's after 1 and I've been tossing and turning for an hour with a sinking feeling deep in my gut.

I should feel happy. I should just try to forget about what Bruce did. Maybe it was a fluke. Everything else is going so good. Moving really quickly. Almost too quickly. Moving as fast as it moved slowly with the bogus Aircraft contract. Now

I see that it was a ruse just to get to me. Why would someone do something like that? Why wouldn't Bruce just come right out and say what he was after from the start? Was he afraid I'd say no if I didn't think it was my last chance.

Mongo is onboard too. I wasn't there when JR told the band that he was leaving, that Aircraft was no more. I'm grateful for that. But I feel like a coward. Hell, I *am* a coward. Who am I kidding? Was it a scumbag move? Mongo shrugged when I offered that to him, on a silver platter, days later. "No more of a scumbag move than me and J jumping ship to go with you," he said plainly. "But I guess I'm a scumbag too. But fuck it, I can't walk away from this."

Mongo

What did she say? Nothing. I just told Cara that I was a scumbag too because I had no problem fucking over the band. Neither did JR. Too bad Zelda didn't feel the same way. She's been a little wacky and emotional since she's been pregnant with Crumbsnatcher # 3. She's all, "How are we going to afford three kids when we can barely afford two? How did this happen?" Then crying. Then throwing things.

Sheeeet. Zelda knows what comes next, I guess. Me quitting my job. I hate the damn job anyway but there's all the necessary garbage that comes with it: health insurance and security and all of that boring crap you need to take care of a family. Zelda's acting like it's already happened. Bruce said it was premature to quit our day gigs before the studio work is done and the concert dates are set up. He says we can salvage a song or two from the Aircraft EP to keep costs down on Cara's LP. Use the tracks for "Mask," at least. It makes sense.

But Zelda wouldn't hear any of it. She just couldn't be happy for me, for us. She kept bawling, which made the babies cry. Then she started shoving things into a Hefty bag. "I can't take this shit anymore! I can't take all of this up and down shit!" A minute later, she was out the door, dragging the kids by the hand, dragging the Hefty bag full of clothes down the stairs and into the street, making a scene. Zelda wouldn't even let me help. Not even when the trash bag ripped and there were Onesies and tiny lacy socks and Weebles all over Court Street. She left a trail of destruction in her path but Zelda didn't seem to notice. She took my car, which had a couple of amps stashed in the trunk, and high-tailed it to her sister's place in Satan Island." (MongoSpeak for Staten Island.)

"If you'd screw the band, why wouldn't you turn around and screw me?" Zelda said, just before she sped off. It was a good question.

She usually cools down after a couple of days—her sister Zana has a habit of getting on her nerves. But this time was different. It's been almost a week and still no Zelda. She hasn't called and she won't talk to me when I call. Zana is all bitchy and up in my business on the phone, saying shit like, "Zelda, it's your loser husband again." But I don't say nothing to her. How can I make them understand that I'm not a loser, that I'm doing this because I want to change things. I have a chance to win and I'll be damned if I don't take it, if I don't give it a shot, at least, because then I'd *really* be a loser, if I got all caught up in the woulda-coulda-shoulda crap.

No one's heard from Danny. JR thinks he might have gone back to Grand Rapids but I know he didn't. He'd rather die than do that. Show the folks back home that they were right, that he couldn't make it in New York.

Roy keeps leaving nasty drunken messages on our answering machines— Cara's, JR's and mine. Yelling, accusing, then crying like a little girl. I just hang up the minute I hear his voice or press "Delete" without even listening to Roy's messages. Hey, how often can you listen to yourself be called shit like a "back-stabbing cocksucking bastard" without it wearing thin?

I don't know what's worse, Roy's yelling or Danny's silence.

6/23/79

When the detectives knocked on my door, I almost lost it. There was something about that knock…heavy and foreboding and full of bad karma. Never mind that it was before 9 on a Saturday morning. A tall cop and a short cop took up my doorway. I quickly scanned my half-asleep brain to try and remember if I had any pot or coke stashed anywhere and concluded that I didn't. Residue, yes, but not anything more than a few flakes. I immediately exhaled.

"Did you know Daniel Galen?" the stocky detective asked.

Did? Past tense. My right knee started to shake. "Sure, I know Danny. Is anything wrong, officer?"

"When was the last time you saw him?" the little one wondered. He was shorter than me and I'm not tall.

"I don't know, a couple of weeks," I said. "We used to be in a band together."

"Used to be?" Chubby Cop asked. "Did it end on bad terms?"

I had to laugh. "Does anything ever end on good terms?" I shot back. Neither of them thought it was funny. "He was upset when the band broke up."

Little Cop was taking notes in a ratty-looking pad. "But you weren't?"

"I'd already moved on," I told them, "to other things." Both detectives nodded. "What happened?" I asked.

"They recovered his body…" the short cop began, and I didn't hear anything else until he said, "Ma'am…are you all right?"

I was sitting on the floor in my hallway and they were crouching next to me. Somehow, they were nicer, more gentle. "Recovered...his...what?"

There was a meaty paw on my shoulder. It was attached to Big Cop's arm. "It appears that Mr. Galen walked off Steeplechase Pier."

"In Coney Island?" I asked.

Both cops nodded. "Witnesses say he just stepped off the edge and disappeared under the water immediately. Turns out, he had stones in his pockets. The toxicology report says he had taken large amounts of muscle relaxers. Valium."

"Where did they find him?" In retrospect, it was a stupid question but I just wondered.

"Down at the Owl's Head Wastewater Treatment Plant. Bodies end up there a lot," Cop # 1 offered.

Cop # 2 continued, "Something to do with the current and the turbines."

"Did he..." I was choking up.

"I don't think he suffered," the short one said. "He was probably unconscious when he hit the water."

"Do you think you can get up now?" the heavy guy wondered. "My knees are killing me." I nodded and let them both help me to my feet.

I asked them inside because I started feeling woozy again. I had to clear spaces for them to sit on the sofa, which was covered with drum skins, the boxes from my new Zildjians and junk mail. "Were you two...involved?" the big one asked, a little uncomfortably.

"No," I told them. "We were friends, sort of, bandmates. That's it."

"Because there was a note in his pocket. It was pretty soggy but we managed to read it."

"What did it say?"

"I can't really tell you but you're mentioned in it. And so are Mr. Martinez and Mr. Clapowitz."

"Throw me a bone, at least," I begged.

"Well, he says he doesn't blame you. He would have done the same thing. He just couldn't go home again."

I bit my lip. "Thank you," I managed to say before a few tears leaked out.

"And he wishes you luck. All of you."

Edith

First, she comes by every five minutes, then I don't see her for five weeks. At least it seems that long. Was it Passover? No, it was after Passover, Memorial Day weekend, I think. And here it is, almost the 4th of July.

Then all of a sudden, Carol appears, like it's nothing with nothing. With roast beef sandwiches, from Brennan & Carr this time. And onion rings. She knows they give me heartburn but she brought them anyway. Such a *shmegegge*, my Carol. But she meant well. She always means well, the poor *schnook*.

Carol was wearing black, not that it's unusual for her, but this was black dressy clothes, not the ratty *schmatas* she usually wears. This time, Carol was wearing a skirt and high-heeled shoes. She looked nice, even with that terrible hair of hers. There was a velvet band around her head. For once, it didn't look like she stuck her finger in a light socket.

She was more than halfway through with her sandwich when Carol told me she'd just come from a funeral. "A memorial, really," was all she said. Someone she used to be in a band with died. She didn't say anything more.

"I haven't been feeling good myself, Carol," I told her.

"Ma, it's always something with you."

"This is different. My arm. My chest."

"You probably just pulled something," she said, shrugging me off like a *meshuga* again.

"No. No, I don't think so."

"Did you tell Dr. Lewy?"

"*Fa*! What does he know?"

"He's a *doctor*, Edie. He knows a lot." Then she let it go. I was tired of the back and forth, and so was she.

This was when we were having rugelach. She knows I'm borderline diabetic with a bad heart, mind you, with the willpower of a flea, yet she brings me rugelach all the time. When I told her this, Carol just shrugged, "They're from Vito's on Avenue U."

"How somebody named Vito can make Jewish pastries..." I started *kvetching*. But they were good, I had to admit. Better than Strauss's.

"They're just cookies, Ma. Anyone can make them."

So, when we were having rugelach (raspberry, my favorite), Carol took something out of her purse. Yes, she was actually *schlepping* a pocketbook and didn't have the paper shoved into her back pocket like a hoodlum. I unfolded it and looked. It was a legal document of some sort. I could tell even without my glasses, which she handed to me anyway.

"What's this?"

"A contract," she said.

"I can tell it's a contract."

"It's a record contract, Edie."

"For your band...Airplane?"

"Aircraft. And no, it's for me. They just wanted me." Now, this was news. Nobody ever "just wanted" my daughter. She was good at losing things, not at getting things. She lost jobs. She lost boyfriends. She lost good money making demo tapes and *dreck* like that. But a contract? Nobody ever gave her a contract before. This was good. This was very good.

"Nu?"

"So...so we're going to make a record. Another record. With me singing lead on it, and playing drums. Then we're going on a tour."

"You're not going to quit your job. It's a good job!" I told her.

"It's a temp job. And no, not yet. I'm not quitting until I have to."

"Who says you have to?"

"Well, when I go on the road..."

Then it started. I was back to my old self. What does my son Irving call me? A bitch on wheels. "Oh, right, so you're going to leave me, sick as I am!"

Carol threw her hands up into the air. Rugelach went flying. "You're never happy, are you?"

She makes it so easy. "I was fine until you..."

"Until I got here?"

"I didn't say..."

"When I don't have a boyfriend, you tell me I'm an old maid. When I do have a boyfriend, you don't like him. When I have a job, it's not the right kind of job. When I play music, you say I'm wasting my time. When I get a record contract, you say I'm abandoning you." Carol got louder and louder as she went on. The veins were standing out in her neck and she gritted her teeth. Sometimes, I liked getting her riled up—it was some reaction, at least, and she wasn't acting like a victim—but not like this. I was afraid she was going to hit me.

"Tell me, Edith, what the fuck do you want?" Carol asked, inches from my face.

I didn't know what to say. "I just…I just want you to be happy, *bubbala*," I told her. It was the truth. What mother doesn't want their child to be happy?

After that, there was nothing left to say or do. There was no eating, no drinking coffee, no nothing. Carol got up to go and I started to hand her back the papers. She pushed away my hand. "That's for you. Keep it. Frame it. Wipe your ass with it. Put it in your little memory box. I don't care what you do with it."

Carol left without kissing me, slamming the door behind her. She slammed it so hard, the house shook. I worried that the Klappermans upstairs would complain but I don't think they were home. Besides, their kids blasted that *chazerai* "We are the Champions" whenever they won a soccer game. What was a little door slamming every once in a while?

So, Carol left and she left the box of rugelach, too. There must have been almost a pound of it, apricot, raspberry and chocolate (her favorite). I ate every last one and even licked the crumbs off my fingers. It wasn't long before I felt the burning in the back of my throat. I couldn't make it to the sink in time. My bum hip was acting up, even in the nice weather. There it was, a big, ugly mess on my clean kitchen floor, with no one to mop it up but me. Story of my life.

6/24/79

JR went down to Kings County Hospital to identify Danny's body. He didn't want any of us to go with him. Not even Fern, although I offered to babysit Jessica so he didn't have to go there alone. Shitty neighborhood, East Flatbush, especially for a balding, skinny white boy named Wilmot to be tooling around in, but he didn't care. Just let some junkie from the PJs try and mess with him, and see what would happen.

We never talked about it afterwards. "It" being Danny's death. I mean, his suicide. JR never said a word about how our former lead singer died again.

Danny's body was sent home to Michigan without ceremony at the request of his parents. They wouldn't hear of Danny being laid to rest in New York, even though he loved it here. Grand Rapids was his true home, they said. Funny, how when the holidays roll around or when someone dies, you find out where their true home is. I don't know if his family had a service for him out there. If they did, we weren't invited.

Still, Fern thought it wasn't right to have nothing. "People bury their cat in the backyard or flush their goldfish down the toilet with more than what poor Danny got," she said. So, this afternoon, the five of us went down to the Narrows, to that little parking area right under the Verrazano, and said goodbye to the boy from the Great Lakes State with the eight-octave range.

Roy still refused to return JR's calls, so the five were made up of me, Mongo, JR, Fern and Jessica, who fell asleep in her car seat the minute we hit the Belt

Parkway. Fern had roses, red ones, for us to throw into the bay. It was crowded along the bike path behind us since it was a Sunday, and a pretty day at that. Fern said we should each say a few words like they did in the movies, then drop our rose into the water.

JR didn't say a word, just whipped the flower onto the rocks so that the petals came off. Mongo said something in Spanish, then translated it for us. It meant, "Good-night, sweet prince." From Shakespeare, from Hamlet, I think. Then he started crying hard, harder than I ever saw a man cry.

Fern leaned over and whispered to me, "PRs are so dramatic." Then she bit her lip and stepped up to the railing. She took a deep breath. "I hope you finally found peace," she said in a voice that was solid and strong. Then Fern dropped her rose into the Narrows. The tide carried it out further and further until we couldn't see it anymore. My eyes watered from trying to find the smear of red in the ugly gray water.

Finally, I gave up and threw mine in without ceremony. "I'm sorry," I said to no one in particular.

We went to the Tiffany Diner a few blocks away from the Shore, on 99th Street. It's the kind of place people go on dates, after movies at the Harbor Theater and after Little League games. Fern and I shared a slice of cherry cheesecake. Jess shared it with us, too. She didn't like the cherry part much and made a face when bit of the red glue got onto the spoon Fern was feeding her with. The guys just had coffee. Nobody talked much, not even Fern, who pretty much talks nonstop.

I hope Danny had a better sendoff in Grand Rapids but somehow I think not. I bet his parents just put him in a hole in the backyard like a hamster in a matchbox coffin and forgot about him. But as for me, I can't forget.

Fern

Not that Danny was one of my favorite people in the universe. But what he did...the finality of it...the selfishness of it...I just can't get over it. I don't think Willie will ever be the same again. None of us will.

We had a little ceremony of our own, under the bridge, near one of those pullouts along the Belt. Nothing much, just flowers and a few words. Just so he didn't go into the ground unnoticed. It wasn't far from the sewage treatment plant where they pulled out Danny's body. Then we went to a diner in Bay Ridge. I don't know why. It's something Italians do after funerals. They eat. Or try to.

The silence in that booth was killing me. It was worse than chatter when you just wanted quiet. So I had to break it. "On the way home, can we stop at Leske's?" I asked Willie.

"Sure, Fern, whatever you want," he said.

"Because they have the best black and whites," I told them. "On the planet. Hands down." Mongo said something like "Umph" and Jessica said "More," meaning she wanted more cheesecake, sans cherries.

I kept at it. "Their frosting is creamy, not hard. Like something you make in an Easy-Bake Oven..." My voice trailed off because I didn't think anyone was listening.

"You can't bury your grief in food," Cara told me, licking her fork.

"Maybe not," I said. "But I can sure try."

Leske's was crowded, as usual. Willie double-parked outside on Fifth Avenue near 76th. I ran in with Cara in tow and Jessica screaming, "Mama!" in the car seat. But I didn't care. Sometimes you just have to cut the cord, you know? Even if you are two years old. It's a cold, hard world out there. Besides, Jess could survive without me for two minutes. Willie has to learn how to calm down his own daughter.

You could just smell the sugar the minute you walked through the bakery's door. It covered you like a blanket and your teeth started to hurt. I got a half dozen black and whites and a rainbow cookie for Jess to pull apart and crumble.

"We're the darkest things in here," Cara said, gesturing to the blonde-on-blonde girls behind the counter. "Except for the blackout cakes."

"Well, it is a Scandinavian place," I told her. I pointed out the bright blue and gold paint job, which are the colors of the Swedish flag. Then I said, "It's not your fault." Cara looked at me like she didn't know what I was talking about. But I know she did. "None of it."

"I know," she said."

"Do you?"

"Danny told me," she shrugged. "In his letter. The cops told me so. They thought I might need to know."

"I'm still pissed as hell at you," I told her. "But I still love you." I grabbed the pastry box and left. Cara didn't say anything in response, just followed me as closely as Jess does sometimes.

Traffic on the Belt was crawling on the way home. What did we expect? It was a Sunday. A warm, beautiful Sunday in June. Everyone and their Aunt Tillie was out for a drive, it seemed. It got so bad that Jessica started freaking out in her car seat. The poor kid had been running on empty the whole day, cooped up in the car, cooped up in the diner, then cooped up in the car again. At least she slept during Danny's ceremony. But that meant she was all revved up with no place to go. (Willie would hate it that I quoted Meatloaf but the hell with it, I just did.) So Jess did the "baby bugout" in the car. She went even crazier when Mongo teased her, chanting "Baby bugout!" It amazes me that guy even has kids. He can be such an ass around them sometimes.

I made Willie pull into one of those parking areas along the Shore, the one right before Caesar's Bay. We let Jess run around a little bit while the four of us shared a joint, kicking rocks and trash, and trying not to look at each other. I don't know what got into me, but I blurted out, "Death comes in threes." Maybe it was the silence that I hated, pressing on me like a rubber band around my head.

"That's an old wives' tale," Cara said, passing me the J.

"Then I guess I'm an old wife," I told her.

"It's true, though," Mongo chimed in.

"Just Puerto Rican voodoo," Cara said.

Willie rolled his eyes. He hated that old school Guinea shit. He was only half Italian, Polish on his dad's side, so he didn't get it. But I was full-blooded Dago, so I got it. I heard stuff like that my whole life. Throwing salt over your left shoulder into the face of the Devil, who lives there, and so on.

"You wait and see," I told them all.

"Ooooh," Willie teased, making ghosty sounds. "Who's next? I hope it isn't me..."

That's when I punched my idiot husband in the arm and he started chasing me like a teenager. But then Jess fell, cut her knee and began screaming bloody murder. We all got back into the car.

Traffic had eased up by then. I bribed my daughter to stop bawling with a black and white cookie. Yeah, I know, I'm setting her up for a lifetime of eating disorders by taking her mind off her pain with food, but the heck with it. We were all tired, cranky and hurting but you didn't see us screaming. Besides, it worked.

I cleaned the dirt out of Jessica's knee with apple juice (don't judge, it's all I had!) while Cara played tiny drum rolls on my girl's tummy. Jess roared with laughter, the tears still wet on her face. Cara laughed, too. It's funny how much Cara's face changes when she laughs. She's usually scowling but when she smiled, when she laughed with abandon (which was rare, I admit it), she just glowed. "You're good with kids," I told her.

Cara seemed embarrassed. "Just this kid," she told me.

"I bet your nieces and nephews would disagree."

"Nephews. All I have is nephews." Cara broke off a vanilla part of the black-and-white and handed it to me. She knew I didn't like chocolate.

"Maybe you'll be the one to have the girl, then," I said.

"Me?" Cara choked. "Me! I'm never having kids. They're one big ego trip... no offense. To most people, but not you, Fernie. I know I'd be a terrible mother. Could you imagine how many different ways I'd fuck a kid up?"

"Fuck up," Jessica piped. "Fuck."

"Sorry," Cara told me. "But you know what I mean."

I did. As much as I loved Cara, I had to admit that she was probably right.

I was surprised when Cara let Jessica hold her hand until Jessie fell asleep. Both of them did. Maybe it was the rocking motion of the stop-and-go traffic. Before Cara drifted off, I caught her sniffing Jess's head. "I love that baby smell," Cara blushed. "The only thing softer than baby skin is baby hair." I think Cara would make a good mother, despite what she said. Just because you have a rotten mother, doesn't mean you'll be one. Look at me. Mine is nothing to write home about but I think I'm okay. So far

When Cara slept, she looked as vulnerable as my daughter did. They held hands until the noise of the train passing overhead near Shell Road woke Cara up and she jolted awake. Immediately her face hardened, her eyes narrowed and those two fine lines between her eyes reappeared.

It was a matter of minutes before we were home. Willie offered to drop Cara off at her place but she said 'no,' she wanted to walk. She wanted to stretch her legs. I think she might have just wanted a drink. And not coffee like I offered.

Before Cara walked off, she said, "Thanks."

"For what?" I asked her.

"For being my friend." I must have looked stunned. I didn't know what to say.

"That's what we are, isn't it? Friends," she added.

"Sure," I told her. "Yes, we're friends."

"Good," she nodded, a half-smile creeping in. "I don't have many of those."

As I watched her go, I realized that she was probably right. And what a God-damned shame.

6/29/79

Bruce had us back in the studio before Danny's body was back in the ground in Michigan. I don't know how he managed to get time on such short notice in Electric Lady but he did. Probably because he booked time after regular business hours. But that was fine for our crew. Besides, it was a good location for all of us, right near the IND train lines and not far from the FedEx headquarters on the West Side, which made it easy for Mongo to get to.

Me and JR slummed it and took the D into the city. He was excited that Bruce wanted to do a bunch of his and Fern's songs plus a few new ones. I guess JR's excitement made him overlook the fact that Bruce was a coke fiend. (JR has no clue that he's a sex fiend, too. Or at least I hope he doesn't.) It's amazing what people will overlook and justify because they have no choices left.

Electric Lady is smaller, more intimate than Sound Lab or Power Station. There's one room at both places that's pretty much an auditorium. For recording symphony orchestras, I guess. But to have the worst (read that as tiniest) room in the best music studio in Manhattan (Electric Lady), you can't ask for much more than that. There's still a Jimi Hendrix vibe floating through the place even though it's been alive and kicking for almost 10 years and Jimi's been gone almost that long. He spent something like a month recording part of "The Cry of Love" here a month or so before he died.

If you ask me, his music still holds up today, what with tracks like "All Along the Watchtower" and "Voodoo Child," but I'm still partial to the "Are You

Experienced" album. "Fire" and "The Wind Cries Mary" being my two favorite tracks, in that order. Although I think I could do better, more kick-ass drum tracks on both songs than Mitch Mitchell could. "Fire" especially. Holds some sentimental value, you could say. Michael used to tell me that he thought I had some kind of crazy fire burning inside of me. A room would burn hotter with me in it, he said. The temperature would rise a few degrees when I walked in. He said that even my touch had heat. Michael, hmmm.

Anyway....

I'm not going to bother writing what went down in the studio. How boring is that? To me, recording is the pits. It sucks. All of that repetition, doing riffs and singing parts over and over again, until you feel like you want to rip your hair out. It's just the nature of the beast. Not that we suck or anything. Far from it.

Even with a studio musician on guitar, we sounded awesome. Bruce got us some guy named Marcus. Marcus Seward or something like that. "The best in the biz," Bruce sniffed, but he says that about everyone and everything. In this case, Bruce was right, though.

To look at Marcus, you're not sure what you're going to get. He actually showed up wearing a kilt. I'd never seen a guy wearing a kilt before in my life, except in a parade. Marcus has long, wooly, red hair which he sometimes pins to his head in a wild 'fro or else has it pushed up under a hat. And not a baseball cap or something normal. A multicolored African cap or a huge beret or a bright orange fedora. But it all works somehow, especially on him.

Once, Marcus even brought his dog with him, a sweet, smart, standard-sized poodle named Tommy. Coolest dog I ever met. Tommy showed up carrying a brown paper bag in his teeth, with of his own snacks inside. Plus it just so happens that Tommy's fur is the same color as Marcus' hair. It's wild.

Marcus is from some place in Indiana no one's ever heard of, Appleville or Applewood, which is probably why he got the hell out of there as quick as he could. He studied classical cello, believe it or not, at SUNY Someplace, but began playing guitar at some ridiculous age, like six, before even picking up the cello. Comes from a musical family, he said, where they had only one rule: no instruments at the dinner table. Damn, imagine coming from a family as normal as that. Did the Finkelsteins have any family rules growing up? Besides keeping Kosher? Maybe no *kvetching* at the table. Well, no one except Edie. She was, and still is, the Queen of Kvetch.

Can this Marcus guy play! He's the kind of guitarist Chuck Berry had in mind when he wrote "Johnny B. Goode." Especially the part that goes, "He could play the guitar just like a ringing a bell." That's Marcus all right. He doesn't like to be called Marc. In fact, he told Mongo that more than once, super politely, sweet as pie. And Mongo got it, eventually. He always does. Eventually.

Marcus really rocked out on the songs, like he grew up playing them. That's how much he dug the music. It was refreshing to see. Nothing like Roy sneaking drinks from a pint of Wild Turkey in his back pocket, thinking nobody saw, his playing getting sloppier and sloppier with each take. I don't think Marcus ever took a drink in his life, though you might assume he's a druggie by the way he looks. Despite all that hair and kilts and kente shirts, he's straight as an arrow.

I would love it if Marcus could come on tour with us but he's booked solid. Tours with the Pauls (McCartney and Simon) and anyone else who's lucky to enough have him. Right now, I'm taking it one day at a time. Something might open up in Marcus' schedule, you never know.

Bruce is talking about "The Cara Funk Explosion" going on tour before the end of the year. He wants to wait till the album comes out. (Notice I said album and not EP.) So we can promote the hell out of it. I'm not nuts about the name but he seems pretty set on it. The folks at Larva are, too. It's an obvious play on The Jimi Hendrix Experience. Maybe too obvious.

I'm afraid a name like that will make people expect too much before they even hear us. Plus I'm a little uncomfortable with being front and center. That's a lot of pressure. Always being "on," always being the one to draw them in. When I told Bruce my fears, he laughed, saying, "Who the fuck are you kidding? You're always the center of attention. You can't help it. That's just the way it is."

JR just smiled and shook his head.

Anyway...

Then there were the backup singers looking like a Gospel choir gone awry but sounding like soiled cherubs. Just the right touch of roughness to their rich, sweet voices, like warm maple syrup and spicy barbecue sauce mixed. But somehow working. Two girls and a guy. Never did get their full names. One was named Lisa and she had the rich voice of an angel. Toured with Jagger, I heard. The singers were amazing, did their thing, and were in and out in a flash, on to the next gig, probably.

Well here I am, saying I wasn't going to describe the recording sessions but then I go ahead and do it. You might say the studio time was nondescript. We got in there and got it done, in between everyone's work schedules. I could sure use some time off, not a vacation exactly, but a break. Only I don't get one as a temp. If I don't work, I don't get paid.

There's always something to do in Accounting, no matter how trivial or boring. Bruce keeps saying I won't be at the *Post* for long, that I might as well give my notice now and enjoy the summer. That shows he doesn't know me well. Michael might say I don't "do" enjoy very well—that I don't truly enjoy anything. Except playing. And sex. With him.

I also don't "do" vacations. I get too antsy. Even in a beautiful place like Antigua, I'd get restless. I always want to be playing, need to be playing. I find myself tapping, my feet, fingers, whatever, even without a pair of sticks in my hands. People kid me about that all the time. I just can't sit still. It was hell in school, especially in grade school when I couldn't control it as much as I can now. But it's still hard today.

Plus, I don't like to tan. I also don't like laying on the beach and frying like most people do. It's pure torture for me. I feel like an egg in a pan. I lay there feeling my skin sizzle, thinking there's got to be something else I can be doing, that I *should* be doing instead of nothing. Scribbling down lyrics, setting up gigs, practicing. Besides, it takes a lot of dark rooms to keep up this pasty complexion. It's my trademark.

I did something I said I was never going to do. No, it wasn't hook up with Michael again. Even though I wouldn't mind it, I can't keep yo-yoing back and forth into his life. It's not fair to him. He deserves more than that. What I did was take a gig with Ste-Mar. But it was only because Marty wasn't on the gig. I would *never, ever* work with that prick again, even if I was starving.

Turns out Steve double-booked a midweek gig and with all of the weddings, graduations and pot-smoking, he must have spaced out about it until the last minute. Steve was bugging out that Marty would find out and rip him a new one, so he quick threw together a band the night before the gig. None of their other drummers could do it. Steve literally begged me. He even said he'd pay me twice my old rate. He'd take it out of his own pocket and eat the loss. Said he'd pick me up, without me even asking. It was an offer I couldn't refuse.

Denise

I never thought I'd see her again. Not for a long while. "The next time you see me, I'll be on TV," Cara whispered to me before our last goodbye. We'd run into each other on the street in Mill Basin, and as always, it was a thrill to see her. Cara always made me smile, no matter what.

Steve didn't tell me where we were going. He just said he had to pick up some musician, that's it. I thought it might be her. When we turned down East 18th Street, I knew it was Cara and my heart did a little joyful leap. It was like I was going on a date or something. With the way Steve carries on and all the garbage at work with girls leaving left and right (I'm office manager as well as chief radiologist at an imaging place on Avenue U), I have very little joy in this crazy thing called life. Cara can always make me laugh no matter how crappy things are. And I think I saw her face brighten when she saw me, too.

"Dennie! What a nice surprise," she said. And meant it. Not like all of those other bullshitty musicians, kissing up to the boss's wife. Cara smiled from deep in her eyes, even deeper than that.

Steve was on his best behavior. (I found out later that he was stuck without a drummer for this gig, down to the wire.) He helped Cara pack her drum kit into the back of the Honda, no easy feat with the band's speakers in there too. I had to hold Steve's trumpet case on my lap. But first, I got out and gave Cara a big hug. She felt good in my arms, a little bony, maybe, but still good. She took my chin in her fingers. "You look like hell," she smiled. "You been crying?" she asked in a quiet voice, so Steve couldn't hear.

"Allergies," I told her.

"Always with the allergies," she said, whining like an old *yenta*. And I smiled again.

"Come on, girls," Steve broke in. "Lundy's awaits." But I could tell by his voice that Steve was smiling, too. He really liked that kid, and not in the sleazy way he liked most women. He truly liked Cara—as a person, as a human being. Maybe there was hope for the old boy yet.

Cara and I chatted away on the short drive to Lundy's. It was Ste-Mar's first gig there but from going out to dinner there many times, I knew it would be hell to a club date musician. Lots of stairs. When we got to the valet parking on Emmons Avenue, I helped them unload the equipment.

The food in Lundy Brothers Restaurant is great. Seafood, plain and simple, and fresh as anything. Passing by, you couldn't miss the huge, block-long building with the Spanish tile roof. It's humongous. And to think it all started from selling clams from a pushcart. It was the Jewish-American dream. But I was always uncomfortable there because all of the waiters at Lundy's were black. They wore spic-and-span white uniforms and white gloves. (To make sure their black skin didn't touch your white food?) But Lundy's was nice and roomy inside, sweeping ceilings, big arched doorways, white stucco walls. Plus the prices weren't bad for the value you got—large portions of good, fresh fish. Still, I couldn't get past the waiter thing. No waitresses either, black or not.

Of course, the gig was on the second floor. Steve, who had stripped down to his tux shirt, was already sweating through it on his third trip up the stairs with a speaker in each hand. Okay, he did have a few extra pounds on him, but this was not the way to start a gig. Cara seemed unruffled, as usual, even though it had to be at least 90 degrees. Nothing seemed to get to her, especially now. It was like Cara was on the outside looking in, removed from the club date insanity. For me, she was the only thing that made it sane. I had a feeling the drummer Steve mentioned might be her, that's why I tagged along—I needed my Cara fix.

The band set up pretty quick. Ackerman was on guitar and some *schlubby schmo* was on keyboards. His tux shirt had serious ring-around-the-collar ("Use Wisk!" as the annoying TV commercial goes) and his tux had wear marks around the wrists and knees. But at least it wasn't Marty, that piece of garbage. Any gig I didn't have to see his sneering mug was a good gig.

It was a graduation party of at least 100 people. Three parents of kids from Sheepshead Bay High's Class of '79 pooled their pennies and had their kids celebrate together. Smart, because not only did they split the cost three ways but they didn't have to worry about conflicting party dates and all of the drama about which friends would go to which party. Besides that, it was a pretty typical gig with teens sneaking drinks, a little puke, maxi and mini dresses in a rainbow of colors, some truly awful tuxedos, a few tears and a handful of shouting matches. The band slipped from "My Sharona" (which has filthy lyrics, by the way, something about how his *schvantz* is running down the length of his thigh. Jeez!) to "Hot Stuff" to "Shake Your Body." Cara really kicked it on the last one, singing lead and playing. It looked like she was going to take flight, she was rocking so hard. All in all, it was a good party. It looked like even Cara was having a blast.

There was a long dinner break, 20 minutes almost, and Ackerman played easy listening music while the guests chowed down and the kids tried to sneak rum into their Cokes. When I told Cara that I was going to duck out for a cigarette (Stevie didn't like me smoking), she said she'd come along. They'd already served the band scallops, pretty good, but the cheapest thing on the menu. "I could use some air," I told Cara. She told me she could too and followed me out. I was hoping she'd do that.

We crossed Emmons Avenue and stood near the railing alongside Sheepshead Bay, which was a little stanky on a warm June night. People were fishing from the footbridge, even though it was dark outside. I lit up axnd took a long drag. Man, that first suck on a cigarette tastes good. "I know I shouldn't smoke but..." I said, my voice trailing off.

"So," Cara said, after a while.

"So," I answered back.

"You guys still together, I see."

"Barely," I told her. "Lana has a room to let. I'm thinking of moving in."

"Doug still there?" she wondered.

I couldn't help but smile. "You remembered his name."

"I'm good with things like that."

"You're good with lots of things," I said. "You ever sign that contract?"

"How did you know?"

I stubbed out the Parliament, which I'd smoked down to the filter. "I'm good with things like that. Feel guilty?"

"At first."

"Well, you shouldn't. We take what we can get in this life."

The seagulls screamed and fought over a piece of fish guts on the deck of a boat. "How about you? Are you taking it?" Cara had the knack of cutting to the chase, of asking questions that had teeth.

"I'm moving out next week," I told her, and she smiled. "You'd like him." An old cocker spaniel walking an even older man nosed around our feet. Cara reached down and stroked the dog's curly head. Then the pair waddled on. "Doug and I still haven't done it yet. I'm moving to Lana's just to get out of the apartment. Doug just so happens to have a room at Lana's, too. It's not a big deal."

The sun had already gone down. There was a faint pink glow in the direction of where the Belt Parkway looped toward Cropsey Avenue and continued to the Verrazano. "I'm happy," I told her.

"You deserve happy," Cara said.

Her hand was on the silver-painted railing. I put my hand on top of it lightly. "And you?"

"Am I happy?" Cara asked. "Happiness is a work in progress."

By the time we got back inside, Steve was already onstage, looking worried. A girl in an apricot-colored dress with poufy sleeves was puking into an ice bucket while her friend held back her hair and her lace bib collar. A boy across from her was sneaking vodka from a pint bottle into his orange juice.

Cara took the stage, took a seat behind her kit, took her sticks and launched into "Too Much Heaven" without missing a beat. I guess that's why they pay her the big bucks.

We didn't get a chance to say much to each other afterwards. Just small talk. Weather, family, politics, and whether *Rocky II* was as good as original *Rocky*. Ackerman dropped Cara off after the gig.

I never saw her again.

7/4/79

It sounds like a war zone outside. I never was one for fireworks. Too loud, too unpredictable. A bizarre thing for someone like me to say, someone who makes a living making a lot of noise, right? But drumming is *my* noise. Does that make sense? My joyful noise, as Michael used to say. Comes from a Bible verse.

The Finkelsteins aren't even Old Testament folks, although we silently live by the "eye for an eye" credo. But Michael told me there was a verse from a psalm, Psalm 100, I believe it was, that went something like "Make a joyful noise unto the Lord, all ye lands…" He said it always made him think of me. It goes on to say, "Serve the Lord with gladness: come before His presence with singing." Blah-blah-blah.

Actually, I kind of like it even though I'm not big on religion. Michael always argued that I was religious in a sense, that I was moral, kind and just. I wonder if he'd still say that now. He was always spouting these Bible quotes to me—he said I brought out the religion in him. "Don't hide your light under a bushel basket," is another one he would say, going all New Testament on me. From somewhere in Matthew, I think, or Luke, or maybe both.

Also, "He who sings prays twice." But that was from a saint. Augustine or Peter, can't remember which. I would joke with Michael that my playing and singing were far from holy. Unholy, if you asked my mother. But Michael would just smile and say that talent like mine came from a special place, from God or Allah or whatever deity you happened to believe in. Or not believe in.

I feel like I'm rambling. Maybe I am. It's late but I'm wired and besides, it's too noisy to sleep. The fireworks…that's where I started. I'm not going to lie, I did a line when I got home. I should have done another shot but when I ran out of rum, I discovered that I only had tequila left and I didn't want to mix liquors. I'd been sipping rum and Cokes since I got back. But they still barely took the edge off my day with the family.

My family… Aileen and Stan picked up Edie and me in their hideous lime green Econoline (a custom color, believe it or not) at 10 am on the dot. Between us four and the two kids, I felt like we were going on a field trip. Or like we were the Jewish Joads from *The Grapes of Wrath*. Except we weren't going to California. Either to or from the nuthouse. But I can't decide which.

We jumped onto the Belt and headed toward Irving and Robin's out in the wilds of Hightstown, New Jersey. If Suburbia could puke up townhouses, this would be it. Rows and rows of almost identical houses attached on both sides, just like Brooklyn except these were newer, uniform and personality-less with grass baseball fields and plastic playgrounds in between. Whenever we drove through Irv and Robin's development, I felt like saying, "Cue the 'Prelude' from *Trouble in Tahiti*." But no one in the van would have gotten the reference. I think the Bernstein song is also called "Morning Sun." I've always loved it.

"Morning Sun's" lyrics list all sorts of things that are supposed to make you happy. This trio sings about suburbia, saying stuff like: lovely day, lovely life, happily married, vitamin B, chlorophyll toothpaste, sweet little son, second to none, colorful bathroom. As if this stuff is all wonderful. But they sound like hell to me. Just like the Twin Rivers subdivision in East Windsor, NJ.

Irv and Robin's place boasts all sorts of modern conveniences like a breakfast nook, rumpus room, central air and central vacuum system, plus two and a half baths. My least favorite feature is the cheesy, metallic wallpaper in the half bath festooned with all sorts of supposedly-funny Holy Roman Empire slogans that weren't funny at all, like: "I love my wife but oh, Euclid!" and "Down with Caligula." I find it so jarring, I can barely pee.

The ride to East Windsor is only supposed to take an hour but on this wacky Wednesday in July, it took almost twice that long. Traffic on the Jersey Turnpike was stop and go, bumper to bumper. Jared and Stewie fought all the way down with "Mom, he's touching me!" and "Mom, he's on my side!" Even though there was plenty of room in the back of Econoline, they insisted on sitting next to each other and annoying each other.

Edie was almost as bad as they were, yelling at them in her Chesterfield alto, then Aileen yelling at Edie for yelling her kids. "I can yell at my own kids, Mommy!" she whined like the big baby she was. And all the while, Stan was sighing like the weight of the world was on his shoulders instead of on his belly.

I don't know why I said I'd go to a barbecue at my brother's but I did and it was my cross to bear.

At one point, Edie said, "All right already!" and smacked my hands.
"What?"

"That *facocta* banging!" I must have been tapping my fingers. I do that sometimes when I feel like I'm going to jump out of my skin. Without even realizing it. It's self-soothing, my friend Nadia, who's an occupational therapist, once explained to me. I sat on my hands the rest of the way.

"*Oy*, I'm *shvitzing*," Edie proclaimed. "The air conditioner isn't reaching us back here." Stan turned up the AC with a sigh. I know he was calculating what this gesture would do to his gas mileage.

We stopped twice—once for the bathroom and once at the QuickChek because Edie needed something to drink. "It's so hot, I'm going to *chalisch*," she gasped dramatically.

"Why don't you just ask for a drink like a normal person?" Aileen snapped.

"Why doesn't Grandma speak English?" Jared asked.

"Why are you so fresh?" Edie barked. "And what? I'm not normal." I whispered to Jared that *chalisch* meant 'faint' in Yiddish, and he seemed satisfied.

"Why doesn't everyone just shut up?" Stan suggested. And no one said another word until we pulled up at the parking spots reserved for Canterbury Court. We each grabbed a bag of food. ("What am I, your slave?" Aileen said to her boys when they didn't.) Jared tried to open the Joyva Ring Jells while Stewie attempted to take a nibble of *halavah* without my sister seeing. Meanwhile, Stan put a milk crate on the ground so Edie could use it as a step to get out of the van. I unfolded her walker to her symphony of *"Oy's"* with each step she took.

Robin was waiting for us at the front door. "You're late…I told you not to bring anything…" she said, instead of hello. "I thought I was going to *plotz* from worry."

I looked at Jared. "Fall down or faint," I told him.

"Again with the fainting," he said.

"Fainting is big with this family," I sighed.

Inside, it was total chaos. Not that Robin isn't a good housekeeper but with three boys, things like soccer balls and baseball mitts become part of the décor. Often, you have to move a tennis racket just to sit down only to find there's a tennis ball wedged up your ass. I think it's charming, while for Edie, it's the source of annoyance and brings forth a symphony of sighs. "Always such a *tummel* in here," Edie whispered, loud enough for my sister-in-law to hear.

My brother Irv was engulfed in a cloud of smoke in the fenced-in patio off the kitchen. He tried his best at barbecuing but the result was always the same: charred meat. However, Robin wasn't "from the cookers" either, as Edie liked to point out at every available opportunity, so it wasn't too much of a let-down. The most important thing was that we were all together. Right? Wrong.

While Irv was apologizing for the burn-fest, the five boys were clamoring to eat. "At least no one will get ptomaine poisoning," I joked.

"This is pork?" my mother gasped, a blackened sausage halfway down her gullet.

"You know I don't keep Kosher, Edie," Robin snapped. "Never have, never will." Then to my brother. "She can't tell me to keep Kosher in my own house, Irving."

Edie huffed and reached for a crisp hockey puck of an all-beef hamburger.

(Why do I write this stuff like it's a short story out of Michael's "Fiction Writing 101"? Maybe it gives me an extra layer of protection, so I can remove myself from the situation. Somehow, it doesn't seem so tragic when you can look at your life like it's fiction.)

And what's this with Michael, Michael. I mentioned him something like four or five times already, haven't I?

Okay, so then, right in the middle of the BurnFest, the barbecue grill ran out of propane. Irv checked with his neighbors on either side but they were out, too. I gladly left with him for QuickChek on a quest to get another propane tank. Before the door shut behind us, I heard more weighty sighs and *oys* from Edie, Robin telling her favorite mother-in-law, "Nobody's gonna starve!" and saw Stan's face reddening to an unhealthy glow. I'm glad I missed another one of his "Aileen, I've had it with your fucking family" outbursts. For the time being.

My brother didn't wait long after the wood-paneled doors of his Town and Country (Robin had a sporty Duster) were shut before he dug into me. "So?"

"So?" I shot back.

"Any news? Mommy tells me you got a record deal."

"Good news travels fast," I told him. "They're mixing the album now. There's talk about a tour in the fall, as soon as the album's ready."

"Fantastic," Irv said, his Eddie Cantor banjo eyes getting bigger. "You don't sound too excited."

I shrugged. "I'll believe it when I'm on the tour bus and I'm holding the album in my hands."

Irv put on his directional and made a right to go left. In New Jersey, it was impossible to make a left turn without going into a jug-handle turnaround. That was one of the many reasons I hated the Garden State. It was even worse than Satan Island. "There you go again with your negativity," he told me. "Just like Mom. It's like a disease."

I thought my head was going to explode. "Just like Mom! Don't you ever say that to me again! I'm not just like Mom any more than you're just like Dad!"

Of course, my brother immediately backed down, groveling with his tail between his legs. Irv was such a wuss. "I didn't mean...Carol, I swear, I..."

We were at the QuickChek by then. I grabbed a propane tank and paid for it while Irv turned in the old one. It was in the back of the station wagon and I was back in the passenger seat before Irv got in again. He tried to shove a tenner into my fist but I waved it away. "My pleasure," I told him.

It felt good to have the upper hand, to have my brother feel like he owed me something. He did, especially since he'd insulted me. Irv took the long way back, winding past apple farms, stopping at Lee Turkey Farm, where Robin had bought a freshly killed and cooked turkey one Thanksgiving, plus the entire dinner from soup to nuts—sweet potatoes, broccoli, stuffing. Hands down, it was better than my sister-in-law's cooking but because the kids teased her about being a JAP, she never did it again. "A Jewish-American Princess? Are you kidding me?" Robin had howled. "In this palatial estate?" she continued, gesturing to the cramped townhouse just like the row of townhouses it was attached to.

Like I said, the only difference between this and Brooklyn was no graffiti or visible homeless people. There was no culture, no museums, no personality, just a clone of the house next door, even if your next door neighbor was named Mohandra. The people who lived there were kidding themselves if they thought it was better than Queens or Brooklyn. In my eyes, it was worse.

Irv parked in the lot in front of the red clapboard building. A sign said that the Lee Family had been decapitating turkeys since 1868. Irv pointed this out. "That's about the same time Grandma Finkelstein was being ravaged by the cossacks," I offered.

"Carol, I'm sorry," my brother told me. "About what I said. You're not like her."

"I'm on my own, Irving," I responded. "I have no one. Not even my family."

"Whose fault is that?" he shot back.

"No one's. Everyone's. I don't know."

"What about that guy Marco?"

"Michael? What about him?"

Irv sighed in frustration. Nope, I wouldn't even throw him a freaking bone. "Is he still around?"

"Yes and no."

"You're not going to tell me anything, are you?"

"Probably not," I sighed.

With that, Irving went inside the farm store to get a half-gallon of apple cider but they were all out. When he slipped back into the driver's seat, he started up the van right away, in a rush to get back home to Horror House. For a while, we drove in silence. It was nice. Until we slowed down almost to a stop when we came to a tree with a deep dent in the trunk about 5 feet off the ground. The propane tank clunked from the seat and onto the floor behind me.

Irv told me in excruciating detail how a 17-year old boy had taken the curve too fast a couple of weeks ago, went airborne and slammed into the oak. The poor bastard didn't even die instantly. With the steering wheel lodged into his chest, the kid screamed in agony until he passed out from the pain. The state troopers all agreed that it was the most horrific accident they had ever seen. Then my brother moved on. Moved the car and the conversation.

I could tell we were getting close to the house. Even though it wasn't easy to do because those subdivisions all looked alike to me. "Can you believe this place used to be farms?" Irv said. Probably rhetorically, even though I don't think he knew what rhetorical meant. I didn't respond. But I was thinking, 'How sad.'

I knew my brother was on a roll and that nothing would stop him until he said what he needed to say. In this way, he was a lot like my mother. He got stuff out no matter who it hurt. He just needed to get it out. "About what you said before. About having no one. Do you really think it's true?"

I shrugged. "Don't be silly," my brother continued. "You have us, your family. We have each other's backs. Always."

"Do we? Or are we biting each other's backs? Always."

"I don't know what you're talking about."

"Of course, you don't."

Irv parked and grabbed the propane tank from the station wagon's floor. By the time we got back inside, all hell had broken loose. Stan's face was beet purple in rage. Robin, Edie and Aileen shouted out trimultaneously at me and Irv,

"Where the hell have you been?"

"What happened?" my brother wondered.

"What didn't happen?" Robin spat. "The boys knocked over a plant. Evan got hit in the eye with a softball…"

"We're leaving!" Stan yelled. And no one argued. No one said they were hungry or that they had to pee. Aileen took back the bags of food that Robin hadn't even wanted anyway. Edie limped to the car park behind her walker, sighing with practically every step. Jared and Stewie had the good sense to say nothing, not even goodbye to their cousins.

Back in the van, Aileen silently passed around a green tube of Pringles Sour Cream & Onion. "Potato chips?" she asked. I waved them away. "You sure? They're newfangled."

"They're less than 50% potato," I said quietly.

"That's it!" Stan screeched, and pulled the van onto the service road so sharply that we all slid into each other. He jammed on the brakes. Stewie's head bounded off the seat rest in front of him but he didn't cry. "I've had it with you, always judging everyone," Stan spat. "You think you're better than everyone else, don't you?"

Aileen and Edie tried to calm Stan down. Jared whimpered quietly because he knew what was coming. I opened the door to harmonious screams from my mother and sister. I got out and started walking in the opposite direction. We had just gotten onto the New Jersey Turnpike and the Princeton Junction station couldn't be far away. Well, it could, but a tow truck gave me a lift to Al's Sunoco which was nearby. Nice guy, not too much of a creep, though he did try to get my number.

Michael

Cara always thought there was someone else. There was never someone else. Not anyone serious, anyhow. I went on a few dates with that Social Studies sub at school. She was nice enough, cute enough but she wasn't Cara. Eventually, I slept with her. Only once. It wasn't bad but it was awkward. It didn't feel right, even though Cara and I weren't together anymore. And even when we were, we didn't have any kind of monogamy agreement. But after being with Cara, there was no being with anyone else. She ruined me for all other women. I'm serious.

When Cara breezes back into my life, I just can't say 'no.' A bad day with Cara is better than the best day with someone else. I know a guy isn't supposed to say things like that but it's true. Fuck it. What do I gain by hiding it? Nothing.

It has been a while, though, since Cara and I were an item. She left a string of half-drunken messages that I forced myself to ignore. It wasn't easy. At weak moments, at lonely moments, my hand reached for the phone. Sometimes I even dialed 332-472…then stopped before the final 2. Once or twice, I dialed all the way and hung up when she answered. Adolescent stuff, right?

This time, when Cara called a couple of days ago, on the 4th of July, I answered on the first ring. In the back of my mind I hoped it was her. I know, I know, I said before that I didn't want to get back onto the Cara Train again. But I found myself missing it, missing her. Missing the ups but not the downs. Not her crippling depression and self-depreciation. But missing looking into someone's eyes that burn with a fire…for you, for everything they see and touch.

So, I picked up the phone and it was Cara. She sounded like hell and started crying immediately. She seemed shocked I'd answered after months of screening my calls. But my heart leapt when I heard her sexy-husky voice. When I breathed her name it was like a prayer.

From what I could tell before Cara started sobbing too hard to understand, she'd had a horrendous day with her family. One of many, take your pick. It's not that I blame them for making Cara what she was (or wasn't) but they certainly didn't help. Unconditional love is nonexistent in that family. To them, love is just a four-letter word *á la* Elton John or Bob Dylan or Joan Baez, whichever you prefer.

I've never seen people related to each other by blood hurt each other like they do. The way they yell and dress down each other. Not really curse, because to Edith, that's *verboden*. No, she'd never utter "the f-word" but she'd think nothing of telling Cara that she was a worthless sack of garbage who'd never amount to anything. That she was *gornisht*, which meant nothing…or less than nothing. Imagine saying that to your daughter? Or to any human being. But with Mrs. Finkelstein, it was SOP. I'm dead serious. And forget the things Mrs. Finkelstein has said to my face. But that doesn't count because I'm a stranger and a *goy* at that. Yeah, she's a real *yenta* who sticks her nose where it doesn't belong. And a really rude person.

Cara had the bad sense to take me to her cousins Sol and Audrey's son's *bris* last year. Maybe for moral support, I don't know. But they needed to make a *minyan* and I fit the bill. For *goyim* like yours truly, a *minyan* is a group of 10 males, age 13 or older, necessary to make an official ceremony like a funeral or a ritual circumcision official. Sexist, I know, but that's the way most religions are. Women don't count.

It was the first *bris* I'd ever been to and it was peculiar, to say the least. The food was good, all sorts of "appetizing," as Edith called it. Jewish delicacies like chopped liver, lox, *schmaltz* herring, all kinds of salads, plus strudel, rugelach, and all of those sickeningly sweet (but oh so good) desserts. All catered from Adelman's on King's Highway, which is the best of the best. And from Meshuga Phil's on Avenue U because Adelman's doesn't "do" bagels.

Although she stuffed her face like a trouper, Edith was all *verklempt* because Audrey mixed meat with dairy, which made the Kosher meal un-Kosher. "But it's my party and I want chopped liver," Audrey pointed out. Rabbi Schraeder didn't have a problem with it either. The *mohel* was supposedly the brother of the famous Jewish comedian Jackie Mason, who was revered among Semitics like Tony Bennett is among Guineas like me.

Edith also had a big problem with me. "How could you bring a *goy* to a *bris*?" she whispered to Cara, a bit too loudly. "This is *mishegas*!"

"No, it's not crazy, Ma," Cara told her. "Audrey needed a *minyan* and Michael makes a *minyan*."

"But you have to be Jewish to be part of a *minyan*," Edith screeched.

Rabbi Schraeder politely butted in. "No, you don't. For him, it's a *mitzvah*." Then the rabbi moved on to the whitefish salad.

"See, it's an extra special blessing to have *goyim* in attendance. And if it makes you feel any better, Edie, Michael's circumcised, so we're good," Cara threw in for good measure. Totally unnecessary but it just showed how angry she was.

Their argument was cut short because it was soon time for the actual *bris*. Traditionally, I'm told this happens before everyone starts eating, but the rabbi was late (he had a funeral beforehand). Besides, Audrey was *hungerik*. And as we all know, it was her party.

Circumcision jokes abounded. Like this gem:

- Did you hear about the *mohel* who didn't charge for circumcisions? He only took tips.

Or:

- Did you hear about the rabbi who made a wallet out of the skins he took from circumcised penises? Rub it and it becomes a suitcase.

If Cara had her drum kit with her, there would have been a snappy roll on the snare to accentuate these punch lines. Someone even brought up that scene from *Roots* when the village boys are going to get circumcised at age 13. Someone tells the cutter: "Careful, or women will weep."

Rabbi Schraeder hustled us into Audrey and Sol's bedroom. It was a glitzy affair, full of mirrors and chrome (on the headboard, over the dresser). There was a pillow covered with a plain, white pillowcase. The rabbi's implements of torture were already laid out on a brand-new, white towel on the bed: something that looked like an X-Acto knife and another tool I later learned was called a Gomco clamp. Man, these Jews were hardcore!

Irv and Robin's eldest, Shawn, who was just *bar mitzvahed* a year earlier, passed out the second he saw all of that surgical steel. I caught him on the way down and propped him in a chair. Rabbi Schraeder said he didn't have to be conscious, just bodily present, to make the *minyan*, so he proceeded.

I positioned myself toward the back so I didn't have to see all the gory details. The godfather held poor little Abe on a pillow on his lap. They removed the baby's diaper. At only eight days old, his raisin of an umbilical cord stump was still attached. That made him seem even more vulnerable. Abie was fine until two of the men held down each of his legs, pinning them to the pillow. All three men looked away as Rabbi Schraeder attached the clamp. Then I turned away, too.

The baby's bloodcurdling screams followed, drowning out the rabbi's prayers. Audrey clawed at the door, begging to be let in but no one would open it. The whole *bris* thing seemed pretty barbaric, very Old Testament, which, of course, it was. All about Abraham making a blood pact with *HaShem* (Jews never said the name of God, unless they were praying, so this literally meant "the name") and every Jew thereafter making good on Abraham's promise.

Then it was over. There was less blood than I'd imagined there would be. Small smears on yet another clean, white, cotton cloth. Abe was given a drop of wine and a Binky, and seemed no worse for the wear. I couldn't say the same for Shawn, who made a sprint for the master bath and hurled up his bagel.

I knew something had gone on in the living room while we were in the bedroom because when the *minyan* returned, Edith's sisters were shushing her up and murmuring to her in Yiddish. *"Shtum, shtum,"* they cooed, as if to a baby.

"I will not be quiet!" Edith protested, as if she *were* a baby.

"All I said was that I'd dance at their wedding," Sarah told her sister. "Jew, Gentile, it makes no difference to me. As long as they're happy."

At that moment, Cara looked mortified. Her usually beautiful, clear, punkish Snow White complexion was mottled with rage. Her hands were balled into fists. Edith cocked her head toward her daughter. "Does she look happy?" she asked.

Iris threw her hands up in frustration. She took a deep breath and ran her fingers across her Jackie O bouffant. "You did this to her! It's you!" Iris shouted. "Why can't you just shut your trap and let her be happy."

Cara and I were out of there before it could get any worse. I put my hands on her shoulders and she allowed me to lead her out the door of Audrey and Sol's apartment. She grasped my fingers as we waited for the elevator, not saying a word. I loved her more than ever—so silent, so brave, so hurt and strong. We quietly started to walk toward the Brighton Beach boardwalk. It was like the sea drew us there. Ocean View Avenue was only a few blocks away. We passed beneath the D train's elevated tracks, passed Brightwater Court and the Shorefront YM-YWHA.

It wasn't until Cara's hands were grasping the railing that separated the Riegelmann Boardwalk from the sand that she started crying. She let out a wail that was so loud, so tortured, that I almost started crying myself. Just one. People stared but she didn't care. I didn't care. The seagulls scattered. Soundless tears rolled down her face and then suddenly, she was done.

But I digress.

So, once again, Cara is back in my life. I decided not to fight it. That only makes me miserable. I'll take whatever she can give. Like I said, it's better than nothing at all. I keep thinking of those old love songs with hokey lines that go "like a moth to a flame." In fact, I put on Billie Holiday as I started writing this. Right now, she's singing "I'm a Fool to Want You," which Frank Sinatra is credited as being one of the writers. All about how the singer is powerless and can't seem to leave this girl, how he keeps coming back to her, how wrong it is but how he can't get along without her. Give it a listen. It's me and Cara to a T.

I mean, I can get along without Cara. But I don't want to. So, when Cara called, I went to her and stayed the night.

7/7/79

The night of the 4th I made it back to the Port Authority in one piece. Late. Feeling beaten up. But still, in one piece. 42nd Street was in all its glory, neon lights blooming like brilliant flowers, creepy men zipping in and out of peep shows, marquees bursting with kung-fu and porn movie titles. Sometimes it was tough to tell which was which. *Screwples...Enter the Dragon...The Ecstasy Girls.*

Being back in New York, I felt relieved, like I could breathe better. Give me an overflowing trash can and puke dried up on the sidewalk over a homogenized suburban subdivision any day. I was home.

By then, I was starving. Did I want Howard Johnson's greasy clam strips or Nathan's crunchy franks? (Nah, the best dogs were at the Coney Island Nathan's anyway, the rest were imposters.) I settled for a Chock Classic at Chock Full o' Nuts: cream cheese on date nut bread. It was dense, thick, supposedly homemade bread. Cheap and satisfying, kind of like me.

I walked down to the D train on the corner of 6th Avenue, not caring that the fireworks were going to start exploding over the East River soon. I'd had enough fireworks for one day.

In my last journal entry, I wrote enough about what happened with my fabulous family. I don't want to think about it anymore, yet I can't stop. I haven't talked to any of them since I left them near Exit 8. Not that anyone has tried to call me to see if I made it home all right. Can you imagine that? Not even my own mother.

Well, screw them. Screw them all.

Oh, and I called Michael, which is nothing new. But this time, he picked up the phone. After something like three months. He came to me and it was good. Like slipping into a favorite pair of jeans. He fit. He felt right. Especially spooning in bed afterwards with him twirling my hair around his finger. I told him the gory details of the July 4th would-be barbecue. "I don't know whether I should laugh or cry," he said. Then in the next breath, "You guys need therapy."

"The Finkelsteins don't do therapy," I told him.

When I got back from the 4th of July fiasco, the light was blinking on my answering machine but I ignored it. I didn't feel like talking to anyone. The next morning, after Michael left, I listened to the message. It was from someone I didn't know, a grad student from NYU doing her thesis on the impact of Electric Lady Studios on American contemporary music. So, why the hell was she calling me? Was it a hoax? I didn't call her back but she called again that afternoon while I was in.

Virginia sounded nervous as she gave me her spiel: grad student, thesis, interview, maybe a film, would I be so kind as to… How did she get my number? The engineer at Electric Lady gave her Bruce's number and Bruce gave her mine. ("No publicity's bad publicity and it will help push the album," Bruce explained when I called him later.) I told Virginia I would think about it. And I am.

Back to Michael. He's the last person I want to hurt and I don't do it purposely. This time, I think he understands what I can give him and what I can't. And he seems okay with it. Time will tell.

But I can see he's stupid in love with me. If I were honest with myself, I would admit that I loved him, too. Maybe not as wild or as deep as he loves me but I truly do love him. Just because you love someone doesn't mean they can make you happy. Plus I can't afford to have anything stand in my way. Not now. I've never been this close before. And if I lost this opportunity, I don't know what I'd do. Well, I do know what I'd do but I don't feel comfortable putting it down on paper. Even seeing those words would be difficult.

But I'd do it. I'd do it in a heartbeat. If Danny could, then so could I.

Virginia C. Smith
Graduate Student, New York University

Testing...Testing...This is Virginia C. Smith. Tape Three, Interview Number 5, NYU thesis project, "Electric Lady Studios and its impact on American contemporary music 1970-1979." In this paper, I will examine several major recordings produced at the seminal Electric Lady Studios beginning with "The Cry of Love" which was partially recorded there. Contrary to popular belief, Hendrix's "Electric Ladyland" was not recorded in Electric Lady Studios, but rather, was recorded in 1968, two years before its opening party on August 26, 1970. Hendrix spent only four weeks laying down the tracks for "The Cry of Love" at the studio before his untimely death on September 18, 1970 in Notting Hill, United Kingdom.

I'll continue this transcription later. I'm scheduled to meet with Cara Funk, a female singing drummer, who just finished recording most of her first album at Electric Lady. Her "Mask" is due to be released on September 4, 1979 and a US tour will commence shortly prior.

I first became aware of Ms. Funk when I heard her laying down drum tracks a few weeks ago at Electric Lady. I persuaded Spike (no last name given), the sound engineer, to give me Ms. Funk's contact information. I then spoke with Trini Otero, the personal assistant of Bruce Lask, an Artists and Repertoire (A&R) Director at Larva Records, who gave Mr. Lask my information. Through Ms. Otero, Mr. Lask supplied me with Ms. Funk's direct telephone number. After a few days, I was able to connect with Ms. Funk. I am meeting with her at 1 pm this afternoon at Mr. William Shakespeare's at 176 MacDougal Street, at the corner of West 8th Street, a stone's throw from Electric Lady Studios. More later.

1:11 pm, at Shakespeare's

(background noise)

SMITH: This is Virginia C. Smith. I am sitting here with Cara Funk, singer/drummer. A note for the transcriber. For clarity's sake, please mark my dialog 'Smith' and Ms. Funk's 'Funk.'…Are you ready, Ms. Funk?

FUNK: Cara, please call me 'Cara.'

SMITH: All right. Cara.

FUNK: So, what's this you're doing again?

SMITH: My thesis. It's a study of American rock albums recorded at Electric Lady Studios and their impact on 20th century music.

FUNK: Or lack thereof. Like?

SMITH: Patti Smith's "Horses."

FUNK: Good one.

SMITH: "Young, Loud and Snotty."

FUNK: The Dead Boys. Yes. How about Sir Lord Baltimore? "Kingdom Come."

SMITH: Another Brooklyn band. Yes.

FUNK: "Physical Graffiti?"

SMITH: I can't include Led Zepplin. Just American bands.

FUNK: Fair enough. Okay, shoot.

SMITH: First, what made you decide on Electric Lady?

FUNK: Well, that decision was made by my manager, Bruce Lask. It has a good reputation and they had some open slots. Bruce signed me a few weeks ago and Larva wants to get an album out by the fall.

SMITH: What's the rush?

FUNK: I'm not getting any younger…or prettier. (Laughs) But seriously, the sooner the better, I always say. Things have a habit of falling apart if you give them enough time.

SMITH: What kind of impact do you think your record will make?

FUNK: Well, I hope people will buy it. I hope they'll like it. But impact?

SMITH: A lasting impression.

FUNK: I hope they find something that speaks to them.

SMITH: Did you write any of the songs?

FUNK: One or two. I'm just starting to find my sea legs as a songwriter. But the song that speaks the most to me is the title track.

SMITH: "Mask." Why?

FUNK: Maybe because it was written about me. It *is* me. We're all hiding behind some kind of mask, aren't we?

(Muffled voices)

SMITH: Yes, we're ready to order. I'll just have the Hamlet Burger with fries. And a Fresca.

FUNK: And I'll have an Othello Burger, no fries, just water…Don't you love it? Mozzarella and black olives. Othello. Desdemona. The black and white thing. Get it? Pretty funny.

SMITH: You were talking about masks. What's yours?

FUNK: Hmmm…Some people might say I hide behind my music. Behind my drums. But I think my mask is what people want me to be, not what I am.

SMITH: And what are you?

FUNK: I don't understand how that has anything to do with American music.

SMITH: It's all about the music, isn't it?

FUNK: I guess so. You asked what I was? A singing drummer.

SMITH: That's all?

FUNK: Isn't that enough?

SMITH: Not a daughter, a sister, a girlfriend?

FUNK: Those are things anyone can be. But a singer…a drummer, that's what makes me different. No one can be exactly what I am, exactly the way I am.

SMITH: And the album?

FUNK: The album is my mark. It's what I leave behind.

SMITH: Sounds like the way other people might talk about having a child. Their legacy.

FUNK: Hmmm. I guess it does…Let me ask you something.

SMITH: Go ahead.

FUNK: How did you find me?

SMITH: I heard you. The studio door opened as I was talking to Spike in the hallway and I heard you sing. It was like nothing I had ever heard before. It was like church. Like heaven and hell rolled all into one.

FUNK: That's intense.

SMITH: But it wasn't the first time I'd heard you. I saw you at the Peppermint Lounge, singing on "Mask," but you weren't doing lead.

FUNK: Right. Danny was. I just backed him up.

SMITH: Then, when I heard you again at Electric Lady, I thought it was… serendipity. Sounds stupid but I did. I started doing some research and…

FUNK: Why me?

SMITH: I thought it would be an interesting juxtaposition to pit albums of moderate success, past records, against one without a track record, and then follow it.

FUNK: Track me. Test me. See what happens, you mean.

SMITH: Yes. I think you'll go far.

FUNK: I hope you're right.

SMITH: If you don't mind, I'd like to follow up with you. A few months down the road. To see where you've been.

FUNK: Sure. And Bruce gave you my bio? To fill you in on the other stuff?

SMITH: Yes.

FUNK: Okay. So I'll see you a few months from now, then. I hope I'm still around.

SMITH: Me, too.

7/14/79

I haven't written in this for a while. A week? Maybe more? I've been really busy. As much as I hate to admit it, everything seems to be coming together. This album. The tour. My life. Even Michael and I are in a good place. He understands where we are and he's good with it. I am, too. I call him when I can. We get together when we can. (And when we do, it's pretty great.) He's really occupied working on a novel and teaching a summer class.

Oh, and I met with that college student a few times. Virginia. She's been interviewing me for her thesis. Something about the history of Electric Lady Studios. Only I can't imagine how all of the stuff she asks me fits in. Personal things that have nothing to do with the studio or Hendrix. Like:

- How old were you when you first started playing drums?
- Did you ever feel like you didn't fit in?
- If you didn't play drums, what would you be doing?

Deep things like that. Things I would never ask myself. And I find myself telling her stuff "off the record" that I wouldn't tell anyone else. Not even Michael. I wonder why that is. I don't know, but in a way, it feels good to get it out of me and into the air.

Ginny's a nice enough kid. From California. Smart but in a silent way, not showy. And deep, like the questions she asks. I'm beginning to think she might have a girl crush on me. But I'm okay with it. Happens all the time. I guess because I do things most chicks don't have the balls to do, that they only dream about. They come up to me at gigs all breathless and flushed and bashful. They tell me I'm great or that I give a voice to things they can't say out loud. They tell me I'm their idol. Then they go back to their quiet little lives and I go back to living out loud.

I've also been meeting with Bruce. I don't know if I'll ever feel comfortable with that guy. With JR and Aircraft, I was comfortable right away. Nothing out of line ever happened and I was never afraid it would. But Bruce is all over the map. Sometimes he treats me like one of the boys and others, he's all moon-eyed and goofy. I bet it has to do with the coke, which I never do with him anymore. I tell him it's because it messes with my vocal cords but mostly it's because I don't want to let my guard down with him.

Lately, when Trini shows me into Bruce's inner sanctum, there's something in her eyes that tells me she knows, that he pulls this weird shit with her, too. Or at least he tries to. She looks me straight in the eye then turns away before she shuts the door. I've seen that look before: it's exchanged between kids who are abused or women who are treated like garbage. They look at each other and immediately *know*, like they have some sort of inner radar. From Trini's look, I get: 'Yeah, he's a pig but who the hell isn't? Besides, the pay is good and I need the job. Everyone else is pretty nice here and I like working at Larva. There's something to be said for free sodas and snacks in the pantry. And sometimes free lunch.'

Yep, I get all of that from a glance. Trini avoids my eyes after that. If I were to tell her something without words, it would be: 'There's no such thing as a free lunch.' And then she'd probably give me a Puerto Rican switchblade look that tells me to mind my own damned business.

After Trini closes the door to Bruce's office, if there's coke residue on the table, I know I'm in for a sidestep or two. If it's clean, I'm usually good. It's cool when JR comes with me but when he doesn't, I know anything can happen. I haven't told him. Haven't told anyone. Not even Michael. Is it my imagination or do the people I pass in the hallway at Larva know, too? Maybe being a skeevy sex fiend is part of Bruce's bad reputation. Maybe it's something they just deal with, that they just ignore because Bruce has the knack of bringing in such good acts. It's easy to turn a deaf ear or a blind eye if the dollar signs add up enough.

Would Bruce try this shit with a guy? Maybe. Something tells me it's part of Bruce's DNA, the bizarreness, pushing the envelope. What's that TS Eliot line Michael is constantly quoting? "Force the moment to its crisis?" That's Bruce to a T. Maybe he's one of those people who push and push just to see how far they can get. Like Marty, only not as mean-spirited.

Why do I seem to attract these wack-a-doos? Could be the music business that attracts them. What does that say about me, then? Guess I'm a wack-a-doo, too.

My snare drum hasn't left my side lately. I carry it like some chicks carry a purse. Bruce jokes with me about it. Says it's like a shield or armor. He's afraid I'll take a swipe at someone with it on the subway if they get "fresh." (Now there's a real Edie word. It surprised me to hear it coming out of Bruce's mouth.

I have no clue how old he is—older than me but younger than Edie—but I didn't think he'd ever say such an Old-World word.)

Only Bruce is wrong about that. I'd never hit anyone with my snare, no matter how tempting. Not even Bruce. I carried it with me to all of our studio sessions at Electric Lady and I usually take it with me to Larva meetings in case we pop into their studio to do some overdubs. You never know.

I *love* this snare. I think I've written about it here before but I'll write about it again. That's how great it is. It took me my whole life to find a snare drum that was perfect, that didn't have to be tuned every five seconds, that didn't sound too sharp and tinny. And I found it in my Pearl. (And yes, I even named her "Pearl.") Pearl and I have been everywhere together, through all kinds of crap, and we're still ticking. She's got a chrome-plated shell and is a 14-incher with a brass nameplate, stainless steel tension rods and stop-locks that help her stay in tune no matter how much you beat the crap out of her. If Pearl were a man, she would be a perfect partner. 14 inches and all.

Why am I waxing philosophical about a drum? To avoid talking about Bruce? I know he has an amazing track record but I also know that the buzz in the biz is that he's a has-been. I usually don't pay much attention to idle chatter like that but my career is on the line. And even if Bruce is a once-was, maybe I'm his ticket back to the A-list. This is why I've been forgiving his transgressions and his creepy passes, which, luckily, I've been able to avoid for the most part. But for how long?

Just yesterday, Bruce handed me a big check. So big, I didn't have enough money in my poor excuse for a savings account to cash it. 10 G's. I had to deposit it and wait till it cleared to take some of it out. At first, I tried to give it back to Bruce. I tried to tell him to wait. But he said, "Wait for what?"

"It's Friday the 13th," I told him. "It's a bad luck day. I don't want to jinx it."

"Your luck has just changed," Bruce responded.

I'd really like to believe him. I keep thinking about what my brother said, that I'm just like my mother, that I'm negativity personified. But the way I see it, I'm just a realist with the facts.

Ellis

I tried to convince her not to leave yet, to wait, but I couldn't. When Cara gets an idea in her head, she's hell-bent. Stubborn. Like most women. Gets this certain look on her face where her jaw is square and set, and there's nothing you can do to get her to change her mind. About anything.

When I told her not to quit yet, Cara said something like, "What's the matter, you don't believe in me either?"

Of course, that wasn't the case. Heck, I've never even heard her play or watched her perform but something tells me that she's outstanding. Anything she does is wholehearted, even setting up a filing system. You should have seen the piles of junk around Accounting before Cara got here. In less than six months, she had us all goose-stepping, had a place for everything and everything in its place. Even Ira seemed happier. Not only did he work harder but he smiled more. I think it all had to do with her.

Cara officially gave her two week's notice today. She didn't have to tell me. She could have just left it up to the temp agency, Payton People, to tell me, since she technically isn't a *New York Post* employee. But Cara always did feel like a full-fledged employee, from Day One. I would have offered to buy out her contract and hired her full-time if I thought she would take it. But I knew she would have seen it as an insult instead of as a compliment. 'What? You don't think I can make it as a musician?' Cara would have snapped. So, I never offered her the job. And to tell you the truth, I couldn't imagine an employee working any harder than Cara did. Plus, having her here as a temp saved us money. No health care benefits, no profit sharing. And I'm a dollars and cents kind of guy. She would be the first to tell you that.

After she told me she was leaving, Cara and I shook hands, all proper and businesslike, but I pulled her in for a hug. Unprofessional, I know, but I've started feeling very close to her. Like a daughter or favorite niece. We smiled at each other when we pulled apart. I told Cara that I knew she was going to make it. She smiled even wider then fumbled in her desk drawer. "For your daughter. Sheila, is it?" She pushed something into my hand.

I thanked her and took it. A cassette tape. "My demo tape," she explained. "It's still pretty raw, just rough tracks. But I think she'll like it. Maybe you, too. Even though it's not Paul Anka."

I laughed. That was a running joke with us.

It's against "company policy," but I'd like to have a little sendoff for Cara. "No parties for non-employees," the rules and regs clearly state. But I'd be happy to have something for her, take the money out of my own pocket. Usually Cara's the one who plans things like that but I'm on my own here. Maybe Ira will help me. Lunch at that Italian place they like. Or Mrs. Fields' Cookies. We'll see.

So, July 27th. That's Cara's last day. I'm really going to miss her.

7/21/79

Nothing sucks worse than a Friday afternoon in an office in the middle of July. It's so dead around here. But hey, if they're willing to pay $8 an hour for me to sit twiddling my thumbs, so be it. I just have to try and keep my forehead from hitting the Seletric's keyboard when I nod off. Lucky for me Ellis doesn't care what I do when there isn't much work. He just cares that I look busy. Scribbling in my notebook looks a lot like pouring over a ledger, so I'm good.

I've been working on the lyrics to a song. It's called "Rekindle" and it's about Michael. Believe it or not, it's the first song I've ever written about him and we've been together a while. It's not that I don't care about him, it's just that I've always hated sappy love songs. (Mind you, Paul McCartney made a ton of money singing his "Silly Love Songs.") But this isn't gushy or hearts and flowers shlock. It's pissed off, if anything. An anti-love song, maybe. Pissed off, not at your lover, but at being in love because love is such a pain in the ass. Think 10cc's "I'm Not in Love," only different, from the girl's POV.

Even when you say you're going to take it slow and take everything in stride, you can't. It's impossible. Who doesn't want to curl up and sleep next to a warm body? Whose heart doesn't do a little leap when he calls? He wants you! He thinks of you! He missed you! Oh, please... Give me a freaking break.

This is what I have so far:

I don't want to be in love.
I don't want you to call.

I don't want to be anyone's turtledove.
I don't want to feel like this at all
Because when you fly, you fall.

We've been down this road before,
The best journey of my life,
But I thought I closed that door
Only to find you back tonight.
Now that ain't right.

Chorus:
Rekindle, the flames burn hot.
Rekindle, I know what I've got.
Rekindle, a moth to a flame.
Rekindle, too cool to even say your name.

That's it for now. Not sure about the turtledove line. But it doesn't suck too bad, does it? It's kind of unique. Maybe not. Maybe it's the same. Love songs are all the same when it comes down to it.

I've got to go for a walk, to get out of this bullpen of desks. Ellis is out at one of his marathon liquid lunches and Ira is on vacation. In Florida. Who in his right mind goes to Florida in July? I think Ira's scoping out places to open his fantasy card store. Says he has a nice little nest egg saved up and he's itching to make a change. Ira was really sweet when I told him I was leaving. "I'm pulling for you, darling," he said, and kissed me on the forehead.

1:11 pm
So, here I am, sitting on the rotting pier near the *Peking*. The Fulton Fish Market stinks to high heaven. My feet are dangling above the East River as I write, tourists and seagulls all around. It's so hot and humid that beads of sweat are rolling down my neck. The big, ugly, blonde brick of the *Post* building is over my right shoulder, beckoning its silent promises of air-conditioning. It sucks out here, but still, it's better than being cooped up inside.

I feel kind of exhilarated. Almost happy. Which is a lot to say for me. Everything's going good. Too good. Now, if only I could get Bruce to stop trying to feed me 'ludes, it would be perfect. Almost perfect. But I bet I'd find myself something else to worry about even if Bruce behaved.

Quaaludes. Man, they're almost as common as herpes these days. Lucky Marty is privy to both, another reason to avoid him like the plague. Marty likes to feed Beryl 'ludes whenever he can. Guys seem to love feeding 'ludes to girls—it's supposed to make us horny. But if you have to rely on a little white pill to make a chick want to be with you, what does that say about you? I only took a pill like that once, a tumenol, and it just made me want to go to *shluffy*, not get busy. Much to the dismay of the guy I was hanging out with.

But Bruce and 'ludes…he seems to have added them to his cocaine repertoire. When coke makes him too hyper and he needs to come down quick, I've seen him pop a downer or two. Seconal, Percocet, Valium, Darvon, Darvocet. His top desk draw is a veritable pharmacy. A rainbow of pink, red, blue, and white pills.

I constantly tell Bruce that he's got to be careful with that shit. He's not a small guy and a human heart can only take so much. But he just shrugs it off. "Big guy, big heart, big tolerance," he's been known to croak, adding, "Besides, if it's good enough for Hendrix, it's good enough for me." Then Bruce will generally go off on a tangent about how he can handle the shit and how Jimi was a skinny fag bastard who couldn't take it. That's when I tell him to can it because nobody talks trash about my Jimi. Not even Bruce.

I should be getting back to the salt mines but I don't want to. There's such a nice breeze coming from Brooklyn Heights. It almost drowns out the stench from the fish market. Ellis wouldn't care, especially now, with me leaving in a few days. Maybe I'll just sit here and try to finish that song. Just a few more minutes.

2:15 pm

Well, the song didn't want to come out. There were too many other things in the way, I guess. It's too quiet here back at my desk. I'm still the only person in Accounting. Ellis is due to come back any minute—or not. He's been out since noon. He always loses track of time when he's had a few. But then, who doesn't?

In a sick way, I'm going to miss this place. I know how much I complain about it but the people are pretty nice in their own freaky way. I'm totally in love with Ira, that's no secret. He helped keep me semi-sane here. Ellis isn't a bad guy, even with all of his lecturing and dispensing of unasked-for fatherly wisdom. He was a good boss, very laid back, even during crunch time. Always made sure we took breaks and brought in a box of Dunkin' Munchkins every so often. And even Bing is good for a laugh, if anything. I'll miss her mangling the English language and bringing in chicken feet and jellied blowfish for us to snack on.

Maybe I'll bake something and bring it in on my last day. A nice bundt cake. Yeah, I bake. I know it sounds very Susie Homemaker but I like it. I find baking very relaxing. Even in July. Who would willingly put on their oven in the middle of the summer? I knew a guy who broke up with a girl because she decided to bake meatloaf on the hottest day of the year. And my friend Mike broke up with a chick because she didn't like Johnny Cash. "I mean, Carol, who doesn't like Johnny Cash?" he asked me. I couldn't think of anybody but her.

I wasted as much time as I could near the *Peking*, with no words coming. Then I wasted another few minutes down by the loading docks. Tom looked happy to see me. I hadn't stopped by for a while. I didn't see the point, really. He seemed shocked when I mentioned in passing that I would be leaving the *Post* next week, like I was breaking up with him, or something. Then Tom asked for my number so we could keep in touch. I told him I didn't think it was a good idea. He didn't get it. "What about us?" he asked.

"Tom," I said as nicely as I could, "there is no 'us.'"

"But...but..." he kept stammering.

Then the conveyer belt slammed into life just as the foreman shouted, "Get your belts on!" All of the truck drivers jumped to their stations, Tom along with them. Some drivers wore their heavy-lifting belts, others didn't because it was just too damn hot. It got loud and frantic in the space of a minute.

I didn't know what else to say to Tom, so I just started walking away. "Do me a favor, just buy my album." I told him. I swear, I meant it half joking.

"Buy it?" Tom shouted back. "I thought I'd at least get a free copy!"

Then he went back to grabbing those piles of newspapers and throwing them into the back of his panel truck. He glared at me like he could have killed me. Ah, well, one of many.

JR

It's almost August. Bruce set the wheels in motion and set up gigs for us right before Labor Day. Supposedly. While I've signed contracts, I haven't seen anything about these gigs in writing. I've asked Bruce for an itinerary a few times and he hasn't come up with anything concrete. Fern has taken over as my manager, making phone calls and bugging Trini, Bruce's assistant. Fern suggested it, said it would better for me just to concentrate on the music while she would be "a bitch on steroids." And it's true. Most of the time Fern can be sweet as pumpkin pie but just cross her and she turns into Helen Wheels.

Fern has been really cool about this whole thing. We have a little money put aside, not much, but it will keep us afloat for a few months. Whenever I waffle and doubt that the tour will ever happen, she tells me that I have to go for it, give it a shot. "Besides, your father's construction business isn't going anywhere," she says, insinuating that if I have to, if things fall through with Cara's band, I can go back to knocking down drywall and putting up sheetrock. I couldn't imagine anything worse, though.

The last few days at work with my old man, I've been dropping hints about taking some time off. But my dad isn't big on taking hints. He's a very cut and dry kind of guy, tells it like it is, shoots straight from the hip. "You walking out on me?" he asked after I was side-stepping telling him about the upcoming tour.

"Not exactly," I half-admitted.

"Either you are or you're not," Big Will said.

"I signed a small record deal," I told him. "There's a tour coming up and…"

"So, you are."

"Yeah. You mad?"

"You know how busy it gets after the summer," Dad said. "But we'll manage. Always do." Then he added, "How long?"

"A month. Maybe more. I leave a couple of weeks before Labor Day."

There was a sigh. He rubbed his grizzled face. "I hate having to count on your brother," he admitted. "You're a lot more dependable than him, a much better worker. Maybe I'll have to get a Polish guy, one of those day laborers who hangs out near Green-Wood. We'll see."

"You sure you're okay with this?" I asked him.

"Do I have a choice?"

"I guess not," I told him.

"Besides, it's time."

"Time for what, Dad?"

"For you to shit or get off the pot." Then my father did something he hadn't done in a really long time. Since I was a kid. He hugged me. "You gotta give this thing a shot," he said. "Or else, you might end up like me."

"That's not such a bad thing," I admitted.

"For me, maybe. But not for you. There's a lot more in store for you. I know it."

And from my father, that was a fucking rave.

7/28/79

My last day at the *Post* was bittersweet. No cake or party since I'm not
technically an employee. (Rubin's rules.) Bing gave me a Chinese good luck coin
but for all I know, it put a hex on me. But the guys took me to Forlini's, Ira's and
my special place. Ellis and Ira did. Ira cried, Ellis didn't. They gave me $50 to
treat myself to something nice, Ellis said. I thought it was a sweet touch. Chaste
hugs all around, manicotti and Italian cheesecake. Then I was off to rehearsal.

Bruce has us rehearsing four sometimes five days a week now. He moved the
tour up to before the album release to create a buzz, he said, to test the waters.
Our first gig is out in California. San Diego, to be exact. It's on August 26th, a
little more than a week before Labor Day. That's like four weeks away. "Why
San Diego?" Mongo asked him. "Why not New York?"

"So you can hang onto your safe, boring little jobs?" Bruce shot back. "So
you can have a safety net? Well, guess what, life doesn't come with a safety net.
Besides, I know what I'm doing. Trust me."

Whenever somebody says "Trust me" my first instinct is not to trust them.
But I've turned over a new leaf. I've become more positive. At least I've tried to.
Some days are better than others. I'm a work in progress, I guess. We all are.

It's strange but when I'm crazy-busy like this, I find myself pining away for
a few free minutes to write in this journal. At first, I think I'm just going to jot
down some thoughts so I don't forget them, but before I know it, I'm writing so
furiously that I can barely read my own handwriting. Then my hand's aching
and when I look back, I've written pages and pages. Journaling is so bizarre

Sometimes I feel like I haven't fully experienced something unless it's documented in this notebook.

I've barely had time for anything but music these past few weeks. Not even meeting with that grad student. Just a few stolen moments with Michael. Haven't even seen Edie. But I have called her. When she gets over the initial pissed off comments like, "You never visit. You never call," she yammers on about things I couldn't care less about. Really, what does Aunt Sophie's blood pressure have to do with me? And who cares that Cousin Sol has the gout? Usually, I just "Yes" and "Uh-huh" her to death, half-listening, while I'm changing a drum skin or eating Arthur Treacher's in front of the TV.

This thing is the real deal! Besides the test tour up the coast of California from San Diego to LA, there's talk of something at the Whisky a Go-Go around Labor Day if the gigs at college venues along the way go well. I can't tell if I'm more nervous or excited. Probably the combo platter.

What if I fall flat on my face? What if nobody comes to these gigs? What if I crash and burn? What if I don't really have what it takes to make it? Well, it's time to shit or get off the pot, like JR's dad Mr. Clapowitz says.

Bruce is going all out with this thing. He's hired a bona-fide Broadway costumer who's worked on shows like *The Best Little Whorehouse in Texas, Zoot Suit* and *Sweeney Todd*. Not that I want to look like a slut or a demon barber. Kent has come up with some amazing costumes. Fanciful, wild, yet functional. It's important that I can move my arms and legs freely behind the drum kit. Plus I hate having something on my head. I bop around so much, hats and earpieces always fall off or slip down over my eyes. Not good. Kent has even come up with some impressive outfits for JR and Mongo. Oh, and for Adam, our new guitarist. Adam seems pretty cool. He gets the job done without all of the drinking and drama that went with Roy.

I keep asking Bruce how much this is costing and he keeps telling me not to worry. "That's my job," he says, patting me on the ass.

"What's your job? Worrying or keeping track of money?" I ask, and he tells me, "Both."

I couldn't believe it when I was holding the album sleeve in my hands. It was only a mockup and it still needed to be color corrected. Plus they misspelled Mongo's name on it and there were a few other typos. But to see it, to hold it, literally took my breath away. Tears filled my eyes.

It was Bruce's brainstorm. He said from the start that I was the female Elvis, so one night when Bruce was on a coke binge, he lifted his head in mid-snort and started scribbling on the back of a deli bill. He kept going, "Oh..oh...This is brilliant...genius."

To me, it just looked like a bunch of chicken scratch, but a few days later, I was cradling a cardboard square. It was filled with a huge black and white photo of me sweating and singing behind the kit—I looked like a wild, uncaged animal. Going down the left-hand side of the album was the word "CARA" and across the bottom was the word "FUNK." In bright, bold capital letters. Just like that early Elvis Presley album, except the lettering was all pink instead of pink and green. The back of the album said "The Cara Funk Explosion" in smaller letters with "Mask" splashed across the middle.

"What do you think?" Bruce asked, beaming like a kid who'd just brought home a kick-ass report card.

"I think I love you," I told him.

"We still need to retouch the photo, maybe take a new one, but the general concept's there," Bruce said. "But I ask you, how could anyone pass this up in a record store?"

I hoped to God he was right.

Edith

I haven't been feeling so good. Maybe it's this *facocta* heat. That's what my daughter Aileen keeps telling me. But I think it's more than that. "If you're so worried, call Dr. Lewy," she says. But I'm sick and tired of doctors. I'm sick and tired of pills and pain and this crappy walker. I'm sick and tired of everything.

I'm a wreck. I look terrible. I'm all bloated. My ankles are like balloons. The water pills don't seem to work anymore. "I'll put you in the hospital for some tests," Dr. Lewy says. "Just a couple of days. It'll make it easier on you to get them all done at once. Plus it's air-conditioned." But I don't want to go to the hospital. I have a feeling if I go in, I won't get out. Alive, that is.

Of course, I don't tell Carol this. Oh, she asks how I'm doing, but I don't tell her much. I'll usually just sigh and say, "The same." You know me, I'm not one to *kvetch* or complain." And who listens anyway? Tell me, who really cares?

I've had this awful pain in my chest that comes and goes. Sometimes it's so strong, I have to hobble over to a chair, sit down and breathe hard until it passes. I hate to use them but I've been popping those nitroglycerine tablets like Tic Tacs. I put them under my tongue, try to breathe deep, hold on and wait until they kick in. Sometimes I'm afraid I won't pull through, that they won't work. But they always do. The pain slips away like water and I go back to normal.

But really, what difference would it make. If I didn't pull through who would really mourn me? I bet my kids would be relieved. Especially Aileen. Carol would be the hardest hit, I think, even though she would be a little bit relieved, too. But I think Irving, that *putz*, would be excited about the few *schekels* I'd leave behind. Not that I have much. Enough to bury myself and a little to spare. But still, he'd be like one of those disgusting neighbors in *Zorba the Greek*, ripping the curtains from around that poor woman's bed before she was even dead. That's my Irving.

But Carol....my Carol is just the opposite. She'll blame it on herself somehow. She always manages to do that. Either she didn't look after me right or she didn't see the warning signs or she didn't visit me enough. Carol will blame herself while the other two will blame everyone and everything else under the sun. When the truth of the matter is, it's nobody's fault. None of it. Life or death or what happens to you in between.

What is it with Carol and guilt? You'd think she was Catholic with all of this guilt. I don't really know what my youngest daughter is religion-wise. She's keeping company with that *goy*. She's not a practicing Jew but she's not a bad person. In fact, Carol is a very good person. Did I ever tell her this? Well, if I did, I bet I didn't say it enough. Story of my life. Never enough.

I can't forget something Carol told me when she was just a teenager. She was quoting some big philosopher. Freddie something. She said, "I could only believe in a god who dances." I punished her for saying that. I told her it was sacrilegious. I even made her go to her room. Then all I could hear was her banging away on her books with pencils—she didn't even have a drum set yet. Maybe I shouldn't have done that. Punished her, I mean. When I think about it, a G-d who dances isn't such a bad thing.

Well, whatever G-d has in store for me, I'm ready to go. I've heard Christians say they're looking forward to "going home to Jesus." Jews never say anything like that. And I'm not only talking about the fact that we don't believe in Jesus. I've never met a Jew who said they were looking forward to dying. Not even the ones who are in pain or terminally ill. Most Jews complain so much about everything anyway that dying is nothing with nothing. For some, it's a relief, almost.

But the truth of it is, I'm scared of dying. What is it? The end of the road? Blackness? Jews aren't big on reincarnation so there's no light at the end of the tunnel for us either. So, we lose either way.

As for me, I think I've been in pain every single day of my life since I had that accident at 19 at the *schmata* shop. It was downhill from there. How horrible is your life that the best you ever were was when you were a teenager. And here I am, not even 60 years old, and feeling all washed up. Sick of it all.

But I'm still scared. I don't want to die alone but I probably will. Another thing I remember Carol used to say. She even put it down as her "motto" in the Sheepshead Bay High School yearbook. It was a play on something Conrad somebody said in one of his books. I yelled at her for that one, too. "You want people to remember you for *that*?" I asked her when I read it.

The quote? "We die as we dream—alone."

8/3/79

I saw Edie last night. She looked like hell. Barely ate the pizza I brought. From Roma, her favorite. "It's too hot to eat," she said. But not too hot to smoke, I guess, because she lit one Chesterfield with another. Until I pointed it out to her. When I heard the Mister Softee song on Coyle, I went outside to get her a pineapple sundae, also her favorite. "Why is everything food with you?" Edie said. "What are you? Some kind of Eye-talian?"

I shrugged in response while Edie sat there smoking and let the vanilla custard melt into a puddle in the waxed paper cup. It was disgusting. A waste. But I refused to eat it. So did she.

I was shocked that Edie noticed my haircut, though. Or "styling" as Matisse, my guy from Vidal Sassoon, insisted on calling it. It took more than an hour, with all of these painstakingly tiny little snips. I must admit, it looks pretty good, especially with all of that "product" in it. I look like a punk-rock porcupine. "Did you go to Cut N'Curl?" Edie asked.

"Something like that," I told her.

"Hmmm. Your hair doesn't look as bad as it usually does," she huffed.

"Thanks," I said. I think my mother meant it as a compliment. Really.

Edie had one of her episodes while I was there. Before I saw it with my own eyes, I thought she was putting it on. But it was terrible. Angina is such a stupid-sounding ailment, sounds too close to "vagina" to be taken seriously, right? But to see it, to see Edie's face go all white and stiff, to hear her breath get all ragged…that's a totally different thing.

At least the tablets were close by. Edie keeps them in that little pouch my Aunt Sarah sewed for her walker. It ties onto the bars and is actually pretty neat. I told Sarah she should patent it but she just shrugged it off. "You could make a mint," I told her. But Sarah just waves me away whenever I say it. That's the problems with the Schwartz women: they don't think big.

Anyhow, Edie keeps everything in that pouch: money, sucking candies fuzzy with age, half-used tissues, her Pocket Word Search, everything. I saw that look on her face and I dug into the pouch for the pills. When I handed her one, she tried to wedge it underneath her tongue, then cursed. "I swallowed it," she cried. (They don't work if you swallow them.) So, I handed her another. In less than a minute, I could tell she was feeling better. Her breathing got more regular and she stopped sweating, or *shvitzing* as Edie would say.

"Ma, I can't leave you like this," I said. "I go on tour in less than three weeks."

"Tour, schmour. I'll believe it when I see it," she told me. No big surprise there. Edie still manages to be bitchy even with severe chest pain. "Besides, what are you going to do for me? What can anybody do for me?"

"Nothing, but…"

"So, if I die and you're on the road, I'll still be dead when you get back."

"Don't talk like that, Ma."

"Why? Somebody has to. I'm sick and tired of your brother and sister tiptoeing around this thing like it's not happening. It's happening!"

We pretty much went back and forth like that. A tennis match of words. 15-Love. Advantage: Edith Finkelstein. *Status quo* with Edie. Which one's Billie Jean King and which one's Bobby Riggs is anyone's guess.

I'm amazed that Michael hasn't swooped in for the kill—meaning, that he hasn't tried to get super-close to me being that he's done with classes for the summer and has all of this free time. If anything, he's swooped out, if that's an expression. He's gone for a couple of weeks—to a writer's camp up in Woodstock. "A writer's retreat," he would correct me. "A camp is for kids." But I say it just to annoy him, which it does. Michael tells me that Juneapple Press is even talking about publishing a chapbook of his poetry. I can't say I'm not happy for him but I do miss him.

Things are okay with JR, too. I thought they would still be uncomfortable but he doesn't seem to mind being second banana to me. I try to keep it all equal. I don't lord the contract over him or the fact that I'm fronting the group now. He's fine with it, seems to be happy that his music is getting out there and that he's still getting a chance.

Danny is the 800-pound gorilla in the room that nobody talks about but is always there, silently eating bananas in the corner. Mongo refuses to even say Danny's name, superstitious PR that he is. And everybody's all but forgotten about Roy once Adam stepped into the band. It's been seamless. Better than seamless since Adam is a hell of a lot better guitarist.

And Bruce…Bruce is being an asshole.

JR is taking a leave of absence from his dad's construction company and Mongo is using up vacation days to go on the West Coast tour. If it works out (which it better), Mongo says he'll just call from the road and give notice. I've been a little buggy without having to go into work. As much as I bitched about it, I think I need structure to my days. I mean, how much can a girl rehearse?

I've been trying to write new songs. And finish old ones like "Rekindle." But it's like the damn thing is haunting me, taunting me. It's still not finished. Maybe I'll take it up with Fern. She's always saying how she wants to collaborate more with me. Oh, Fern is preggers again. Not the best timing, with her husband taking a break from work to chase the rock-star dream. But babies seem to happen at the worst times. Like I did. Not that it's their fault. Or that it was mine. But sometimes I still think that Edie holds a grudge and it's been almost 30 years.

I'm getting tired of writing in this thing so I might put it down for a while. Shoveling the same shit over and over again, and my arm's getting tired.

Aileen George
Cara's Sister

How did you find me? I know my number's listed, but still. If my mother wants to talk to you, that's her business. Let's get one thing straight: I *am* not my mother. I don't want to say anything about my sister. She's DIME. Do you know what that stands for? Dead in my eyes. Got it?

Carol's always been selfish, always been spoiled. Did she ever tell you about the time she left that suitcase in the middle of the floor and I tripped right over it? Broke my jaw. That will ruin anyone's summer. Especially when you're 19. The first thing I thought of was my mother and what happened to her at that age. I'm sure you know the story about my mother. I'll be damned if I end up like her. Bitter. Broken. Settling for less because you think you're not worth more.

But I told you I wasn't going to talk about Carol. Or my family. Understand?

If she thinks the world is standing there holding its breath, waiting for her to come out with a record then she's got another thing coming. She'll see. It's always the same. Carol's a loser. Why can't she just get a nice job, settle down and be happy? Like me? Oh, I know she probably thinks my life is a living hell, but guess what, I've got a nice townhouse in Georgetown—don't call it "Canarsie"—a decent husband who's a good provider and two nice kids. That's something, isn't it? Don't answer that. I'm not talking to you anymore. Not about Carol. Not about me. Not about anything.

This interview is over.

8/11/79

Dear Diary,

I can't believe it's so long since I've written! I've been so busy! Things are moving so fast! I think I might actually make it! Thanks for always sticking by me, Diary! I love you!

What bullshit. I can't believe I've been writing in this stupid book for so fucking long. I don't know why. Michael hasn't even asked about it. Besides him, nobody knows it exists. Nobody cares about it but me. And I've written things in here that no one would know about if I didn't write about them. So, why bother? I don't know.

Even when I'm not writing in this journal, I'm thinking about writing in it. Even when I don't have much to say. Bizarre. It's like having a jones for something or someone.

Although my days are pretty full, time seems to be crawling by. I'm dying to get out west but in another way, I dread it. What if I can't deliver? What if nobody comes to the gigs? What if we suck? What if we suck because of me?

Edith doesn't sound great and she looked like crap the last time I saw her. Not to mention the angina episode I saw firsthand. I feel bad leaving her, even though there's still my brother and sister to look in on her. Aileen's been very standoffish. Even more than usual.

Unfortunately Bruce hasn't been. That dude seems to be everywhere. Plus he's slimy like a snake. I have to keep dodging his hands. But it's nothing I haven't done before. I got used to dodging Marty's grabbiness and got pretty good at avoiding Howie's pathetic whack-off routine. I try to tell myself that Bruce is just an extension of those guys. Same side of different coins. Without Marty's abusive personality and nasty comments, without Howie's sad eyes. Bruce, I can handle. I've dealt with his kind before.

But with Bruce, there are a lot more drugs around than Marty ever had. And Marty's glove compartment was a like a Rexall. Maybe that's why I'm feeling so shitty. Even a line or two makes me feel like crap the next day. But there's that amazing sensation you get the first millisecond you take a snort or a toke...utter release...euphoria. But just for a minute. Then it's gone. Gone, baby, gone.

Irving Finkelstein
Cara's Brother

Is this thing rolling? Okay. I guess I'll just let you ask the questions. I'll have a cup of coffee. Dark and sweet…the way I take my women. Just kidding, I've never… Not that I wouldn't. If the opportunity presented itself, I mean… But don't tell my wife. Robin wouldn't get the joke.

Where should I start? At the beginning, I guess. I don't really remember when my sister started drumming. I'm the oldest of the three of us. Aileen's the typical troubled middle child. She's always been a pain in the ass, as far back as I can remember. She's always had a chip on her shoulder.

Carol…or should I call her Cara? Okay. Cara's the ignored youngest kid. By the time she came along, my folks' marriage was already on the skids. What do I remember most about my childhood? Screaming and yelling sticks in my head most. As a little kid, Cara was scrawny and always sick. Like I said, I don't really remember the first time she picked up the drumsticks. If she says she was 10 then I was almost 15. And by then I was out of there as much as humanly possible. Sorry. I don't remember too much.

I married Robin when I was barely 21. It seems like I was always married to Robin. Damn, I've been with her almost half of my life. The kids came soon after we tied the knot, one after the other. All boys. Robin didn't want Jewish-sounding names. She was afraid they'd hold the kids back in life. Their bad genes would hold them back enough, I told her, but she didn't think that was very funny. She doesn't have much of a sense of humor, my Robin.

Carol, she's a fantastic aunt. Maybe because she's a big kid herself. I don't think she ever really grew up, know what I mean? Maybe it's because my parents split when she was so little. She wasn't even five. Maybe she felt like she was robbed. But my folks were better apart than they were together. It was a lot quieter after Jake moved out. Edie had one less person to rag on. But my mom would still scream and yell at us kids like a banshee. Still does. Just like she did to my dad. She screamed at him till the day he died. Late with child support. The stinking kids need new shoes. You name it, she yelled about it. Sometimes I think he got cancer on purpose just so he could get away from Edie and get some peace.

I remember once when my folks were still together, my father slipped in the shower. He fell so hard he cracked his head on the soap dish. You know, the ceramic kind that's attached to the wall. There he was, lying at the bottom of the tub, unconscious, and my mother's standing over him yelling that he was getting blood all over the place. Not only that, but he broke the soap dish, too. I can still hear her yelling, "You're always making a mess for me to clean up, Jakie!" Man, you just can't make this stuff up.

It was worse on Carol than it was on me and Aileen because Carol was there longer. Me and A got out of the house as fast as we could. We got married. Not to each other. To Robin and Stan. While Carol, being just a kid, was stuck there. For years, it was a one-on-one cage match between Carol and Edie, and Edie always came out on top. She was bigger, stronger and meaner. My mother could dress you down, make you feel worthless and have you in tears in the space of five minutes. Then she'd yell at you for being hysterical, which made you even more hysterical. If Carol didn't have the drums, something to bang on, I don't know what she would have done. Bashed Edie's head in, maybe.

Like I said, my baby sister is really good to my boys. Plays with them, listens to them. Gets them the coolest presents, and for no reason at all. Hot Wheels. *Star Wars* action figures. Space Legos. She gets kids. They love her to pieces and she loves them back. You can just see it.

Hey, what is this for again? And you really think she has something? You really think she's going to make it? The truth? Hmmm. We'll just have to see about that, won't we? To me, Carol's just my little sister. Nothing special. Just a kid. Even though she's pushing 30. But don't tell anybody. I don't know if she wants anyone to know her real age. Between you and me, Carol's a little bit vain. But not because she's stuck up. Because she was so damned fugly when she was a kid. Buck teeth, a real toothpick, no chest, fuzzy hair that went all over the place. And a nose that she never quite grew into. A real mess.

Do I ever think Carol will be a superstar? You mean, like Mick Jagger or Rodney Dangerfield? No. Definitely not.

Hey, do you mind if I get some cheesecake?

8/15/79

They still haven't found that Etan Patz kid. It's like he disappeared off the face of the earth. Sometimes I wake up in the middle of the night and think about him. It's really fucked up, I know. But I get up to pee and I'm lying awake and Etan's crooked, trusting smile pops into my head. His ragamuffin clothes. His honest blue eyes. His scruffy, do-it-yourself haircut. I lie in my bed wondering if he's scared or hungry or safe. Or dead. Where and how he disappeared. Sometimes I imagine running into him on the street, taking him by the hand and bringing him to the 61st Precinct on Coney Island Avenue, but maybe buying him a Carvel cone on the way. Or anything else he wanted. Isn't that weird?

I've been having a rough time sleeping. A million things go rushing through my pointy, little head. Not all bad. Just lots of stuff.

Like:
- I hope I don't miss my flight next week.
- I hope my mother doesn't get sick.
- Should I take my sharkskin jacket or will it be too hot for it in California?
- How much money should I bring?
- In cash or traveler's checks?
- What if we don't sell one ticket?
- What if Bruce shows up at my room in the middle of the night?
- What if Michael's cheating on me with some super-sensitive, super-cute writer chick in Woodstock?
- Do I care?

- Shit yeah, I care.
- What if Ginger Baker shows up in LA, like Bruce says he will.
- What if he doesn't?
- Should I wax my legs?
- Will it hurt?
- Damn right it'll hurt.
- Why wax your legs if you're not going to sleep with anyone.
- What if I sleep with someone?
- Are Michael and me monogamous, or what?
- What does 'or what' mean?
- What does anything mean?
- My heart is beating like my bass drum. Am I having a heart attack?
- I have to pee again. Maybe I have a UTI.
- Maybe if I rub one out I can get back to sleep.
- Maybe if I rub one out it'll make me more agitated.
- Should I smoke a joint to relax?
- If I do, I'll get the munchies. I wonder if I have any Bugles or Fiddle Faddle left in the cabinet.
- No, I finished them last night and swore I wouldn't buy that crap again.
- What if Bruce tries to sneak pot or coke or 'ludes on the plane?
- The plane? I've never flown before. What if I freak out?
- Should I take a Benadryl so I fall out during the flight?
- What if the Benadryl makes me too dopey afterwards? Or hyper? I've never taken it before. Nix the Benadryl.
- What if I get plane-sick?
- Why can't I finish that "Rekindle" song? Maybe I should get up and try to work on it some more.
- I should get up anyway. I heard Beverly Sills say on *The Mike Douglas Show* that when you have insomnia, you shouldn't lay in bed and worry. Instead, you should get up and sit in a chair and think of it as your "Worry Chair." Bev's a notorious insomniac. It sounds crazy but it makes sense.
- Could a folding chair be a "Worry Chair?"
- Where did I put the folding chair?
- I wonder what's on TV at 3:18 am. *I Love Lucy* reruns?
- There's nothing good on TV at 3:18 in the morning.
- I wonder if Michael's awake. Anyway, there's no phone in his room. That's what he told me, at least.
- I shouldn't have had that ice cream sandwich at midnight. The sugar's making me wired.
- It's not the sugar. I'm just wired.
- Maybe it's the Chinese food that's making me hyper. That shit is filled with MSG. Damned Chinese bastards.
- It's not the Chinese food.
- Maybe I should have a shot of Amaretto.

- Don't I have half a joint stashed somewhere? But where?
- I don't think I should check my snare with the rest of my drums when I fly. It's too delicate.
- Yeah, but do I want to be lugging a drum onto a plane?
- I hope I have a window seat.
- Do I really want to look out the window? It might be freaky. And if I have to pee, I'll have to bug two people to get up.
- I seem to be obsessed with pee lately. Maybe I have a fetish.
- Also, if I sit in the window seat, that means Bruce will be in the middle and he'll have me cornered. Who knows what he might try under one of those little airplane blankets.
- I should be okay if Mongo or JR sits next to Bruce. But what if he got them seats somewhere else?
- Don't worry about things before they happen, Cara. You'll put yourself into an early grave.
- Breathe deeply and slowly. Just relax. Breathe. In. And out. In. And out.
- Maybe I should try some lavender oil on my forehead. Dennie said it works wonders for her. Sweet of her to give me some.
- God, I miss Dennie. I wonder if she's still awake.
- It's too late to call anybody. After 4 am now. Just suffer through it alone. Insomnia's like menstrual cramps. Nobody can help you. And no one else gives a shit.
- But I'll be exhausted in the morning. I have to get up by 10 to get to rehearsal at JR's by 11. Maybe I can sleep afterwards.
- No, I can't take a nap after rehearsal. I have to pop into Larva then. Bruce wants me to sign off on the posters.
- Posters! I never imagined I would ever be on a poster. Front and center. All decked out in this black velvet cape, peaked sleeves and all. Skintight jeans. Black leather boots laced thigh-high. "Like a slutty version of the Evil Queen from *Snow White*," Bruce said. "Guys dig that," Bruce said.
- God…Bruce. I'm fucked.
- I can hold my own with Bruce. I've had my share of creeps clawing at me. But he's my manager. I have to travel with him, for God's sake.
- It'll get better with Bruce. It has to.
- Why does it have to get better? It can get worse. Things always get worse. The bad shit never goes away. Don't you know that, you idiot?
- Edie looked terrible the last time I saw her. But then again, does Edie ever look good? Her skin is always so chalky and flaky. The veins were pop ping out on her swollen ankles. They looked pretty bad. Maybe I should call Dr. Lewy.
- What will I look like when I get to be her age?
- Will I ever get to be Edie's age?

- Why not? I'm in okay health. I don't smoke…cigarettes. I drink a little, drug a little. But who doesn't? I'm a nun compared to Bruce.
- Oh, Bruce. Damn it, Bruce…

See what I mean? No wonder I can't sleep. It goes on and on, snowballing down the hill until my thoughts become an avalanche and the avalanche crushes me. I'm dead meat by the next morning. Exhausted. Like I've been through the mill. But I guess I have been through the mill. The mill of me.

I'm my own worst enemy. I've been told that more times than I can count. I wish I could get away from myself. I wish I could take a vacation from myself. At least for a little bit. I wish I could quiet the voices in my head. But I guess these voices in my head are what makes me me.

They *are* me.

Bruce

Let's get one thing out of the way. I know what people say about me. That I'm a total piece of shit. But the difference is I know I'm a piece of shit. Now ask me, do I care? What do you think?

Although "total piece of shit" might not be so accurate. There's a Yiddish word that's perfect. *Schnorrer*. A user, a grabber, a taker. But that's how you get anywhere in this business. You take. And yeah, you give back, but only because you've taken first. You never just give for the sake of giving. I've got no talent except making something out of what's already there. Using other people's talent. I've said it a thousand times and I'm getting tired of listening to myself.

I'm trying to tie up loose ends before that Funk chick's first tour starts next week. Or should I say, Trini is. The key to success is hiring good help. I'd be in the toilet without Trini. She makes me look good, which is a tall order, especially these days. I'd be lying if I said I didn't know that everyone at Larva is banking on me failing big time with Cara. And falling hard. Again. They might be right but the failure wouldn't be through any fault of Cara's. I take the blame entirely. It's a manager's job to mold their artist, to bring out their best qualities. But I think I just make her nervous instead of more confident. I can be pretty intimidating, I've been told.

I'm the most out of control I've ever been in my entire life. And that's saying a lot. Hey, I'm a fat fuck, too. I'm the fattest I've ever been. I'm an ugly, roly-poly fucking Elvis Presley. My clothes hurt. Trini keeps ordering the stuff I like the next size up but she still can't seem to keep up with me these days.

And I know my lifestyle doesn't help. The blow, the pills, the drink. But do I care? To me, there's only one way to live and that's to the fullest. If I wanted to be a priest, I would have converted and become one.

Trini keeps bugging me to get a checkup. It's been two years since my "annual" physical and I guess the brass at Larva is bugging her to bug me. But I'm putting it off until after the tour. I'm in the talking stages for local gigs after we get back from the West Coast. Great Gildersleeves, Max's Kansas City, The Roxy. It'll only delay my physical a month or so longer. What's going to happen in a month? Either nothing or everything.

In the next few weeks, the piper will be paid. Or he'll be killed. One or the other. My gut tells me that it's going to be good. And my gut is never wrong, especially big as it is these days.

It'll be good to spend time with Cara. Maybe she'll finally let down her guard. I can't help but wonder who fucked her over and how hard. She must have had a hell of a past. Holds herself tight and proud and close to the vest. Never lets on what's going on inside. I have a feeling it's dark and delicious. And that's just the way I like them. Troubled. With an edge. That's Cara. Troubled with a capital T.

The second I got a glimpse of her at CBGB's, I got a woody. That's the way I tell true talent, even with guys. Not that I'm a homo or anything because I'm not. But Cara made me stop dead in my tracks. And she wasn't even behind the kit yet. It was before she even took to the stage.

So far, I haven't gotten through to her. Into her pants, I mean. Oh, there's been some kinky stuff, some lookie-loo stuff that she's gone along with. Even though she really wasn't into it. I could tell it made her uncomfortable even though it was strictly "look but don't touch." I get off on that kind of shit. I admit, I'm an old horndog from way back.

Not that I'm into that penetration crap. I'm really not into pussy. I don't like getting all messy and dirty, getting girl cream all over my Johnson. Too intimate, being inside somebody's body. Know what I'm saying? I'm more into making a mess. Let me ask you, what guy doesn't like making a girl's *tuchus* look like a glazed donut? What guy doesn't like splooging on a fine set of knockers?

For me, sex has always been about control. I get off being in the driver's seat. I never feel more powerful than when I'm turning down a perfectly good act or twisting one off on some pretty little wannabe's kisser. Same difference to me.

Now don't go judging me. Everybody in this business does it. Well, practically every manager. Even the chicks. Don't let anybody tell you otherwise. I shoot straight from the hip. Always did, always will. Not that I'm one to kiss and tell or name names but... Even "People who need people." Even "Gypsies, Tramps and Thieves." Even pretty blonde girls with a "Heart of Glass." Take it from me.

And what difference does it make? Really. It's only bodies, only matter. An exchange of body fluids. Like blowing your nose into a tissue. What? You find that offensive? It's true. We're not made of gold; we're just hunks of DNA. Just

11 elements. We're molecules. Nothing more. That's all any of us are. A shitload of molecules. Some molecules just have more talent than others.

8/22/79

I fly out to San Diego tomorrow. It'll be just me and Bruce. He wants me to go out there a few days earlier with him. To sort things out. Get a feel for the place. Get a feel of my ass is more like it! I was a little shocked when Trini handed me the plane tickets and I looked at the date. Bruce didn't even tell me about the date change himself. Trini broke it to me when I told her that the flight date was wrong. There won't even be that extra layer of protection of having the guys with me because they're flying out later. JR always keeps an eye on me. Mongo, too. They've always been great fending off weirdos in clubs, putting off a sound guy who got a little too familiar. I haven't been around Adam enough but he seems like a decent guy. I think he'd have my back as well.

Just take it as it comes, Cara. Don't get yourself bent out of shape over something that might not even happen. Bruce might be fine. He might not be the skell you think he is. He might just be one of those guys who *has* to try, who *has* to flirt, no matter who the chick is. Coming onto a girl makes him feel like a man. Bruce might surprise you and turn out to be a cool, fatherly kind of guy. Yeah, fatherly as in incestuous. But we'll see.

There I go, thinking the worst of people. I hope Bruce pleasantly surprises me. Stranger things have happened.

I'm not sure what to pack. Trini took care of the big stuff, the costumes, new leathers and boots. My stage duds, I guess you'd call them. I kept asking her how much money I'm into Larva for so far and she kept telling me not to worry about it. Just like Bruce. Except I do worry about it. I worry about everything.

So far, I've got one big suitcase stuffed with socks, bras, underwear, jeans and t-shirts. I don't wear shorts, no matter how hot it is. They're not my thing. Especially hot pants and culottes. Whoever invented culotte shorts should be shot. A real fashion "don't" in my humble opinion. Same thing for sandals. Maybe because I don't like my feet. I've got long gorilla toes plus calluses all over the sides and soles of my feet from banging on pedals for a couple of decades. Most of my clothes are black or gray, so that makes packing easy, too.

The DHL truck already came to take my drums and hardware. But I'm hanging onto the snare. I'll carry that on with my backpack full of shit to keep me amused during the five-hour flight.

Toothbrush, toothpaste, the usual toiletries. And birth control because you never know. I've been off the pill because Michael and I have been so on again/ off again. We've been using rubbers, which aren't my favorite, but they do the job. I packed a few condoms. That plus a three-pack of Today sponges should be enough, just in case. Besides, it's not like there aren't any drugstores in Southern California.

It would have been nice to see Michael before I left. Not that I'm too hung up on him or anything. But he was invited to stay at the writer's conference a couple of weeks longer, and on their dime. Besides putting out a small chapbook of his poetry, it seems that they liked a short play he wrote as a final assignment. It won first place in a competition. It's about a female drummer in the society music trade who's trying to make it. (Sound familiar?) He calls it "Different Drummer." The Woodstock Playhouse is even going to put on a whirlwind production. Just a week to rehearse it and get everything in order. It premieres over Labor Day weekend. He starts teaching the next day or so after that. Too bad I'll still be on the West Coast when they're doing his play. I would have really liked to see it.

I went to see Edie today. Her stomach's been on the fritz, so I only came with a pint of chicken egg drop soup from Great Wall Kitchen. She could barely get down a bowl but I think she was grateful I brought it. It's hard to tell with Edie. She'd been in bed, even though it was a nice, sunny day, not too humid. She didn't even have a fan on and was shivering under a thin blanket. I wanted to call Dr. Lewy, but Edie wouldn't hear of it. She wouldn't even let me take her temperature. She did get up to have the soup, though. But she didn't even have one cigarette the whole time I was there. That's how I knew she was sick.

I brought her a bunch of flowers. Nothing fancy, just a mixed bouquet from the Korean grocer's on Knapp Street. Instead of saying "Thank you," Edie said, "Flowers? I'm not dead yet."

"They're just flowers, Ma," I told her.

"They're nice," she managed to say, then told me where the vase was. I had to stand on a kitchen chair (barefoot, so I would scuff the ancient Naugahyde) to reach it. I made her a cup of tea, Lipton, "not that Chinese crap," to have with her fortune cookie, which read, "You are going on a long journey."

When I laughed and told her that *I* should have gotten that fortune, she seemed confused. She seemed even more confused when I reminded her that I was heading to California tomorrow. "Oh, that's right," she said, but I could tell she didn't have a clue. Something's up with her, I don't know what, but it's not good.

I stayed a little bit after the tea (I had "that Chinese crap" with some ice in it) but I could see that Edie was tired. Bone tired. And she hadn't done anything but gotten up out of bed. She wouldn't let me call Aileen or Irv. She wouldn't let me call anybody. When I got up to leave, I had a big, empty feeling in my chest. "I won't see you for a while," I reminded her.

"Right," my mother said. "Good luck. Really. You'll do fine, Carol. You always do." From Edie, that was epic.

I kissed her cheek, which felt cool and waxy. Then she pulled me in for a hug and didn't let go. The way she held me, you would have thought I was going to the Andromeda Galaxy instead of San Diego International on Laker Airways. "It's just for a couple of weeks," I told her when I pulled away from her. Edie didn't say anything but I knew there was something on her mind. "What?" I asked but she just shook her head and waved me away.

When I looked back at her, my mother was crying. I should have gone to her but I didn't. How many times did she leave me alone and crying when I was a kid? Not that it's right but I just don't know how to deal with Edie when she sobs. She doesn't let herself cry a lot, but when she does, it's like the flood gates open. Then they don't want to close.

So. I did the easy thing instead of the right thing. I just kept walking toward Nostrand Avenue and didn't stop until I got to the B-44 bus.

I felt weird leaving my mother. I feel weird leaving tomorrow. But I guess I have to. It's almost like I'm trying to find excuses not to go. I'm scared shitless to confront my own destiny, I guess.

It's almost midnight and I don't feel tired. I know I have to put this damned notebook away. I'll slip it in my backpack so I can take it out on the plane and write in it some more. But that's it for tonight.

Trini Otero
Personal Assistant to Bruce Lask

Look, I'm only talking to you because you're a friend of Miss Funk's. She mentioned you and your project. More than once. She's one of the good ones. I liked her from the start. She treated me with respect from Day One, looked me in the eye, and always thanked me. Even if I only handed her a pen. Too many of the people who pass through these doors get blinded by all those gold and platinum records on the walls. They talk to you like you're a servant. Or worse, they don't even acknowledge you at all. Like you're a speck of spit on a bathroom mirror. For 30 years, my mother's busted her *culo* cleaning up after people like that, so I notice right away. Miss Funk isn't like them at all.

You've got to understand, I signed a confidentiality agreement when I took this position. Despite the fact that Mr. Lask can be a bit of an SOB sometimes, I like this gig. The money's good and I'm good at what I do. Plus I can't afford to lose my job. All I've got is a GED but Larva didn't care. They hired me anyway. Maybe they saw a spark in me. Something. I don't know what they saw but they hired me. That was three years ago, even before Mr. Lask came back. Basically, they gave me to him as an administrative assistant because nobody else wanted the job. I'm a tough little spic from Spanish Harlem so maybe they thought I could handle him. And I can. To a certain extent, I can. Only I can't control what he does when he leaves this building or behind closed doors. They understand and don't expect anything more of me. He's a grown ass man, after all, and I can't regulate everything that goes into his mouth or up his nose.

Don't quote me on that, I've said too much already.

I can't say anything more about what happened. All I know is that about 7 am this morning, Mr. Lask called me to call 911. He was having trouble breathing and he couldn't move his left side. Besides that, he wasn't making must sense. The ambulance took him to Bellevue's Emergency Room, which is where I should be right now. But he gave me implicit orders to stay right here so I could give Miss Funk instructions when she lands. As far as I know, she's on that plane. That's what I told her to do. Laker Airways confirmed that she checked in at the gate and that's where she was when I spoke to her. I sure hope she proceeded without him. That's what she was instructed to do, anyway. But Miss Funk strikes me as one of those people who ultimately does what she wants, not what she's told. That's another thing I like about her. She's not a pushover.

Listen, you're going to have to leave now. Please don't make me call Security. And I will. You seem like a really nice kid so I don't want to get you in trouble.

There goes the damned phone again. I have to get that. Now, you've got to excuse me. I think you know the way to the elevator.

8/23/79

I can't believe that motherfucker didn't show up! I was all checked in and waiting at the gate when the flight attendant at the desk paged me over the loudspeaker. I had a phone call, she said. Phone call? Who the fuck knew I was there? It was Trini. She said that Bruce was delayed, something about circumstances beyond anyone's control, that I should get on the plane and go to San Diego as planned. She'd reach me again when the plane got to San Diego. Trini told me to check with the desk at the gate the second I landed and she'd update me then.

I swear, I felt like running, running and never coming back. But I got on the plane. And here I am.

My boots are off and my legs are stretched out across Bruce's empty seat. They're resting on my snare drum, which is actually in Bruce's seat. Flying isn't as scary as I thought. I actually like looking out the window. It reminds me of the old Aircraft song "40,000 Feet." Maybe I should put it into our set list.

I've had my journal out for the past hour, thinking maybe I could jot down a few lines and finally finish "Rekindle" but that isn't happening. So, I started writing this crap. But I'm scribbling circles and swirls and mountains and clouds. It's what I see out the window. Plus tiny roads like veins. And cars that sparkle like stars. And houses that look smaller than dollhouses. The lakes and rivers are an unnatural blue. And there's not a cloud in the sky because we're above the clouds. We're above everything.

I'm worried about Bruce. What the hell happened to him? Did Security stop him with a noseful of coke? Did he try and sneak a few joints stashed up his ass? I mean, who would want to look there? Or did he just oversleep?

Speaking of sleep, I'm going to try and get some rest. I tossed and turned all night last night.

12:35 pm

I can't sleep. The second I drift off, I start to dream that I'm falling and then I jolt awake. Or else the little bugger in Seat 28A behind me starts to kick the back of my chair and I jump. But the good news is, I started to work on "Rekindle" again.

I don't want this to end.
I don't want to be your friend.
I don't want to see your face.
I just want to erase
The part of you that's become a part of me.

I know it's an awkward rhyme but it feels right, somehow. Maybe the song is done. I'm not sure. It doesn't exactly feel done. One of my English teachers back at Sheepshead High used to tell us, "A poem is never finished, only abandoned." I can't remember who said that originally, but it's true.

Oh, and I started jotting down ideas for a new song. I think I'll call it "Holding Lilacs and Laughing." It's about my mother.

1:53 pm

I feel like I've been on this freaking plane forever. I feel like I'm never going to get out. Not that I'm afraid it's going to crash. Even worse would be the plane going back and forth from coast to coast for eternity. That's my idea of hell. Like that character in *The Devil in Miss Jones*. (Yes, I watch porn movies now and then. So what?) For Justine Jones, a raging nymphomaniac, hell was being locked up with a nut job who's more interested in catching imaginary flies than giving her an orgasm. Everybody has their own private hell. For Edie, it would be a place without Chesterfields. For Michael, it would be having piles of paper but no pen to write with. For me, besides being on this plane forever, it would be the prospect of never, ever making it. Of coming close (like Justine Jones and her fleeting climax) but never getting there.

2:13 pm

The pilot just made an announcement that we're supposed to land in two hours. Two more hours! I feel like I've been on this 747 for two days!

I have a heavy feeling in my chest like something's wrong. Really wrong. Of course, something's wrong because Bruce isn't on this flight. But something more. I'll call my sister when we land. My mother didn't answer her phone when I tried calling her from LaGuardia before I left.

4:01 pm

The stewardess just said that we were making our initial descent into San Diego International Airport. But I knew we were. Either that or we were going to crash. My stomach is doing flip-flops like it does on the Cyclone. Like its bottom is falling out. I hate that feeling. Not nauseous but not right. I like having my feet on solid ground. There's something so unnatural about being up in the air.

For the first time since takeoff, I feel scared. If that guy in 27C looked a little bit friendlier, I'd ask him if he wouldn't mind holding my hand. But he seems to be a button-down type like Ellis—three-piece suit, briefcase, wingtips, a pile of papers—and he looked at me like I might have herpes when I scooted past him to my seat. He gave me hard-eyes the one time I had to disturb him to use the bathroom. I mean, jeez, guy, it's a five-hour flight. A girl's gotta pee sometime.

Maybe I should concentrate on something else. Far off, I can see the ocean. It's covered in mist. I can even make out the waves breaking. Do I see seals or surfers? It's a couple of people in wetsuits, with surfboards. There are sand dunes and a road snaking beside the sea. And everybody looks blonde.

Toto, we're not in Brooklyn, anymore.

Sheree Ross
Fight Crew, Laker Airways

I knew it was her the minute she disembarked the aircraft. If she were trying to get on my plane, I would have stopped her. 1979 has been a bad year for hijackings: the Serbs, the Slavs, and of course, the Cubans. Always the Cubans.

She had a wild look in her eyes. Agitated. A bit crazed. And it was a little more than jetlag. I would have guessed she was on drugs but apparently, that's the way she always is. Running a little faster, a little hotter, than everyone else. But I knew it was Carol Sylvia Finkelstein, Seat 27A, the second I laid eyes on her. Black jeans and T-shirt, black hair, oversized black leather jacket with a tear at the elbow, worn black leather motorcycle boots. Bright red lips against pale, pale skin, like a rose in snow. Instead of a cute, little purse, she was carrying what looked like a big hat box. She wasn't LA or even San Diego people. No, she wouldn't fit in here. I could just tell.

The crazy lady had been calling the desk at Gate 13 for almost an hour. Something urgent, she said. No, not quite *said*, more like *screeched*.

Anyway, I grabbed Seat 27A as soon as I could, weaving my way through the sea of bodies coming off the jet bridge. "Miss Finkelstein?" I asked. She looked startled that I knew her name.

"Yes," she said. I told her that someone had been calling, a woman, who sounded upset. She didn't give her name or leave a number. "Trini," she said with a sigh of relief.

"Maybe," I shrugged. But before we could get any further, the phone at Gate 13's desk rang again. I grabbed it.

Instead of saying hello, there was a jagged voice that demanded, "Is she there yet?" I didn't respond, just handed the telephone to Miss Finkelstein. The other woman's voice was shrill and garbled. I couldn't figure out what she was saying but 27A's mouth hung open slightly and her white skin became whiter.

"But I just saw her yesterday…" 27A said, holding the receiver slightly away from her ear.

"So did I," the woman yelled, louder now, so loud that I and everyone else nearby could hear. "But she's still dead! She laid down for a nap and she never got up, Carol!"

"Mommy's dead?" Miss Finkelstein said in disbelief. And again, so that maybe she might believe it this time. "Mommy's dead."

I was afraid she would crumble to the ground. "Miss Finkelstein, would you like to sit down?" I pushed the wheeled stool behind the desk closer to her.

"No," she said. "No, thank you."

There were more garbled words from the East Coast and 27A responded in a voice that got quieter and quieter. Then another passenger asked me about a connecting Pan Am flight to Fresno. When I looked up, the telephone was dangling off the hook and Miss Finkelstein was walking away. She stopped abruptly, sat on a bench and scribbled something in a notebook. Just before she disappeared into the crowd, she tossed the notebook onto a seat.

8/23/79 Later

4:33 pm (New York Time)

My sister Aileen just called me at the airport to tell me that my mother was dead. Edith Schwartz Finkelstein died at approximately 11:00 am, Eastern Standard Time. Alone. Aileen found her when she came to do Edie's laundry. Mom was in bed. She might have been there since I left her last night.

I'm still in shock. I gave my mother my travel information, never thinking anyone would have to use it to contact me. It was probably sitting on the kitchen table where I'd left it, scribbled on a pad that had "Keep on truckin'" printed across the top. On the chipped Formica table were that pad and the Thom McAn shoebox I returned to Edie.

"So, when are you coming back?" the hysterical woman who was my sister asked.

"I…I just got here. I can't come back."

"What?!" Aileen screamed. "You're not going to leave me to clean up this shit. You always leave me to do the dirty work. Well, not anymore, I…"

"Look, Mommy's already dead. Me coming back home isn't going to change anything. Is it?"

That's when the telephone receiver just fell from my hand. It suddenly had gotten very heavy and I couldn't see why I needed to hold onto it anymore.

Michael

Cara didn't even come to her own mother's funeral. I know Jews usually bury their dead within 24 hours but her sister Aileen was willing to wait until Cara got back. Aileen said that when she last spoke to Cara, she was still in the airport. I mean, how fucking hard is it to jump back on an airplane when you're still at the airport?

No one has heard from Cara since. Not her family, JR, Mongo, not even the record company. A nice Latina lady named Trini called me a few times when I was still in Woodstock. (I'm back in Brooklyn now.) It seems that Cara wrote me down as her emergency contact on the Larva paperwork. I'm her beneficiary, too. Cara's manager is still in the hospital, hooked up to a bunch of machines, Trini said. He had a major stroke before he left to meet Cara at LaGuardia. His heart is working at 50% capacity and it doesn't look good. He isn't breathing on his own and they don't expect him to pull through.

Then, this afternoon, a worn out black-and-white composition book arrived in the mail with a Laker Airways return address. There was a note paper-clipped to the front of it, on pink perfumed stationery. It was from an airline employee named Sheree Ross. She's the one who overheard part of Cara's conversation with her sister. Sheree also caught a glimpse of Cara walking away toward the baggage claim, and before she disappeared from view, she saw Cara leave this notebook on a chair.

Although Sheree lost Cara in the crowd, she managed to rescue the notebook. My name and address was scribbled on the inside cover. "It seemed important,"

Sheree wrote on the coral notepaper in flowery, girly script—she even dotted her "i's" with tiny hearts. "I thought you might like to have it."

Tucked into the notebook was an old, black-and-white picture of a woman with an armful of flowers. On the back, it said, "Me, holding lilacs and laughing." It looked vaguely like Cara. It could have been her mother from many years ago but I'm not 100% sure who it was.

I had no idea Cara was actually keeping a journal, even though I must have suggested it a thousand times.

So, I'm going to sit here and read it from cover to cover, starting at the beginning. Maybe then I'll find some answers.

Publisher's Note

While this book is inspired by real people, places and some actual events, *Different Drummer* is a work of fiction and in no way meant to be a historical accounting. Any resemblance to persons, either living or dead, is purely coincidental. This book is intended solely for entertainment purposes.

Acknowledgements

Different Drummer began as a final assignment for David Winn's "Workshop in Fiction 2" at Hunter College in 1982. I'd like to thank Professor Winn for his encouragement during our meetings and for telling me "This should be a book."

I'd like to thank my husband Peter for his brutal honesty, love and support, and for helping me find the right words post-chemotherapy. He was the book's first reader, diligently taking notes as he read it on his Kindle in bed.

I'd also like to acknowledge Debbie James, who the book is dedicated to. Our friendship endured several decades, four husbands (between the two of us), various triumphs and tragedies. In 2009, when Debbie was in advanced end stage breast cancer, she traveled halfway across the country to "say goodbye" to a handful of people. I was honored to have been among them. When I told Deb she had to hang on because I was working on this book, her response was, "Write fast." Although it ultimately wasn't fast enough, at times I felt like Deb was looking over my shoulder, smiling. I took great joy in writing the character inspired by her because it felt as though Debbie was alive again.

And a big thank-you to Vinnie, for taking another chance on me.

Thanks also to my friends and family, and even to the truly evil individuals who inhabit several characters.

CGB

About the Author

Catherine Gigante-Brown is writer of fiction, nonfiction and poetry. She was born in Brooklyn, where she still lives with her husband and son. Her first novel, *The El*, was published in 2012.

Also available from Catherine Gigante-Brown.

The El

A stirring historic novel set in Depression-era Brooklyn, *The El* weaves an unforgettable family saga.

In the shadow of the elevated train (called "The El," for short), a loud, lusty Italian-American clan resides: Poppa, the kindly patriarch; Bridget, his loving wife and mother of their six grown children; Rosanna, their eldest, who is married to Tony, an evil, dangerous drunk; Kewpie, their nubile teenage daughter and Tiger, their scrappy ten-year old son. A stark drama quickly unfolds as a terrible secret is revealed.

Told through the eyes of a quirky, colorful array of characters, the Paradisos struggle through seasons of joy, loss and desire, and experience simple delights. Here, the ordinary becomes extraordinary. It is a place of unconditional and unrequited love, where the unimaginable is indeed possible and the whims of a violent alcoholic threaten to destroy the idyllic applecart of the family's existence.

The El is simultaneously homey and horrific, innocent and erotic, magical and shocking. It is a complicated mosaic of light and dark, full of savory flavors and vivid, memorable images.

If Pete Hamill and Joyce Carol Oates could have a literary lovechild together, it would be *The El*...with a bit of *50 Shades of Grey* thrown in for good measure.

Volossal Publishing